A DANGEROUS COLLABORATION

A
DANGEROUS
COLLABORATION

A VERONICA SPEEDWELL
MYSTERY

Deanna Raybourn

BERKLEY
NEW YORK

BERKLEY
An imprint of Penguin Random House LLC
1745 Broadway, New York, NY 10019

Copyright © 2019 by Deanna Raybourn
Penguin Random House supports copyright. Copyright fuels creativity, encourages diverse
voices, promotes free speech, and creates a vibrant culture. Thank you for buying an authorized
edition of this book and for complying with copyright laws by not reproducing, scanning, or
distributing any part of it in any form without permission. You are supporting writers and
allowing Penguin Random House to continue to publish books for every reader.

BERKLEY and the BERKLEY & B colophon are registered trademarks of
Penguin Random House LLC.

Library of Congress Cataloging-in-Publication Data

Names: Raybourn, Deanna, author.
Title: A dangerous collaboration / Deanna Raybourn.
Description: First Edition. | New York: Berkley, 2019. | Series: Veronica
Speedwell mystery series
Identifiers: LCCN 2018043155| ISBN 9780451490711 (hardcover) |
ISBN 9780451490735 (ebook)
Subjects: | GSAFD: Mystery fiction.
Classification: LCC PS3618.A983 D36 2019 | DDC 813/.6—dc23
LC record available at https://lccn.loc.gov/2018043155

First Edition: March 2019

Printed in the United States of America
1   3   5   7   9   10   8   6   4   2

Cover art and design by Leo Nickolls
Book design by Kristin del Rosario

To all of the intrepid adventuresses
just waiting for their journeys to begin . . .

A DANGEROUS COLLABORATION

CHAPTER

1

London, March 1888

"What the devil do you mean you're leaving?" Stoker demanded. He surveyed the half-packed carpetbag on my bed as I folded in a spare shirtwaist and *Magalhães's Guide to Portuguese Lepidoptery*. It was a weightier volume than one might expect, featuring an appendix devoted to the butterflies of Madeira and certain flamboyant moths found only in the Azores.

"Precisely what I said. I am packing. When I have packed, I will leave this place and board a train for the coast. There I will leave the train and get onto a boat, and when it stops at Madeira, I will have arrived." My tone was frankly waspish. I had dreaded telling Stoker of my plans, expecting some sort of mild explosion at the notion that I had at last secured an expedition, however minor, to which he was not invited. Instead, he had adopted an attitude of Arctic hauteur. I blamed his aristocratic upbringing for that. And his nose. It was very easy to look down on someone with a nose that would have done a Roman emperor justice. But I could not entirely blame him. As natural historians, we had balked at our enforced stay in London, each of us longing for the open seas, skies that stretched to forever, horizons that beckoned us with spice-scented winds. Instead, we had found ourselves employed by the Earl of Rosemorran to catalog his family's extensive collections—interesting and modestly profitable work that stunted the soul if endured for too long. One could count only so many stuffed marmosets before the spirit rebelled. The notion that I was to escape our genial confinement whilst he labored on would have tested the noblest character, and Stoker, like me, bore a healthy streak of self-interest.

"At Madeira?" he asked.

"At Madeira," I replied firmly.

He folded his arms over the breadth of his chest. "And might one inquire as to the expected duration of this expedition?"

"One might, but one would be disappointed with the reply. I have not yet formulated my plans, but I expect to be away for some months. Perhaps until the autumn."

"Until the autumn," he said, drawing out the words slowly.

"Yes. Look for me in the season of mists and mellow fruitfulness," I instructed with a feeble attempt at a smile. But even a nod to his beloved Keats did not soften his austere expression.

"And you mean to go alone."

"Not at all," I told him, as I tucked a large pot of cold cream of roses into my bag. "Lady Cordelia and I shall travel together."

He gave a snort of laughter that was distinctly lacking in amusement. "Lady Cordelia. You know her only experience with shipboard life is the Channel steamer, do you not? Her notion of rough travel is not taking the second footman. And I do not even like to *think* of what Sidonie will have to say on the matter."

I winced at the mention of Lady Cordelia's snippy French lady's maid. "She will not be coming."

His mouth fell agape and he dropped the pose of icy disdain.

"Veronica, you cannot be serious. I know you long to shake the fogs of London out of your clothes as much as I do, but dragging Lady Cordelia to some benighted island in the middle of the Atlantic makes no sense at all. You might as well haul her to the North Pole."

"I should never attempt a polar expedition," I assured him with a lightness I did not feel. "There are no butterflies to be found there."

He gripped my shoulders, his thumbs just brushing the tops of my collarbones. "If this is because of what I said earlier today," he began, "what I *almost* said—"

I raised a hand. "Of course not." It was a pathetic attempt at a lie. The truth was that both of us, in an unguarded moment, had very nearly given voice to sentiments we had no business declaring. I could still feel the pressure of his hand, burning like a brand at my waist, as his breath stirred the lock of hair pinned behind my ear, warm and impulsive words trembling on my lips. Had his brother, the Viscount Templeton-Vane, not interrupted us . . .

But no. That line of thought does not bear consideration. The point is quite simply that we *were* interrupted, and as soon as the viscount left, I had taken tea tête-à-tête with Lady Cordelia, Lord Rosemorran's sister and a good friend to both Stoker and to me. By the time we had shared the last muffin between us, we had decided upon a course of action that we knew would surprise and quite possibly annoy the men in our lives. Lord Rosemorran had behaved with his characteristic good-natured vagueness, offering money to fund the venture and raising objections only when he realized his sister's absence would mean taking care of his own children.

"Call one of the aunts to help you," Lady C. instructed with unaccustomed ruthlessness. "I am thoroughly exhausted and a holiday is just what I require."

Lord Rosemorran gave in at once, but Stoker was being bloody-minded as usual, not least because so much hung between us, unsaid but thickening the air until I thought I would never again draw an easy breath.

"It is quite for the best," I said, forcing the last of my shirtwaists into the bag. "This business with the Tiverton Expedition has been demanding. A little peace and quiet to recover from it will do us both a world of good."

On the surface, it was a tolerable excuse. The investigation we had just concluded* had been harrowing in the extreme, entailing all manner of reckless adventures as well as a few bodily injuries. But Stoker and I throve on such endeavors, matching each other in our acts of derring-do. No, it was not physical exhaustion that drove me from the temperate shores of England, gentle reader. It was the recent entanglement with Stoker's former wife, Caroline de Morgan, a fiend in petticoats who had very nearly destroyed him with her machinations. I longed to repay her in kind. But I had learnt long ago that revenge is a fruitless pursuit, and so I left Caroline to the fates, trusting she would see her just deserts in time. Stoker was my concern—specifically the powerful emotions he stirred within me and what, precisely, I was going to do about them. It seemed impossible to assess them with the cool and dispassionate eye of a scientist whilst we were so often together. After all, a proper examination of a butterfly did not take place in the field; one captured the specimen and took it away to regard it carefully, holding it up to the light and accepting its flaws as well as its beauties. So I meant to do with my feelings for Stoker, although that intention was certainly not one I meant to share with him. Knowing how deeply he had been wounded by Caroline, I could have no hand in hurting him further.

Luckily for me, Lady Cordelia had been desperate, insistent upon

---

* *A Treacherous Curse*

getting right away, and I seized upon her invitation with alacrity, determined to make my escape without revealing our purposes, even to Stoker.

"I daresay I will have nothing more interesting to write about than butterflies, so do not be surprised if I am a poor correspondent," I warned him. "You needn't trouble to write if it bores you. I am sure you will have far more interesting activities to occupy your time. I am sorry if it leaves you in a bit of a lurch with the collections," I finished, buckling the carpetbag.

"I will manage quite well alone," he replied as he turned away, his expression carefully blank. "I always have."

As he no doubt intended, Stoker's parting words haunted me for the better part of six months. Madeira was beautiful, lush, and fragrant and offering tremendous opportunities for my work as a lepidopterist. But more times than I cared to admit, whilst hotly in pursuit of a sweet little *Lampides boeticus* flapping lazily in a flower-scented breeze, I paused, letting the net drop uselessly to my side. Articles for the various publications to which I contributed went unwritten, my pen resting in a stilled hand while my mind roamed free. Every time, my thoughts went to him, like pigeons darting home to roost. And every time, I wrenched them away, never permitting myself to think too long of him for the same reason a child learns not to hold her hand too close to a flame.

In the summer, when the late-blooming jacaranda poured the honeyed musk of its perfume over the island, it was necessary—for various reasons I shall not detail here—to call in the doctor to attend both Lady Cordelia and me. By the time we had regained our strength, half a year had passed and our thoughts turned to England once more. Long afternoons had been spent upon the veranda of our rented villa as we rested like basking lizards in the sun. We were both slimmer than we had been when we set out. Lady Cordelia's pale milk skin had gathered a cinnamon dusting of freckles in spite of her veils and broad brims, but I had tossed my hat aside, turning my face up to the golden rays.

"You look the picture of health," she told me as we boarded the boat in the port of Funchal. "No one would ever imagine you had been under a doctor's care."

I plucked at the loose waist of my traveling suit. "You think not? I am skin and bone, and you are little better. But some good Devonshire cream and plates of English roast beef will see us right again," I assured her.

Absently, she linked her arm with mine. "Do you think they have missed us?"

"The frequency of their letters would suggest so." "Frequency" was not quite the word. Every mail ship had brought fresh correspondence. The earl and his children had written regularly to Lady Cordelia, and I had received my share of the post as well. Colleagues in lepidoptery had much to say, and there were weekly letters from Lord Templeton-Vane, Stoker's eldest brother. He wrote in a casual, conversational style of current affairs and common interests, and as the months passed, we became better friends than we had been before.

And from Stoker? Not a single word. Not one line, scribbled on a grubby postcard. Not a postscript scrawled on one of his brother's letters. Nothing but silence, eloquent and rebuking. I was conscious of a profound and thoroughly irrational sense of injury. I had made it clear to him that I did not intend to write letters and expected none. And yet. Every post that arrived with no missive from him was a taunt, speaking his anger as eloquently as any words might have done. I had sowed the seed of this quarrel, I reminded myself sternly; I could not now complain that I did not like the fruit it bore.

And as I stood arm in arm with Lady Cordelia on the deck of the ship bearing us home, I wondered precisely what sort of welcome I could expect.

. . .

"What in the name of seven hells do you mean you want to 'borrow' Miss Speedwell? She's not an umbrella, for God's sake," Stoker grumbled to his eldest brother as the viscount entered our workroom. (Such demands often comprised the bulk of Stoker's conversation; I had learnt to ignore them.) "Besides which, she has only been home for two days. I very much doubt she has even unpacked."

Lord Templeton-Vane bared his teeth in what a stupid person might have mistaken for a smile. "Stoker, how delightful to see you. I hadn't noticed you behind that water buffalo's backside. Perfecting your trade, no doubt," he mused as he looked from the moldering buffalo trophy to the pile of rotten sawdust Stoker was busy extracting. As a natural historian, Stoker's lot was often the restoration of thoroughly foul specimens of the taxidermic arts. The backside of a water buffalo was far from the worst place I had seen Stoker's head.

His lordship clicked his tongue as he gave Stoker a dismissive glance. "Besides which, I hardly think Miss Speedwell requires assistance in arranging her affairs." He lingered on the last word just a heartbeat too long. The viscount had a gift for silken suggestions, and I suppressed a sigh of irritation that he had exercised it just then. Stoker and I had scarcely spoken since my return, exchanging cool greetings and meaningless chatter about our work. But I had hopes of a thaw provided the viscount did not scupper the possibility.

I looked up from the tray of *Nymphalidae* I was sorting and gave them both a repressive stare. "I am not your nanny, but if required, I will put either of you over my knee," I warned them.

Stoker, who topped me by half a foot and some forty pounds, pulled a face. His brother's response was slightly salacious. He lifted an exquisite brow and sighed. "One could only wish," he murmured.

I ignored that remark and brushed off my hands, putting my

butterflies aside. "My lord," I said to the viscount, "before you explain further, perhaps we might have a little refreshment."

His lordship looked pained. "I abhor tea parties," he protested.

It was my turn to snort. "Not that sort of tea." With Stoker's grudging consent, I retrieved a bottle of his best single malt and poured out a measure for each of us. We settled in and I studied my companions. In certain respects, they could not have been more different, yet in others they were startlingly similar. They shared the fine bone structure of their mother; from high cheekbones and determined jaws to elegant hands, they were alike. It was in coloring and musculature that they varied. While his lordship was sleek as an otter, Stoker's muscles, honed by his long years of work as a natural historian and explorer, were heavier and altogether more impressive. He made good use of them as he worked on the mounts that would form the basis of the Rosemorran Collection. Whilst we sorted the family's accumulated treasures from centuries of travel, the earl had given us the use of the Belvedere, the grand freestanding ballroom on his Marylebone estate, as well as living quarters, modest salaries, and a few other perquisites such as entertaining visitors when we chose.

Stoker, as it happened, was not entirely pleased with our current caller. His relationship with his eldest brother was difficult at the best of times, and it was apparent from his lordship's expression of feline forbearance that he was rather less inclined than usual to tolerate Stoker's bad temper. Stoker, for his part, was determined to play the hedgehog, snarling with his prickles out.

The viscount gestured expansively towards the specimen Stoker had been stitching when he arrived. "Why don't you go and play with your buffalo? I have business with Miss Speedwell."

Stoker curled his lip and I hastened to intervene before bloodshed broke out. "Poorly played, my lord. You know that Stoker and I are colleagues and friends. Anything you have to say to me can be said freely in front of him." I had hoped this little demonstration of loyalty would settle Stoker's hackles, but his mood did not change.

The viscount's expression turned gently mocking. "Colleagues and friends! How very tepid," he said blandly. He took a deep draft of his whisky while Stoker and I studiously avoided looking at one another. Our investigative pursuits, invariably dangerous and thoroughly enjoyable, had drawn us together, forcing a trust neither of us entirely welcomed. We were solitary creatures, Stoker and I, but we had discovered a mutual understanding beyond anything we had shared with others. What would become of it, I could not say. In spite of six months' distance, I still thought often of that last significant meeting, when words had hung unspoken but understood in the air. I had alternately cursed and congratulated myself on my narrow escape from possible domesticity—a fate I regarded as less desirable than a lengthy bout of bubonic plague. I had been so near to making declarations that could not be undone, offering promises I was not certain I could keep. My vow never to be relegated to the roles of wife and mother had been tested during a moment of vulnerability. Stoker was the only man I knew who could have weakened my resolve, but it would have been a mistake, I insisted to myself. I was not made for a life of ordinary pursuits, and it would take an extraordinary man to live with me on my terms. It was a point of pride with me that I hunted men with the same alacrity and skill that I hunted butterflies. Only one sort of permanent trophy interested me— and that had wings. Men were a joy to sample, but a mate would be a complication I could not abide. At least, this is what I told myself, and it was perhaps this elusiveness that made me all the more attractive to the opposite sex.

His lordship included. He was lavishly lascivious in his praise, his conversation usually peppered with deliciously outrageous comments. I never took him seriously, but Stoker took him *too* seriously, and that was the root of their current lack of sympathy with one another. Like stags, they frequently locked horns, and although neither would admit it, I suspected they enjoyed their battles far more than they did the civil affections they shared with their other brothers.

Stoker was glowering at the viscount, who held up a hand, the signet ring of the Templeton-Vanes gleaming upon his left hand. "Peace, brother mine. I can feel you cursing me."

"And yet still you breathe," Stoker said mildly. "I must not be doing it right."

I rolled my eyes heavenwards. "Stoker, behave or remove yourself, I beg you. I still do not know the purpose of his lordship's call."

"I do not require a reason except that of admiration," his lordship said with practiced smoothness. Stoker made a growling noise low in his throat while his brother carried on, pretending not to hear. "I missed you during your sojourn abroad, my dear. And, as it happens, I do have business. Well, business for you, dear lady, but pleasure for me."

"Go on," I urged.

"Tell me, Miss Speedwell, in all your travels around this beautiful blue orb of ours, have you ever encountered the Romilly Glasswing butterfly?"

"*Oleria romillia*? Certainly not. It was as elusive as Rajah Brooke's Birdwing and twice as valuable. It is unfortunately now extinct. I have only ever seen one preserved specimen in a private collection and it was in dreadful condition."

The viscount held up a hand. "Not entirely extinct, as it happens."

My heart began to thump solidly within my chest as a warm flush rose to my cheeks. "What do you mean?"

"I mean that there are still specimens in the wild. Do you know the origins of the name?"

I recited the facts as promptly and accurately as a schoolgirl at her favorite lesson. "*Oleria romillia* was named for Euphrosyne Romilly, one of the greatest lepidopterists in our nation's history. She founded the

West Country Aurelian Society, the foremost body of butterfly hunters in Britain until it merged with the Royal Society of Aurelian Studies in 1852. She discovered this particular glasswing on the coast of Cornwall."

"*Off* the coast of Cornwall," the viscount corrected. "As it happens, the Romillys own an island there, St. Maddern's, just out from the little port town of Pencarron."

"A tidal island?" I asked. "Like St. Michael's Mount?" The Mount was one of Cornwall's most famous attractions, rising out of the sea in a shaft of grey stone, reaching ever upwards from its narrow foundation. On sunny days it was overrun with parties of picnickers and seaside tourists and other undesirables.

The viscount shook his head. "Not precisely. St. Michael's is accessible on foot via a causeway whilst St. Maddern's Isle is a little further out to sea and significantly larger than the Mount. There are extensive gardens as well as a village, farms, a few shops, a quarry, even an inn for the occasional traveler seeking solitude and peace. It is a unique place, with all sorts of legends and faery stories, none of which interest me in the slightest, so I cannot recall them. What I do recall is that the Romilly Glasswing makes its home upon this island, and nowhere else in the world. And this has been an excellent year for them. They have appeared in record numbers, I am told, and they dot the island like so many flowers."

I caught my breath, my lips parted as if anticipating a kiss. Nothing left me in such a heightened state of expectancy than the thought of finding a butterfly I had never before seen in the wild. And glasswings! The most unique of all the butterflies, they traveled on wings as transparent as Cinderella's slipper. Ordinary butterflies derive their color from scales, infinitesimally small and carrying all the colors of the rainbow within them, reflecting back the jewel tones associated with the most magnificent butterflies. Moths and more restrained specimens of butterfly have scales with softly powdered hues, but the most arresting sight is by far the butterfly without any scales at all. The wings of these butterflies are crystalline in their clearness, patterned only with narrow black veins like the leaded glass of a cathedral window, the thinnest of membranes stretching between them. It seems impossible that they can fly, but they do, like shards of glass borne upon the wind. Their unique wings make them delicate and elusive, and the Romilly Glasswing was the most delicate and elusive of all. The largest of the glasswings, an adult Romilly could span a man's hand if he were lucky enough to catch one. I lusted for them as I had lusted for little else in my life. But it was no use to me.

I forced a smile to my lips. "How kind of you to share this information," I said in a toneless voice. "But I no longer hunt, my lord. My specimens from Madeira were all gathered after their natural demise. I have lost the drive to thrust a pin into the heart of a living creature. My efforts are directed towards the vivarium that Lord Rosemorran is graciously permitting me to develop on the estate."

Once the derelict wreck of a grand freestanding glasshouse, the vivarium had been my own pet project, undertaken at Stoker's suggestion. While he tinkered happily with bits of fur and bone and sawdust, I had been permitted to stock the restored structure with exotic trees and the larvae of a number of specimens. I had nurtured them carefully as any mother, bringing several species to life in my bejeweled little world.

"You should know that better than anyone," I reminded the viscount. "You were kind enough to send me a grove of hornbeams and luna moths to feast upon them."

The viscount crossed one long leg over the other, smoothing the crease in his trousers. "I remember it well. You gave me quite the education upon the subject of the luna moth. What was it you said? That they have no mouths because they exist only to reproduce? One is not certain whether to regard them with envy or pity."

He arched a brow at me and I gave him a quelling look. "Precisely," I told him, my voice crisp. "And while I am glad to hear the Romilly Glasswing is not extinct, I must leave its pursuit to others."

The words pained me. I had only within the last year discovered in myself a reluctance to carry on my life's work as I had always known it. The pursuit of the butterfly had given my existence meaning and pleasure, but it had dried up for reasons I did not entirely understand. Madeira had been an experiment after a fashion, a short expedition to test my mettle. And I had failed to conquer my reluctance to kill. The few inadequate specimens I had brought back had made the entire affair pointless, and I could not justify further expeditions if I had no better expectations than the results I had achieved there. It chilled me to think that I might never strike out again, net in hand, for foreign climes and exotic lands. The notion of being forever immured in Britain, this too-often grey and sodden isle, was more than I could bear. So I did not think of it. I pushed the thought away whenever it occurred, but it had crept back over and over again as our ship had neared England, returning me to the complacent little life I had built within these walls. It teased the edge of my consciousness as I drifted off to sleep each night, that little demanding voice from a place that longed for adventure. *What if this is all there is?*

Stoker grasped his lordship's meaning before I did. "Tiberius does not mean you to hunt them," he said quietly. "He has found you larvae. For the vivarium."

I smothered a moan of longing. "Have you?" I demanded.

His lordship laughed, a low and throaty chuckle of pure amusement. "My dear Miss Speedwell, how you delight me. I have indeed secured permission from the current owner of St. Maddern's Isle, Malcolm Romilly, for you to take a certain number of larvae for your collection. While not a lepidopterist himself, he is an ardent protector of every bit of flora and fauna unique to his island, and he believes that if the glasswing is to survive, there must be a population elsewhere as a sort of insurance policy."

My mind raced with the possibilities. "What do they eat?"

The viscount shrugged. "Some shrub whose name escapes me, but Malcolm did say that you might take a number of the plants with you in order to make the transition to London as painless as possible for the little devils. Now, I am bound for St. Maddern's Isle for a house party to which Malcolm has invited me. It seems only natural that we should combine our purposes and I should escort you to the castle."

"What a splendid notion," Stoker put in smoothly. "We should love to go."

"Stoker," the viscount said firmly, "you are not invited to the castle."

"Castle!" I exclaimed. "Is it really so grand as that?"

His lordship favored me with one of his enigmatic smiles. "It is small, as castles go, but it is at least interesting. Lots of hidden passages and dungeons and that sort of thing."

"What of ghosts?" I demanded archly. "I won't go unless there is a proper ghost."

The viscount's eyes widened in a flash of something like alarm before he recovered himself. "I can promise you all manner of adventures," he said.

I could scarcely breathe for excitement. Stoker gave me a long look as he drained the last of his whisky, put down his glass, and walked silently back to his buffalo.

His brother leaned closer, pitching his voice low. "Someone is not very pleased with us."

"Someone can mind his own business," I said fiercely. "I am going to St. Maddern's Isle."

"Excellent," said Lord Templeton-Vane, his feline smile firmly in place. "Most excellent indeed."

CHAPTER

2

"He means to seduce you, you know," Stoker said after the viscount had left. He was removing rotten sawdust from the badly mounted water buffalo, punctuating his words with vigorous gestures and showering the floor and himself with the smelly tendrils of moldering wood. He had stripped off his shirt as was his custom when he worked, but the nasty stuff had stuck to his tumbled black curls and to the sweat streaking the long, hard muscles of his back and arms. I paused for a moment, as I always did when Stoker was in a state of undress, to admire the view. I had given him the better part of an hour to master his temper, but it seemed it had not been enough. I adopted a tone of generally cheerful reasonability.

"Of course he does," I agreed.

He stopped and fixed me with a disbelieving stare. "You know that?"

I sighed. "Stoker, I am twenty-six years of age. I have traveled around the world three times, and I have met scores of men, some of whom I have known far more intimately than you can imagine. I promise you, I can smell a burgeoning seduction from across the room. I am no fainting virgin," I reminded him.

"Then why in the name of bleeding Jesus are you going with him?"

"He promised me Romilly Glasswings," I said simply.

"And that is all it takes? Bought with a butterfly?" he said in a particularly harsh tone.

"Oooh, how nasty you can be when you are sulking," I observed.

He turned to his buffalo, wrenching out the sawdust in great, choking clouds. The original taxidermist had thrown in whatever he could to absorb moisture—sawdust, newspaper, bits of cloth. The stuffing had made cozy nest material for all manner of rodents. Tiny bones flew through the air with horrifying regularity as Stoker worked in a frenzy. After a few moments, he stopped.

"I am not sulking. I am concerned," he told me, his voice soft and gentle now, but the words clipped at the end, as if admitting them caused him pain.

"I can take care of myself."

"That is what I am afraid of."

"I will not be gone long. His lordship and I settled the details before he left—a fortnight at most."

He nodded, his witch-black hair gleaming in the lamplight. I waited for him to rouse himself to temper again, waited for the inevitable repetitious clash of wills, but it did not come. When Stoker and I disagreed, a frequent occurrence if I am honest, it was a thing of beauty—volcanic and ferocious. I took it as a mark of the highest affection and respect that he fought with me as he would a man, and I gave him no quarter either. Our rows were legendary on the Marylebone estate, with frequent wagers amongst the staff as to which of us would prevail. (The safest bet, I need not reveal, was always upon me.)

But this time Stoker simply refused to rise to the occasion. I knew he was angry at his brother's presumption. Any invitation or gift that had come from the viscount in the past had been met with rage on Stoker's part. The skeletons in their cupboard of childhood troubles danced vigorously. The viscount's overtures were intrusions, Stoker believed, encroachments on something he held dear and that belonged to him—me. Even though our relationship had not progressed past a firm friendship and perfect companionship, he resented any attempt by the viscount to win me to his side. I anticipated our quarrels on these occasions. I enjoyed them. But this time, Stoker merely worked at his buffalo, his jaw set and his gaze averted.

"Well, I suppose I ought to pack," I said finally. "We leave in the morning. His lordship wants to take the early train from Waterloo."

"Don't forget your hot-water bottle," he said, baring his teeth in a ghastly impression of his brother's smile. "I should hate for you to get cold in the night."

I returned the smile. "Do not worry on that account," I told him. "I know well enough how to keep warm."

I rose in good time the next morning, fairly fizzing with anticipation as I washed and dressed and gulped a hasty breakfast. Is there any feeling as delicious as the beginning of a new adventure? To be perched upon the precipice of a fresh endeavor, poised for flight, the winds of change ruffling the feathers, ah, that is what it means to be alive! I glanced around my quarters, but to me they had assumed an air of emptiness. Everything I truly cared about was packed into my carpetbag; the rest was merely trappings. I gathered two last items for the journey—the latest installment of the adventures of Arcadia Brown, Lady Detective, and the tiny grey velvet mouse I had carried since infancy. Wherever I had ventured in the world, from the misty foothills of the Andean mountains to the lush islands of the South Pacific, Chester had been my constant companion. He was a little the worse for wear these days, his velvet thinning in some places and one of his black-bead eyes a trifle loose. But I would have sooner traveled without my head than without my stalwart little companion.

I stepped outside and drew in great breaths of morning air, but not even the choking soot of London could stifle my elation. At my feet, the dogs—Stoker's bulldog, Huxley, and Lord Rosemorran's Caucasian sheepdog, Betony—romped along as I made my way to the Belvedere to take my leave of Stoker. He was already there, immured once more in his buffalo. To my acute disappointment, he wore a shirt, and his usually disordered locks were rather neater than was their habit.

"Good morning," I said in a cordial tone as I rummaged in a biscuit barrel for a few scraps to throw the dogs. They quarreled over the largest—a bit of moose antler from the Canadian wilderness—before Huxley surrendered it as a courtship gift to Bet. She rolled ecstatically on the ground, waving her enormous paws in the air and upsetting a model of the *Golden Hind* made out of walnuts as Huxley watched, his deep chest puffed out proudly.

Stoker merely grunted by way of reply.

"I am leaving, then."

He withdrew his head from the buffalo. He appeared tired, and he was wearing his eye patch, a certain sign that he had fatigued himself. It was a reminder of an accident he had suffered in the Amazon that had nearly taken his eye and his life. He still bore a slender silver scar that ran from brow to cheek, and from time to time, he had recourse to the black patch to rest his weaker eye. I never minded as—coupled with the golden rings in his lobes—it gave him the look of a buccaneer. A rather bored buccaneer at present. His expression was bland as he gave me a casual glance. "Oh? Pleasant journey."

He resumed his task and I stared at him, slack-jawed. I had expected an argument. I had *depended* upon it. There were few things I enjoyed more, and a set-to with Stoker was just the thing to cap my ebullient mood. The fact that the past few days had seen us somewhat at odds with one another made me all the keener to resume our usual banter. After six months with no word from him, I had anticipated a row to shake the rafters upon my return. Instead he had been blandly cordial, unreachable even, and his apathy goaded me far more effectively than any display of temper might have done.

"Is that it?" I demanded. "No dire warnings about your brother's wandering hands? No glowering silences or raging tantrums?"

He backed out of the buffalo again, his expression inscrutable. "My dear Veronica, you must make up your mind. Do you want silence or savagery? You cannot have both."

Ordinarily such a remark would be heavily larded with sarcasm, his rage barely held in check. But this time there was only that maddening calm, a newfound self-possession I could not prick. If he meant to wound me, he could have chosen no sharper blade than indifference.

"You are quite right," I remarked acidly. "Do forgive the interruption. I'll let you get on with your buffalo. I expect to be back in a fortnight. If I am not, it's because I eloped with your brother to Gretna Green."

His sangfroid never slipped. He merely smiled and returned to his specimen, calling over his shoulder, "Mind you ask for separate lodgings. He snores like a fiend."

Silence dropped between us with all the finality of a stage curtain. That was it, then. I turned on my heel and left him without a backwards look. Carpetbag firmly in hand, I strode to the front of Bishop's Folly, admiring the unholy muddle of architectural styles that had been assembled courtesy of several generations of Rosemorran earls. The Folly was well-named, for there was not a builder's fancy that had been omitted—buttresses, vaults, towers, crenelations, the Folly boasted them all.

Just as I rounded the corner, the great front door swung back and Lady Wellingtonia Beauclerk, the present earl's great-aunt, emerged, calling a greeting. I paused to give her a smile.

"I am so glad you happened to come out," I told her. "I had no chance to say good-bye."

"It was not happenstance," she said as she came down the short flight of stone steps to the drive of loose chipping. "I was looking for you. I've not yet welcomed you back from Madeira and here you are off again, like one of your pretty butterflies." Her tone was light but her eyes were shrewd. "One might even think you were running away from something."

I gave an involuntary glance back at the Belvedere, where Stoker still labored. "Don't be absurd, Lady Wellie."

"Are you certain there is nothing you would like to share with an old woman?" she prodded, lifting her walking stick to gesture vaguely in the direction of my person.

"Absolutely not," I returned.

She did not bridle at the sharpness of my tone. She was obviously preoccupied as she brandished a newspaper at me. I could not quite read the headlines, but the text was enormous and the story clearly lurid.

"Have you seen the newspapers? This Whitechapel murderer business is whipping up hysteria."

"I'm afraid I have heard nothing."

Her brows raised. "Lucky you. Prostitutes in the East End, child. Someone has been ripping them up and all of Scotland Yard has been thrown into tumult."

I thought of our previous involvement with the Yard* and the head of Special Branch in particular. "Poor Sir Hugo," I said lightly. "He must be keeping busy."

She gave me a narrow look. "It is not just on Hugo to solve these atrocities," she replied with a firmness that belied her eighty-plus years. "It is a national disgrace to have this monster stalking our streets and our police force unable to apprehend him. England ought to be better than this."

---

* As related in *A Curious Beginning, A Perilous Undertaking,* and *A Treacherous Curse.*

In Lady Wellie's estimation, the Empire was the center of the universe and England the center of the Empire. Nothing else mattered but this blessed isle. The whole of her father's life and hers had been devoted to its service, secretly, as each had fulfilled the function of an éminence grise, the power behind the royal family, always guiding, protecting, shielding, not for love of the family themselves but for love of the land and people they governed. Her blood was red as St. George's Cross. She was, without doubt, the most patriotic individual I had ever known, and she was not above using anyone or anything in order to serve her goals. She was ruthless and hard-edged, and when she smiled, it was a crocodile's smile, full of guile. I quite liked her, if I am honest, but that morning I was eager to be on my way.

Her shrewd dark eyes missed nothing. "I know you want to be off. I'll not keep you. But tell me where you mean to be in case I should like to write to you."

I rattled off the castle's address, watching as she pursed her lips. "Malcolm Romilly's place. I knew his grandfather. Waltzed with him at Victoria's coronation ball. He trod on my toes, but he was a very good kisser. Quite a skillful tongue," she said with a dreamy look.

I smiled in spite of myself and pressed her hand. "Good day, Lady Wellie."

She lifted a withered hand. "Godspeed, child."

His lordship and I had arranged to meet at Waterloo Station, and I very nearly missed him in the teeming throng of travelers that balmy late September morning. The platforms were heaving with people of every description, starched nannies with their screaming charges, turbaned gentlemen making their way with courtly elegance past nut sellers, and pale, thin girls selling the last of the summer flowers, bawling out their wares in harsh cries to make themselves heard above the plump matrons offering meat pies for the journey. Through them all strode City men of business in their pinstriped rectitude, discreetly ogling the aristocratic ladies gliding past without glancing to the left or right, little dogs and ladies' maids trotting in their wake.

The viscount found me at last. "Miss Speedwell," he said, coming to my side with long strides that earned the admiration of more than one passing lady. "I was beginning to despair of ever finding you in this melee. Come, I have secured our compartment and the porter will see to your bags."

A very upright porter with the posture of a broom handle took my bag from my hand and gave me a searching look. "Shall I wait for the lady's maid, my lord?" he asked the viscount.

Lord Templeton-Vane waved him off. "Miss Speedwell is a modern lady. She does not travel with a maid."

If his lordship had told the man I intended to travel stark naked with a pumpkin on my head, he could not have looked more appalled. He swallowed hard and gave a half bow that was both respectful and condescending. "Very good, my lord."

"And I will carry my own bag, thank you," I said, retrieving my carpetbag with a gesture that brooked no argument.

He gave a little sniff—offended either at my intransigence or the fact that he would see no tip from me—before drawing himself up to his full height and turning to the viscount. "In that case I will bid you a happy journey, my lord. The hamper and your small case are in the compartment and your larger bags are marked for Pencarron and stowed in the luggage van. Good day, sir," he finished with a hopeful look at the viscount. His lordship obliged him with a substantial coin and the fellow gave me a dismissive look as he strode away.

The viscount turned to me. "My dear Miss Speedwell, two minutes in and already you are causing a scandal. Whatever shall I do with you?"

I did not trouble myself to reply. He offered his arm and we were soon comfortably established in our private compartment. As the train drew from the station in great gusts of steam, he settled back against his seat, regarding me thoughtfully. "I suppose I ought to have considered better the impropriety of our traveling together," he said.

I shrugged. "I am no stranger to impropriety. It troubles me not in the slightest," I assured him. "After all, I work for a living. I am hardly a lady."

His handsome upper lip quirked into an effort at a smile. "And yet you speak with such distinction and your manner and gestures are thoroughly elegant. Tell me, Miss Speedwell, how did you come to be?"

The tone was casual but the gaze that fell upon me was watchful. It occurred to me then that his lordship might have penetrated the truth about my identity. It was an imperfectly kept secret at best. Stoker knew, as did their second brother, Sir Rupert, along with an assortment of government officials, a few Irish malcontents, and our own royal family. Being the semi-legitimate daughter of the Prince of Wales came with a few drawbacks, not least the lack of recognition from my own blood relations. I had made my own way in the world, no thanks to them, but I concealed my birth from prying eyes. Permitting my story to become publicly known would rock the monarchy, I had been warned, although they needn't have bothered. I had as little desire to be pestered and fussed over as they had of being deposed. The fact that one villain had already attempted to put a crown upon my head was enough to convince me that the life of royalty was not for me.

But the question I pondered now was how much of this Lord Templeton-Vane knew. I gave him a noncommittal smile. "It is a dreadfully dull story, I'm afraid. My mother died when I was a year old and I never knew my father." That much was true, strictly speaking. "I was brought up by two of my mother's friends, a pair of spinster sisters who were like aunts. One of them encouraged my interest in lepidoptery, and I discovered that I could make a comfortable living with my net as well as see the world," I finished lightly.

His lordship said nothing for a long moment. "I think you underestimate how interesting a person you are," he remarked finally.

"I have always said that it is interesting people who find others interesting."

"And how neatly you turn my observation to a compliment! That takes real skill."

"I am merely observant—as are you, my lord."

He canted his head, a gesture I had seen Stoker perform a thousand times. "I think that we have progressed beyond 'Miss Speedwell' and 'my lord.' I would take it as a mark of generosity on your part if you would address me as Tiberius."

"Very well. If you wish."

"I do. Veronica," he replied, drawing out the syllables as if reciting an incantation. Without warning, his expression darkened.

"Is there something wrong?"

He shook his head. "Not precisely. But I have taken a liberty of which you might not approve. You see, I remembered only this morning that Malcolm Romilly is a Roman Catholic, rather a fussy one. He would not approve of my traveling with a young lady unchaperoned."

"I am hardly a young lady!" I protested.

"Young enough," the viscount corrected with a wry twist of the lips. "And delectable to boot. No, I'm afraid Malcolm's sensibilities might be offended and we can't have that. But I realized a little polite fiction might smooth the path. He could hardly think it amiss if we travel together as an affianced couple."

I blinked. "You want me to pose as your fiancée?"

"Yes," he said, obviously relishing the idea. "That small pretense will serve us quite nicely."

"I hardly think it necessary," I protested.

"Oh, but it is," he told me with an unmistakable air of satisfaction. "Malcolm can be a stickler about such things. What if he took offense and decided to withdraw his offer of the glasswing larvae? How dreadfully disappointing that would be." His voice trailed off suggestively, letting the insinuation do its work.

I had, as he had known, no choice. "I will not lose the glasswings," I said forcefully.

"Then we are in agreement," he said, settling back with a broad smile. "And you will naturally forgive me for taking the precaution of sending a wire to our host with that information just before we departed." Before I could respond, he gestured with an elegant hand, imperious as Jove. "Now, if you will reach into the hamper beside you, you will find a bottle of rather good champagne. I think a toast is in order."

The next hours passed in a haze of succulent food and drink and amiable company as the viscount and I talked and laughed and thoroughly enjoyed ourselves. The champagne was not the only delight to be found in the hamper. His lordship—or Tiberius, as I had been instructed to think of him—had laid in a supply of delicacies to last the better part of a week.

"I thought the journey was to be completed by nightfall," I told him as I helped myself to a tiny pie with a featherlight crust and a filling of herbed chicken.

"And so it should be, but there is no reason for us to deny ourselves as much pleasure as possible along the way," he remarked. I might have taken that for a proposition, but he merely selected a sandwich of the thinnest, whitest bread filled with slivers of perfectly roasted beef and lashings of horseradish sauce. "Divine," he pronounced.

"You have a crumb upon your lip," I told him. He put out his tongue in search of it and missed. Laughing, I moved forward and touched my fingertip to the corner of his mouth. I had not considered the intimacy of such an action. It was the sort of thing I might have done to Stoker, and I had come to enjoy a similar although less intense rapport with the viscount.

But if I was slow to appreciate the familiarity of the gesture, Tiberius was not. He held my gaze with his, all mockery fallen away as he leant forward. He parted his lips, taking my finger into his mouth as he removed the crumb. His eyes locked with mine, he gave a gentle suck, and I felt the blood beat in my veins.

He released my finger and sat back with a slow, deliberate smile. "Delicious. As I suspected it would be," he told me. And I knew he did not mean the crumb.

For the rest of the journey—and make no mistake, to travel from London to the tip of Cornwall takes *hours*—the viscount behaved with almost perfect decorum. He still made the odd remark that might have been construed as inappropriate by Society's standards, but nothing that imperiled my virtue, slight as it was. And he did not touch me again. Instead he applied himself to my comfort, insisting upon opening the window when the compartment grew stuffy and asking intelligent and penetrating questions about lepidoptery. I was no fool. I was familiar enough with the machinations of men to know when I was being catechized simply so that a gentleman might appear to marvel at my accomplishments, thereby endearing himself to me. But Tiberius was more skilled than most. I almost believed that he was sincerely impressed with the breadth of my knowledge.

Almost. To test him, I spent the better part of an hour describing the Gypsy moth in exhaustive detail. If I am honest, which I have sworn to be within these pages, I will admit that I embroidered most of the facts and invented some out of whole cloth. Throughout my recitation, he kept his expression attentive and even offered thoughtful comments from time to time.

"You don't say," he remarked at one point. "The Gypsy moth has a furry tail and feeds solely on Madagascar lizards. How frightfully interesting."

"No, it isn't," I corrected. "Because I made it up. *Lymantria dispar* do not have furry tails, nor do they eat lizards. No moth does. I was merely testing your ability to pretend to be interested. It is a prodigious skill, my lord. You lasted fifty-seven minutes."

He looked aggrieved, then smiled. "You were supposed to call me Tiberius," he reminded me.

"And you have no need for this pretense. Why play at being interested in moths, of all things?" I asked.

"I am not interested in moths," he admitted. "But I am interested in you."

"That," I told him without a blush, "is entirely apparent."

"Good."

He sat forward, hands resting upon his knees. They were good hands, like Stoker's, beautifully shaped, although Tiberius' were unstained by chemicals and glues and the various other nasty things that habitually fouled Stoker's. These hands were strong and clean, the nails trimmed and the moons stark white.

"You have never done a day's work with those hands," I told him.

"No, but I've done many a night's," he said, reaching one out to cup my cheek.

"My lord," I began.

"Tiberius," he reminded me, leaning forward still further until his name was a breath across my lips. I was just trying to make up my mind whether to let him kiss me—the viscount was after all a very handsome man—or to give him a polite shove, when the train jerked to a stop, flinging him backwards onto his seat.

"Oh, look. We've arrived in Exeter," I said brightly.

CHAPTER

3

After changing trains at Exeter, we carried on to Padstow, where we changed yet again, the trip requiring a further leg on a smaller railway to Pencarron and then a transfer to a quaint little quay full of fishing boats bobbing at anchor. They were brightly painted, as were the houses clustered on the hillside that rose sharply above the curved arm of the shore.

The sea air was bracing and fresh, and Tiberius, with no sign of resentment at his thwarted attempts at lovemaking, drew in a breath and let it out in an exultant sigh. "There is nothing like sea air to mend what ails you," he pronounced.

"I did not know you were fond of the sea," I told him as we made our way from the tiny station down to the waiting boats.

"Indeed I am. A naval career is one of the things I envied Stoker bitterly."

"The fact that you envied him anything at all would come as the most appalling shock to him," I returned.

His mouth twisted into a wry expression. "I envy him more than any other man I have ever known," he said.

"Tiberius," drawled a familiar voice, "how very touching. I did not realize how much you cared."

I whirled to find Stoker lounging idly, one leg crossed over the other at the ankle, his arms folded.

"How on earth—"

"There was an express from Exeter," he told me. "Tiberius ought to have taken it, but I suppose he was too enchanted with your company to want to shorten the experience."

"How is it," I demanded, "that we did not see you on the train from London?"

"I traveled third class," he told us with a grin as a porter came trundling up with an assortment of smart shagreen cases stamped with the viscount's initials.

Tiberius' mouth thinned. "How very predictable of you, Revelstoke."

He seldom used Stoker's proper name, and it was a measure of his displeasure that he did so.

Stoker shrugged and picked up his single piece of baggage, a small battered naval chest. I turned to Tiberius. "Will Stoker's arrival present difficulties with your host?"

"I doubt it, since I expected this very course of action on his part," was the smooth reply.

Stoker fixed him with a penetrating look. "What do you mean?"

"I mean, dear brother, that you are as easy to anticipate now as you were in childhood. I wired Malcolm this morning that my brother would be joining the party and I hoped he could be accommodated. Just before we departed, I received an affirmative reply." He bared his teeth in a semblance of a smile. "I know how much you like to play the prodigal brother, so I have arranged for the fatted calf."

With that he turned on his heel, signaling the porter to follow. I looked to Stoker, whose expression was one of naked astonishment edged with resentment.

"Why so vexed?" I asked. "You obviously wanted to come and now you're here."

"True," he replied slowly. "I just resent like hell being Tiberius' foregone conclusion." He looked at me for a long moment. "What about you? Are you bothered that I have come?"

His jaw was set, his lips tight, belying the easy tone he had adopted. He was trying for nonchalance and very nearly achieved it. But I knew him too well for that.

I turned on my heel to follow Tiberius. "I have not yet decided," I called over my shoulder. "Try not to use your kennel manners. We are guests."

It was almost dark then, well past sunset with only the fading purple light of evening to illuminate the horizon. Off to the west, silhouetted against the violet sweep of the sky, a pointed black shape rose, thrusting itself upwards.

"St. Maddern's Isle," Tiberius said as I joined him, and there was a note in his voice I had never heard before, some strong emotion he was struggling with and very nearly concealing. But I heard it, and I saw it in the expression in his eyes before he looked away, brushing at some invisible lint on his sleeve.

"Come, Veronica. It would be best to make the crossing before nightfall."

I followed him down to the quay and took his hand as he helped me into a narrow boat. Stoker followed, leaping nimbly into the boat with the grace of a seasoned sailor. A local fellow of advanced years sporting fisherman's clothes and a Cornishman's accent tugged at his cap and welcomed us aboard.

"Trefusis, I'm called. You'll be the guests of the master of St. Maddern's. I'll have you over in a trice, my good lord, and your lady and t'other gentleman as well. Your bags will come over on the next boat, but you'll be wanting to get across before the storm comes."

"Storm?" I asked. The sky was as yet a soft plum color, with gentle gauzy wisps of clouds just masking the first glimmer of starlight.

"Aye, but not to fear, lady. A bit of a squall, no more. Gone by midnight and a fair day tomorrow," he promised. "Now, stand you here if you like for the best view of St. Maddern's Isle as we approach." I did as he advised, and Tiberius came to stand behind me. Stoker remained in the stern of the boat, feet planted wide apart, hands thrust into his pockets as he lifted his head, sniffing the air. A mist had risen, shrouding the island and its castle from sight until we were quite close, and then, without preamble, a soft sigh of wind blew the shreds of fog away and there it was, looming above us, black and forbidding and utterly enormous from the vantage of the tiny boat in the open sea.

"There she be," the Cornishman Trefusis said proudly. "The Isle."

He beached the little craft and clambered into the water as Tiberius vaulted smoothly over the side of the boat. I dropped into his waiting arms, rather more solid limbs than I would have expected. To my surprise, there was nothing flirtatious in his embrace. He held me firmly against his chest as he strode with apparent ease through the thigh-deep water. When he had placed me solidly upon my feet on the shingle beach, he offered the Cornishman a coin before Stoker bent his shoulder to help old Trefusis turn the boat towards Pencarron. The Cornishman tugged his hat brim and set his course for home as Tiberius and I looked to the castle, Stoker standing just behind.

Tiberius had fallen silent and merely stood for a long moment, his gaze fixed upon the black stone built upon the eminence. He was sunk in some sort of reverie, and for a fleeting instant, something dark and terrible touched his face.

"Tiberius?" I asked gently, drawing him from his thoughts.

He shook himself with visible effort. "My apologies, Veronica. I had not thought to be here ever again. It is a curious and winding road, the path of fate."

"Certainly," I said briskly. "But the wind is rising. Should we not make our way up to the castle?"

"Of course. I seem to have misplaced my manners. What you must think of me for leaving you standing about!" He had found again his usual mocking tone, and when the starlight shone upon his face, I saw that his expression was guarded once more.

Before I could reply, he put a firm hand beneath my elbow and guided me towards the cliff towering above us, Stoker following silently behind. As we approached, I saw a staircase had been cut into the stone, switching back upon itself over and again as it rose towards the castle.

"There is a funicular on the other side of the island," Tiberius told me as we began to mount the steps. "But it is a temperamental beast and means a walk of a few miles to go around that way. If you can bear the climb, this is much more direct."

"Nothing would suit me better than a chance to stretch my limbs after the train journey," I told him truthfully as I clambered ahead.

"If you get tired, I'll push from the back side, shall I?" Stoker asked nastily.

"Do shut up," I muttered as we pressed on.

Iron lanterns had been set at periodic intervals in the stone and someone had lit them; they glowed like small golden stars against the vast black reaches of the cliffside, pointing the way ahead. We climbed for what seemed hours, ever further, ever higher, until at last we reached the top and the last step led us to a stout stone wall fitted with a high archway.

I glanced upwards as we passed through. "Is that a portcullis?" I asked over my shoulder.

But it was not Tiberius' voice which replied. "It is indeed, dear lady."

The archway led us into a courtyard thick with shadows, illuminated by starlight and torchlight and the glimmer of dozens of golden windows set within the black walls. A broad door had been thrown back upon its hinges, letting more light spill over the paving stones. Standing just before it, silhouetted against the warm glow, was a figure of a man. He stepped nearer, letting the light fall upon his face.

It must have once been an almost handsome face, I judged. The features were regular and agreeably arranged, and his physique was that of a common country squire, heavily muscled in shoulder and thigh. He looked the sort of gentleman England had made a speciality of producing, stalwart, principled, and with an air of dutiful determination about him, the kind of man who would have been in the first charge at Agincourt. But a second look showed eyes that were a little sunken, as if from sleepless nights, and there were deep lines incised from nose to chin that looked as if they had been drawn on with an unkind hand. If this had not persuaded me that he was troubled, a single glance at his hands would have done so. His fingernails were bitten to the quick, a slender thread of scarlet marking the end of each.

But his smile was gracious as he threw open his arms expansively. "Welcome to the Isle. You must be Miss Speedwell. I am your host, Malcolm Romilly."

"How do you do?" I asked, shaking his hand gently.

"And you, sir, must be Revelstoke Templeton-Vane," he said, moving forward to shake Stoker's hand.

"Stoker, please," he urged his host. Stoker answered to his surname as seldom as possible.

Malcolm Romilly turned to the viscount at last. "Tiberius. It has been a long time."

"Indeed," Tiberius replied coolly. "I hope you are keeping well."

Mr. Romilly gave a small and mirthless laugh. "Not as well as you, it seems. I am delighted to make the acquaintance of your fiancée." The words were cordial but there was an undercurrent of something inexplicable swirling beneath.

Behind me, I felt Stoker stiffen like a pointer at the remark, but

Malcolm Romilly was already speaking again, urging us in the door. "Come inside, won't you? There's a storm brewing and we have rooms prepared for all of you."

Stoker fell in step behind me. "Fiancée?" he murmured in my ear. "We shall speak of this later."

"There is nothing to discuss," I told him, still mightily put out that he had taken it upon himself to come to Cornwall. I had been anticipating a few weeks to straighten my disordered feelings and instead he was there, inches from me, causing every nerve to tingle and my thoughts to leap about in a most unsettling manner.

To my surprise, Stoker let the matter drop then and we followed our host into the great hall of the castle. It was exactly what one hoped a castle would be. The vast stone hall was furnished with an enormous fireplace—the sort for roasting half an ox or an annoying child—at one end and a minstrels' gallery at the other. The ceiling was vaulted and ribbed in an elaborate Gothic pattern of lozenges, each painted in hues of scarlet or blue, surrounding the heraldic mermaid emblem of the Romilly family. Along the stone walls hung the usual assortment of weapons and armor and other trinkets of warfare that interested me not at all. There was even a tapestry of great antiquity, faded and gently nibbled by moths. When I squinted, I could just make out that it seemed to depict a scene of mermaids luring sailors to their doom.

"I know it all seems a bit Gothic these days," Malcolm Romilly explained with an apologetic little bob of the head. "But the great hall is the pride of the Romillys and we cannot bear to change it. The rest of the castle is far more comfortable, I promise," he assured me.

I smiled. "I am accustomed to living rough when required. I hardly think a castle would challenge that."

There was a silken murmur of soft, padded feet upon the stone as a black cat slipped into the room. "Hecate, come back," chastened the lady following the cat. She was holding her skirts in both hands, moving swiftly to retrieve her pet. Somewhere on the dark side of thirty-five, she was dressed expensively in a gown of austere black satin. The fabric shimmered in the light, heightening the pastel rose of her cheeks, and I noticed her eyes were an unusual pale blue-grey. She was an attractive woman, but her greatest asset was her voice. It was low and melodious as she scolded her cat, sweeping the animal into her arms. It settled down comfortably, preening a little as she cradled it.

"Malcolm, I simply cannot find Mertensia. She knows that you were expecting guests and she is not here to welcome them," she protested.

Mr. Romilly gave her a wan smile. "You fuss too much, Helen. Mertensia will be in the gardens, I have no doubt." He turned to us. "You must forgive my sister. Mertensia is a tireless plantswoman, and her gardens here are renowned. If she is not elbow-deep in the soil, she is brewing up concoctions in her stillroom or coaxing bulbs to flower out of season."

He turned and gestured for the lady to come forward. "Lord Templeton-Vane, Miss Speedwell, Mr. Templeton-Vane, my sister-in-law, Mrs. Lucian Romilly. Helen, this is the Viscount Templeton-Vane and his fiancée, Miss Speedwell, and the viscount's brother."

She smiled. "Of course, Lord Templeton-Vane, I remember you well. We met once before here, although you had not yet succeeded to your title."

Tiberius bowed low over her hand. "I recall," he said softly. There was an undercurrent I could not place, but before I could puzzle over it, Helen Romilly turned to greet me, her smile of welcome firmly in place. "Miss Speedwell, welcome to the island. And Mr. Templeton-Vane. I must say, I do not think I would have known you for his lordship's brother if Malcolm had not said it is so. You are very different upon first look, although I think I detect a faint resemblance about the eyes," she observed.

"You are too kind," Stoker said archly, bowing over her hand. I rolled my eyes heavenwards, but Helen Romilly seemed pleased with the gesture.

"And who is this beautiful creature?" Stoker asked, stroking the head of the cat with practiced gentleness. It half closed its eyes, a low purr beginning to rumble in its throat.

"Hecate," Helen Romilly replied. "How curious! She hates strangers, but she seems to have taken a liking to you."

"Stoker has a great appeal to animals and other creatures incapable of rational thought," Tiberius put in with a bland smile.

Just then, a figure in grey materialized in the doorway. "Mr. Malcolm, the rooms are prepared."

The woman who appeared was dressed in bombazine, the unmistakable jingle of a chatelaine at her waist proclaiming her the house-keeper. Her hair was winged back on either side of her face in an old-fashioned style, the pins covered by a neat cap of black lace.

"Thank you, Trenny. My dear guests, Mrs. Trengrouse will show you up. Dinner has been put back half an hour to accommodate your arrival. When you hear the gong, it will be time to join us in the drawing room."

He stepped back, giving a little bow of welcome, and we moved to where Mrs. Trengrouse stood, lamp in hand, as he made the necessary introductions. "Welcome, my lord, Miss Speedwell, sir," she said, greeting each of us in turn as she led us through a narrow stone passage which gave way to a still narrower set of stairs cut into the stone. "I am afraid the castle has not yet been fitted with gas, so you will need a lamp or a candle if you mean to move about in the evening. Please watch your step upon the stairs. They are very old and quite uneven."

They spiraled up into the darkness and I turned to flick Tiberius a glance. His face was immobile, set in an expression that looked very much like one of grim determination. I followed Mrs. Trengrouse and Tiberius followed me and Stoker followed him like a crocodile of school-children.

"You are up here, my lord, on the first floor," she said, indicating a door on the landing. It stood open and I could see a round bedchamber furnished in deep blue. "It is the largest of the suites in the tower because the structure narrows as it rises. Hot water has just been brought up and your bags are on their way. Your things will be unpacked before you have finished bathing," she promised.

He made a noncommittal noise and went inside, closing the door behind him.

"Miss Speedwell," she said, gesturing for me to follow. "I have put you just above his lordship. It means an extra flight of stairs, but the views make it quite worth the climb. Mr. Templeton-Vane, I have put you on the top floor in the smallest chamber, the Bachelor Room."

"That's me put in my place," Stoker murmured as we climbed to the next floor.

My bedchamber was very similar to Tiberius' except that it was of slightly more modest proportions and my furnishings were of violet velvet. It was a surprisingly comfortable room, with a welcoming fire kindled upon the hearth and a tub of water giving off fragrant steam. There was a tall, narrow window embrasure facing west, and I imagined the views over the water would be spectacular as the sun rose behind the castle, glittering across the sea. A pair of cozy armchairs flanked the fireplace, and the bed was an old-fashioned four-poster, hung with more violet velvet and spread with heavy linen sheets of near-blinding whiteness. A soft fragrance permeated the air, and I sniffed appreciatively.

"'Tis the potpourri Miss Mertensia makes for me to keep in the linen press," Mrs. Trengrouse told me. "And the flowers," she added with a nod towards the tall vase of exuberant hydrangeas standing upon a polished oak chest. "She always does the flowers for guests. Not much for conversation, but she likes folk to feel welcome," she said with a slight air of defensiveness. She was obviously devoted to her mistress, and I gave her a reassuring smile.

"It is very charming, Mrs. Trengrouse, and far too grand. I shall feel like a princess."

She broke into a smile, and her face, sad in repose, was transformed. "That is very kind of you to say, Miss Speedwell."

She turned to leave, but Stoker raised a hand. "I daresay I can find my own way, Mrs. Trengrouse."

"I daresay you could, sir. From here, the stairs lead only to your chamber. There is no proper bathtub in your room, for the stairs are too narrow, but hot water will be brought so you can wash at the basin."

"You needn't show me," he assured her. "I am used to looking after myself."

He did not even glance at me as he left, and I turned away, feeling somehow chastened by that parting thrust.

But Mrs. Trengrouse had other matters on her mind. She moved swiftly to plump a pillow. "There. That's better now."

"It is good of you to take such trouble."

She turned to me in obvious surprise. "It is my job, miss."

"Have you been at the castle long?" I reached for my hatpin and tugged it loose. I wore a hat for travel and for any possibly dangerous enterprise—hatpins were among the most effective weapons I owned—but there was never a time I did not find them tedious in the extreme, no matter how luscious the flowers I insisted upon as embellishment.

Mrs. Trengrouse moved forward, never hurried, but with a swift competence I would come to discover characterized all of her actions. "Since I was twelve years old. I came as a nurserymaid when the late Mrs. Romilly bore Mr. Malcolm." She took my hat and shook the dust from it.

"Then you are a friend to them indeed!"

Her smile was one of the gentlest reproof. "I would never presume, miss. I see you have come without your maid. Shall I take this for you and have one of the girls give it a good brushing?"

"That would be most appreciated, thank you."

She inclined her head. "If there is anything you want while you are here, you have only to ask. It is Mr. Malcolm's express wish that his guests have every comfort."

"I will remember that," I promised her.

She left me then, closing the door gently behind her. I undressed and slipped into the bath, the warm, scented water lapping at my skin as I thought of Tiberius, in the room just below, doing exactly the same. I wondered precisely how long it would be before he attempted to make the trip up the narrow, winding stair. And I thought of Stoker, in the room just above, and wondered what further surprises the evening would hold.

A short while later, there was a scratch at the door and an apple-cheeked maid appeared. She was young but tidy, with a spotless apron and neat dark plaits pinned at her nape. "Good evening, miss," she said as she bustled in, the skirts of her starched cotton frock snapping. "Mrs. Trengrouse said as you had no maid of your own I was to wait upon you during your stay."

"That really is not necessary," I began.

She pressed her lips together firmly. "I am afraid Mrs. Trengrouse insists, miss."

"Of course she does," I murmured. "Very well, you can begin with the unpacking."

The girl was as quick as she was determined, and in the veritable blink of an eye she had unpacked my solitary bag, hanging the clothes upon pegs in the wardrobe and arranging my comb and brush and pot of cold cream of roses on the washstand. My lepidoptery gear—specimen jars, ring net, pins, field notebook—was deposited in the bottom of the wardrobe. My books were placed in a tidy stack on the mantelpiece, and the boots I had worn during my travels were set outside the door to be collected by the boot boy. An enormous cake of soap smelling of herbs had been provided, and by the time I had rinsed off the suds and patted myself dry, she had shaken the wrinkles from my one evening dress and assembled a regiment of hairpins.

She stroked the fabric of my evening dress as I slipped into my dressing gown, knotting the belt at my waist. "'Tis a fine color, that is, miss," she remarked, turning the fabric this way and that to catch the light. "What d'ye call it?"

"The dressmaker pronounced it azure," I told her, "but to me it is the precise shade of the Morpho butterfly."

"The what, miss?" I seated myself at the dressing table and she began to dress my hair.

"*Morpho didius*," I explained. "A beastly great butterfly native to South America."

"South America! Fancy that," she said, gathering my hair into loose waves to pin at the crown of my head. "Imagine someone going all the way to South America just to catch a butterfly. They'd have to be daft," she added.

I did not bother to tell her I had journeyed much further in my quests. "What is your name?" I asked her.

"Daisy, miss. And if you want me, day or night, you've only to ring the bellpull by the fireplace and I'll come."

I gave her a careful look and decided against delivering a lecture upon the evils of domestic servitude in exchange for low wages.

She jerked her head towards the floor, indicating Tiberius' room. "I saw his lordship on my way up," she said, plucking a hairpin from between her teeth. "The word belowstairs is he is your intended, miss."

"Well, then it must be true," I temporized.

She gave a little sigh. It was highly irregular to gossip with the servants, I reminded myself, but I had never stood on ceremony, far preferring to establish myself on a friendly footing with those around me, whatever their station. We chattered on while she finished my hair, arranging it so cleverly that not a single pin could be seen. Then she helped me into my gown, giving the bustle a brisk shake so that the folds settled into elegant swags.

"There you are, miss," she told me. "Fine as a pheasant." She gave me a broad wink as she left, and I realized that my time on St. Maddern's Isle might be a good deal more diverting than I had even anticipated.

The gong sounded shortly after I finished dressing and I made my way carefully down the stairs, holding my skirts well above my ankles so that I would not trip. It was a measure of Tiberius' newfound distraction that he made no comment about the sight of them as I reached the bottom, where he waited. He always looked splendid in the black-and-white severity of evening clothes, and he had brushed his dark chestnut hair until it gleamed. But a tiny dot of crimson just below his ear showed that he had cut himself shaving, a curious development given that his lordship was usually as fastidious as a cat.

"Shall we wait for Stoker?" I ventured.

"Stoker has gone ahead," his lordship replied, clipping the words.

He led me through a series of rooms and passages in the labyrinthine castle, and I realized that he knew his way comfortably around. He was indeed no stranger to this place, I reflected. He paused outside a closed door, and as he hesitated, he reached for my hand.

"Tiberius?"

He said nothing, merely turned his head, his grey eyes glittering feverishly, his hand grasping mine with the strength of a drowning man. He opened the door to the drawing room, where a quartet of people had already assembled. Malcolm Romilly was deep in conversation with Stoker, the pair of them poring over what appeared to be a barometer of some antiquity. Helen Romilly rose from her perch on a sofa, dislodging an irritated Hecate the cat and towing in her wake an exceedingly young man with almost startling good looks. He wore an expression of acute boredom.

"My lord, Miss Speedwell, may I present my son, Caspian Romilly? Caspian, say hello to Lord Templeton-Vane and his fiancée." This was no boy; Caspian Romilly was eighteen at the very least and perfectly aware of his arresting appearance. He had his mother's eyes and rosebud lips, but his stern brow and excellent nose were clearly the stuff of Romillys.

He greeted us with an inaudible voice and a marked lack of enthusiasm, but just then his mother's cat took a decided swipe at the hem of my gown, and she clucked her tongue. "Caspian, darling, do please take her in hand."

He gave an elaborate sigh and rolled his eyes but did as she asked, gathering up the sullen animal with surprising gentleness and coaxing her out the door.

"Such a lovely boy," his mother murmured. "Quite a way with animals. He's terribly sensitive."

"He wants whipping," Tiberius murmured into my ear as Helen Romilly turned away at her brother-in-law's approach. He and Stoker had left off their discussion in order to join us, and I saw Helen Romilly's gaze rest a moment too long upon Stoker. It was always a surprise to see him in evening clothes since he wore them so well, his careless good looks and deep ebony hair setting off the severe black and white. The garments were indifferently tailored, but he would suit a burlap sack, I thought, and Helen Romilly seemed to agree.

For his part, Malcolm Romilly looked pale and tense in his evening clothes, but they were well tailored and his stickpin was of heavy gold, set with an unusual stone.

"I see you are admiring my carnelian," he told me. "We are rich in such gems here upon the island. The rocks are heavy with seams of carnelian, jasper, agate. Semiprecious, of course, but worth the effort just the same. If you would like a souvenir of your travels, you must visit the jeweler in the village. He has an assortment of our local gems."

"Is the island large enough to support a jeweler? I had no idea," I told him. "I confess, I was dreadfully unaware St. Maddern's Isle even existed before his lordship mentioned it."

Malcolm Romilly gave me a singularly sweet smile, as sad as it was genuine, as he poured out small glasses of wine for the company. "We have been in seclusion, Miss Speedwell. You are the first guests we have invited in three years."

"Lucky for us," Stoker said as he took a glass.

"Have you been here before, Mr. Templeton-Vane?" Helen Romilly asked Stoker as she accepted a glass of wine from her brother-in-law.

"I have not had that pleasure, Mrs. Romilly," Stoker told her. "I was always deeply envious of my brother when he returned from one of his holidays here. I can only count myself fortunate to be included in this one." He lifted his glass towards his host and sipped.

She gave a hard little laugh. "I shall be interested to hear your impressions of the place. It always seems a curious dream when one is here. I am never entirely certain I haven't been away with the faeries when I return to the mainland."

"Surely you mean the piskies, Helen," Malcolm Romilly corrected with a smile. "After all, we are part of Cornwall."

Her look at him was level and long. "Just as you say, Malcolm."

There were odd currents of tension in the room, swirling and eddying about us, and before I could determine what it all meant, Mrs. Trengrouse appeared in the doorway.

"Dinner is served."

CHAPTER

4

The table was set with a handsome silver service, a line of elaborate epergnes marching down the center of the table, each lavishly filled with striped red-and-white roses that perfumed the air. Before I could remark upon them, a disheveled-looking lady of perhaps thirty appeared, slipping into her seat next to Stoker with a hasty glance of apology towards Malcolm Romilly.

"Mertensia," he said with the merest hint of reproof.

"I know, Malcolm, but I was gathering rose hips and I quite lost track of time," she protested.

"And apparently the location of your looking glass," her sister-in-law said with a smile that did not quite take the sting from her words. "You haven't even changed your gown!"

Mertensia Romilly looked down at her plain dress of striped cotton in apparent surprise. "So I haven't. But I washed my hands," she added brightly, flashing palms that were crossed with scratches and old scars but scrupulously clean.

Helen Romilly flicked a glance towards Mertensia's untidy hair and gave a little sigh before turning to her soup—a delicious mushroom consommé served in the tiniest of dishes. Malcolm made the introductions and his sister peered at Tiberius.

"I remember you," she said.

Tiberius inclined his head. "Miss Mertensia. Always a pleasure to renew our acquaintance."

Then Miss Mertensia's gaze fell properly upon Stoker for the first time. She colored heavily and I suppressed a sigh. I had seen it all before. Women, particularly those of original tastes, were invariably drawn to him. A metaphor involving moths and flames came to mind. Stoker was faultlessly kind in these situations.

"I understand you are a keen gardener," he ventured. "I should very much like to see the gardens whilst I am here."

She blinked at him and colored again as she made an inaudible reply. He applied himself to his soup as she turned to me.

"Do you like gardens, Miss Speedwell?" she asked, her gaze penetrating.

"Only inasmuch as they provide haven for my butterflies," I told her. She sniffed and devoted her attention to her food with all the enthusiasm of a laborer who has toiled long and hard and earned her bread. I realized then that Miss Mertensia no doubt divided people into "garden" people— worth knowing—and "nongarden" people, who were obviously not.

Malcolm Romilly turned to me. "My sister is responsible for overseeing the extensive gardens here at the castle, as well as the glasshouses and stillrooms. She is the castle's very own white witch," he added with a faintly teasing smile.

Miss Mertensia rolled her eyes heavenwards as she finished off her soup. "It is not witchcraft, Malcolm. It's medicine, only of a more traditional sort than those rubbishy fellows in Harley Street with their stethoscopes and condescending moustaches."

Helen Romilly leant forward to catch my eye. "Malcolm tells us you are a lepidopterist. You must explore the gardens whilst you are here, Miss Speedwell. They are absolutely enchanting. Mertensia has the greenest of thumbs!"

"I shall make a point of it," I assured her.

Miss Mertensia looked up sharply. "Go where you please; in fact, I will even show you the best places to hunt butterflies if you like. The little wretches are always eating my plants. But mind you don't explore alone, at least not the far end of the gardens."

If I was taken a little aback at the edge to her tone, I strove not to show it. "I shouldn't dream of intruding, Miss Romilly."

She gave a grunt of approval as she returned to her food, switching her empty dish of consommé with Stoker's.

"Mertensia!" Helen Romilly exclaimed. "You have the manners of a peasant."

"Do not distress yourself," Stoker said lazily. "Miss Romilly is welcome to the rest of my soup."

"What difference does it make to you?" Mertensia demanded of her sister-in-law. "My manners are no concern of yours."

A sudden chill seemed to settle over the table. No one spoke for several long seconds, each of them punctuated by the ticking of the mantel clock. Finally, Helen Romilly cleared her throat.

"You are quite right, Mertensia. I ought not to have offered criticism where it is not welcome. I forget sometimes that we are not truly family although Caspian carries Romilly blood," she finished with a nod towards her son.

Mertensia's eyes narrowed and she opened her mouth, but before she could speak, her brother stirred himself.

"Mertensia," Malcolm Romilly said in a steady, authoritative voice. "That is enough." His sister shrugged, clearly more interested in her dinner than in sparring with her brother's widow. Malcolm looked to his sister-in-law. "Helen, please accept my apologies. Of course you and

Caspian are family. You were much loved by Lucian and he was much loved by us." He raised his glass, the dark red wine catching the candlelight like a handful of garnets. "A toast, then. To the memory of my late brother, Lucian. And to burying the past."

Helen Romilly gave him a sharp look, but the rest of the company merely echoed the toast and sipped. Only Malcolm Romilly did not drink. He stared into his glass as conversations began around the table amongst the dinner partners.

"Are you scrying?" I asked him in a teasing tone.

He roused himself. "I beg your pardon?"

"The old folk custom of looking into a crystal ball or a bowl of water to tell one's future. I have never seen it done with a glass of wine, but I am certain it could be attempted."

He gave me a curiously attractive smile. "I am glad his lordship thought to bring his brother and you, Miss Speedwell. I think with strangers amongst us, we might behave better than otherwise."

He fell silent again, staring into his wine for a long moment before giving himself a visible shake. "Forgive me. I seem to be woolgathering and I am failing in my duties. Now, Tiberius tells me you have a passion for my glasswings. Has he mentioned my intention to make you a present of some larvae?"

"It is very generous of you."

He waved a hand. "I am very happy to think that a colony of them might find a home in your vivarium. It is a miracle they have survived as long as they have. The slightest alteration in habitat or climate, and we might have lost them. In fact, for some years, we thought we did. It was the most delightful surprise to find them thriving once more."

We fell to talking of other things—the natural beauties of the island, the difficulties of living in so remote a place—and although we turned at times to talk to our partners, we conversed easily upon a variety of topics. The food was excellent, the consommé being followed by several courses of fish. From fried soles sauced delicately with lemon we proceeded to roasted turbot and curried lobster, all of it freshly drawn from the sea around the Isle, our host assured me with obvious pride.

"Our waters are some of the most bountiful in all of England," he boasted. "Luckily for us."

"Indeed?"

He smiled. "We are a Catholic family, Miss Speedwell, and it is Friday," he reminded me.

We were partnered again during the sweet course, and after we had finished it, I remarked upon how clever the confection had been.

"Clever?" he asked.

I gestured towards my empty crystal dish. A sorbet had been served with tiny plates of the most elegant cakes I had seen outside of a patisserie. "The rose sorbet. It is a perfect complement to the roses in the centerpieces. *Rosa mundi*, are they not? The rose of the world?"

As luck would have it, my remark came during lulls in the other conversations, and I distinctly heard the sharp rasp of a spoon scraping over china.

"Rosamund," Helen Romilly whispered.

Malcolm Romilly gave her a thin smile. "It seems Miss Speedwell is the only one to notice my tribute. It is fitting, is it not? A mass of roses to commemorate Rosamund."

The rest of the company was silent, expressions varying from numb horror (Helen Romilly) to acute boredom (Mertensia). Only Tiberius was smiling, a small, cruel smile.

I looked to our host. "Who is Rosamund?"

He did not look at me, staring instead at one of the striped roses. Unlike the others, this one must have been imperfectly arranged, for it drooped away from the epergne, brushing wilting petals against the tablecloth.

"She was my wife, Miss Speedwell. At least, she was my bride," he corrected in a still, small voice.

"She disappeared on their wedding day," Mertensia supplied bluntly. "It's been three years and no one has seen or heard from her since."

Stoker turned to her, his brow furrowed. "You do not know what has become of her?"

Mertensia's laugh was brittle. "You don't know the story?" She glanced from Stoker to me and back again. "Goodness, where have the pair of you been? On the moon? It was the most shocking scandal of 1885."

"In 1885, my brother was fighting for his life in the jungles of Amazonia," Tiberius told her with a quiet sternness I had not expected.

"And I was somewhere in the foothills of the Himalayas," I added. "I am still not entirely certain of the exact location. The maps of that region are imprecise at best."

Mertensia was not cowed. "Still, newspapers do exist," she replied. "And poor Malcolm was on the front page of every one. It isn't every day an English gentleman misplaces his bride."

"That will do, Mertensia," her brother murmured.

"I should say so," Helen Romilly put in. "This entire conversation is in very poor taste."

"I'm surprised *you* should think it in poor taste to speak of the dead," Mertensia riposted.

A delicate flush touched Helen's cheeks as she looked unhappily at her plate. Whatever Mertensia had meant by the barb, it had clearly struck home, and I found myself intrigued by the relationship between the two.

"I say," Caspian said, stirring himself to his mother's defense. "That isn't entirely fair, Aunt M—"

Helen made a gesture of restraint at her son, and Mertensia bridled.

"Do not call me that. The very notion of being an aunt is lowering. Aunts should be withered old women of seventy with spaniels called Trevor who lie at their feet as they knit antimacassars."

"We have wandered a little far from the subject," Tiberius put in, giving a thoughtful look in Malcolm's direction.

Malcolm dragged his eyes from the wilting rose. "Yes. Thank you, Tiberius." He forced a smile. "My dear guests, it has been a long day for everyone who has traveled so far to get here, and I think a good night's sleep is in order. We will retire directly. But first, raise your glasses once more, if you will. To the woman I loved, to my bride. To Rosamund."

"To Rosamund," came the various murmurs around the table. Malcolm Romilly finished off his wine, drinking deeply while the rest of the company sipped politely. We made noises of good night and sleep well, and in the dispersal of the group to bed, no one but I noticed that Tiberius put his glass down untouched.

I am an excellent sleeper but that night I tossed and turned as if on a bed of nails.

"Blast the man," I muttered as I thrust my bedclothes away. I meant Stoker, of course. I had traveled to a fascinating place in the company of an intriguing aristocrat who was wildly skilled in the flirtatious arts. There were diverting undercurrents of tension and mysterious things afoot. Best of all, the prospect of my own colony of glasswings danced in my head. I ought to have been held fast in the arms of Morpheus, slumbering sweetly as I dreamt of butterflies and blue seas. Instead, whenever I closed my eyes, I saw only *him*.

With a few elegant curses, I wrapped my dressing gown about me and made my way up the staircase that wound, tight as a snail's shell, to Stoker's room. I did not bother to knock and he did not look surprised to see me. He was sitting in the embrasure, looking into the black night. I sat beside him, noticing the spangle of stars and the bright pearl gleam of the moon as it hung, full and low.

"I suppose you think I owe you an explanation," I began ungraciously.

He did not turn to face me. "You owe me nothing," he said, his voice a little weary. "It is the nature of whatever is between us that we make no demands upon each other."

"Don't," I ordered, my hands curling into fists in my lap. "Don't be understanding and accommodating. It is upsetting."

He turned his head, a small smile playing about his lips. "I haven't been, if it consoles you. I sulked for the better part of the time you were in Madeira. No, I lie. I raged for the first few months, then I moved on to sulking."

"Is that why you did not write? To punish me?"

"I did not write because you told me not to," he reminded me gently.

"Since when do you do as you're told?" I demanded.

He gave me a long look. "You are angry with me. What a novel experience. I've been on the receiving end of your annoyance, your impatience, your frustration. But never your anger. It's colder than I would have expected."

"It can be colder still," I warned him. "But I am come to make amends."

"For what?" he asked, arching a brow in a perfect imitation of Tiberius. "For dashing off to Madeira? For running away with my brother? You seem to have made a habit of fleeing, Veronica."

"For a woman bent upon taking to her heels, I seem not to have got very far. I am right here," I said.

By way of reply, he canted his head and deepened the arch of the brow. It was an inquiry and it was a measure of our understanding that I knew what he was asking.

"I have no wish to discuss particulars with you," I told him firmly. "But neither do I wish to be at odds. So let us have it clearly understood.

At the end of our last adventure, I may have permitted myself to indulge in rather warmer feelings than I am comfortable owning, feelings to which I very nearly gave voice. Were it not for Tiberius' timely arrival in the glasshouse that day, I might have said things I would now regret."

He opened his mouth, but I held up a hand. "I am glad Tiberius came, and I am glad I never said what I might have that day. And I am glad I went to Madeira. We needed time, the both of us, and I think we still do."

"Time?"

"Time," I repeated firmly. "For the duration of our acquaintance, I have understood that Caroline de Morgan was some sort of evil influence upon your life, a malign presence that very nearly destroyed you. It is a credit to the resilience of your character that you survived her the first time, and it is a further credit to you that you survived a second. But I think neither encounter came without scars." I flicked a glance to the long, silver line that marked his face. It might have been dealt at the claws of a jaguar, but Caroline de Morgan was every bit as responsible for the damage as the jungle creature that had flayed him.

His expression was inscrutable, and I went on, calmly. "We have, both of us, acknowledged that our bond is unlike any we have shared with another on this earth. This friendship, this strange alchemy that knits us together, it is too fine a thing to let it be tarnished with whatever corrosion she has left behind. I think there can be nothing more between us until and unless all ghosts from the past have been exorcised."

He looked as if he wanted to protest, but instead he turned his face to the moon, watching the silver-white light play upon the black waves. "What do you propose?"

"Nothing," I told him simply. "I propose we do nothing at all. We simply carry on as we have in the past, friends and colleagues, nothing more. Not until you have fully recovered from the damage she has inflicted."

His hands tightened on the sill of the window. "I have recovered," he told me flatly. "Caroline is nothing to me."

"Your knuckles have gone white at the mention of her name," I pointed out.

With visible effort, he loosened his grip, turning to me, his voice low and dangerous. "Veronica, it is entirely natural that I should harbor some ill will towards a woman who has done everything in her power to destroy me. She married me under false pretenses. She committed adultery with my best friend and abandoned me to die in a foreign country. She dragged my name through the mud and the muck not out of necessity but with real delight. She is everything that is vile and tainted in the world, and if you don't think I deserve to want to take her apart bone by bone with my bare hands—"

He broke off, his breath coming hard. "I will not explain myself further. I thank you for your visit but this conversation has ceased to be productive. I will wish you a good night."

I rose and went to the door. He held it open but did not meet my eyes. "You will see that I am right," I told him. "You have contained your rage for too long and that is a poisonous thing. Let go of it and you will let go of Caroline."

I was scarcely over the threshold before he slammed the door behind me. Then, as if he knew I was still there, he slowly and deliberately threw the bolt, barring me from returning.

Wakeful and unhappy, I sat up for a while writing a letter of some length to Lady Wellie. I was a little troubled at leaving her so abruptly and hoped a deceptively jolly account of my travels and the unique setting of St. Maddern's would amuse her. I took great pains over describing the people I had met and the little I had glimpsed of the castle.

I wrote:

It is a curiously homely place for a castle. The structure itself is of great antiquity but the interior has been redecorated several times. From Tudor galleries to the Jacobean dining room, it is exactly what one would most like a castle to be. I am told the views are spectacular, but have seen nothing yet as we arrived in darkness and it seems the weather is prone to change as often as a dandy's underlinen. A storm has risen, howling like the proverbial banshee around my turret room, and I am thankful I am not of a nervous disposition else I would be cowering under the coverlet with only my eyes peeping over the top as I wait for morning.

I dropped my pen, making a note to finish the letter the following day.

A storm was fully howling as I blew out my candle, and somewhere in the depths of my dreams I noted the clashing of thunder, the cymbals of the gods, but still I slumbered on. I woke later than was my custom. I had no work, no Stoker clamoring for attention, no dogs or correspondence or obligations. I rose, stretching, and went to the window, flinging the casement wide.

Before me, the sea spread like jeweled skirts, shimmering in the morning sun. In the distance, three rocks punctuated the horizon, strung like beads on a chain, but apart from this, there was nothing at all for the eye to see except the blues of sea and sky stretching to the end of eternity. Strong winds whipped the water into white-capped waves and the scent of the brisk sea air was intoxicating. I had not realized exactly how high we had climbed into the darkness, but I felt on top of the world, as if I could reach out and touch the toe of heaven. After scribbling a quick postscript to Lady Wellie about the stunning views, I washed and dressed and made my way down to breakfast with my letter tucked in my pocket. There was no sound from the room above me, indicating that Stoker was either sleeping in or already abroad. Tiberius' door was firmly closed but I did not knock.

I helped myself to a full plate of eggs and bacon and tomatoes from the hot chafing dishes on the sideboard. As I took my chair at the table, Mrs. Trengrouse glided in with a fresh pot of tea and a rack of toast.

"Good morning, Miss Speedwell. I hope you slept well in spite of the storm?"

A tiny furrow appeared between her silvering dark brows. She took her responsibilities seriously as housekeeper, I reflected. With no wife for Malcolm Romilly, and Mertensia clearly uninterested in domesticity, the running of the household would fall upon her shoulders. She did not seem to mind the responsibility. In fact, I would venture to say that she throve upon it. Her chatelaine was as brightly polished as the previous day, but her collar and cuffs had been changed for crisp white linen. Belgian, I guessed.

"Entirely," I assured her. She placed the teapot and toast rack within easy reach of me and rearranged various dishes of jams and butter and honey until I had everything I could possibly desire.

"I shall be fat as a Michaelmas goose by the time I leave," I mused. "I am dreadfully hungry and everything is so delicious."

She beamed. "We take great pride in our kitchens, and the sea air has that effect upon everyone."

"I seem to be the only one about. Where are the others?"

She made her way down the sideboard, peering into each chafing dish and arranging the contents more attractively. "Mrs. Romilly takes breakfast in her room. The gentlemen—Mr. Romilly, Mr. Caspian, his lordship, and Mr. Templeton-Vane—ate earlier and are on a ramble about the island. Visiting the threshing floors and the fishing boats. And Miss Mertensia never breakfasts. She stuffs a roll into her pocket and eats while she works in the garden," she said in a tone of fond exasperation. She drew back the draperies to let in the strong morning sunlight.

"Rain later, I'm afraid, so if you want exercise, you might care to walk in the gardens this morning," she advised.

"I rather thought Miss Mertensia discouraged that sort of thing."

She looked shocked. "Heavens no, Miss Speedwell! She is merely protective of her gardens. You would be most welcome, I am sure." She beckoned me to the window. "You see the walled garden here? That is a little pleasaunce planted four centuries ago for the ladies of the house to take the air and sun. Now, through the west gate is the kitchen garden, which is tidy and productive, but hardly of any interest to the casual visitor. Far better, in my opinion, is the east gate," she instructed, pointing to a large wooden door set in an arch of the stone wall. "It isn't locked, just pass through and you will be in the flower gardens and herbaceous borders. Beyond is another wall dividing the formal gardens from the orchards with a little yew walk at the end. At the far reach of the yew walk is a strong black gate with a skull and crossbones, you cannot miss it."

"A skull and crossbones! Are there pirates about?" I teased.

"No, but it is a warning just the same. That is Miss Mertensia's poison garden, and you mustn't enter without Miss Mertensia to guide you," she said severely. "The plants there have been collected over many years and some of them are quite dangerous indeed. Even brushing up against them can be lethal, to say nothing of breathing in the air around them."

"Goodness, is she not afraid of the danger to herself?"

"Miss Mertensia knows more about plants than half the Western world," she told me with an unmistakable note of pride. "She has been consulted by any number of expert horticulturists on the subject. She receives many requests to visit the garden, but guests are permitted at her invitation only."

"I shall certainly wait for mine," I assured her. She inclined her head and I finished my breakfast, pausing only to collect my hat before striking out for my walk. I followed her advice, making my way through the formal gardens and into the orchard, the branches of the fruit trees heavy with dark purple damsons and the air thick with the odor of ripeness.

What Mrs. Trengrouse had not told me was that each of the gardens was set upon its own terrace, divided by stout stone walls and accessed by staircases hewn into the living rock of the island. Once I had descended to the bottom of the orchard, I turned back to look at the castle. It stood proudly upon its clifftop, the stone burnished to dark gold in the strong morning light. Banished was the forbidding black fortress that had loomed above us in the darkening night. It was as if a faery had cast a spell of enchantment over the place, gilding it to splendor. Set within the lush gardens, it harmonized perfectly with the landscape that had borne it. Overhead, gulls wheeled and screamed, reminding me that this place was set within a sparkling sea.

A bench had been placed within the orchard—no doubt for just such meditations—but I carried on, descending around the walled poison garden towards a lower terrace. Through the forbidding gates, I had just seen the bobbing figure of Mertensia Romilly, heavily gloved, with a protective hat and veil, her clothes covered by a sturdy canvas apron as she worked amongst her perilous plants. I waved a greeting to her and she slipped out of the gate, throwing back her veil and pulling her hands free of the stout leather gauntlets, which covered her to the elbow. She carried a trug looped in the crook of her elbow, the ruffled crimson petticoats of cut poppies just peeping over the edge.

"Good morning, Miss Speedwell," she said, giving me a short nod. Most young ladies who made a pretense of gardening were content to do no more than cut roses and carry around a pretty basket in a picturesque pose. Not Mertensia. She had a spade in her other hand and her sleeves were rolled up to bare forearms scratched from thorns and nettles. Her skirts were streaked with mud, and perspiration pearled her hairline, but she looked entirely happy.

I took in the long view down towards the village nestled at the foot of the mount. "The gardens are extensive," I observed. "Surely you don't manage them entirely on your own."

"Old Trevellan is still about to advise. He was gardener in my grandfather's day. His grandsons help with some of the pruning and digging, particularly the vegetables, but I like to manage the flowers and herbs myself. And no one touches the poison garden but me," she said with a nod towards the tall iron gates behind her. They rose some ten feet in the air, fastened with a stout iron chain and a notice strictly forbidding entry.

"I suppose that is to keep out the curious," I remarked.

"It is to protect people from themselves," she said sternly. "Even breathing the wrong plants in there is dangerous."

I regarded her thoughtfully. "I wonder at your keeping them then if they are so perilous."

She shrugged. "Plants develop poison as a protection against predation. Should I keep one out simply because it has learnt better than its brothers how to defend itself? Roses have thorns and yet no one ever thinks to ban them from a garden for being prickly."

"A simple thorn has never killed a man," I pointed out.

"That one has," she told me, guiding my gaze towards a tall plant that reared up against the gates. Through its lacy leaves, I could just make out the thorns, each one as long as my finger and sharp as a needle.

"*Senegalia greggii.* A catclaw acacia from Mexico," she told me. "Capable of holding a man in its grasp until he dies of inanition. When it flowers, the blossoms appear on yellow spikes that are a warning to give it a wide berth."

"It is magnificent," I told her truthfully. "It reminds me of a certain butterfly—*Battus philenor*, the Pipevine Swallowtail. It will poison a bird that eats it. The bright blue of its hind wings is a warning to birds to leave it or suffer the consequences."

"Exactly," she said with obvious satisfaction. "Nature knows how to take care of itself."

I glanced at her gauntlets and veil. "I see you take a number of pre-cautions for working in your garden."

She nodded. "One cannot be too careful in a poison garden. The Medici had one, you know. It was where they grew the plants they used to dispatch their enemies."

"And that inspired you to create one of your own?" I ventured.

She shrugged. "Why not? It is far more interesting than monkey puzzle trees and herbaceous borders. Proper gardening is *dreadfully* dull. This adds a bit of discomfort to the mix. And things are more enjoy-able when there is just a little discomfort to sharpen the edge."

"Do you really think so?"

"Of course. And so do you, if you only stop to consider it. Isn't a meal more pleasurable when the appetite is strongest? Isn't sleep sweetest when the fatigue is greatest?"

I blinked at her. "My dear Miss Romilly, you are a philosopher!"

"Mertensia, please. We do not stand on ceremony here. And do not look so surprised that I bend towards philosophy," she said with a touch of asperity. "There is nothing to do on this island but read and think. I have done much of both."

"And what have you concluded?"

"That poison is no different from medicine," came the prompt reply. She gestured towards the silken scarlet flowers heaped in the trug. "Take my poppies, for instance. In small doses, a preparation of the milk soothes the fiercest pain and gives sleep and respite. Too much, and death follows."

"Do you make many medicines from your plants?" I asked.

"As many as I can." She pulled a face. "Malcolm would prefer if I spent my time making bramble jam and weaving lavender bottles, but even he has had cause to thank me for a digestive tisane from time to time. We've no doctor on the island, and so my remedies must suffice for smaller ills."

"And greater ones?"

Her expression soured. "There is a doctor in Pencarron who is summoned for matters beyond my ability."

I looked her over from square, capable hands to clear, unlined brow. "I cannot think there is much beyond your ability."

For the first time in our short acquaintance, Mertensia Romilly smiled. Her teeth were small and white and even, just like her brother's. "There is much I am not permitted since I have never studied formally. But the old ways are not forgot, not on this isle."

Abruptly, she gestured towards my dress. "That is clever," she said, peering closely at the curious arrangement of my costume. On the right-hand side, from just above the ankle to just above the knee, a deep pocket had been stitched, just wide enough to permit a furled umbrella to be tucked neatly away, ever at the ready should I require it but without encumbering my hands.

I spread my fingers. "A butterfly hunter needs her net," I reminded her. "Mr. Templeton-Vane devised this for me so that I can secure my umbrella when I am on the hunt. But I have found it generally useful in keeping one's hands free."

"And you carry no reticule," she noted.

I demonstrated the further modifications to my ensemble, interior pockets fitted into the seams of my dress, deep but easily accessible, and one secret compartment located just under my modest bustle. "And if I button back the skirt, you will see that I am wearing trousers underneath." I showed her. I had a few variations on my hunting attire but all modeled on the same basic principle: a narrow skirt, slim trousers, and a fitted jacket of serviceable and handsome tweed. Underneath was a well-tailored white shirtwaist, and my legs were protected from brambles by flat leather boots that fitted like a man's and laced to the knee. The original design had been my own, but the pockets were entirely Stoker's doing, both in conception and in execution. He had learnt to stitch as part of his training both as a surgeon and as a taxidermist. The fact that he occasionally used those skills to alter or mend my clothes was a particular pleasure to me.

"It's the cleverest thing I have ever seen," she pronounced. "At first glance, you look like any other countrywoman, but you can move like a man in it."

"I can move like a scientist," I corrected. "And that is more to the point."

She smiled again, and I sensed a softening in her. Mertensia had put me in mind of a hedgehog before, prickly in her defenses, but she had clearly found in me a kindred spirit.

"I could send you the specifications, if you like," I told her. "Any competent dressmaker could run it up for you."

She nodded slowly. "Yes, I think I would like that."

I took advantage of the moment of rapport to put a question to her. "I was surprised to hear of the disappearance of your brother's bride. What do you think became of her?"

Her face shuttered immediately. She picked up a shovel, clutching it with practiced fingers. "Speculation is the refuge of an idle mind and mine is seldom without occupation. Forgive me, Miss Speedwell. I must get on."

"Veronica," I corrected. "After all, you do not stand on ceremony," I added with a smile.

Mertensia did not smile back.

CHAPTER

5

Mertensia recovered enough from her momentary brusqueness to walk with me to the edge of the terrace, pointing out the path that would lead me eventually to the little village nestled at the foot of the castle. Patches of fog had drifted inland, draping wisps of gossamer mist over the trees. "If you mean to go to the village, go now. There will come a storm later and you won't enjoy the walk back if it's raining. Do stop in at the Mermaid for some cider. We grow the apples here in the lower orchard and it is like nothing else you will ever taste," she promised. "Mind you do not go into the pubs," she added. "Their trade is with the sailors who call in on their way to Ireland. The inn is the only suitable establishment for unaccompanied ladies."

The grounds were cleverly laid out so that they seemed quite private right until the end, the path winding through copses thick with trees in the full glory of their late summer foliage, dressed in coats of glossy green in every shade imaginable. The air was humid and heavy, pressing close against me as I walked, drawing beads of perspiration from my temples. I picked my way down the path, into the mist-shrouded trees. The formal gardens gave way to orchards and then to wilder patches of forest, little copses that had been so cleverly planted they gave the impression of much larger woods.

I kept to the path and in a very short time found myself at the foot of the mount on the main street of the village. It was a bustling little place, boasting a shop, a church, three schools, an inn, a trio of pubs, and a smithy, all dating from the Tudor period to judge from the architecture. The half timbering was old, but the plastered bits had been freshly white-washed, and the windows in each were gleaming. It had a tidy, prosper-ous look. The blacksmith was busy at his forge, shoeing a horse whilst a farmer waited. A few of the island's women were gathered at the shop, purchasing stamps or exchanging gossip as they waited to be served, falling to interested silence as I posted my letter to Lady Wellie. Strangers were clearly a matter of note in so small a place, and I gave them a cordial nod as I emerged from the shop. Down the street a buxom maid poured a pail of water onto the steps of one of the pubs, sluicing it clean. In a patch of sunlight in front of the church, an elderly woman sat tatting, her cat at her side, licking daintily at its paws. It was as peaceful a place as any I had seen, and I felt a curious somnolence steal over me. It was like walking into a storybook village, a sleepy place where folk never changed and life went on as it always had throughout the centuries.

Even the inn seemed like something out of time, I decided, as I pushed through the door and entered the low-ceilinged main room. The sign out front had depicted a fairly lascivious-looking mermaid, but within all was peaceful. Chairs and tables were scattered about, good plain oak, so darkened by time and polish that they were black as walnut. I glanced about for a proprietor, and to my surprise, the elderly woman from in front of the church appeared, cat trotting neatly at her heels.

"Good day to you, Miss Speedwell," the woman said in a curious, creaking voice.

"How did you—" I paused and began to laugh. "Of course. It is a small island, after all."

She smiled, displaying a surprisingly beautiful set of teeth. "Old Mother Nance knows more than you might believe, my dear." She gestured with one long-fingered hand. "Come into the parlor and sit by the fire. The mist is rising and it won't be long before the sun is gone. You must warm yourself and take some cider," she insisted. She guided me into a smaller parlor where a merry fire was burning upon the hearth. It was much colder in this room with its stone walls and tiny windows and she noticed my shiver.

"This is the oldest part of the inn," she told me. "Built into the living rock, it is. You can feel the damp, can you not? The whole island is laced with tunnels and secret passages."

"Not surprising for a property owned by a Catholic family in the reign of Elizabeth," I pointed out.

She laughed, a small wheezing sound that shook her bony shoulders. "Lord love you, my dear. You think they practiced secrecy because they were recusants? Nay, the Romillys were smugglers, child. That is how they made their coin and crafty they were with it. There's not a square inch of this island that doesn't hold a secret." She turned away and busied herself for a moment before returning with a tray upon which perched a tankard. "Take it and drink," she urged.

"Only if you will drink with me," I told her.

She seemed pleased at the invitation. She fetched herself a tankard and we toasted before I sipped. Mertensia had been right. The cider was sweet and cold, but behind the bright apple taste was a sharp note of something dark and complex, like an excellent wine.

"You mark the difference," Mother Nance said.

"Miss Romilly mentioned that the local apples are unique," I agreed.

"Grown in the bones of a dead man," she said solemnly.

I stared at her in horror.

"Heaven bless you, miss! Not a real dead man," she said, wheezing again in amusement. "'Tis only the legend that the island was once a giant who strode across the seven seas before curling up to sleep. It is said the sea washed over him as he slept and he never waked again and only his bones were left, picked clean by the creatures of the deep and that is how the island came to be."

"I suppose a place like this is thick with legends," I said.

"That we are. We've our giant and a mermaid and more ghosts than we have living folk."

"Ghosts—" I began, but we were interrupted by the boisterous arrival of a young boy, his dark hair tumbling over his brow as he bounded in. The cat twitched its whiskers at him but did not move.

"Hello, Gran," the boy said, dropping a kiss to her worn cheek.

"Hello, poppet. Miss Speedwell, this is my grandson, Peter. Peterkin, this is Miss Speedwell from up the castle. You say a proper hello to the lady."

He bowed from the waist in a gesture of such refined courtliness it would have done credit to a lord. I inclined my head. "Master Peter. It is a pleasure to make your acquaintance."

"How do you do?" he asked gravely.

His grandmother gave him a fond look. "He's a right little gentleman, isn't he?" she asked me. "Always reading books about his betters and practicing his manners."

"Good manners will take him far in the world," I observed.

"And he will go far," Mother Nance said sagely. "I have seen it."

"Seen it?"

"Gran is a witch," the child said calmly.

There seemed no possible reply to this that could achieve both candor and politeness so I opted for a vague, noncommittal murmur.

Mother Nance gave another wheezing laugh as she petted her grandson's curls. "Miss Speedwell thinks you've told a tale, my little love, but she'll soon discover what's what."

The boy gave me an earnest look. "'Tis true, miss. Gran is a witch. Not the nasty sort. She shan't put a spell on you and give you warts," he said seriously. "She sees things. She has the sight."

"The sight?"

"Things come to me," Mother Nance said comfortably. "I do not ask them to come, mind, but come they do. Things from the past and things that have yet to be."

"And ghosts," her grandson reminded her.

"Aye, I have had more than a few chats with them that walk," she agreed. She narrowed her gaze at me, but her expression was still kindly. "Miss Speedwell is a skeptic, poppet. She believes in what her eyes can tell her. She has yet to learn there is more to see than what the eyes can perceive."

"I am skeptical, as you say. But I am willing to be persuaded," I told her.

She laughed and exchanged a look with her grandson. "Persuaded! Lord love you, there's no persuading to be done. Either you believe a thing or you don't. And your believing doesn't make it so. The ghosts don't care if you see them or not," she added.

I thought of Malcolm Romilly's missing bride and experienced a shiver of curiosity.

"Have you seen ghosts?" I asked the boy.

He nodded gravely. "Twice. I saw a dark fellow with a funny sort of tin hat. He were on the beach, lying as still as the dead. Then he seemed to rise up and he kept looking behind him at the sea as though he were seeing something awful."

"A Spaniard," his grandmother said promptly. "An Armada ship was wrecked upon these shores, and one or two sailors washed up, half-drowned and despairing."

"What became of them?" I asked.

"One was a priest, a chaplain to the vessel which sank. He was welcomed by the Romilly family, and it is said they kept him on secretly and he held masses for them, although no one ever saw a trace of him within the castle."

"And the man on the beach?" I pressed.

"He drew his sword when the islanders came down to the shore," the child told me calmly. "He did not have time to do more than that."

"You mean they killed him?"

"He was an enemy," he replied in the same matter-of-fact way.

"Never you mind, Miss Speedwell," his grandmother said with a laugh. "We're a far sight more welcoming to most visitors."

"I am glad to hear it," I said, taking another deep draft of my cider.

"There's another ghost that walks," her grandson went on. "But I've never seen her because she doesn't leave the castle."

My pulse quickened. "A ghost in the castle? A lady?"

"The bride," he said, his dark eyes rounding in excitement. "She walks abroad in the night in her wedding gown, waiting to wreak her vengeance on those left behind."

A chill passed over the room, but before I could respond, the boy leapt to his feet. "I am hungry, Gran."

"There is cold meat pie in the larder," she told him. "Mind you wash first."

He scampered off and she completed several more stitches on her tatting before she spoke. "He was talking of Miss Rosamund, of course," she said mildly. "Mrs. Romilly, as she was when she died."

"You think she is definitely dead, then?"

Her gaze was piercing as it held mine. Her fingers fairly flew as if enchanted, never faltering, but she did not look down at her work once. "She must be," she told me. "Otherwise how could her ghost walk? No, some folk want to believe she is still alive. But mark me well, miss. Rosamund Romilly is a dead woman. And she is coming for her revenge."

I stared at her, but Mother Nance continued to stitch away, as placidly as if she had just told me the price of corn.

"Is that one of the things you have seen?" I asked after a moment.

She slanted me a sideways, inscrutable look. "Mayhaps."

"Do you read tea leaves? Or peer into a bowl of dark water when the moon is full?"

Mother Nance pursed her lips. "You're a nimble one, aren't you, miss? You've made a habit of skipping lightly through life, no matter what perils besiege you. Troubles fall away from you like water off a duck, do they not? You've a high opinion of your abilities." I started to speak, but she held up a hand. "I don't say it is a bad thing. Too many women think too little of themselves, content to live by a man's lights instead of their own. No, your pretty ways have served you well, and you could no more change them than a hen could learn to crow. But you won't always be so lucky, you know. And mind you remember, 'tis no more than Fortune's favor that has saved you thus far. If she should choose to turn her back upon you, there be none that can save you."

She looked like a Delphic prophetess then, warning of doom, and I wondered how much of the effect was put on for visitors. "Thank you for the warning," I told her sincerely. "Shall I cross your palm with silver?"

She flapped a hand. "I am no Gypsy fortune-teller, miss. Save your silver for the traveling fair. The second sight has come down in our family through the centuries, a gift it were, from the first lady of this island."

"The giant's lady?" I hazarded.

"Bless me, no! The giant laid himself down to sleep before history was a thing that was known. And long after, when his story had passed into legend, the first fishermen of Pencarron began to sail these waters. One night, when the moon was full upon the water, and the silver light shone down, one of the fishermen, a comely lad with hair as black as night, trapped a mermaid within his net. She promised him anything if he would free her, and he was a poor lad, so he asked her for a purse of gold. But the mermaid had taken a liking to the boy, handsome as he was, so she told him if he would free her and take her to wife, for half the year she would swim with her own kind and be free as the wind itself upon the waves. But for the other half, she would live with him, bringing with her all the wealth under the sea."

I interrupted her at this point. "There is wealth under the sea?"

"Of course there is!" she cried. "Pearls and coral made by the fishes, and gold and silver from ships sunk in tempests. All the treasures of the kings of earth are nothing as compared to the wealth that lies beneath." She leant a trifle nearer, pitching her voice low. "And there is ivory as well, from the bones of those who have gone down to their deaths."

I gave an involuntary shudder, and she seemed pleased. "Aye, miss. All the wealth you can imagine, as much as all the lords of creation and more again, this the mermaid promised her comely lad. And he agreed, taking her to wife but always minding that he must let her go free for half the year to swim the seas with her sisters."

"Were they happy?" I wondered.

"Happy as a mortal can be when wedded to merfolk," she said sagely. "The little mermaid gave him a son in due course, and wealth, just as she promised. And with the wealth, the poor fisherman built a castle upon this island, which he gave in time to his boy, the mermaid's son, and so it was that the Romillys came to live upon this island, with the blood of the merfolk in their veins. They want to be better than they are, but we who have lived here for all the centuries in between and share their blood, we know the truth. The castle folk are sprung from a fisherman's son and his mermaid mother."

"Share their blood? Then you are related to the Romillys?" I asked.

"Why, everyone on this island is related to the Romillys," she told me. "Most from the wrong side of the blanket. But we are all bound by the pellar blood of the mermaid who began it all, and it is from her that the sight comes."

"Does everyone on the island have the sight?" I asked, goggling at the idea of an entire island full of clairvoyants.

She gave a comfortable chuckle. "That would be a fair thing, would it not? No, miss. The sight used to be a common gift, but it is not so anymore. In my mother's time, only she and my auntie had it, and I am the last pellar witch on the island."

"Has no one else in your family the sight?"

Her expression turned faintly disgusted. "Not a single one of my children has it. They take after their father, and him a fisherman from over Pencarron way. I ought to have known better than to marry an outcomer, but I loved him and who can argue when love will have its way?"

"Who indeed?" I mused. I finished my cider and rose. "Thank you for a most interesting visit."

She put aside her tatting and gathered herself slowly to her feet. "It was good of you to come, miss. Mind you come again. And mind you mark my warning," she said, coming so close I could see the faint flecks of black in the grey of her eyes. "Rosamund Romilly does not rest easy. Take a care for yourself and any you love."

"I will," I assured her. I emerged from the little inn into a patch of sketchy sunlight, my head fairly swimming with stories of mermaids and ghosts and pellar witches. The boy Peter was sitting outside, pitching conkers, but he scrambled to his feet when he saw me.

"Are you going back to the castle, miss?" he asked.

"I am. It must be getting on time for luncheon, and I should hate to miss it."

"Indeed," he said longingly. "Mrs. Trengrouse runs a proper kitchen, she does. Sometimes she gives me a bit of apple tart when I've done a job or two for her. Did you have a nice chat with Gran?" he asked politely.

"I did, thank you. She is a most interesting woman. She was telling me about the mermaid who founded the families on this island."

"Oh, aye? That's fine for girls, I reckon," he said soberly. "But mermaids are not a thing for boys."

"How frightfully limited you are in imagination if you think so," I told him with a smile. "A boy might properly love a mermaid story."

"I don't think so," he replied. "You see, a boy wants a sort of *heroic* story, and mermaids are fine if all you want to do is loll about in the sea, but I want stories about people who *do* things."

"Ah, like the Spanish conquistadors who washed ashore?"

"And pirates," he said, rolling his eyes ecstatically. "I love pirates."

"Of course. I had quite a fancy for them when I was your age."

He blinked. "You, miss? You liked pirates?"

"Naturally. Boys are not the only ones who want to sail the seven seas in search of plunder," I assured him. "In fact, that's rather my vocation."

"You have been to sea? Actually to sea," he said, waving his arms to encompass the horizon. "Not just the bit between Pencarron and here?"

"Not just that bit," I said. "I have been as far as China and back again."

"That," he told me seriously, "is all the way."

"It is indeed."

"Did you ever fight anyone with a sword?"

"I regret to say, I have not. But I was caught in the eruption of a rather nasty volcano and shipwrecked, so I have had rather more than my fair share of adventures."

His eyes shone in admiration. "I say, that is good. But you ought to know how to fight with a sword. Shall I teach you?"

"What a gallant offer," I replied. "Do you know how to fight with a sword?"

"Not yet. But I met a pirate just now, and I mean to ask him to teach me."

"A pirate! Well, we are living in interesting times indeed. Did he sail up under the banner of a skull and crossbones?"

Peter's expression was painfully tolerant. "Well, of course not, miss. A pirate would not want folk to *know* he's a pirate, would he?"

"I suppose not," I admitted. "But you were clever enough to penetrate his disguise?"

"I was. I told him I knew him for a pirate and that if he didn't want me to tell folk, he would have to teach me to use a sword properly."

I gave him a thoughtful look. "It is a dangerous business to blackmail a pirate, young Peter."

"I am not afraid," he told me with a stalwart air. He put his hands into fists at his hips. "When he has done and I have mastered it—which I think will be in a week or so—I will teach you."

"That is a most excellent plan. I shall look forward to it." I paused and put out my hand. "Thank you for escorting me to the gate, Master Peter. You are a true cavalier."

He swept off his cap and made a low bow, as graceful as any Stuart courtier, as I passed through the gate and onto the path to the castle. I returned the way I had come, up the path that wound from terrace to terrace, each forming a little wooded place or patch of wilderness. As I moved through the last copse, the sunlight faded, replaced by thick grey cloud and a mist that seemed to materialize from nowhere at all. One moment I was walking jauntily through damply dappled woods, the next I was surrounded by wisps of incoming fog.

"Bloody islands," I muttered. The path before me was obscured as the cloud rolled in, smothering sound and stifling even the shrieks of the gulls. They sounded faraway now, and eerie, as if they were crying, and I shook myself free of the fanciful notion that they were shrieking a warning.

Even as I told myself there was absolutely nothing to fear, I heard a footfall upon the path. It was the unmistakable sound of a boot upon the gravel, and then another, and still another, coming closer to me. Someone was walking up from the village, and I had a sudden, thoroughly ridiculous urge to run.

"Don't be so missish," I told myself firmly. I walked with deliberation back towards the castle. But the prickling feeling between my shoulder blades returned. The footsteps did not stop. They sounded, each a little louder than the last, and in between, the gulls shrieked their muffled screams.

I quickened my steps. Surely whoever was behind could hear me as well? I had made no effort to disguise my presence. They must know I was there, and yet there was no greeting, no friendly hail through the mist. I stopped sharply, and the footsteps stopped as well. There was no sound except the beating of the blood in my ears. Even the gulls had fallen suddenly silent.

My mouth went dry and my hands dropped instinctively to my wrists. It had long been my custom when walking abroad to stick my cuffs with minuten, the tiny headless pins of the lepidopterist's trade. Useful for mounting specimens, they were equally useful for fending off unwanted attentions. Unfortunately, I had left the little box of them in my room along with the knife I habitually carried in my boot. That had been a gift from Stoker—a souvenir of one of our murderous little adventures—and I had had recourse to use it once in defense of his life. I almost never went without it, but something about this peaceful little island had lulled my defenses. Even my hatpin was not to hand, for I had worn a modest cap instead of my usual enormous brimmed affairs. I had nothing except my wits and my courage, I realized, and I intended to make the most of them.

I set off again, quickening my pace further still. I must have caught my pursuer off guard; the footsteps did not resume until I had gone a little distance. But then I heard them, coming on, faster now. I looked ahead to where the orchard wall stood atop the next terrace. It was above the mist. If I could reach it, I could see clearly who was behind me, closing the gate if need be. I had noticed on my way down that the key was in the lock.

I stopped in my tracks. Mertensia was in the garden by the orchard. If I was being followed by some sort of miscreant bent upon bad behavior, I would be leading him directly to where she was, possibly endangering her as well. There might be safety in numbers, I reflected, but I would not have it said that Veronica Speedwell was afraid to fight her own battles.

Hardly realizing what I was doing, I whirled upon my heel, hands fisted as I raised my arms and unleashed a Viking berserker battle cry and launched myself down the path, directly at my pursuer. There was a flurry of activity, limbs entangling as we went down. Somehow my pursuer got the upper hand and landed atop me, driving the air out of my lungs as I fell. He was a weighty fellow and I shoved with a massive effort, but could not dislodge him. I drew back my knee and rammed it upwards, earning a howl of pain and outrage for my efforts.

"Unhand me or I shall tear you apart like hounds on a fox!" I demanded with the last of my breath.

"I should bloody well like to see you try," came a familiar voice in a low, grating growl. He gave a great shudder and rolled off of me and onto all fours, panting heavily. I struggled to my knees and whooped air into my lungs. When I could speak again, I used one of his favorite oaths.

"Stoker, will you kindly tell me what in the name of bleeding Jesus you are doing here?"

"Returning to the castle, obviously," he said as he staggered to his feet. "Until you decided to assault my person. Really, Veronica, what on earth possessed you?"

"I thought you were a criminal assailant," I admitted. "You ought to have declared yourself."

"To whom?" he demanded. "I had no idea you were here. That wretched fog is obscuring everything."

"I heard *you* plainly enough," I told him. I was unsettled by coming upon him so unexpectedly. We had left things so badly fixed between us that I could hardly anticipate a cordial conversation, and the knowledge irritated me. "Why have you come back on your own? I thought the gentlemen of the party were taking a grand tour of the island together."

"Yes, well, one can only admire so many lumps of rock before a quarry grows tiresome. I decided to explore the village instead. I had a pint with the innkeeper and then the blacksmith and his apprentice and a brace of farmers turned up for a little refreshment."

"The innkeeper? I suppose you mean Mother Nance? She might have warned me you were lurking about the village. And you must be the pirate her grandson told me about," I added with a glance at his eye patch.

"Ah, young Peter. That boy is going to go far in life. He has the natural instincts of a criminal. He has managed to blackmail me into teaching him how to use a sword."

"I know," I told him darkly. "What I do not know is why you decided to get to know the locals. Unless . . ." I let my voice trail off suggestively.

"Unless?" he prompted.

"Unless you are curious about Rosamund Romilly's disappearance and decided to ask a few questions."

"Certainly not," he said stoutly.

"Liar!" I whirled on him. "Swear to me on whatever you love best in the world that her name did not come up in conversation. Swear on Huxley," I ordered.

"For God's sake, you're dancing around like a damselfly. Of course it came up," he told me in a flat voice. "Rosamund's disappearance was a nine days' wonder. It was the most interesting thing to happen here in three centuries, but no one knows anything. No one saw anything. And there are as many versions of what happened to her as there are people on this island."

I stopped in front of him, forcing him to halt in his tracks. "Stoker. Indulge my curiosity." I raised my chin.

He gave a gusty sigh. "Veronica, have you ever talked to a Cornishman? A proper one? For more than three minutes running? They are the most superstitious folk in the British Isles, and that's saying something. For every fellow who suggests she ran away with a lover or threw herself from a cliff, there are five more saying she was taken by piskies or mermaids or knackers or, just possibly, a giant."

I blinked at him. "A giant?"

"The Cornish love their giants."

"Dare I ask about the knackers?"

He folded his arms over the breadth of his chest. "About two feet tall with blue skin and pointed ears and content to make their homes underground. Something like an Irish leprechaun from what I gather, only one isn't supposed to ask much because they're thoroughly bad-tempered and malevolent."

"They sound just the sort to make off with a bride on her wedding day," I pointed out.

"Veronica, in the name of seven hells, please tell me you are not giving serious consideration to the idea that *knackers* abducted Rosamund Romilly."

"Of course not." I pulled a face. "But what the people around her believe is almost as significant as what actually happened. Very often, golden nuggets of truth may be found in the deepest waters."

"That is a dreadful analogy. To begin with, gold is usually found in shallows," he said.

I held up a hand. "No lectures on metallurgical geology, I beg you. Besides, I have no doubt they were having a very great laugh at your expense. I would wager that pulling the leg of the casual traveler is a well-established sport in this part of the world."

"Of course it is," he replied with an unexpectedly agreeable air. "Which is why I stayed long enough to buy every man a pint and winnow out at least a little kernel of wheaty truth from the chaff of gossip."

He slanted me a mischievous look. "Very well," I told him tartly. "Yours is the better metaphor. Tell me, what grains of truth did you discover?"

He shrugged. "Precious little for all my trouble. Discounting the piskies and knackers—"

"And giants," I added.

"And giants"—he nodded—"it seems there are only two possibilities."

"Death or departure," I supplied.

"Precisely. If she left, how and under what circumstances? Was she abducted? Did she flee, alone or with the help of another? And if so, why has no one heard a whisper of her whereabouts since?"

"And if she died, was it by her own hand, misfortune, or murder?" I finished. "Very tidy. A taxonomy of possibilities. It is practically Linnean in its purity." I paused. "Tell me, what do you think of our host?"

Stoker did not hesitate. "Agincourt," he said, and I understood him perfectly. With that rare sympathy that we shared, he had seen Malcolm Romilly precisely as I had, a bulwark of English predictability in this strange and otherworldly setting.

A rush of pleasure surged through me. This was how it had so often been between us, repartee serving as the language of the heart for us. Where others might whisper little poetries, Stoker and I engaged in badinage, each of us certain that no one else in the world understood us as well as the other.

But just as I began to hope that his mood of the previous night was well and truly behind him, some almost imperceptible withdrawal occurred. His posture, always inclined to lean towards me like an oak to the sun, straightened and he took half a step backwards, his tone suddenly cool. "Personally, I am inclined to think that she took a boat and left. It is the simplest explanation, after all."

"On her wedding day?" I protested. "Surely not."

His sapphirine gaze was level and hard. "I do not pretend to understand the motives of women," he said.

I ignored the barb and replied only to his words. "I suppose such a thing would be possible," I reasoned. "The currents around here must be dangerous."

"That was brought to my attention many times by my drinking companions," he informed me. "They also like to think that she is haunting the island, but that was no doubt a story for my benefit as an outsider. They've created a sort of cottage industry about her disappearance. Peter tried to sell me a charm to protect me against her ghost."

"How much did it cost you?" I knew him too well. He would never have passed up an enterprising child bent upon earning a coin.

He reached into his pocket, producing a bit of shell strung upon a ragged string. "Two shillings."

"Two shillings! Highway robbery," I said with a lightness I did not feel, "particularly as you've already agreed to teach him to use a sword."

He thrust the unlovely item back into his pocket. "He is a bright boy and someone should encourage his initiative." I was not surprised at his justification. He was forever distributing coins to the filthy waifs who trundled to our doors with barrows of fruit or half-read newspapers or bits of nasty embroidery stitched by consumptive sisters. He was the softest of touches.

I fell into step beside him and we started up the path again, walking for a few minutes in silence. We had passed many hours in comfortable quietude with one another, but this constraint was new and unwelcome, and I was uncertain of how to put it right. I only knew that I could not take back the words I had spoken the previous night. He might disagree with my position, but I could no more change it than I could change the course of the sun. "I hope you are at least consoled that I am in no danger from whatever attentions your brother may offer. I am perfectly capable of taking care of myself, as I have just demonstrated with ample effectiveness," I said with a penetrating glance at his manly areas.

He gave me a level look. "I would never make the mistake of thinking you needed anyone."

With that, he picked up his pace with a long-legged stride, leaving me to gape after him. "You ought to hurry if you want to beat the storm," he called over his shoulder. "I hear it's going to be absolutely monsoonal."

He did not turn to see if I followed, which was probably for the best. He would not have appreciated the gesture I directed to his back.

CHAPTER

6

I arrived back at the castle just as the deluge began. Mrs. Trengrouse was waiting at the door. "I will take those boots if you please, miss," she said. "And I have brought your slippers."

"How very kind." I smiled. "And desperately efficient. I should have tracked mud all over your lovely carpets otherwise."

She took my boots, holding the muddy things at arm's length away from the pristine linen of her apron. "The others have just gathered in the dining parlor for luncheon," she told me. "If you would like to wash, there is a small water closet just behind that bit of paneling." She nodded towards a length of linenfold. I pressed it experimentally and it sprang open to reveal a tiny modern room devoted to hygienic purposes.

"What a clever arrangement. I should never have known it was there," I said.

She gave a satisfied nod. "The castle is full of such devices. There was no way to build up or out beyond the original structure, so the masters of St. Maddern's have had to be clever in putting in cupboards and water closets and boot rooms and the like. They are fitted in wherever, which makes it all a bit higgledy-piggledy. But if you discover you are lost, you've only to give a shout and one of the maids will come and find you. The small dining parlor is just along this corridor," she added.

I thanked her and, after washing my hands and tidying my hair, made my way to the dining parlor. "Miss Speedwell!" Malcolm Romilly said with alacrity. "Now the company is at last complete. Please, do be seated," he said, gesturing towards the round table in the middle of the room. It ought to have been a bright chamber, for the long windows faced the sea, but the gathering storm had darkened the room and a large candelabrum had been lit in the center of the table, the fitful light throwing shadows about the room.

Malcolm Romilly drew the curtains—heavy lengths of dark blue silk—against the storm, making the room cozy and womblike. "Much better," he murmured, taking his seat. A sideboard had been laid with all manner of things: a tureen of piping-hot soup, roasted chickens and a vast ham, bowls of pickles and wedges of good cheese. There were dishes of curried lamb and a duck salad, venison pie, and an enormous baron of cold beef, as well as baked macaroni and fresh bread rolls. Beside these sat the expected cruets and sauceboats and pickle dishes offering every accompaniment from chutney to peaches bottled with brandy and spices.

"It is an old custom," Malcolm told me as we filled our plates informally. "Called a groaning board. Centuries ago, the master of St. Maddern's would keep a table for anyone on the island who might be hungry, with an assortment of dishes left from the family dinner the night before. Somehow, the custom was adapted and the groaning board is for the castle folk and the dishes are all made fresh, but it does make for a curious variety."

"It looks delicious," I told him, adding a slice of ham to my plate.

"All of the meat and vegetables come from the island, and the cherry compote is from Mertensia's stillroom," he said with a fond look at his sister. We had taken our seats and at the sound of her name, Mertensia roused herself.

"Yes, this was rather a good lot, if I say it myself," she said. She turned to Stoker. "You must try a spoonful of it."

"Certainly," he said happily as she ladled out enough cherry compote to feed four men. Stoker's sweet tooth was legendary and it seemed that Mertensia had discovered this.

Caspian Romilly lifted his plate to his aunt, his expression deliberately innocent. "May I have some as well, or is it only for the gentlemen you fancy?"

"Caspian," his mother murmured in the mildest tone of reproof. "You mustn't twit your aunt."

"I wasn't," he replied, widening his beautiful eyes to mock innocence. "I was encouraging her."

Mertensia's gaze fell to her plate, two bright, hard spots of color rising in her cheeks.

"Delicious," Stoker pronounced, brandishing a spoonful. "And unexpected. Is there some spice?"

Mertensia looked up, her expression almost pathetically grateful. "Cardamom."

"A family recipe or your own addition?" he inquired.

"My own," she told him, watching with greedy eyes as he spooned the last of the dark, sticky stuff into his mouth.

After luncheon we went our separate ways. Helen claimed a headache, retiring to her room to rest, while Mertensia said she had work in the stillroom. Stoker and Tiberius chose a desultory game of billiards while I went to my room to finish the latest Arcadia Brown adventure. The exploits of my favorite fictional detective were always thrilling, but that afternoon I was conscious of a certain restlessness, a mental itch that I could not scratch with tales of audacious deeds. It occurred to me that it might prove useful to prepare for rearing my glasswings with some specialized knowledge of their natural habitat of St. Maddern's Isle. I put aside my book and made my way down to the library in search of some materials—maps, journals—that could orient me in my new field of study.

As I passed the family wing, I collided with Helen Romilly. She fell to the floor, landing hard upon her bustle.

"My dear Mrs. Romilly, please accept my apologies," I began as I bent to assist her.

She looked up at me, her eyes vague. "Am I on the floor?"

I smelt the heavy spirits on her breath and sighed. "I am afraid so. We were neither of us looking where we were going. Allow me to help you."

It took two tries, but she managed to get her feet under her just as Mrs. Trengrouse appeared, chatelaine jingling. "Mrs. Romilly," she said in a steady voice. "Are you unwell?"

"I think," Helen said slowly, "that I am."

"What are you doing out of your room, then?" Mrs. Trengrouse inquired, putting a steadying arm to the lady's waist.

"I was looking for my cat," she pronounced. She stared at me a long moment. "This young woman was helping me."

"Veronica Speedwell," I reminded her.

"Yes, of course. I ought to have remembered because Mertensia mentioned how curious a name it is. You are called after plants, aren't you?" she asked, weaving a little.

I put an arm around her other side, helping Mrs. Trengrouse to keep her on her feet. "I am indeed," I said as we began walking her slowly towards her room. "No doubt you've seen speedwell. It's a prettyish little plant with purple flowers. Most unassuming."

I kept up the patter of plant talk as we maneuvered her into her room and onto her bed.

"There, now," Mrs. Trengrouse said soothingly. "You have a nice rest."

Helen Romilly thrust herself onto her elbows, giving me a long, level look. "You have done very well for yourself," she said with a slow wink. "A viscount! And a wealthy one! So many fellows with titles these days haven't tuppence to rub together. But you have done very well," she repeated, her head nodding like an overblown peony upon the stem. She roused, weaving a little as she leant near to me, her tone confiding. "Heed my advice, my dear. Get him to the altar at once. A woman cannot survive in this world without the help of a man." She narrowed her eyes at me, blinking hard. "You're a very handsome girl, beautiful, in fact. But it will not last, and you are getting older by the day, my dear. *Older by the day.*"

With that she collapsed back onto the bed, and Mrs. Trengrouse tucked in the coverlet around her as she tossed fretfully, raising her hands in front of her face.

"My poor Caspian," she muttered as she stared dully at her hands. "What will become of him?"

Mrs. Trengrouse made consoling noises but Helen would not be settled.

Helen struggled to sit up in the bed. "Hecate," she began.

"I will send Daisy to find the cat," the housekeeper promised her.

She seemed satisfied at this and collapsed against the pillows, snoring gently before Mrs. Trengrouse even finished tucking in the coverlet around her. She flicked a knowing glance towards the washstand and collected a small bottle there.

"Hair wash?" I asked, reading the label as we left the room.

"Gin," she corrected. She slipped the bottle into her pocket. "She has always liked a bit of a soother, she has. Bless her. She loved Mr. Lucian. It was a terrible blow when he died."

"He sounds an interesting fellow," I suggested.

She beamed. "Oh, what larks he got up to! Always merry as a grig, playing a tune or painting a picture. He went to London to make his fortune, did our Mr. Lucian. We thought he might become a famous actor like that Mr. Irving, but he never did get the right parts. And the pictures he painted were never quite good enough. The story of his life, I fear," she said with a rueful smile. "Never quite good enough. The disappointments were difficult and they took their toll. Well," she finished with a brisk gesture, "I must get on and set Daisy to finding that cat. Thank you for your trouble just now, miss. I know you will not speak of it."

She gave me a hopeful look, and I hastened to reassure her that I would not share with anyone that I had seen Helen Romilly sprawled upon the floor. "Certainly not. A lady's private peccadilloes are her own business."

"Bless you, miss," Mrs. Trengrouse said as she bustled away.

I had very nearly reached the closed door of the library when I heard raised voices, one young and clearly upset, the other more sober and restrained but brooking no interruptions.

"But you must!" the younger cried. It took little imagination to conclude the speaker was Caspian.

His uncle responded flatly. "Must? I must do nothing. I cannot believe you would approach me in this fashion. I will not fund such an endeavor. You must look to yourself for the money."

"But I have not the means," came the anguished response. There was a pause and when he spoke again, it was in a pleading tone of such despair, a stone might have been moved to pity. "I am begging, Uncle Malcolm. For Mama's sake."

"I am not persuaded," Malcolm Romilly replied with a coldness I would not have thought him capable of.

"Then you can go straight to hell," Caspian told him, biting off each word. I heard the scrape of chair legs and the slamming of the chair against the floor as he must have thrust himself to his feet. I had just enough time to move a few feet down the corridor and pretend to be deeply immersed in the study of a painting when Caspian emerged, his color high and his hands clasping and unclasping furiously.

He brushed past, taking no notice of me in his rage, and I crept to the open door. Malcolm Romilly was righting the chair—or at least attempting to. It had been broken in Caspian's fit of temper, and his uncle stared down at the pieces ruefully. He glanced up then.

"Ah, Miss Speedwell. Please come in." A tiny smile, half-embarrassed, touched his mouth. "You must have heard something of my nephew's departure, I gather."

"It would have been difficult not to," I admitted. "I do not mean to pry."

He took up the pieces of the chair and put them behind the door. "It is hardly prying when Caspian was shouting fit to shake the rafters. I have not seen my nephew in some years, and I am sorry to say I detect no improvement in his character. Caspian can be ... difficult. He wants settling down." He gestured. "Do come in, Miss Speedwell," he urged.

It was an impressive room, lined with bookshelves and furnished with several groupings of comfortable armchairs as well as a handsome mahogany desk and a pair of high Stuart armchairs covered in ruby velvet that had been gently nibbled by moths. "Family treasures from the days of Queen Anne," he told me. "The fabric has long since been discontinued and I could not bear to re-cover them." The whole room had the same shabbily contented air as those chairs. The maps hanging upon the wall were foxed; the bindings of the books were so well-worn, the gilt titles were rubbed down to the leather. But an air of serenity hung over the place, and the view from the windows was incomparable.

Or at least it would have been had a heavy fog not obscured the view. Grey mist hung like shrouds at the windows, swirling about the casements like fingers of the dead, looking for a way in.

He gestured for me to take one of the Stuart chairs in front of his desk, and I did so, spreading my skirts smoothly over my knees and returning to the subject of his nephew. "So many young men his age do want settling down," I said with some sympathy. "Perhaps a long voyage," I suggested. "To dangerous lands. A few perils are just the thing to shape a young man's character."

The smile deepened. "And a young woman's. I understand you have traveled the world on your expeditions. You are V. Speedwell, the regular contributor to the *Journal of Aurelian Contemplations*, are you not?"

"I had no notion you read it!" I exclaimed. "You made no mention of it at dinner, and Tiberius led me to believe you were not terribly interested in butterflies."

"I must confess, my knowledge is limited to our own glasswings, but after our conversation last night, I rooted out the latest copies of the journal. My father used to subscribe and I never got around to stopping them from coming. I was terribly impressed with your articles."

"You are too kind," I murmured.

"Not at all," he assured me. "I will tell you, Miss Speedwell, I rather suspected that Tiberius had inflated your interest in the glasswings as a means of securing your invitation. He is such a curious fellow, I admit I have never entirely understood him in spite of our many years of friendship. It is the difficulty in making friends with a man so much cleverer than oneself," he finished with a self-deprecating smile.

I made the proper noises of protest, and he held up a hand. "I harbor no illusions about my abilities or my defects, I can assure you. I am aware of my limitations and my worth, which is more than most men, I think." His genial gaze turned thoughtful. "I wonder, will his lordship make any difficulties about your hobby when you are married? Surely the Viscountess Templeton-Vane cannot continue in trade."

His manner was deliberately nonchalant, but there was a tautness to his hands as he rested them upon his desk and a bright inquisitiveness to his gaze. There was something about my relationship with Tiberius that unsettled him, but I could not imagine what it might be.

I smiled. "I would never give up lepidoptery, not for any man," I told him truthfully.

"What if he insisted?" he pressed.

"I should insist harder," I assured him.

"Yes, I rather think you would," he said with a slow nod. He was silent a moment, then seemed to give himself a little shake as he assumed the manner of a genial host once more. "I do hope you are finding your visit a pleasant one."

"I am indeed. The island is a fascinating place."

He brightened. "Do you really think so? In that case, I must apologize for the fog. If not for the cloud, you could see all the way to the Three Sisters."

"Three Sisters?"

He took down one of the framed maps upon the wall and pointed. "Here we are in the castle. Just to the west, off this little bit of beach, lie three smaller islands in a row, each more barren than the last." They were marked out in thick black ink upon the map, a delicate chain of islands set in a perfectly straight line pointing towards the horizon. I realized then that these were the little isles I had spied from my window upon rising that morning.

"Why are they called the Three Sisters?"

He smiled. "Are you familiar with Cornish folk, Miss Speedwell? We are a superstitious lot. We cannot see a simple geological formation without attaching a myth to it. But sometimes, just sometimes, there is more than myth at work. The story goes that when the castle was built, this isle was the only one, but that the owner of the castle had four beautiful daughters, so beautiful he was jealous of them, and guarded them so that they would never love anyone but him."

"He sounds a dreadful bore," I remarked. "And possessive to boot."

"No doubt," he said. "And no doubt his daughters agreed, for three of them built themselves a boat in secret, and one day, when he was not watching, they set out to sea in their little craft, determined to escape him once and for all."

"What happened to them?" I asked.

"It is said that the father was so angry, he summoned up three rocks from the depths of the sea and the little boat was dashed upon them, killing his three eldest daughters."

"How could a mere man raise islands, no matter how powerful his rage?" I asked.

"Ah, he was no ordinary man," Malcolm Romilly told me. "Have you heard of pellar families?"

"I have made the acquaintance of Mother Nance," I replied.

"Ah, then you have met our resident witch," he said with some satisfaction. "It's all nonsense, of course, but the legends draw sailors to our shores and coin to our businesses, so we must nurture them."

I cast my mind back to the stories of my childhood. I remembered clothbound books of faery stories and one, of drowned blue, that talked of mermaids and selkies and other magic of the seas. "Mother Nance told me that pellar families are given special powers, derived from consorting with mermaids, I believe."

"Indeed! A pellar family is a family not to be trifled with in these parts. In each case, an ancestor has rendered aid to or fallen in love with a mermaid. In return, they were given a precious gift. In some cases, it is the second sight or an ability to foretell doom. In others it is healing magic or a way with animals."

"And the Romillys are a pellar family?"

He smiled ruefully, the expression warming his face to real handsomeness. "You mustn't believe Mother Nance's tall tales," he teased. "The first Romilly to own the Isle came over with William the Conqueror and was given this island in return for his service. He married a Saxon maiden and built a proper castle here to maintain William's defenses and then set about breeding a line of very dutiful descendants who have served their kings ever since. Dull and worthy people," he finished, the smile deepening.

I protested. "Mother Nance's story is much more engaging."

"Ah, yes, the one where the first Romilly caught a mermaid in his net. There's a third story, somewhere in between, that says my ancestor married the last of the pellar maidens, the youngest of the sisters who perished upon the rocks. She did not set sail with her sisters, so she alone survived, bringing pellar blood into the family."

"A much better story," I told him. "But you must finish it. What happened to her father, the sad old man who cursed his daughters?"

He shrugged. "The legends do not say. Perhaps he walked out into the sea and drowned himself. That has been a popular method of ending one's misery here. Or perhaps he drank himself to death or was struck by lightning or died in his bed of comfortable old age." He fell quiet a moment and I wondered if he were considering his missing bride and the dire fate she might have met. His eyes were shadowed, and I hastened to fill the silence.

"Or perhaps his youngest daughter avenged her sisters and helped him along," I suggested.

He raised a brow. "My dear Miss Speedwell, what a ghoulish imagination you have!"

"It seems like a rough sort of justice. One could hardly blame her," I argued.

His smile was sad. "No, one could hardly blame her. Well, that's enough of me prattling on about family stories. I am quite certain I have bored you to sobs." He hung the map back on the wall.

"Perhaps you would care to walk out a little. The rain has stopped, I think."

He led the way out onto the terrace beyond his study, guiding me down a series of staircases until we came to a tiny stretch of beach on the western edge of the island, the same that had been marked upon the map. It was a mixture of rock and shingle and sand, liberally festooned with seaweed. Heavy drops of fog pearled our hair. "Here now, you can see the Sisters properly," he told me, pointing in the distance. The shifting patches of mist obscured the islands on the horizon, but now and then a bit of wind would blow the edges of the cloud ragged and I could just make out the three shapes.

Malcolm gestured towards the small rowing boat beached at the water's edge.

"The storms will come and go for a few days more. It always happens at summer's end on the Isle, but once they clear, one of us will be happy to row you to the First Sister, if you would like. The nearest one is little better than a rock, but the views are superb and the bird life is most interesting. It makes for quite a pleasant outing with a hamper from Mrs. Trengrouse," he added.

"I should like that," I told him.

"I must warn you against rowing yourself," he advised, his expression suddenly anxious. "We leave the boat about, but we really oughtn't. The passage between here and the First Sister is deceptively calm. The currents change often, and it takes a strong rower to navigate the challenges."

"I am a good rower, but I promise not to take a boat without permission."

He smiled and he looked boyish suddenly and winsome. "Good. If the sea is calm enough, you can take the oars for a bit. My father always insisted on every houseguest who wanted to take a boat being given a test—if you could not row right round the island, you were forbidden from so much as getting into a boat. I am not quite so draconian. But it is good to be cautious in these waters, and I would not have you miss one of our best beauties out there," he added with a nod towards the Sisters.

"It sounds quite tranquil."

"It is. One would think the Isle could provide such peace, but we are a bustling little place, what with a blacksmith and cider presses and quarries. On the Sisters, one has only the gulls for company, and the occasional seal."

"And perhaps a mermaid?"

"Perhaps. Although they have been in short supply these past centuries."

He fell silent then and I thought of his lost bride and wondered about her fate. Had she met with mischance, falling to a murderer's dastardly intentions? Or had she run away from a marriage she could not face? If she had left of her own accord, that raised the question of how she had made her escape. Did she take a boat, veil tossing in the wind? Had she rowed herself to one of the Sisters to meet someone? More to the point, what had driven her to abandon her bridegroom on their wedding day? It seemed impossible that this attractive man could have said or done anything to frighten or alarm her.

And yet. Had I not just witnessed a fine display of temper directed at his nephew? For all his courtly ways, Malcolm Romilly had a way with rage. Had Rosamund ever borne the brunt of it? Had he frightened her somehow?

They were questions I could not ask. I turned to Malcolm, who still stared at the Sisters. "I wonder . . ." he whispered.

"Mr. Romilly?" I prompted.

He shook himself. "Malcolm, please. I apologize for my inattention. Building castles in Spain, I'm afraid. A common failing of mine, as anyone will tell you. Now, I suspect you would like to know more about the glasswing butterflies," he said, turning to guide me back up the staircases and into the library. He moved to the bookshelf behind his desk, running his hand down the rank of books before plunging in to retrieve a large volume bound in bottle-green kid. "Here we are. *Butterflies of St. Maddern's Isle* by Euphrosyne Romilly. She was an ancestor of mine, one of the first aurelians," he told me.

He handed it to me and I opened it to find pages of illustrations, each carefully tinted by hand. "These are originals!" I exclaimed.

"Oh, yes. Grandmama Euphrosyne had that book bound in order to keep her collection of illustrations in one place. Not only did she document every butterfly found upon the islands, she included sketches of their habitats and notes on their habits—eating, mating, duration of pupation, and other quite technical terms with which I am thoroughly unfamiliar. It is quite comprehensive."

"It is amazing," I breathed, hardly daring to touch the book.

"Take it with you," he urged. "Study it at your leisure."

"Are you quite certain? It is almost impossibly valuable," I warned him. "I realize it is important to your family collection, but within the history of English lepidoptery, this book is incalculably rare."

"I am entirely certain. There are notes of where to find the glasswings that might prove useful to you. Things haven't changed all that much on the island in a century," he told me.

I thanked him profusely and clutched the book to my chest as I left him. I turned at the door to thank him again, but he was not looking at me. He had moved to the window and was staring out at the grey sea stretching to the horizon.

CHAPTER

7

I hastened to my room with my trophy and read through teatime. I missed the bell entirely, so engrossed was I, and Mrs. Trengrouse appeared a little while after with Daisy bearing a tray. "A little morsel, miss," the housekeeper explained, shooing the maid from the room as soon as the girl had placed her burden upon the narrow writing desk. "Tea is served downstairs, but I thought you might like something special," she told me, and I realized this was a sort of reward for my discretion with respect to Helen Romilly's inebriation. Mrs. Trengrouse went on. "There is a plate of wine biscuits and a glass of our own red wine if you want a bit of proper refreshment. The grapes are grown here on the island on the vineyard head."

I looked up from my book, blinking hard. "Vineyard head?"

"The spit of land to the southwest. The soil and winds make it suitable for the growing of grapes. 'Tis not a fine vintage, mind you, but quite nice enough for the luncheon wines," she assured me.

"I am certain it will be delicious," I told her.

She paused and looked at the enormous book in my lap and the notebook tucked under my chin. "If you would like to work comfortably, I can have one of the lads bring up a proper table. The writing desk is fine for a lady's letters, but that book is far too cumbersome. You would want to spread your things out a little, I should think."

I thought of the narrow stairs approaching my room. "That sounds like a great deal of trouble."

"Not in the slightest," she told me. She left, and I returned to my book, nibbling absently at the wine biscuits and tasting the wine. It was light and flinty with a hint of something unusual, a mineral quality that I attributed to the rocky soil of the island. I preferred the heavier vintages I had sampled in Madeira and put it aside, devoting my attention to the biscuits instead. Richly spiced and tasting strongly of pepper, they were delectable and I was just finishing the last crumb when a knock sounded at the door. A burly lad entered when I bade, carrying a plain table in one hand.

"Where shall I put this then, miss?" he asked in the soft Cornish accent of the local folk.

"Under the window, thank you," I instructed. He set it neatly into place and then returned in a moment with a chair, upright but comfortable and well padded. "On Mrs. Trengrouse's instructions," he told me, touching his brow. I smiled to myself. I had certainly worked my way into the housekeeper's good graces, it seemed.

A moment later, Daisy reappeared, box in hand. "Extra pens and ink, paper for writing and blotting, and a penknife in case you forgot your own. Pencils too," she said.

"Let me guess, Mrs. Trengrouse's instructions," I hazarded.

She grinned. "Right you are, miss. I hear you went down the village way today. Did you meet anyone of interest?" She had turned away from me, using the corner of her apron to wipe nonexistent dust from the corner of the desk. I could see only her profile, but something about the curve of her lips seemed sly.

"I did. I met Mother Nance from the inn, the one who claims to be a pellar witch."

"Oh, and did she tell your fortune, miss?" Her manner was a shade too eager for casual curiosity.

"Not in so many words," I told her in a cool tone.

She rubbed harder at the sleek wood. "You ought to ask her, miss. She knows everything, does our Mother Nance. She can tell things that haven't yet come to pass."

I smiled thinly. "I prefer a bit of mystery in my life." I gestured towards the tray of refreshments. "Thank you for your efforts, Daisy. You may take that away."

She did as she was told, reluctantly it seemed, bobbing a swift curtsy as she took up the tray and vanished.

I passed another hour in happy contemplation of the butterflies of Euphrosyne Romilly until the words swam together on the page and my posture had grown stiff, then prepared myself for the evening meal. Dinner was a strained affair. Helen was pale and quiet after her afternoon's imbibing, content to sip at a glass of sparkling water and feed titbits under the table to her cat. Caspian was clearly in a sulk following his quarrel with his uncle, while Malcolm ignored him entirely. Mertensia talked animatedly with Stoker about various plants and the pests who fed upon them while Tiberius was content to apply his attention to the excellent food and the even better wine.

As the meal wore on, a curious mood seemed to steal over the group, a tension whose source I could not entirely place. It was not until we finished our sweet course that Malcolm made an announcement.

The conversation had just wound down to a natural silence when Malcolm put down his cutlery and patted his mouth. Then he took a long moment, surveying each of us as his gaze traveled around the table. "I feel the time has come to take you all into my confidence. I did not invite you here simply for the pleasure of your company."

He paused, seeming to steel himself. "I invited you here for a specific purpose, and I can only plead necessity as my defense. I hope that each of you will hear me out and decide to offer your help, for God knows, I have need of you all."

He drew in a deep breath as we exchanged glances, our faces betraying varying degrees of bewilderment. Only Tiberius did not seem surprised, and it was to him that our host turned first. "With the exceptions of yourself, Tiberius, and your brother and Miss Speedwell, everyone here was present when Rosamund disappeared. It was the darkest hour of my life. Things have not improved materially since then," he added with a bitter twist of his lips. "Mertensia and I have withdrawn from society. We see no one. How can we? We tried to pick up the threads of our lives. We attempted normality. But every time we encountered friends, there were the awkward silences. The pauses in conversation that went on just a little too long. The subjects upon which no one would ever speak—Rosamund, weddings, drownings. And each time I felt myself withdraw further from people. It felt somehow safer. I believe Mertensia's emotions were much the same."

He paused and his sister gave a grave nod. She had not eaten, I noticed, but merely tore a bread roll to bits in her fingers.

Malcolm went on. "In the end, it became too much even to see family. And that is why Helen and Caspian have not been here."

"We would have come—" Helen Romilly began.

Malcolm held up a hand. "I know. But it all just seemed so much simpler to close the doors and pull up the drawbridge, so to speak. And as time wore on, it became even easier to keep to ourselves. But now I believe it is necessary for us to discover what became of Rosamund once and for all. Only by writing a final chapter to this story can Mertensia and I move on to another. If we do not do this now, we will be immured here, and I think that way madness lies."

He paused again, letting his words settle like stones falling to the bottom of a pond.

"Put simply, I have invited you all here because I need your help." He looked slowly around the table. "Each of you possesses some skill that I think would be useful under the circumstances." His gaze was apologetic as it fell upon Stoker and upon me. "As for Mr. Templeton-Vane and Miss Speedwell, you came here expecting a peaceful holiday, and I do not intend that you should disrupt your plans on my behalf. But perhaps the fresh and observant gaze of scientists would not go amiss in this undertaking."

"What undertaking?" Helen Romilly demanded.

"He has some bee in his bonnet," Mertensia pronounced. "We had a great-granny who went entirely off her head, poor lamb. I shouldn't wonder if he hasn't done the same."

"Mertensia," her sister-in-law said in frigid tones, "I hardly think it is appropriate to speak of your brother in such terms."

Mertensia Romilly gave her a scathing look. "I forgot how tiresome you could be, Helen. Thank you for reminding me."

Before they could continue their spat, Malcolm intervened. "It has been three years since that dreadful day, but to me, it is as if it were yesterday. I think of her constantly. And always there remains the question, 'What became of her?' Did she wander off and lose her way? Did she fall into the sea? Did she run away?"

Helen's expression was patient, as if she were speaking with a backwards child. "I thought it was quite agreed that she left the island of her own accord. It is not pleasant to think that she might have changed her mind about the marriage, but it is the only reasonable explanation."

"That is what I believed," Malcolm replied. "And it is that belief that has tortured me for three years. Why did she leave me? It was the most logical if painful explanation. I endeavored to accept it. I tried to reconcile myself to the fact that she would rather flee with no money, no prospects, than remain here and be my wife. It is a bitter thing for a man to believe," he added with a thinning of the lips. "I knew that is what the gossips believed. It is certainly what the scandal sheets printed often enough. And these last years that has been my torment. Until now."

He rose and went to the sideboard. One compartment of it was locked and he produced a key, fitting it to the door. From inside he drew an unwieldy bundle wrapped in a length of cloth.

"Mertensia, ring for Trenny."

He held the bundle cradled in his arms as his sister did as she was bade. When Mrs. Trengrouse appeared, his instructions were brief. "Have the table cleared, Trenny."

She gave a doubtful look to the bundle held tightly against his chest but nodded, gesturing to Daisy to whisk away the porcelain and cutlery.

"The port," Mrs. Trengrouse began.

"The ladies will not withdraw tonight," Malcolm told her. "And you ought to stay, Trenny. You are a part of the family, after all."

She shepherded Daisy from the room and took a post near the door, closing it against prying eyes or ears from the rest of the staff.

Malcolm stood at the head of the table, looking us over as we watched with expectant eyes.

"I presumed Rosamund ran away, as much as it destroyed me to believe it. I was led to this conclusion by the fact that she took her traveling bag, a small affair of scarlet carpetwork. It was the same bag she had brought with her when she first arrived on the island. She had marked it with her initials, and there was no other like it in the world. The fact that the bag disappeared when she did seemed incontrovertible proof that she had taken it and run away."

He opened his arms, letting the fabric slip aside to reveal a scarlet traveling bag. The initials R.I.A. were worked in white wool just beneath the handle. It was moldering, with a thick coat of lush green mildew staining the sides, but there was no mistaking the bag.

Mertensia's expression was almost angry. "Where did you find that?" she demanded.

"In one of the priest's holes," he told her.

I sat forward in my chair, gripped by excitement. Priest's holes were common in Catholic households during the time of the Elizabethan priest hunters. Fitted in such a way as to escape detection, these tiny secret chambers could hold a man, perhaps two, for weeks at a time as agents of the Crown searched for them. All the most interesting ghost stories featured priest's holes, I remembered.

"Why on earth would you be poking about the priest's holes?" Mertensia asked. "I thought they were all blocked up or refashioned years ago."

"I was preparing to write a new version of the history of St. Maddern's," he explained. "I didn't tell anyone because I was not certain I could bring it off." His expression was slightly abashed. "I am no man of letters, after all. I thought I would have a look through the priest's holes, perhaps take some preliminary notes, and then settle to writing over the winter. But I found this instead," he finished, his gaze fixed upon the bag.

Helen Romilly's eyes were wide in her pale face and her son looked bewildered. "What does this mean?" he asked.

He had put the question to his uncle, but it was Tiberius who replied. "It means that Rosamund Romilly never left this island alive."

"That seems a stretch," Caspian protested.

Tiberius regarded him dispassionately. "Is it? If a lady runs away, she takes a bag. Even Miss Speedwell, who has traveled the world five times over, always takes a bag." He flicked a glance to me and I nodded slowly.

"I cannot imagine a lady embarking willingly on any sort of voyage without even the most modest assortment of possessions."

Tiberius went on. "So let us carry it out to the logical conclusion. If she left and took no bag, she did not leave of her own free will. Or she never left at all. Either possibility points to foul play."

Mrs. Trengrouse covered her mouth with her hand as Mertensia gave a little moan. "It cannot be," she murmured. She reached out blindly, her fingers groping for some comfort. It did not escape me that they landed upon Stoker's sleeve.

"What do you want from us?" Tiberius asked Malcolm.

A brief smile touched our host's mouth. "I should have known I could count on you for plain speaking, Tiberius. I need your help in discovering what became of Rosamund."

"You want us to help you hunt a murderer," Tiberius replied sharply.

At this Helen Romilly shrieked a little and half rose. Stoker patted her hand and she resumed her seat. Mrs. Trengrouse shook her head sadly while Mertensia regarded her brother with horror.

"Malcolm, you cannot be serious," she began.

"I am, I assure you, entirely in earnest," he told her. "This bag means that Rosamund never left the island alive."

"But murder—" Mertensia said.

"What else can it be?" Tiberius asked softly. "If she never left, taking her wretched little bag with her, then she must be here. And who else would hide her traveling bag except someone who wanted to make you think she left of her own accord?"

Put so bluntly, the question laid a pall upon the gathering. We were all silent a long moment, each of us grappling with the enormity of what we had just heard. Malcolm carefully laid the decrepit bag upon his chair and took up his glass.

"What do you want us to do?" Tiberius asked.

"I hoped each of you would bring your skills to the question of Rosamund's fate." He paused, his gaze resting upon Tiberius. "Tiberius, you are my oldest friend, and I find myself in need of support. We were close as brothers once, and I think you will not now refuse me."

Tiberius stirred. "Naturally, I will do whatever I can. I do have a few contacts in London who might prove useful. I will write in the morning and make inquiries. Discreetly, of course," he added with a graceful inclination of the head.

"Thank you, Tiberius. I am grateful," Malcolm Romilly replied gravely. "I cannot imagine there has been any further development, but if there is the slightest chance, we should ask." He seemed about to say something more but fell silent instead. There was an odd undercurrent between the two men, as if something more significant than words had passed between them, only a flicker and then it was gone as Malcolm Romilly moved on, looking to Stoker and to me.

"I had no thought of asking either of you to help, but when you unexpectedly joined our little endeavor here, it did occur to me that, as natural scientists, you are trained observers. There must be something the rest of us have overlooked. A fresh perspective from those who are experienced at observation must be useful and I am desperate enough to throw myself upon your generosity and implore you to lend your skills."

He turned his head slightly. "Mertensia, Caspian. You are both Romillys. The local folk are loyal to us. It is possible that someone has seen or heard something. They might be willing to tell you."

He took a deep breath. "Helen, that brings me to your particular talents."

She inhaled sharply, the jet beads at her throat dancing in time. "Malcolm, surely there are better ways—"

Mertensia regarded her brother in dismay. "Malcolm, this is not wise," she started.

He held up a hand, silencing them both. "I am resolved."

"What talents?" Stoker inquired.

"My sister-in-law is renowned for her abilities to contact those who have passed beyond the veil," Malcolm said. "She is a spiritualist."

"Not just any spiritualist," Caspian put in proudly. "She is rather famous. Perhaps you have heard of Madame Helena?" He finished with a flourish, bowing to his mother, who looked deeply unhappy.

"Malcolm, really," she began again, but her brother-in-law shook his head.

"Helen, I know you must think me inhospitable. I have not invited my own brother's widow and son to enter his family home for years. I have not answered letters. I have fulfilled the very least of my obligations and nothing more."

Helen shook her head. "You have continued the allowance that was Lucian's. You were not obligated to do so," she said in a low voice.

Malcolm brushed her remark aside, and for an instant I saw a flash of the man he must have been before tragedy and isolation had worked their worst upon him. He was decisive and unflinching and new blood rose to his cheeks, giving him a more animated look than I had yet seen. "It is not enough. I have failed," he said firmly. "I have scrutinized my own conduct, and believe me when I say that I am the first to condemn myself for being consumed with my own difficulties and giving little consideration to yours. I wish to make amends, truly. But I understand if you do not wish to clasp the olive branch that I extend."

"It is not that, Malcolm. You must not think so." She stopped, biting her lip until the blood rushed into it.

He rose and went to her, putting out his hand. "Shake hands with me, Helen. Do this for me, and let us be a proper family once more."

Her eyes flicked briefly to her son and she summoned a smile that did not touch her eyes. Slowly, she reached out and took the hand he offered. "Of course, Malcolm. Whatever you wish."

"Then it is settled," he said. "Tonight we will begin our investigations in earnest. With a séance."

"No," she put in sharply. "That is, I cannot possibly summon the spirits with so little preparation. I must have time."

"You do not have to do this," her son said. "Uncle Malcolm has done little enough for us."

Malcolm flushed but did not reply. Helen gave her son a look of mild reproach. "Your uncle is right. We have the chance to be a proper family. And if I can help, I owe it to him. I will do this," she said, more firmly than before. But as she reached to her son, her hand trembled, and something like dread settled in her eyes.

I moved forward as if to look into the bag, but Malcolm met my gaze, his expression bleak. I paused, checking my enthusiasm. To me, it might rank as evidence to be met with scientific inquiry, but to him it could only be a painful reminder of the wife he had lost. Worse still, it was no impersonal item, but her traveling bag, doubtless packed with her most intimate possessions. There would be time enough to ask for its examination later, I decided. I stepped back.

"Tomorrow," Malcolm said firmly, picking up the decaying bag. "We will begin."

As with my visit to Stoker's room the previous night, I did not bother to knock. I entered Tiberius' bedchamber under a full head of steam, surprised to find that he was already undressing. He gave me a wicked glance.

"Why, Veronica, this is all so terribly sudden. Will you still respect me in the morning?"

"You dreadful man. I ought to have known. Stoker warned me, but I would not listen. You've dragged me down here for some nefarious purpose and I mean to know what it is."

I stood with my back firmly against the door as I waited for his reply. He stripped off his evening coat and waistcoat and began yanking at his neckcloth, long fingers plucking irritably at the silk. "Dragged you? My dear Veronica, I had only to mention the glasswings and you were fairly begging to come."

"Semantics," I said firmly. "Now, what is this all about? What is Malcolm Romilly playing at with this gathering and what the devil happened to Rosamund?"

He arched a brow at me. It was an effective gesture, one Stoker often attempted and rarely achieved. "Excellent questions. I wish I knew the answers."

"What do you mean?"

He plucked at his studs, removing each and dropping them to a tray upon the washstand before removing his collar and cuffs. "Lucky for you the master of the house didn't see you creeping into my bedchamber like a lady of imperfect virtue. Malcolm is something of a prude, you know. He would be mightily shocked if he knew you were here right now."

"He will be more shocked if he has to treat you for the injuries I am about to inflict if you do not begin answering my questions."

He gave a short bark of laughter in spite of himself. "God, I was right to bring you," he said, stripping off his shirt. His musculature was not as impressive as Stoker's but it was a glorious thing in its own right. He was long and sleekly sensuous as a Praxitelean statue, and under other circumstances my fingertips would have itched to discover if that marble perfection was as solid as it looked. He took up a dressing gown of black silk and knotted it about his waist.

He gestured towards the chairs by the fire. "Would you like to make yourself comfortable? Or would you prefer the bed?" He chose the bed for himself, lounging against the pillows and patting the coverlet invitingly.

I remained where I was. "Tiberius."

He gave a gusty sigh. "Very well." He laced his hands behind his head and stared up at the canopy of the bed. The fabric had been gathered in a complex starburst pattern, pleated elaborately and most likely at great expense. "To repeat what you have already learnt this evening, three years ago Rosamund and Malcolm Romilly were married here in the castle. On their wedding day, Rosamund disappeared—apparently in her wedding gown and veil."

"Apparently?"

"No one saw her leave," he said in a flat monotone. "The wedding cake was left to molder, the ropes of flowers dropped their petals. It was all frightfully reminiscent of Miss Havisham. Finally, Malcolm accepted that she was gone and was not returning. Now, with the discovery of that dreadful bag, it seems he has decided he wants to rake it all up again, hence the party. He has brought together the only people he believes he can trust to investigate the problem."

"Why not go to the police?"

"The police?" Tiberius pulled a face of mock horror. "My dear Veronica, the police would have been quite happy to hang him for her murder, only it was rather difficult without a body. They made no secret of their suspicions, and one or more of them spoke to the press with disastrous results. You and Stoker were both abroad at the time, but believe me when I tell you I have seldom witnessed a more brutal evisceration by our newspapers. You had only to read one to be convinced that Malcolm was an unholy combination of Bluebeard and Henry VIII. The scandal nearly destroyed him. That is why he is so skittish about my being discreet with any London inquiries I might make—for fear it might all be raked up again."

I was not surprised. Similarly vicious stories had circulated about Stoker during his divorce proceedings. As he was not present to defend himself, the tales had done their work and even now many people believed the worst of him.

"How dreadful," I murmured.

"Yes, well. The dangers of an unfettered press," Tiberius returned. "In any event, the result is that Malcolm and Mertensia withdrew entirely. Neither of them has been off this island since, and they do not issue invitations. That is why I suspected something was afoot when I received his letter asking me to come."

"Why did he ask you particularly? You said you had not seen him in some years?"

He did not answer for a long moment, and when he did, I smelt evasion in his reply. "Our paths have not crossed for a while, but we have been friends from boyhood, close as brothers. Closer, in my case," he added with a thin smile. "You will have observed that Stoker and I are not especially devoted."

"I think you are more attached to one another than either of you would care to acknowledge," I told him. I canted my head, studying his long, elegant form. "I find it hard to imagine you as a child with boyhood friends. What were you like?"

"Incorrigible," he replied with some relish. "Although not as savage as Stoker. I was always refined in my tastes, even as a lad."

"Was Malcolm? Is that what drew you together?"

"Heavens no!" He seemed genuinely amused at the idea. "We were as different as chalk and cheese. Malcolm was a better oarsman, I was a more skilled rider. He liked maths, I preferred poetry, preferably the erotic sort. I was an enthusiastic adherent of Ovid," he added with a vague attempt at a leer. "And my temperament was more in hand than his. Malcolm had a temper, rather a ferocious one."

"Indeed? He seems rather mild," I replied. Apart from the scene with Caspian, I amended silently.

Tiberius' eyes widened. "His temper is the reason he was sent down from school," he told me with obvious relish. "He choked a boy, bigger and older than either of us. It did not diminish my regard for him," he hastened to add. "If anything, it rather increased it."

"He choked a boy? Are you entirely serious?"

"As the grave, my dear Veronica."

"Did he have good cause?"

"Is there ever good cause to choke a fellow human being?" he asked, blinking slowly.

"I can think of at least a dozen," I replied.

He laughed. "Remind me never to fall afoul of you, although I cannot say the proximity of your person, even if homicidal, would be unwelcome."

I might have pressed the issue of why Malcolm Romilly had invited him, but I knew Tiberius well enough to know when a pursuit was futile. I changed tack instead. "Why did you accept Malcolm Romilly's invitation to come here?"

Again he did not meet my gaze, preferring instead to stare up at the canopy. "I told you. Malcolm and I have been friends for a long time. A few years' absence doesn't wipe all that away. He asked for my help and I am giving it."

"I don't entirely believe you."

"Very well. I was bored in London and I suspected Malcolm's little problem might present an interesting diversion."

"Try again."

His expression was mocking. "You doubt my veracity. I am wounded. I should demand a forfeit," he said, thrusting himself onto both elbows, his body stretched in languid invitation.

"Do be serious," I urged.

"I find seriousness to be the least seductive of all the virtues."

"I didn't know any virtue tempted you," I replied. "And you have quite neatly evaded my question. *Why did you come?*"

"Save your breath to cool your porridge, as my old nanny used to say," he told me with a malicious gleam in his eye. "You'll get nothing out of me. I am closed as an oyster."

No matter how hard I pried, Tiberius would tell me nothing more. The storm had risen, hard rain beating against the windows as wind shrieked and howled as it swirled around the tower. He rose from his recumbent position.

"It is time for you to go to bed, Veronica."

I did not move. "You had a purpose in bringing me here. I don't believe it was simply to do me a good turn and send some glasswings my way. You still have not told me my role in all of this."

He rubbed his chin thoughtfully. "I don't know," he said, and it was as close to honest as I was likely to get from him. "All I can tell you is I suspected Malcolm might have something up his sleeve. I suppose I hoped that with you and Stoker here, strangers amongst them, he might behave a little better and not make the whole thing so bloody awkward."

"If you knew this was going to be a difficult situation, why accept the invitation in the first place?"

To my surprise, he decided to answer. "Have you ever turned over a stone just to watch the nasty things wriggling underneath?"

"I think every child has."

His mouth thinned into a cruel smile. "I am no longer a child. There's a baser word for what I like to do. Let us simply say that kicking over this particular stone amuses me."

"Then let us hope you do not get stung."

CHAPTER
8

I was not entirely surprised to find Stoker sprawled in an armchair in front of the fire in my room.

"You should not be here," I told him with some severity as I closed the door. "If the maid finds you in the bedchamber of your brother's fiancée, it will cause all manner of talk."

He waved a hand. "Let them gossip. It might bring Tiberius down a peg or two."

"Your concern for your brother is touching." I took the chair next to his, propping my slippered feet upon the hearth.

"Tiberius has a distinctly nasty side which you have never seen," he reminded me.

"So you have mentioned. I might point out that while I am perfectly well aware that his lordship can be imperious and willful, to me he has been unfailingly courteous."

"Only because he wants something. He has lured you down here with the promise of glasswings but he has an ulterior purpose, I'd stake my life on it."

I refused to give him the satisfaction of agreeing with his suspicions although I entertained a host of my own. "Your cynicism is fatiguing, Stoker. It is entirely possible that his lordship simply thought to do me a good turn. You forget he has already provided me with luna moths and a grove of hornbeams for the vivarium."

"Making it all the more likely that when he imposes himself upon you, you will agree to his terms—no matter how ridiculous."

"Such as?" I demanded.

"Such as this ludicrous masquerade of pretending to be his fiancée," he said, lifting his brows in a gesture of exquisite mockery.

"You know why he felt it necessary. A respectable woman cannot travel alone with a man to whom she is unattached. It was the simplest means of offering me protection against the positively medieval norms of our society. Besides," I added with a touch of malice, "I rather enjoyed the masquerade. Who would not appreciate the attentions of a gentleman of such sophistication?"

He shook his head, then leant back in his chair, crossing his legs at the ankles and lacing his fingers behind his neck. "I refuse to believe your head could ever be turned by the façade of elegant manners and excellent tailoring. I credit you with better judgment than that."

"Tiberius is one of the most eligible men in London. Only a fool would refuse to at least consider the prospect of marriage to him. You have a decidedly low opinion of my pragmatism," I told him.

"I have a lower opinion of my brother. You do not know him, Veronica, not really. He plays the gentleman, but he is nothing of the sort. He sharpened his claws on the back of my childhood and he has got worse with age."

"Why?" I was curious in spite of myself. I liked the viscount and had little desire to hear Stoker's flagellation of his character, but I was careful enough of him to be inquisitive.

Stoker shrugged. "He was old enough to pick up the servants' gossip

and realized I was Mother's son but not Father's." Stoker seldom discussed the fact that he was the product of his mother's brief liaison with
an artist commissioned to paint her portrait during what might best be
described as a "difficult patch" in her marriage to the previous Viscount
Templeton-Vane. After bearing Tiberius, the heir, and Rupert, the spare,
she had produced Stoker, a brilliantly blue-eyed cuckoo in the nest. The
youngest, Merryweather, dated to a hectic period afterwards in which
the viscount and his wife had attempted to reconcile.

He went on. "He used to torture me about it, but after a while he lost
interest."

"He simply 'lost interest'? That doesn't sound like Tiberius. He's te-
nacious as a wolverine. What did you do to *make* him lose interest?" I
demanded.

Stoker gave me a bland look. "I might have set fire to his bed. Whilst
he was in it."

"Enchanting. What do you know of his relationship with Malcolm
Romilly?"

Stoker paused to think. "By the time Tiberius made friends with
Malcolm, he and I had little to do with one another. Tiberius was not
terribly happy at home, and neither was I. We both spent as much time
away from the family seat at Cherboys as possible. Tiberius came here
for school holidays and I eventually ran off to join the circus," he added.
In his case, it was no mere turn of phrase. Stoker had indeed run away
with a traveling show before joining Her Majesty's Navy. His youth had
been a singularly adventuresome one.

"Tiberius is forty," I reminded him. "Those holidays were long ago."

"But formative ones," Stoker said, rubbing thoughtfully at the
shadow darkening his jaw. His battle to keep his beard in check was
ongoing and uphill. "And he kept returning, long after they left school. I
think Tiberius was happiest here. Father couldn't berate him for every

little misstep. There were no expectations put upon him. And with Malcolm's parents gone, they had the run of the place."

"What happened to the elder Romillys?"

"Dead. Their boat capsized on a rough sea between here and the mainland. I can't remember the rest of it, but both of Malcolm's parents were drowned. Malcolm was only twenty-two or so. He inherited the property and guardianship of Mertensia and Lucian."

"What a dreadful responsibility for so young a man," I mused.

"Indeed. I sometimes think Tiberius envied him that."

"Why so?"

"My brother spent the better part of two decades waiting to wear a dead man's shoes." The last Lord Templeton-Vane, Stoker's presumptive father, had died only the previous year. With his passing, Tiberius inherited the title, the country seat, the London town house, and the family fortune. Little wonder he had chafed at the waiting.

"His friendship with Malcolm is one of long duration, then," I ventured.

"The longest of his life, I should think. Although with Malcolm's retreat from the world, I don't think they have been in communication for the past few years."

"Since Rosamund Romilly's disappearance." I stared into the fire for a long moment, drawing up my feet and wrapping my arms about my knees. "What do you think of Malcolm's plan to play the investigator?"

"I think he is a desperate man who cannot face the notion that his wife ran away."

"Without her bag?" I asked, turning to face him.

"Why not? If she were desperate enough to get away, she might leave everything behind."

"Desperate! What could possibly drive a bride from her own wedding feast to running away like a common criminal in a matter of hours?" I broke off.

"What?" he demanded.

"Tiberius did mention a story from their boyhood. It seems Malcolm Romilly once choked a boy at school—so severely he was sent down for it."

"There you are," Stoker said with some satisfaction. "He might have frightened his bride by a display of temper that had her rethinking her entire future with him."

"But if she did run, where did she go?"

"I do not know, and furthermore, I do not care. I have had my fill of runaway wives," he added, bitterness twisting his mouth. His own former wife had left him to die in the Amazon and then dragged his name through the gutter in order to win her divorce. I could well understand his reluctance to involve himself in another marriage's woes.

He went on. "I shouldn't be surprised if she were living somewhere in the Argentine with a farmer husband and eight brats. After all, it is the simplest explanation."

"Shaving yourself with Occam's razor these days?" I asked sweetly.

"Always. How many brides succumb to nerves on the day? How many get cold feet thinking of the commitment they have undertaken? How many cannot face it in the end?"

"Well, that is a cruel trick to play upon poor Malcolm if it's true," I pointed out.

"I have experience with the cruelty of women," he reminded me.

"How much do you know about Malcolm and the others?"

He stared into the fire. "I cannot say I know much about any of Tiberius' friends. The last time he was here, I was rather occupied in Brazil," he reminded me, gliding neatly over the fact that he had been recovering from life-threatening injuries and being jilted by his faithless bride. Stoker had spent the better part of three years under the influence of strong drink and women of negotiable affections; that is to say, his consolations were bottoms—those of both bottles and whores. I had had my own opportunity to experience the viciousness of the former Caroline

Templeton-Vane, thanks to our most recent foray into the investigative arts.* I shuddered at the memory and decided to bring the conversation back to the subject at hand.

"Still, it is an interesting puzzle," I said.

"If you have half an ounce of sense, you will leave it be," he told me, his tone unusually stern. "You needn't play the game just because Malcolm wants you to."

"Game! I hardly think such an inquiry could be called a game. The man is clearly distraught and in need of answers."

"He would be better off letting the dead lie," Stoker replied.

"You were interested enough to listen to gossip about her disappearance at the tavern today. Besides, a moment ago you said she ran off, now you refer to her as dead," I mocked. "Make up your mind. Is she a wayward bride or a murder victim?"

"She is none of my concern, and if you are wise, you will make her none of yours."

"Oh, do go away and stop bossing me about," I told him. "I already told you that you should not be here."

"Ah, yes. Poor brother Tiberius' reputation," he said in a mocking tone.

"Never mind the fact that my own reputation would be in tatters," I reminded him.

He slanted me a quizzical look. "Your reputation has never concerned you much before."

I did not turn to meet his eyes. "You are in a nasty mood and I am tired. Have you said all you came to say?"

"In point of fact, I came to apologize. I have already apologized to Tiberius as well."

---

* *A Treacherous Curse*

I raised a brow in his direction. "You have apologized? Of your own free will? Do you have a fever? Shall I call someone?"

He passed a hand wearily over his face. "Go on. I deserve that, and a hundred more just like it."

I turned to him, almost concerned. "You are contrite and reasonable. I don't much like it."

He shrugged. "I am sincere. I acted rashly, coming down here and thrusting myself into your little escapade. But Tiberius has always known how to prod me. If I did not know better, I would say he wanted me to come. But he denies it."

"You and Tiberius have spoken?"

"After a fashion. He is still maddeningly opaque when it comes to his intentions with regard to you, but we all know this engagement is a thorough sham."

I rolled my eyes. "His intentions with regard to me are nothing I cannot manage, and even if they were, they are not your affair."

He fell silent a long moment, and I would have given a piece of my soul to have known his thoughts. My own were so disordered, I could not trust myself to speak. It was the smell of him, I thought idly. Whenever he was near, I detected leather and honey and something more—unplaceable but fresh and sharp like the wind off the sea.

I turned my head and studied his profile, the proud thrust of the nose, the long, elegant line of the jaw as his head tipped back. A lock of black hair fell across his brow, curling just above his eye. His collar was undone and the pulse beat slow and steady in the hollow at the base of his throat. His hands rested lightly on the arms of the chair, strong, capable hands that had held my life within them more than once. They were the hands of an aristocrat, beautifully shaped with long, tapering fingers, but also the hands of a workingman, broad of palm and heavy with calluses. They were hands that had never failed me.

I looked again to the pulse beating at the base of his throat and heard its echo in my own ears.

I swallowed hard, my lips parted. *Now*, I realized. This very moment, when everything slowed and time itself seemed to hold its breath. This was the moment to mend whatever I had torn. I had only to say the word and declare myself. Three short syllables stood between this present wretchedness and the terrifying bliss of baring my soul to him. I had pushed him away for his own sake, I had convinced myself. I had taken my own cowardice and framed it as an act of generosity. I had told him he needed to exorcise Caroline, but I was the one she haunted, that monstrous beauty with a soul as dark as sin. I was the one who trembled at the thought of being compared to her, of being found lacking somehow. For all my bravura displays of confidence, Caroline had become my bête noire, pricking my self-certainty because I feared above all things in the world becoming just such a woman—capable of inflicting the most profound of wounds upon someone I loved.

But no more. As the fire crackled upon the hearth and the little clock chimed the hour of midnight, I counted the strokes as they ticked off, telling myself that when it reached twelve, when the last echo faded away, I would take my heart in my hands and speak the truth at last.

One. Would I preface it with an apology for my capriciousness? The casual injuries I had dealt him?

Four. How could the seconds slip past so quickly? My heart beat faster, each thud quicker than the chime of the clock.

Seven. So few seconds left before I would speak and change our lives forever.

Ten. Only two more chimes and I must speak. But how to begin?

Eleven. Stoker.

Twelve. It was time.

I drew in a deep breath and my lips parted, joy and trepidation stretching my heart so full I could scarce contain it within me.

Suddenly, he turned his head to meet my gaze. "You were quite right, Veronica," he said in a casual tone.

"I—I'm sorry, what was that?" I had begun to speak, had pushed the first syllable from me but nothing more. His remark cut smoothly across my words.

"Last night, what you said about Caroline. I did not want to hear it, and I daresay I was forty different varieties of rude, but you were right."

I felt dizzy, the heat of the fire suddenly much too hot even as my hands and feet went very cold. "I was?"

He smiled, a ghost of his usual grin. "Do not take it too much to heart and lord it over me. I am unaccustomed to eating crow and I find it not to my taste. But you were right."

I forced my voice to lightness. "It is my usual state of affairs," I quipped with a smile so fragile it seemed made of glass.

He went on, oblivious to my piercing anguish. "I gave it much thought last night. As ever, you know me better than anyone. You see in me what I cannot see in myself, and that is the purest form of friendship."

"Friendship," I said in a faint echo.

He leant forward, eager in his obvious sincerity. "Friendship. I have come to realize that you have been right to insist upon preserving that above all else. Romantic inclinations, physical impulses, those are of the moment. They do not last in the way that real companionship does."

"Like a dog," I said dispiritedly. So I was to be little more than Huxley to him, a dutiful companion at arms, waiting to join in his endeavors, earning a pat on the head and a marrowbone for my troubles.

"It is a new thing for me, to count a woman as my closest confidante," he went on. "I have not always appreciated the camaraderie of the fairer sex. I have not always been willing to listen to the counsel of women, but you are so like a man sometimes that I find myself coming around."

"I am like a man," I repeated dully.

"Well, not in looks, obviously," he said, still sober as a parson. "But in your manner. You are forthright and direct in conversation, playing none of the games that ladies play. You offer only the truth, however painful."

I scrutinized him for signs of malice, but there was nothing in that open, guileless gaze except conviction. "What a martinet you make me sound," I murmured, forcing the words past the ache in my chest.

He smiled kindly. "No, never that. More like a devoted governess at times, always willing to give a dose of medicine when needed, no matter how disagreeable."

There was no possible response to that observation, so I made none. I merely stared at the fire and wished for a quick and painless death.

He yawned and stretched. "Lord, it's late. I ought to let you get to sleep. But I wanted to acknowledge your remarks last night. I was in danger of making a very great fool of myself, but you pulled me back from the brink. Thank you for that."

"Well, making a great fool of oneself is something I know a little about," I said lightly, tasting the words as bitter as pith on my tongue.

He rose and put out his hand. "So let us shake hands upon our new understanding. Friends, boon companions, partners in work and even these ridiculous investigative pursuits you seem to attract."

I took his hand and he shook mine with the heartiness usually reserved for one's stalwart drinking companions.

"I am glad we understand one another at last," he told me. "I have missed our conversations."

"As have I," I told him truthfully. I forced another smile as he bade me good night.

He closed the door quietly behind him as he left. I sat for a long while, staring into the flames and thinking about what a close thing it had been. I had perched on the edge of the precipice, ready to leap, only to find I had no wings at all.

"Clever Veronica," I said wryly. "You thought to protect him from being hurt and instead you have mauled yourself."

The fact that I had saved him from further pain was a very small consolation.

The next morning I took a hearty breakfast alone again. According to Mrs. Trengrouse, the gentlemen had scattered to their various occupations—Malcolm to estate business, Tiberius to his correspondence, Caspian to some frivolity or other (this said with an indulgent air), and Stoker for a row around the island. I was not surprised at the last. Stoker never liked being confined indoors for too long; he had a keen appreciation of the therapeutic effects of physical exertion. I understood the inclination well.

I tamped the impulse to charge out in search of my own exercise and instead read the newspapers, relieved to find the Whitechapel killer had not struck again. But there were endless stories about the murders in gruesome detail and the ghoulish speculation turned my stomach. I flung them aside and settled instead to writing up a plan for accommodating my glasswings in the vivarium in London, but it was no use. I could not banish the cloud which had descended after my conversation with Stoker.

Determined to exorcise my prickly mood, I threw down my pen and went to change into my hunting costume, emerging from my room just as Stoker descended from his.

"Good morning," I said cordially. "How was your sail?"

"Instructive," he replied. His hair was ruffled and his cheeks flushed from exertion. His mood was markedly better than I had seen in some time. He hesitated, then grinned. "I've found something you will enjoy. Come with me."

I needed no further encouragement. For just a moment it felt like an adventure of old, and I followed, my spirits rising with every step. He led the way through the pantries, buttery, carvery, and assorted other domestic offices, greeting the staff and startling a scullery maid busily engaged in a frantic embrace with the boot boy in the game larder.

"How dreadfully unhygienic," I remarked as they scuttled out.

We moved on through the kitchen proper, where Stoker collected a sandwich from the cook—not one of the dainties she usually cut for tea but an enormous affair stuffed with rare roast beef and good Cheddar and spread lavishly with mustard. He gave a little moan of satisfaction as he bit into it, and she beamed at him.

"I do like to see a gentleman with a healthy appetite," she said, urging another on him. "You're a fine figure of a man, you are. You need another."

I waved her off. "If he has another, he'll not keep that fine figure for long."

Stoker blew her a kiss and pointed to a low door set in the far wall. "That's where we are bound."

"Where does it lead?" I asked.

"The wine cellars, miss," the cook replied promptly. "Mrs. Trengrouse is down there now, but 'tis proper dark, it is. Mind you take a lantern."

I busied myself lighting one since Stoker was still ravishing his sandwich. At his encouragement, I led the way through the little door and down the flight of stone steps. There was a pool of warm yellow light at the bottom, and I could see Mrs. Trengrouse with a sturdy-looking man in the rough clothes of the islanders, working together to fill a large wine barrel from a smaller cask.

She looked up as we descended. "Good morning to you both. Come to explore the tunnels again, Mr. Templeton-Vane? Did you meet Mr. Pengird yesterday when you gentlemen rode about the island?"

Stoker swallowed the last of his sandwich and inclined his head. "I did indeed. Manager of the vineyard, I believe?"

The fellow nodded. "Aye, sir. That I am."

"Mr. Pengird has just brought the first pressing of this year's grapes," she told us. "We have no fine vintages of the island wines, I'm afraid.

Everything is mixed together and let ferment. Mr. Malcolm believes that the dregs of the old wine give the new wine character."

"Right he is," Mr. Pengird said stoutly. "We've made wine in these parts since the days of Elizabeth. The older the cask and the older the leavings from the mature wine, the better the new wine. And this year's grapes are a rowdy bunch, they are. Just you taste." He put down the small cask and drew off two tiny glasses, handing one each to Stoker and to me.

"Will you not taste, Mrs. Trengrouse?" Stoker asked kindly.

Before she could reply, the vintner gave a bark of laughter. "Not our Mrs. Trengrouse," he said with a jovial nod towards the housekeeper. "She's teetotal, she is, sober as a judge."

Mrs. Trengrouse shook her head. "It is not fitting for a housekeeper to indulge in spirits, Mr. Pengird."

He laughed again, urging us to drink. Mrs. Trengrouse gave us a sideways look but said nothing. The grape juice, unmatured and unfermented, tasted harsh and sour to me, but Mr. Pengird helped himself to a portion from my unwiped glass.

"That'll put hair on your chest, it will, missus," he promised.

Mrs. Trengrouse gave him a quelling look. "I can finish the rest of the cask, Mr. Pengird," she said. "I am sure you have other tasks awaiting your attention."

"Oh, not me, missus," he said with a broad smile. "I've only these casks to bring up for the master. He does love the first tasting," he added, pouring out a little more into the glass he held and finishing it with a pronounced smack of the lips. "'Tis sweet this year," he said with a wink, "on account of my Anna and her dainty feet."

"I beg your pardon?" I asked faintly.

"We tread the grapes here, missus, just as in the old days. Some vineyards use a stone, but not for us, no. We choose the fairest maidens on the island to have a go at pressing the grapes, and this year my Anna had the honor of the first pressing."

Stoker and I exchanged slightly queasy glances. Little wonder Mrs. Trengrouse did not drink the local wines! She darted us an apologetic little look while she stuck the cork firmly into the large barrel and handed the small cask back to Mr. Pengird. "Thank you, Mr. Pengird. I will be certain to convey to the master what a treat this year's vintage will be."

"You do that, missus," he said with another wink. He gathered his little casks and moved to the far wall, to an iron gate set in the stone.

Stoker took the lantern from me. "I wanted to show Miss Speedwell the tunnels, Mr. Pengird. If you are leaving that way, we will go with you."

"Aye, sir," said Mr. Pengird before he turned to me. "Now, you see, miss, the whole island is riddled with them. Natural caverns, they is. The first fellows used them for living in, until the castle were built and the houses and the village proper. Then the tunnels were put to use as a place to hide away in case of invasion. More than once a ship of villains landed on these shores and sailed clean away again when they found not a soul on the whole of the island."

"What are they used for now?" I asked.

"Lord love you, missus, they'm used for nothing at all save keeping a man dry when the rains come and he has to get from one part of the island to another."

"Where precisely do the tunnels go?" Stoker put in.

Mr. Pengird tipped his head, scratching his broad belly. "Well, now, let me have a think. There's the great tunnel that led from the main beach to the village, but that's been wrecked for seventy year or more. Caved in, it did, and killed a few good men and ruined a batch of Napoléon's best brandy, it did." He gave me a wink. "Them days, the tunnels were used for smuggling, and it's no crime to tell it now, for the present master would never hold with such doings. But his grandfather weren't so proper, and he liked him a bit of French brandy and some silks for his missus. Many's the load that were brought through the tunnels in those days."

"But that tunnel has been blocked for the better part of a century?" Stoker prompted.

"Aye, sir. That leaves the two small tunnels, one from the village up to the castle, and one from the castle down to the western beach, the one that overlooks the Sisters," he explained.

Mrs. Trengrouse lifted her own lantern from a peg on the wall. "I will leave the gate unlocked so you may come back up this way when you have finished."

Mr. Pengird scratched himself again. "I'll lead you to where the tunnels branch and then you can find your way," he told us. "Farewell, Mrs. T.!"

She bade him good-bye and the last we saw of her was a pale face shining in the darkness of the receding cellar. Pengird led us through the iron gate and into a cave that gave way almost immediately to a narrow tunnel. There was enough room for Stoker to stand upright, but little more than that, and I wondered how the smugglers and seamen had managed through the centuries.

Mr. Pengird must have intuited my thoughts, for he called back, "This is why we use the small casks to bring the wine," he explained. "More trips but a shorter distance by far. Now, mind your heads, for the land slopes away here and down."

The tunnel took a sharp drop at this point, growing steep, punctuated at places with short flights of steps cut into the living rock and handrails of knotted rope. In other places, the floor of the tunnel was flat enough to permit easy walking, but we were always descending, and I thought what a devilishly hard time they would have hauling heavy goods.

Once more Mr. Pengird anticipated me. "The last master put in a hydraulic lift, he did, for bringing goods up from the beach. Used to bring his wife's mother up that way, for the lady were so stout she could not climb it herself," he added with a wheezing laugh. Suddenly, the tunnel divided and he stopped.

"This is where I leave you." He pointed to the right. "This branch goes to the village, it does, right up into the smithy." He indicated the left branch. "Here'm what you want. Just follow it straight down to the beach and you'll not come to harm. The tide is out, so you've naught to fear from the sea, but mind you come back up sharpish. The tide'll turn in three hours and you'll not want to be caught at the bottom."

"Is it dangerous?" I asked.

"Only if you've not the legs to carry yourself up," Pengird returned with a grin. "But the beach is covered and the tunnel floods up the first twenty feet or so. Nothing but the sea beyond until you reach the First Sister." He touched his cap and set off, shouldering his empty casks and whistling a merry tune.

Stoker and I turned towards the beach tunnel, holding the lantern aloft to cast the light as far as we could down the dark hole. "Mind your step. It's slippery here," he warned. He put out his hand and I took it, feeling the whole world in the warmth of that clasp. The air in the tunnel was fresher than I would have expected, smelling of seaweed and salt.

"We're close now," he called, and just as he did I noted a lightening just ahead. The tunnel made a slight curve and we emerged onto a narrow shingle of rocky beach. Offshore, thrusting upwards out of the sea, the smallest of the Sisters lay, its barren rock lapped by the grey waters. A gull stood atop, giving us a baleful eye across the water.

"She doesn't look terribly inviting, does she?" I asked Stoker. But the beach itself was heavenly. The sun had emerged for a brief time, gilding the stones and warming the air. I stripped off my stockings and shoes and settled myself at the water's edge to wait as I dabbled my toes in the surf. The water was frigid and I drew my feet back as gooseflesh dimpled my legs.

Stoker did not join me. Instead he stripped off his clothes without a word and strode into the waves, plunging ahead with a strong swimmer's stroke until only his seal-dark head was visible.

He swam for some time, back and forth, parallel to the horizon and across the current until at length he emerged from the sea, taking up his trousers and pulling them on with deliberately provocative slowness. Water dripped from his black locks, running down the solid breadth of his chest and the flat plane of his belly. I turned back to the horizon. I pretended not to watch, but set my face to the sea, studying the gull as it flapped away from the tiny isle, wheeling overhead and making mournful noises as it searched for a likely fish. There was a flash of movement on the rocks at the edge of the shingle, a bird, no doubt, coming to inspect the shingle for an unlucky crab.

Stoker eased himself down onto the beach, pulling on his shirt but leaving it open and affording me a tantalizing glimpse of the hardened muscles that moved easily under his skin. I reminded myself forcibly that we were only to be friends, as established by the conversation of the previous night. No alluring display of masculine charms should distract me from that.

"You will catch your death swimming in water that cold," I told him sternly. "You might take a cramp and drown."

A tiny smile played about his lips. "How good of you to concern yourself with my health. But you needn't fear. I have no intention of drowning."

"They say it is a peaceful death."

Stoker shuddered. "It isn't."

I said nothing, and after a moment he went on. "I've seen it. Twice. Sailors who went overboard, once during a storm and that was not so terrible. At least it was quick. We saw him thrashing and fighting the waves as they rose higher and higher, but we couldn't come about. There was no chance to save him, and believe me, there was nothing peaceful about it."

"And the other?"

He shook his head. "A rigger slipped from the mast. He missed the deck by inches and plunged straight into the sea. It was calm that day. If he'd known how to swim, he could have saved himself. But he never learnt."

I raised my brows and he explained. "Most sailors never learn. They think a quick death by drowning or shark is better than lingering on when there is no hope. This fellow was one of those. He couldn't keep himself afloat. In the time it took us to come about, he was gone. But we could hear him, gurgling and choking and screaming for help until there was nothing but silence—that terrible silence that was worse than all the begging in the world."

I shuddered and he leant a strong shoulder into mine.

"No more dread stories of death on the high seas," he promised. "Shall we make ourselves an adventure today?"

"I am surprised you men haven't got together to go and shoot something. I thought that was what gentlemen did for fun," I said lightly.

He laughed and the warm honey of the sound filled me to my bones.

"I thought we had established that I am no gentleman. Besides, I no longer hunt."

"Neither do I," I admitted with a rueful smile. "I thought my reluctance to capture live specimens was an aberration, an effect of being confined to London, but as it happens, I was no more successful in Madeira. I restricted myself to taking specimens which had died of natural causes."

"Speaking of Madeira," he began slowly.

I broke in, cutting him off ruthlessly. "Young Caspian is something of a devil. I forgot to tell you that he and Malcolm were having a row yesterday. Something about Caspian needing to make his own way in the world. I don't know what the precise trouble was, but money seems to be the answer."

I held my breath, waiting for him to retrieve the subject of Madeira, but he was content to let it lie. For the moment. He shrugged. "I suppose Caspian is asking for money which Uncle Malcolm will not supply," Stoker guessed.

"That would be my assumption."

Stoker rubbed his chin thoughtfully. "I wonder how much of an allowance Malcolm has made to Helen and how much she shares with Caspian. He might have exceeded it on some trifle. Gambling? Women?"

"Those are the likeliest dissipations for a young gentleman," I agreed. "Just once, I wish a fellow would ruin himself with extravagant purchases of fossils or a penchant for expensive footwear."

Stoker snorted. "I have seen Caspian Romilly's shoes. He is not indebted to his cobbler."

"His mother might be," I suggested. "Not indebted to a cobbler. But she might be a source of trouble. I have seen evidence that she drinks. Perhaps she has an unfortunate admirer, someone with whom she has been indiscreet."

"She is still a handsome woman," Stoker said in a pensive voice.

"More so than her sister-in-law." The words slipped from my mouth before I could halt them.

A sudden gust of wind stirred Stoker's hair like a lazy hand. "Oh, I don't know," he said, keeping his gaze averted from me as a tiny smile played about his lips. "Mertensia has her own charms."

This observation did not trouble me in the slightest as I am not prone to such petty emotions as jealousy. A trifling irritation I could not place made my voice sharper than usual.

"As does her brother."

"Yes," Stoker agreed, his voice suddenly chill. "A castle tends to improve a man's attractiveness exponentially."

"It isn't his castle I find attractive," I returned with a feral smile.

Stoker thrust himself up from the shingle. "We should go back. It's suddenly grown quite cold."

Without waiting, he collected his boots and made his way across the shingle. Very cold indeed, I reflected.

CHAPTER
9

The rest of the day passed slowly. Every time I glanced at the clock it seemed to have stopped, the minutes ticking by like cold treacle as I tried to settle to something, anything. I had no wish to see Stoker. The tepid companionship he offered—the companionship upon which I insisted, I reminded myself coldly—seemed a small and wretched thing in the light of day. Over the months in Madeira I had persuaded myself that I must take a rational and sober course. But now, in proximity to him with a puzzle to solve, old emotions, once firmly banked, had burst once more into flame and the veritable inferno threatened to consume me. And Stoker's easy camaraderie and casual nudity did nothing to help. I thought of how nonchalantly he had stripped himself bare in front of me, as if I were no more than one of his sailor chums. He had taken me at my word, agreeing to be the best of what we had always been, partners with no regard to our respective genders.

And yet. In spite of my declarations and good intentions, that was simply not good enough. It was as if I had taken a blade to a fine painting, slicing the canvas to shreds, and now I complained I could no longer see the picture. I sat and loathed myself in silence for a little while before taking myself firmly in hand.

I wrote again to Lady Wellie as well as to Lady Cordelia before writing up my plan for the glasswing exhibit in the vivarium. Then I rewarded myself with a few chapters of Arcadia Brown's latest exploits with her faithful sidekick, Garvin. She was involved in solving the theft of priceless cameos from the pope's private collection in the Vatican, and I had just come to the particularly gruesome murder of a member of the Swiss Guard when a sudden clap of thunder nearly startled me out of my skin. The storm that had risen and quelled had revived itself, bringing with it lashing rain and gusty winds. I was surprised to find that I had filled the afternoon and it was teatime, and I went in search of the others, finding them in the drawing room, with Mertensia looking miserable over the tea things.

"I've been forced to play Mother," she told me through gritted teeth. "What will you have? China or India?"

"China, please." She poured a cup of steaming amber liquid and thrust it into my hands, letting some of the tea slop into the saucer. "God, I'm a fright at this. Why must we do it . . ." She trailed off, clearly irritated at the responsibilities of hospitality. She was a prickly creature, and I was determined to make cordial conversation with her even if it were against our collective will.

I sipped. "You mightn't enjoy playing the hostess, but no one can gainsay your expertise in the garden."

"I wish I were there now," she told me. "I understand plants. People are a different matter entirely."

She hesitated, then nodded with obvious reluctance towards the empty space on the sofa beside her. I sat and sipped at my tea, refusing cake and sandwiches and bread and butter.

"It's all so pointless," she said at length and with some bitterness. "Why must we sit around so stupidly, having precisely the same conversations with exactly the same people, day after day? I would far rather have a quick cup of tea in the garden and then get back to my work."

"Surely not on a day like today," I teased with a glance to the window. Ribbons of rain silvered the glass.

"Especially on a day like today," she countered. "Plants behave differently when they are wet. I learn something new every time I am near them. You must feel the same about butterflies," she challenged.

"Butterflies do not fly in the rain," I reminded her.

She tipped her head as though the thought had never occurred to her before. "What do they do in the rain?"

"Cling to a handy bush or shrub, shelter under a leaf. Their wings are made of overlapping scales, so tiny they are almost imperceptible to the naked eye. If the scales collect too much moisture, the wings will be too heavy to lift the butterfly from its perch. Part of the charm of hunting them is the knowledge that they thrive in good weather in temperate climates."

"But I know I have seen our glasswings flutter about in the rain," she said.

"That is what makes them special," I told her. "The distinction of the glasswing is that it lacks the scales of other varieties. It is the scales that lend color to a butterfly's wing. A creature without those scales is colorless but magnificent in its own way and able to fly in the rain. Perhaps it is an example of Mr. Darwin's theories on adaptive evolution," I suggested.

"You mean the weather here is so changeable that in order for a butterfly to thrive, it would adapt to the conditions in which it lives?"

"Something like that."

"You are a follower of Mr. Darwin's theories?" she asked.

"I am interested," I corrected. "I tend towards Mr. Huxley's more reserved approach. I am an empiricist and believe what I observe. Stoker tends to give greater credence to Darwin," I added, and at the mention of his name, Mertensia flushed.

She covered her blushes by munching at a prawn sandwich, and I took the opportunity to change the subject.

"I am sorry if I distressed you yesterday with my question about Rosamund. Impertinence is rather a bad habit of mine."

She brushed the crumbs from her fingers. "Not so impertinent after all," she said. "It seems Malcolm had a purpose to this gathering the whole time."

"Did he share it with you?"

"He did not." Her dark eyes were wary. "It seems he has been keeping secrets from me," she added with an attempt at lightness.

"You didn't know about the traveling bag?"

She shook her head and took up a piece of cake but did not eat it.

"It must have come as a shock," I supposed. "To have so much uncertainty about her fate and then to learn that your brother believes she never left the island alive—it is ghastly."

Her eyes flashed to mine. "I never believed Rosamund left the island," she said with brutal finality.

"What makes you think she never left?" I pressed.

"Because she would never have walked away from her life's ambition at the moment she achieved it," Mertensia told me.

"Then what do you think became of her if she did not leave the island?" I pressed.

Her lips parted and she looked down at her hands, almost in surprise, it seemed. The piece of cake had been crumbled to bits. She wiped her fingers and put her tea things aside, her movements deliberate. "You must excuse me now. I have spent the morning cutting hydrangeas and must put them into glycerin if I am to preserve them for the winter."

She left me then and almost immediately Helen Romilly slipped into her place. "May I pour you another cup, Miss Speedwell?"

I assented and she played Mother. Her hand was steady, I noticed, and she passed me the cup with a small smile.

"I must thank you, both for your kindness and your discretion," she began.

"Think nothing of it," I instructed.

She held up a hand. "Please. You were very understanding and I have no excuse for my behavior, only that it is difficult being here again."

"You were here for the wedding, were you not?"

She nodded, her dark hair gleaming in the lamplight. At her throat was pinned a mourning brooch, a lock of hair woven into a crosshatched pattern forming the center.

"Lucian's," she said, putting a finger to the brooch. "I do not like coming here, but I feel closer to him, knowing this place was so dear to him."

"You must miss him terribly." I sipped at my tea and watched a tiny wrinkle etch itself between her brows.

"Not as much in London. Here he is always present because this was his home, but in London we were always changing lodgings, forever buffeted by the winds of chance," she said. Her voice was light, but there was a strain in her manner and I wondered exactly how happy her marriage had been.

She went on. "My husband was an optimist, almost childlike in his belief that the next great thing was about to happen. He had great power to make others believe it too, or at least he made me believe it," she added with a gentle smile. She turned and beckoned to the cat, Hecate, who leapt lightly onto her lap and settled herself, regarding me with lamplike eyes. Helen's hands, beautiful and slim, fell to stroking the animal as it purred.

"There is an otherworldliness to folk from these parts," she told me in a low voice. "They believe in piskies and faeries and all sorts of things we grow past when we are adults. It is almost as if they never quite leave childhood behind."

"They are more remote," I reminded her. "They live on the edge of the world, it must seem to them."

"Indeed. It worries me sometimes to think that Caspian might have inherited some of that out-of-touch quality. There is a morbidity to the

Romillys, a refusal to face the world as it is. It is frightening," she told me, her hands never pausing in the slow petting of the cat.

"I think all mothers worry for their children."

She smiled. "No doubt you think me silly. But Caspian is all I have left in the world. I want him to do well and I want him happy."

"Those things are not mutually exclusive," I suggested.

"No, but the Romillys seldom make happy marriages."

"It sounds as if yours was," I reminded her.

"It was," she told me firmly. "But mine was the exception, because we did not live here, I think. It was good for Lucian to get away from here. But now I have brought his son back and I wonder if it were a very great mistake."

"Surely it is good for him to know his family."

"Yes," she agreed, but there was a note of hesitation in her voice.

I thought back to the scene between uncle and nephew I had overheard the previous day. "Do you worry about Malcolm's influence on your son?"

Her eyes widened and her hand stopped, earning her a rebuke from the cat. She resumed petting as she shook her head. "Certainly not. Malcolm is a gentleman. He and Mertensia might be prone to melancholia, but that is the worst one can say about them."

I hastened to repair the damage. "Forgive me. I heard that Malcolm was intemperate once at school and laid violent hands upon another boy."

"Oh, *that*," she said with a short laugh. "The boy he choked was a nasty little brute. He was playing the bully to one of the younger boys and Malcolm wouldn't stand for it. He threw himself at the larger fellow and wouldn't be shaken off. The headmaster insisted upon his expulsion for it, but he came home a hero."

"You're quite certain of the circumstances?"

"Of course! Lucian saw it all. They had been sent to school together and the headmaster expelled them both at the same time. He used to tell that story whenever Malcolm's name was mentioned, he was so proud of his elder brother for holding his own with a boy twice his size."

I fell silent, wondering why Tiberius had not seen fit to share the mitigating details of the story. Did he know them? Or had Helen invented them?

She went on. "No, my fears with regard to Malcolm have nothing to do with his temper. They are rather to do with his judgment. I fear this house party will be a calamity."

"What do you think he means to achieve?"

She shrugged one elegant shoulder. "Exactly what he says. To discover once and for all what happened to Rosamund. I only hope he can live with whatever he finds."

"What do you think happened to her?"

Helen shook her head. "I do not know. I cannot believe Rosamund would have run away. It would have been so out of character."

"Did you like her?" I asked on impulse.

She gave me a level look. "You are forthright, Miss Speedwell. One is not supposed to ask such things."

"That means 'no,'" I replied.

Her mouth curved into a smile. "Very well. I did not. She was very pretty, arrestingly so. But there was something hard about her, I thought. Watchful. It was as though she were always assessing, calculating, waiting to discover what part she should put on to play a role."

"What role?"

She spread her ringed hands. "Mistress of this castle. She was a governess, Miss Speedwell. She had been trained to serve, to fit in, to be unobtrusive. But something drove her, some determination to better her station. I did not fault her for it, mind you. Women in this world have to compete and there is only so much to go around. If she managed to stake her claim here and made good, I was prepared to accept her as Malcolm's wife."

"Your attitude is a very modern one," I told her.

"I am, unlike the Romillys, a realist. I know too well what the world is like," she reminded me. "Hence my advice to you yesterday about securing the viscount while you have him. Although I think your inclinations lie elsewhere," she added with a flick of her gaze towards where Stoker stood at the fireplace, quietly making his way through a plate of cream buns.

I murmured something indistinct into my teacup and she laughed, leaning forward to tap my knee. "Do not worry, my dear. Your secret is safe with me. Betrothed to one brother and cavorting with the other on a beach while he is disrobed! Another woman might be shocked, but I take my hat off to you," she said.

I thought back to the flicker of movement I had detected out of the corner of my eye while we were on the western beach. "You saw us."

"I did."

"Would it help if I confessed that I am not, in fact, actually betrothed to Tiberius? It was a stratagem because he worried that our traveling together would offend Malcolm's Catholic sensibilities."

"Are you his mistress?" she inquired bluntly.

"Certainly not," I returned. "Tiberius is a friend, nothing more. He has arranged for me to add several specimens of the Romilly Glasswing butterfly to my collection."

"And his brother?" she asked, her eyes straying once more to Stoker.

"We work together. We are employed by the Earl of Rosemorran to establish a museum."

"How disappointing!" she said with a smile.

I bristled. "Because I am in trade?"

She rapped my knee with her knuckles. "No, my dear. I, too, am in trade, after a fashion. No, I meant your chaste connection with the younger Templeton-Vane. I saw well enough what is under those clothes, Miss Speedwell. Permit me to observe that you are wasting an opportunity there."

I could not help but agree. She made a compelling point.

. . .

At dinner that night we dutifully made our way through several courses of excellent and largely untouched food, our conversation stilted. Helen did not appear.

"Mama never likes to be in company before a visitation," Caspian explained.

"A 'visitation'?" I asked.

"That is what she prefers to call these encounters," he told me. He was pale and darted several tight-lipped looks towards his uncle, but otherwise his mood was gravely courteous.

"How did your mother discover her abilities?" Tiberius queried.

Caspian shrugged. "She has always been sensitive to atmospheres. After my father died, she was inconsolable. She called upon a medium in order to speak with him but we never heard from him."

Mertensia snorted. "You make it sound as if it were a social call."

"In many respects, that is precisely what it is," he insisted. "She establishes a connection with the world beyond, and if the spirit she wishes to speak with is inclined to communicate, he or she will respond. If not, Mama is given her congé."

"Not at home to visitors," I quipped.

His smile was warm. "Just so."

"How fascinating," Tiberius said, his gaze inscrutable as it rested upon the young man. "I must make a point of speaking with her on the subject."

"I am certain she would be amenable to that," Caspian returned.

I looked to where Malcolm sat, toying with a dish of fruited custard. I leant closer to him, pitching my voice low. "Are you quite all right? I know it is not my place to remark upon it, but you have hardly touched your food." I did not add that his wineglass had been filled four or five times by my count.

He looked at me a long moment, seeming to focus only after an effort. "How kind of you to ask. I confess, I find this all more difficult than I had expected."

"I can only imagine. But you needn't carry through with it," I pointed out. "You have only to say the word and it is finished."

"How can it be finished until I know?" The question was anguished, and I felt a rush of pity for him. He seemed to recover himself then, for he touched my hand lightly. "You are very gracious, Veronica. Tiberius is a lucky man."

Tiberius! I was grateful that our host had not yet discovered our deception, particularly as I had been indiscreet enough to disport myself on a beach with a wet and naked Stoker. The memory of him, striding from the waves, seawater rolling off of his body like a son of Poseidon . . .

"Veronica?" Malcolm's voice recalled me to the present.

I smiled. "Sometimes I quite forget I am an engaged woman."

"I am not surprised," he said, touching my bare finger. "You wear no betrothal ring."

"He hasn't given me one."

Malcolm's expression was shocked. "Then he is derelict in his duty—no, not duty. For it would be a pleasure to put a jewel upon that hand."

To my astonishment, I realized Malcolm Romilly, grieving bridegroom with a missing wife, was engaging in a flirtation. True, he was slightly intoxicated, but not wildly so. Still, there was something at the back of his eyes I did not like, something calculated. I eased my hand out from under his just as Mrs. Trengrouse entered.

"The clock is striking ten, sir," she said in a toneless voice. "It is time."

We rose slowly and made our way to the drawing room. As I passed Mrs. Trengrouse, I saw that her expression was unhappy, a trifle nervous even. I gave her a reassuring smile.

"I am certain all will be well," I told her, sotto voce.

"From your lips to God's ear, miss," was the fervent reply. "I will go and order hot drinks for afterwards. Some revivifying may be in order."

"An excellent notion." She followed us to the door of the drawing room, closing it after us. I could hear the rattle of her chatelaine as she bustled away, no doubt concealing her concerns for her master in the demands of her position. Far better to go and supervise the clearing up of the dinner things than loiter outside the door.

Helen was already in the drawing room, and I saw at once that it had been arranged a little differently—no doubt to her specifications. The drapes were drawn tightly against the night sky, and two tall tapers, church candles of beeswax, had been lit in holders that stood on either side of a sturdy wooden chair. This was set at a round table covered in a dark cloth, and other similar chairs had been arranged to encircle the table. A third candle, small and low, rested in a dish in the center of the table. No fire had been kindled in the hearth, and I was surprised at this, for the storm was still blowing, the wind moaning softly at the windows like a voice asking permission to enter. The soft metallic ping of rain-drops against the glass was the only sound beyond the rustling of our skirts as we ladies took our places, the gentlemen coming after.

Helen directed us, taking the chair between the tapers for herself. Malcolm was seated at her right hand, Caspian at her left, and Tiberius was almost opposite. I occupied the spot between Malcolm and Tiberius, while Mertensia took Tiberius' other hand and Stoker seated himself next to Caspian. We exchanged glances, none of us entirely comfortable, it seemed. Helen was dressed in her usual black, severe and unrelieved except by the mourning brooch at her throat. A veil of black lace rested on her coiled hair, and her eyes were enormous, the pupils inky against the pale irises.

"Let us begin," she said in a low voice. She put out her hands, indicating that we should do likewise. Tiberius took mine with a light clasp, his fingers warm, and I felt the weight of his signet ring. Malcolm's grip was firmer, a slight callus between his middle and forefinger where his pen rested when he wrote. He shifted his hand, putting his palm flat to mine and folding his fingers over as if we were preparing for a waltz. I gave his hand a slight squeeze of reassurance and glanced across the table to where Mertensia was holding Stoker's hand tightly, her knuckles white in the dim light.

"I must ask that you do not speak," Helen instructed us. "No matter what occurs. You must not intervene when I am communing with the spirits. It is dangerous, for me and for you," she said ominously. She closed her eyes, breathing deeply, once, twice. A third inhalation went on for a long time, and she expelled the breath slowly through slightly parted lips. As the breath escaped, a hum began to sound, nothing at first, a mere vibration. But then it gathered strength, filling the air.

"Spirits, can you hear me?" Helen demanded in a louder voice than she had yet used, one unlike I had heard from her before. It was a voice that would have done Sarah Siddons proud, ringing past the footlights and into the rafters. The invocation was delivered three more times, each punctuated by a low breath and a hum as she began to sway in her chair.

Suddenly, the candles guttered and one of the tapers blew out. Mertensia sucked in her breath and I felt Malcolm's hand flinch in mine.

"Spirits," Helen said, coaxing now. "Speak to me. I can feel you near." The second taper blew out in a rush of cool wind. Mertensia gave a low moan of protest and I heard Stoker's murmur of reassurance.

"Silence! No one must speak but the dead," Helen rebuked. "Come, spirits! Come and speak with us now. I call upon Rosamund Romilly, if you are here, make yourself known to us." The rush of cool wind came again, and this time a series of raps.

"Don't," Mertensia begged.

But Helen carried on, commanding Rosamund to make herself known to us once more. The raps came again, slow and inexorable, closer now.

"Rosamund, is that you?" Helen demanded. "Rap once for yes!"

The silence was infinite, stretching out between us as the darkness pressed in from all sides. We circled the single flame, like cave dwellers desperate for solace against the terrors of the night, I thought. It danced wildly, casting shadows over our faces, making sinister masks. I realized that Helen had opened her eyes and was staring into the flame, never blinking, her black pupils reflecting the light.

We waited, the silence growing taut and unbearable until at last it came.

A single knock.

Malcolm's hand grasped mine convulsively as Helen moved almost imperceptibly forward in her chair. "Yes, spirit! Tell us again. A single rap if you are Rosamund."

Again it came, one knock. Mertensia moaned again and closed her eyes. I saw Stoker's fingers tighten over hers in support.

Helen spoke, her voice coaxing. "Rosamund, tell us now. You are in the spirit realm. That means you have left your body. Is this true?"

Another single knock.

"Rosamund, were you murdered?" Helen breathed out the words barely above a whisper. Beside me, Malcolm clasped my hand like a drowning man. I thought I heard him murmur in protest, half begging not to hear what he knew he would.

We waited in the silence, the candle flame flickering. It settled, the golden light holding almost still for a long moment. Then, without preamble, it streamed sideways, flaring once before it blew out. In the sudden darkness, I heard a new sound, tentative at first, then gaining strength. Soft at first, so distant and quiet I almost thought I imagined it. It was a harpsichord or spinet, constructed with strings, I realized, and the melody was old—something Baroque and complicated with trills and a slow, slightly melancholy rhythm.

"It is music," I said in some surprise.

"No, it isn't," Mertensia burst out. "It is Rosamund!"

"Will someone light a bloody candle?" Tiberius demanded. I heard the rasp of a lucifer being struck and Stoker's face sprang into view, illuminated by the small flame. He held it to one of the tapers, but it would not take light. It guttered out at once and Mertensia made a small noise of protest. Stoker struck another lucifer, cupping one hand to protect the tiny flame.

"Mama!" Caspian cried. His mother was slumped senseless in her chair. He shook her gently until she came to with a start.

"What has happened?" she demanded. Then she heard the music, sitting forward, clutching at her son's sleeve. "Rosamund," she breathed.

Stoker's lucifer burnt out and he struck another.

"There are lamps in the hall," Malcolm told him.

"You mustn't," Mertensia cried, curling her hands into fists at her temples. "We must stay together! Do not leave," she pleaded.

Malcolm half started from his chair. "The music is getting louder," he said, still holding fast to my hand.

Stoker vanished with the tiny flame, plunging us once more into darkness before returning a moment later with a small lamp lifted just high enough to throw his face half into shadow. "The music is louder in the passage."

"The music room," Malcolm managed in a strangled gasp.

We rose almost as one, Malcolm, Stoker, and I at the front of the little band, leading the way towards the music room. The door was closed but we could hear the music clearly, growing louder with every step. The trills and flourishes seemed to surround us in the passage, music conjured from nowhere, teasing and tormenting as snatches of it danced around us.

"She is still here," Helen said in a strangled voice. Her son supported her, one stalwart arm at her waist. To my surprise, Mertensia supported her other side, gripping her sister-in-law's hand with her own grubby one. For once, Helen did not pull away. She seemed, instead, grateful for her kindness.

Instantly, the music stopped, the last notes cut off sharply but an echo of them lingering in the passage. Malcolm burst through the doors of the music room, leading us as he held the lamp aloft. In the center of the room stood a harpsichord, the lid lifted, music scattered upon the floor. Attached to the harpsichord was a bracket for a candelabrum fitted with slim white tapers. The scent of blown candles filled the air and a slender wisp of grey smoke spiraled lazily upwards. Stoker put his finger to the smoking wick.

"Still hot," he murmured.

"What does that signify?" Malcolm demanded.

Stoker opened his mouth to speak, but paused as Tiberius came forward. He moved like a sleepwalker, slowly, inexorably towards the harpsichord. He put out his hand and lifted something from the seat, turning towards Malcolm with an expression I had never seen before.

Clutched in his fist was a single striped rose.

He held it up, but Malcolm did not touch it. He stared in horror, his white lips parted, his breathing heavy. Suddenly, with a choking gasp, Helen slid to the floor, crumpling into a heap of black taffeta.

Caspian bent to his mother just as Mrs. Trengrouse bustled into the room.

"Mr. Malcolm, I am sorry. I'm afraid the storm—" She broke off at the sight of Helen Romilly huddled on the Aubusson.

"Fetch a vinaigrette, Trenny," Malcolm said wearily. "I think it is going to be a long night."

CHAPTER
10

By unspoken agreement, we reassembled in the drawing room, where a fire had been kindled against the rising storm. The draperies were drawn to shut out the pounding rain, but a restlessness seemed to have settled over the group. Helen had been roused from her swoon and was settled on a sofa, a rug over her knees. Caspian disappeared and returned a few moments later with her cat, Hecate, dropping the animal onto his mother's knee. The creature turned a few times, kneading its claws, before gathering its legs underneath and assuming a posture of watchful rest upon its mistress's lap.

"Thank you, darling," Helen murmured to Caspian. He shot her a fond smile and then ducked his head, as if embarrassed at being caught in the act of a kindness.

The rest of us said little, listening to the ticking of the clock and the crackle of the flames, and after a long while, Mrs. Trengrouse reappeared, leading Daisy and another maid bearing platters of sandwiches, bread and butter, and bouillon cups of steaming beef tea. There were pots of strong black tea as well, and Mrs. Trengrouse set the maids to serving. "Mind you all have a cup of the beef tea. It is sustaining and should prevent anyone else from succumbing to shock."

"Strong drink, you mean," Mertensia put in. She was seated on a sofa next to Helen, not touching her sister-in-law but keeping a curious eye upon her. Whatever fright Mertensia had taken during the séance, she seemed determined to recover herself. I knew well the inclination to explain away the inexplicable. It was easy to forget the things that waited in the dark when one was warmed by the light. But there was a tautness to her expression that made me wonder if she had been more frightened than she would like to remember.

"Mertensia!" her nephew called sharply.

His aunt shrugged, and Helen bestirred herself. "Never mind, Caspian. It is true that I drink more than I ought. It is the only thing that quietens my head." She trailed off, letting her words hang in the air.

"Be that as it may, no one can deny that what happened tonight was sufficient to disturb the stoutest constitution," Malcolm said evenly. "I confess that I myself was startled."

"Startled!" Caspian's handsome mouth curled in scorn. "You looked as if you had seen a ghost. That is—" He stopped abruptly, a warm flush creeping up his cheeks. "You never expected that, did you?" he demanded. "You thought Mama's gifts were a joke, but now the laugh is on you because she did conjure something."

"Something? Or someone?" Mertensia asked softly.

Silence blanketed the room save the sound of the crackling fire and the rising wind and Stoker, munching happily at a slice of cake he had unearthed behind the sandwiches. I pulled a face at him, but I knew better than to remonstrate with him when he was indulging his sweet tooth.

"I presume Rosamund played the harpsichord," I said to Malcolm. He turned to me in surprise.

"Why, yes. She was quite accomplished. It was an old-fashioned pastime for a modern girl. She took no end of japing about it, but she refused to give it up. She could be stubborn like that," he added, his expression faraway as he no doubt thought of his beautiful bride.

"And that was her instrument?" I pressed.

He nodded absently. "It was a wedding gift, I don't know from whom. She demanded that it have pride of place in the music room. The evening before the wedding, when there was a reception for our guests and a dinner to celebrate the upcoming nuptials, she spent it in there, playing hour after hour. The same Baroque melodies."

"Like the one we heard tonight?" Stoker asked.

Malcolm nodded again. "I think so. They all sound alike to me," he said, his manner slightly abashed. "I am afraid I don't understand music. Never did."

"The Romillys, none of us, are musical," Caspian put in. "Which is why the music room is usually shut up."

"Is it?" I asked.

Malcolm shrugged. "There are instruments in there that my grand-parents played, badly, I recall. But after their time, no one took an interest save Lucian. My father had been made to practice as a boy and loathed it, so when he inherited the castle, he left the room shut and that was the end of it apart from Lucian noodling away as a boy. He was the only one of us who had any sort of feel for music. I don't suppose I have been in it more than a dozen times in the whole of my life."

"Until tonight," I observed.

"Until tonight. I certainly never went in there after Rosamund . . ." He did not finish the sentence.

Caspian gave a sharp bark of laughter. "Perhaps ghosts know how to pick out a tune," he ventured.

"Don't be stupid," Mertensia snapped. "We have had enough talk of ghosts for one night."

"Yes, but we have made a start," Malcolm said. There was a boyish earnestness to him that was oddly touching.

"You want to do this again?" I asked.

"I do. I believe we have only scratched the surface. My God, if Helen has managed to make contact with her so quickly and so comprehensively, imagine what Rosamund could tell us."

His eyes were almost feverish, and his sister stared at him as if he had taken leave of his senses. "You cannot be serious, Malcolm. It's the rankest chicanery."

"How dare you—" Caspian leapt to his feet, his fists balled at his sides.

Mertensia rose, standing toe-to-toe with her nephew, lacking a few inches but nothing in courage. "I do dare," was the stout reply.

"Mertensia, Caspian, we have guests," Malcolm reminded them.

"Guests?" Mertensia whirled to look at her brother. "I hardly think so. Tiberius has been coming here since he was a boy, and as for the others, what secrets have we now? We are beyond polite conventions, brother. We have been since you asked them to search for a dead woman."

The gentlemen had risen as soon as Mertensia got to her feet. Only Helen and I remained seated, but she rose now, gathering the cat to her breast. "Malcolm," she said in her usual gentle voice, "I will try again tomorrow if you insist. But I am not certain it is wise. Perhaps Mertensia is right. Perhaps it is best to let the dead bury the dead."

Malcolm's mouth set in a mulish line. "Do you know what the past three years have been like? No, none of you can imagine," he said, looking from each of us to the next. "I have been as one insensible, sleepwalking through my days. I cannot put her memory to rest because I do not know what became of her. I have been driven halfway to madness, and you would have me stop now?"

"But what if the truth is too terrible to bear?" Mertensia asked in a voice of surrender.

"There is no truth so terrible as the unknown," he replied.

"Very well," she said. "I am against this. I do it under protest, and I think it unwise. But I will do it for you."

He reached out and clasped her hand. He turned to their sister-in-law.

"Helen, I do insist that you try again tomorrow. After dinner, we will attempt once more to contact Rosamund."

"As you wish," she murmured. "I will do my best." But I noticed that the hand that stroked the cat trembled and the smile she offered her brother-in-law did not meet her eyes.

We neglected the sandwiches, but the beef tea and hot whiskies did not go unappreciated. When we had drunk our fill, the party began to break up, with Helen retiring first, followed swiftly by her son and Mertensia. The rest of us filed out a few minutes later, each taking a lit taper from the housekeeper, who stood stationed by the foot of the stairs. Stoker disappeared up the spiral stairs while Tiberius gave me a low bow, his expression thoughtful as he closed his door. I took the opportunity to slip back into the corridor, following the housekeeper's shadow until she reached the dining room.

"Mrs. Trengrouse?" I called.

She whirled, her face as white as the taper I held aloft. "Miss Speedwell. What can I do for you?"

"I rather wondered if I might do something for you," I began. "Anything that affects the family must affect the rest of you who live here. And the burden of keeping everything running smoothly falls upon your shoulders."

"That is true, I suppose," she told me in a low voice. "I have the devil's own time keeping the maids from losing their wits. They are silly girls, every last one of them."

"Naturally they are influenced by such a tragic story."

"The tragedy is that he fell in love with her at all," she said suddenly.

I canted my head. "Is it?"

She spread her hands, sturdy, capable hands that were no doubt more accustomed to keys and chatelaines than handkerchiefs and vin-aigrettes. "I should not have spoken," she began.

I put an impulsive hand to her arm, the black bombazine rustling under my touch.

"Were they ill suited, do you think?"

"What difference does it make now?" she returned sadly, her tone one of resignation.

"I thought her relationship with Mr. Malcolm might shed a little light upon why she might have run away. You must admit, it is unusual for a bride to flee her own wedding."

She hesitated, then beckoned me into the dining room. She poured us each a tiny measure of brandy and handed me a glass. "I think we might be excused a medicinal dose," she told me. I smothered a grin, wondering how often the allegedly teetotal housekeeper indulged in such a remedy. She tossed off the drink, putting a hand to her mouth when she was finished. I sipped mine and waited for her to speak. She busied herself a moment, locking the brandy away again in the tantalus before turning back. She plunged ahead as if she had made up her mind to speak hard truths and wanted the task done as quickly as possible. "I would never say a word against Miss Rosamund," she told me sternly. "But she and Mr. Malcolm were as different as chalk and cheese."

"Some say opposites attract," I reminded her.

She leveled a glance at me. "I know a thing or two, Miss Speedwell, and I recognize a lady with experience of the world when I see one. Have *you* ever found that opposites attract?"

"No," I admitted. Emboldened by her frankness, I pushed further. "In what ways were they not suited?"

Mrs. Trengrouse shook her head. "It is difficult to explain if you haven't known Miss Rosamund. She was unlike any woman I have ever met."

"How so?"

"She was a lovely creature, perhaps the loveliest I have ever seen, all dark hair and eyes like sloes. But there was something more, an expression I cannot quite describe. As if she were in on some great joke the rest of us didn't know. I used to wonder sometimes if she were laughing at us, but I think it was something different. She was a world apart, quiet sometimes, watchful. I never quite knew what she was thinking."

"That sounds uncomfortable," I mused.

"Oh, now, miss, don't take it like that," she begged. "I'm not saying a word against her. But I wondered sometimes if she were the right one for Mr. Malcolm. She was so very clever, and he and Miss Mertensia, well, they're simple folk. My little lambs, I called them when they were small. Under nurserymaid I was, when they were small. Their mother was poorly after she had her babes, every one. She would take a dark turn, staring out the windows for months on end, never holding her littles or taking an interest in them. It was left to Nanny and me to care for them."

"Childbed takes some women that way," I observed with a shudder. All the more reason never to engage in the practice of reproducing, I decided.

"That it does," she agreed. "And after Miss Mertensia were born, the mistress never quite recovered. Just black moods and melancholy. So I played with them and sang them songs and made them rhymes and taught them their letters. And in time I moved up in the household. Nanny left to live with her sister on the mainland and I was put in charge of the nursery. When the old master died and the housekeeper gave notice, Mr. Malcolm couldn't bear to think of having anyone else in charge of things. 'You know us better than anyone, Trenny,' he told me. 'You must take the helm,' and so I did." She had changed, her cool propriety giving way to a casual Cornish warmth as her accent broadened and her choice of words became more colloquial.

"They are lucky to have you," I told her.

She looked pleased. "Very kind of you to say." Her expression turned a little sly. "I remember your man, his lordship, from a long year back. He first came when he and Mr. Malcolm were schoolboys together. A charmer he was, even then. I could see he would be a handsome gentleman when Mother Nature finished with him."

"Yes, his lordship is very attractive," I agreed.

"And jealous of what belongs to him I should think," she added, her expression perfectly neutral.

I realized then that Stoker and I had indeed been seen together upon the little shingle of beach, him brazenly unclothed and me entirely unconcerned.

Before I could speak, she leant close and I smelt the sharp spiciness of good lavender on her clothes and the merest hint of brandy upon her breath. "It isn't my place, miss. God knows it isn't," she said fervently. She gripped my arm suddenly, and all semblance of the gentle housekeeper was gone. Her eyes were pleading, tears dampening the lashes. "But if you don't wish to marry his lordship, break it off. Miss Rosamund didn't and look where it has got us."

"You think she ought to have broken her betrothal?"

"Aye," she said, her fingers tightening on my arm. "If she had her doubts, she might just have left him, might have saved him years of misery and wondering what became of her. Why could she not have called off the wedding?" she demanded. "She might have saved him so much torment if only she had taken her courage in her own two hands and refused to go through with it."

"Then you think she ran away," I ventured. She blinked furiously, seeming to recollect herself. She dropped my arm and took a handkerchief from her pocket. She wiped her eyes and blew her nose lavishly.

"What else could it be, miss?"

I did not like to speak of murder to Mrs. Trengrouse. It was all so sordid and out of keeping with her tidy ways. In her world, mess and disorder were things to be mended. I knew from my own careful taxonomies that there was a tranquility to be found in order. My solace was the pinning of specimens and the lettering of Latin labels—not so very different to the starching of sheets and the roasting of ducks. To defile the housekeeper's serenity seemed somehow unkind and so I temporized.

"I am sure she had her reasons," I told her. "For marrying Mr. Malcolm and for leaving."

Mrs. Trengrouse's expression was doubtful. "Perhaps it is as you say, miss."

She dried her eyes again and pocketed her handkerchief, her manner once more brisk.

"I shall not ask your pardon for my intemperate speech," she said formally, her Cornish accent smoothing into something more mannered. "But I would never have unburdened myself to a guest were the situation not so—"

I would have touched her arm once more, but it was clear the moment for such intimacy was past. "Think nothing of it, Mrs. Trengrouse. People often forget that staff are as deeply affected by the goings-on in a house as the family themselves."

She paused, then nodded slowly, the candlelight sparkling off the silver threads in her dark hair. "Most people never think of such a thing. You are a most singular person, Miss Speedwell."

"Thank you, Mrs. Trengrouse. I shall take that as a compliment."

They say that curiosity killed the cat, but I am no cringing feline. I waited until the castle slept, the only sound the roaring of the wind about the tower, then rose and put on a dressing gown. I omitted to wear slippers, preferring chilled feet to the noise of soles scraping upon the stones. I stepped out onto the landing of the turret stair, groping carefully rather than lighting a candle and risk alerting Tiberius—or anyone else—to my presence. There was no sound from Stoker's room above, and no light shone down the stairs. I put my foot to the first step and ran headlong into a broad chest. Strong arms came about me, and a hand clamped over my mouth.

Warm breath that smelt of peppermint humbugs stirred the air next to my ear and there was the softest brush of lips as he whispered.

"Not a sound. Tiberius is wakeful."

I gave a nod and Stoker withdrew his hand from my mouth but his arms were still firmly clasped about my person. "I presume you mean to investigate the music room?"

I nodded again and the arms relaxed as the lips brushed my ear again. "Then I am coming with you."

It was just as well that I should not speak. The unexpected proximity of him had set off a most interesting and violent reaction within me. I felt warm—very warm *indeed*—where his body made contact with mine, and unbearably cold where we did not touch. I attributed the sensation to the chill of the stone stair upon which I stood and the thinness of my night attire.

With a purposeful gesture, I pushed him away, fancying I detected a glint of something like amusement in his expression. It must have been a trick of the fitful moonlight slanting through the open arrow slit of the tower, I decided, following him silently down the winding stair. We crept past Tiberius' closed door, and I paused, detecting no sound from within.

At the foot, a nightlight burned in a glass chimney set upon a stone plinth, casting feeble light towards the end of the wide passage. Keeping to the shadows, we made our way to the music room, slipping like wraiths through the half-closed door. Stoker shut it softly behind us as a precaution before lighting a single candle from one of the music stands. The sudden flare of light nearly blinded me, but I bent hastily to the task at hand. I inspected the harpsichord thoroughly, from its lacquered case to the strings that formed its innards, running my hands over the ivory and black keys, careful to draw no sound from them.

"What precisely are you looking for?" Stoker inquired. He had made no move to help me, merely stood with his back to the door, arms folded over his chest as he watched me.

"I will know it when I see it," I pronounced.

He grinned. "You don't know, do you?"

I pulled a face. "I am not mechanically minded," I admitted. "Have you any suggestion?"

He came forward, standing very close behind as he reached over my shoulder to point. "The likeliest way to accomplish a trick like this is to fashion a clockwork mechanism to create the effect of an instrument playing itself. It would have to be housed just here," he added, his arm brushing mine as he reached.

I peered closely into the lacquered cabinet of the harpsichord, but I saw nothing amiss, no devices or contraption that might have accounted for the instrument playing by itself.

I stepped back, frustrated. "How could it have been done, then?"

Stoker shrugged. "It cannot. Not with this instrument. Someone had to actually touch the keys in order to make the music." He trailed his forefinger along the edge. "A handsome piece," he said, "and an expensive one, if a little gaudy for my taste."

He was not wrong. Each panel of the instrument's case was painted with a different allegorical scene of passion—Venus and Adonis, Jupiter and Europa. They had sprung from the brush of a master, I realized, rendered with uncommon skill and delicacy.

"The artist has put in little jokes," I told him. I bent to show him a goat with a wreath of laurel tipped drunkenly over one horn, a puppy stealing a beribboned slipper.

"Clever," he murmured, peering closely. "He has managed to give the animals almost human expressions." His shoulder was pressed companionably to mine, and if I turned my head, even the slightest, my mouth would brush his cheek. I straightened at once, brushing in my haste against the rack above the keyboard, sending sheets of music tumbling to the floor, a single harsh note ringing out in the silence.

"How clumsy of me!" I exclaimed, diving beneath the harpsichord to retrieve the sheets.

As I went to replace them, I noticed another picture I had not yet seen, one that had been concealed behind the display of sheet music and positioned just where a musician might see it when playing by heart. Situated above the keyboard, this image was the most beautiful of all, an exquisite depiction of Jupiter and Leda. The god was in the midst of his transformation from swan to man, his form beautifully sculpted and entirely human, but his arms still broad and powerful wings, stretching to embrace his beloved. She was crowned in roses, her face turned into the strong column of Jupiter's neck. He was in profile, but something about his posture caught my eye. I leant near, holding the candle close to the painted face. It was small, the entire figure of the god no bigger than my finger, and I had to stand quite near to see it clearly.

"How lovely!" I breathed. I pointed and Stoker came to stand behind me, looking at the god and his ladylove in the throes of their erotic embrace.

"Rather gives one ideas," he murmured. I swallowed hard and darted a glance at him, but he did not look at me. Rather, his gaze was fixed upon the little painting. He bent swiftly and gave a sudden exclamation.

"You unspeakable bastard," he muttered. He turned to me. "Look."

"I did. It's lovely," I began.

"No," he instructed, taking my shoulders firmly in his grasp and forcing me to bend closer to the painting. *"Look."*

For a moment I was conscious only of his hands gripping me through the thin fabric of my nightdress. I could feel the warm clasp of each finger just at my collarbones, and the thumbs, pressing either side of my spine, stroking gently as he pushed me. I bit back an involuntary moan as my eyes fell upon the image of the god and I saw for myself what he meant.

"But—"

"Exactly," he said with grim satisfaction.

"But that means—"

"Not now," he cautioned. "We can discuss it when we have finished here. For now, we ought to conclude our investigation in this room and make good our escape before we are discovered."

"I meant only to search the instrument," I told him truthfully. "What else should we examine?"

He thought a moment, his eyes gleaming in the low light.

"Unless Helen actually conjured the dead—a possibility I refuse to countenance," he said resolutely, "or a clockwork mechanism which we have not discovered was used, then some human took the opportunity to play the specter, picking out that melody on the harpsichord."

"Impossible," I told him. "How could anyone elude us so swiftly? There had been a matter of mere seconds between the playing of the last note and our arrival into the empty room, insufficient time for anyone to have escaped past us and down the corridor without notice."

He gave me a coolly superior look. "I cannot fault your logic, Veronica, but you fail to take it to its natural conclusion. Obviously, the phantom must have found another means of egress."

I opened my mouth to protest, but there was no point. He was right, and I chafed at my own shoddy logic. I could not account for it—the conclusion was so patently obvious—but I was deeply aware of a certain mental confusion stemming from my disordered feelings for Stoker.

A whole minute never passed that he did not touch me in some fashion—putting a hand to steady himself when he squatted to examine the base of the linenfold paneling or brushing my arm as he reached for a candle. I moved away with a decisive gesture, putting several feet between us. He gave me a quizzical look, but I ignored him until he stretched up to feel a panel some distance above his head, his shirt pulling high over his taut, muscular belly. His trousers slid a little, revealing a sharply cut iliac furrow which my fingers twitched to explore.

"Nothing there," he said cheerfully.

I growled by way of response and bent to the panel in front of me, kicking it in my frustration. To my astonishment, it leapt open at the blow, revealing a narrow passageway behind.

"You've done it!" he praised, coming up behind me and putting a hand once more to my shoulder. The passage was dark and smelt of cold stone, and I was suddenly grateful for his presence.

I paused to examine the hinges, not surprised to see them gleaming with oil.

"Someone has attended to these recently," I pointed out.

"No doubt planning their exit from the music room much as a conjurer might plot out a trick," he agreed, coming forward to sniff the oil.

Stoker retrieved a lit candle and gestured for me to precede him into the passage. I gathered my courage along with the skirts of my nightdress. "If I am going first, I ought to take the light," I said, taking charge of the situation. He acquiesced, handing it over and following me as obediently as a lamb as we made our way down the passage.

I was conscious of him behind me, too close for my own peace of mind, I reflected darkly, and I wrenched my attention to the task at hand—investigating the passageway.

Running the length of an interior wall, the little corridor had no doubt at one time been a means of moving from one part of the house to another. I had to push hard at the other end to force open the door. I emerged into the library, just behind a high-backed porter's chair. The door here was neatly concealed by a narrow map case.

"Useful to have a passage such as this if the Romillys were hiding recusant priests," Stoker said as he emerged into the library. It would

have helped to move someone quietly from one part of the castle to another. In extremis, a clever Romilly might have permitted the queen's
soldiers to discover it, gambling that perhaps they would look no further
and the rest of the hidden chambers would go undetected.

Without further discussion, we secured the panel and crept back
the way we had come, pausing at the music room. Just as I was about to
close the panel, I heard a footstep and Stoker and I turned as one to see
that the doorknob was turning.

In the space of a heartbeat, he had thrust me back into the passage
and pulled the panel closed behind us. In his haste, the candle blew out,
plunging us into complete darkness. The passage was small and narrow,
and we dared not move with only the thin oak panel between us and
whoever had come into the music room. My back was pressed against
the stone and my front was pressed against Stoker, a surface every bit as
unyielding but much warmer. His heart beat slowly under mine and his
exhalations ruffled the hair at my brow.

His mouth moved against my ear, intimate, caressing. "Veronica,"
he murmured, his voice almost soundless in that small, confined space.

I turned my head to touch my lips to his cheek, whispering the
words against his skin. "Yes." It was not a question. It was a declaration,
an invitation. He moved against me, and I stifled a moan, biting my lip
so hard I tasted the sharp salty copper of my own blood on my tongue.

His mouth moved again. "You are standing on my foot."

I reared back, hitting my head on the stone wall behind me. I smothered a lavish curse and realized that there was a faint glimmer of light in
the passageway—a crack in the linenfold paneling. I put my eye to it just
in time to see the glow of a single candle illuminating the music room,
held aloft by Mrs. Trengrouse. She was wearing a sober dressing gown
and nightcap. She walked forward slowly and took only two or three
steps, as if steeling herself against what she might find.

She held the candle high, moving it from side to side in a slow arc.

"Miss Rosamund? Is that you? Are you here?" Her voice trembled, and I held my breath, knowing that Stoker and I dare not reveal ourselves, as much for fear that she would faint dead away as for the lack of any possible excuse for our presence. Far better to wait for her to withdraw, then beat a hasty retreat to our own rooms. I slid a little aside, guiding his head to the crack so that he, too, could see. We were awkwardly arranged, with Stoker half-stooped and one strong thigh braced under my bottom so that we could both watch. I slipped a little and he caught me, planting one palm flat against the paneling, creating a sort of armchair for me out of his own body. The warmth of his flesh was almost unbearable and I wondered for a brief and irrational moment if he were deliberately provoking a physical reaction in order to annoy me. To show him I would not be goaded, I perched upon his thigh, making a point of wriggling just a little before turning my attention back to Mrs. Trengrouse.

She stood still for a long moment, listening, I suspect, and I fancied I could almost hear her heartbeat as well as my own in those seconds as they ticked by. "Go away," she said with sudden ferocity. "You will not harm this family!" I froze, certain she had spotted the gleam of our eyes in the crack of the paneling, but she made no move to command us to come out, and I realized she was not speaking to us at all. "Go away, Miss Rosamund," she called, a trifle more gently. "It is time for you to rest."

With that, she left, closing the door behind her. We listened to her footsteps as they faded away. After several minutes, Stoker eased his posture, setting me onto my feet and releasing his arm. I nearly pitched over, for my legs had gone quite numb in the chill of the passageway. He took my hand as we crept out of our hiding place. We dared not light the candle again, but we knew the way well enough. There was no sign of Mrs. Trengrouse in the corridor, and we hurried hand in hand past the various closed doors. Stoker started up the turret stair, and just as I started up after him, I heard a noise behind me. I made a shooing gesture and Stoker continued on as I turned. After a moment I heard the almost imperceptible click of his door closing.

The noise I had detected was a sort of strangled gasp, stillborn in the throat, the sound choked by emotion. I turned to see Helen Romilly at the opposite end of the great hall. The nightlight by the turret stair had blown out, and there was only her candle to light the distance between us. Against the inky shadows of the staircase behind me, my white dressing gown must have appeared ghostlike, the hem trailing along the ground like the draperies of a phantom. My face, half-shielded by my black hair, would look as if it floated above my body, making a wraith of me.

"Rosamund!" she cried, starting forward a half step. "Did I summon you? Go away," she urged.

I did not move, but just then a gust of wind blew from an opened window in the turret, billowing my dressing gown about me and tossing my hair.

She gave another gasp and her candle fell from her trembling hand, the fitful flame guttering out as it landed upon the stone with a dull thud. She called again in the darkness as she fumbled for it.

"Rosamund! You must go," she moaned. "You must leave us in peace."

I did not wait to hear more. I could hardly reveal myself to her. She would be utterly humiliated if she discovered I was no ghost, and I had little inclination to subject myself to further histrionics. It seemed a quick retreat was the easiest for both of us.

Without another thought, I slipped up the stairs, making my way on silent feet into the shadows above. As I ascended, a pool of warm light spread beneath me, rising through the darkness. She had relit her candle and was making her way to the turret. I hurried, very nearly tripping over the hem of my dressing gown as I charged up the stairs, determined to elude her.

I came to Tiberius' door and flung myself through it, easing it closed just as the golden light illuminated the step below. I had closed it sound-

lessly; Helen would not find a ghost this night. But while I had success-
fully eluded both the housekeeper and Helen, I had created a new
problem for myself.

Lounging upon his bed in his dressing gown of black silk, Tiberius
surveyed me through heavy-lidded eyes, his mouth curving into a thoroughly salacious smile.

"Well, my dear Miss Speedwell. What a delightful surprise," he said,
tossing aside the book he had been reading.

I put a finger to my lips to urge him to silence. I did not know where
Helen was, and she might well be just outside the door.

"Oh, don't worry," Tiberius assured me in a whisper as he levered
himself off the bed and made his way to my side, his lips grazing my ear
as he took my hand. "I will be as quiet or as loud as you like. I am yours
to command," he told me. And then his mouth settled on mine.

CHAPTER

11

I will admit to a certain susceptibility where Tiberius' amorous efforts were concerned. Between my own healthy libido and the length of my self-imposed and unaccustomed chastity, I was ripe as a plum for the plucking. And we might indeed have plucked had I not come to my senses. As much as I enjoyed Tiberius' exertions—he had graceful, deft fingers and the nimblest tongue of any man I had ever met—experiencing them only made me deeply aware of Stoker and the thwarted embraces we had shared.

Stoker. The thought of him propelled me to instinctive action. With no little measure of regret, I removed my hands from the viscount's person and placed them flat upon his chest, giving him a small shove.

At least it was *supposed* to be a small shove. He ended up flat on his back on the hearthrug, contemplating the ceiling. When he had recovered his breath, he folded his hands over his lean stomach and regarded the coffered ceiling thoughtfully. "You need only have asked me to stop, Veronica. I have never yet taken a lover against his or her will, and I certainly wouldn't begin with you."

I reached a hand to help him up. "I am sorry. I suppose I was rather more forceful than I intended."

He smoothed his dressing gown back into place, tying the knot of the belt where I had yanked it loose in a moment of reckless abandon. "Still, that was rather nearer the mark than I expected. Two minutes more and I wager you wouldn't have been able to stop yourself."

He poured out a measure of whisky and handed it to me, taking another for himself.

"Two *seconds* more and I wouldn't have," I admitted. I sipped deeply at the whisky to calm my jangled nerves and persuade my insistent lust to quiet itself.

He eyed the bed, then turned, regretfully I think, to the chairs in front of the fireplace. He settled himself, crossing one long leg over the other. "I suspect I have my brother to blame for this," he ventured.

I took the other chair, propping my feet upon the still-warm hearth. "There are no significant developments in that quarter," I told him.

"But there never will be if you and I become better friends, is that it?"

"Something like that."

He smiled, a curiously kind curving of the lips that was devoid of his usual mockery. "You walk with hope, Veronica. God, how I envy you that. Life is a brutal business when one has nothing left to hope for."

He rolled his glass between his palms, staring into the amber depths of the whisky.

"Do not try to engage my pity," I warned him. "You are handsome, wealthy, privileged beyond belief, and you have hobbies to amuse and engage you."

He arched one brow in my direction. "Music and art are poor substitutes for love, my dear."

"I was not referring to those, my lord. I meant instead your penchant for puppeteering. Goodness, how you do like to tug the strings."

His gaze was quizzical. "I haven't the faintest idea what you mean—" he began.

He did not affect innocence well. There was something a trifle too mocking about the mouth, a little too knowing in the eyes. I gave him a thin, mirthless smile.

"We are all so many marionettes to you, are we not? How you enjoy this! I know you brought me here for some purpose beyond butterflies," I said flatly.

He lifted his glass in a toast to my décolletage. "My dearest Veronica, with assets such as those, you can hardly blame a man."

"And," I went on as if he had not spoken, "for a purpose other than dalliance. You could as easily have attempted a seduction in London. But you had a reason for coming here—a reason to do with Rosamund."

He hesitated a fraction too long before replying and it was that pause which told me everything. "I cannot imagine what fevered fancy has caused you to think such a thing."

"I saw the harpsichord."

"Of course you did," he returned politely. "We all did. It was sitting in the music room."

"I mean that I *saw* it. Specifically, I saw the panel above the keyboard, and I recognized a familiar face."

"My, my, Miss Speedwell," he said after a long moment, "what sharp eyes you have."

"The better for hunting butterflies," I replied. "Noticing details and, more importantly, understanding their significance, makes the difference between a dilettante and a prolific in my profession. And it is an excellent likeness."

"Do you think so?" He rubbed one hand over his chin. Unlike Stoker, his lordship did not battle constantly against an unruly beard. His jawline was but lightly shadowed, lending him a slightly roguish air. "I only sat once for the artist, but I think he did a rather good job of capturing my profile. He made Jupiter's shoulders too heavy," he added thoughtfully. "Mine are more elegant." Having just had the features in question under my questing hands, I could confirm his lordship's assessment, but I said nothing. He heaved a sigh and drained the last of his whisky.

"How long were you in love with Rosamund?" I asked gently.

"From two minutes after I first met her until . . . what is today?" he asked.

"You were married to another woman," I pointed out in a reproachful tone.

"I was doing my duty," he countered.

"But you still loved Rosamund?"

"One could not help it. She was simply the most enchanting woman I ever met, if present company will take no exception."

"None taken," I assured him. "Will you tell me about her?"

He shrugged. "What is there to tell? She was not as classically beautiful as you are, but she had your quickness, your liveliness, a joie de vivre that was utterly irresistible. I wanted her from the first."

"Where did you meet her?"

"Here. Malcolm was hosting one of his bloody house parties and Rosamund was a guest. Mertensia and Rosamund had been inmates together at some school for acidulated females. Malcolm was rather at loose ends when his parents died and didn't quite know what to do with his younger siblings, and so they were both packed off to school. Lucian made a success of it, but Mertensia wept the entire term. She managed to make friends with Rosamund and together they formulated a plot to get Mertensia away from the school and back home to St. Maddern's."

"Rather daring for schoolgirls," I mused.

"Indeed. I think Mertensia rather felt she owed her something for it. Rosamund was in disgrace at the school for her part in the scheme, and only Malcolm's intervention persuaded the powers that be to let her stay on after Mertensia left. I suspect he made a handsome donation to the school as well," he said.

"Why should he?"

He shrugged. "The Romillys are dreadfully old-fashioned. Devoted to outmoded notions like loyalty and fidelity. Mertensia couldn't bear the idea that Rosamund should suffer on her account, and as she was a scholarship pupil, Malcolm's flinging a little money their way would be quite welcome."

"So Mertensia came home to St. Maddern's and Rosamund stayed on at the school?"

"She was training for a teacher." A tiny smile played about his lips. "You cannot imagine anyone less suited for the profession."

"Was Rosamund not clever?"

"Clever! The girl was clever as a monkey and twice as mischievous. She was too high-spirited for such a drab life. But it was the only one open to her. Her parents were dead and there was nothing on the horizon for her but genteel poverty unless she earned her crust."

"I know the feeling," I said.

The smile deepened. "Since making your acquaintance, I have been more than once forcefully reminded of Rosamund. It has been both a joy and a torment."

He said nothing more for a long moment, then cleared his throat abruptly. "So, Rosamund began her profession as a teacher but found it did not suit her. She left in order to undertake private employment."

"Was she more successful in this enterprise?"

"She was not. As I said, she was clever. Too clever to waste her youth and beauty teaching dull-witted children to lisp their ABCs. But she had a living to make. She took a series of assignments, each more unsatisfying than the last. Finally, some three years ago, she made up her mind to leave England and accepted a post in India. It was not due to start until the autumn. There was a period of some months during which she was at loose ends, with neither home nor occupation. She wrote to Mertensia, who immediately invited her to spend the summer here. It had been many years since their last meeting."

"That was the summer you met her?"

His lips twisted. "'Met.' So tame a word for it. It was not a meeting, Veronica. I was introduced to her and it was like finding part of myself that had been somehow walking the earth without me. She was my other half when I had not realized I was incomplete."

I said nothing; my throat was too tight for words.

He went on in a faraway voice, staring into the fire. "Malcolm had settled into comfortable bachelorhood, and I was much the same, content to indulge myself with what we shall call impermanent companionship. I believe you understand what I mean."

I thought of my own eminently sensible indulgences of the flesh—there is no better remedy for low spirits and a poor complexion than a healthy and revivifying bout of copulation, I believe—and nodded.

"And yet I was occasionally conscious of a flicker of dissatisfaction. I enjoyed my dissipations thoroughly. I made a practice of them that would have put the most jaded and accomplished reprobate to the blush. But there were times when I was aware of a certain envy beginning to gnaw at me."

"Envy?"

"Not a word you might immediately associate with the likes of me, I know. I do not inspire pity, as you have so astutely pointed out," he said, making a sweeping gesture with his arm. "I am wealthy and titled and I am not uncomely. I have been dreadfully indulged and have got my way in almost every situation."

"You are thoroughly spoilt, you mean."

"Ah, that touch of asperity! You are the only one of my acquaintance who is unafraid to spice her conversation with that particular pepper. It is one of the things I adore most about you."

"You are proving my point," I warned him.

He smiled lazily. "Did you know that if you rub a cat's fur the wrong way with a piece of silk, you can make sparks? Little flickers of electricity conjured from your bare fingertips. It is the nearest thing to being a god. That is how I feel when I spar with you."

"I am glad it amuses you."

"Amuses! My delectable Veronica, 'amusement' does not begin to plumb the depths of my regard."

"You were telling me about how you fell in love with another woman," I reminded him.

"Yes, I was. I have always thought it a ridiculous expression, to say that one falls in love, and yet that is precisely how it was. One moment I was myself, as I had ever been. The next, I was over the precipice and into the abyss."

"And she felt the same?"

"She did," he said, a sudden fierceness in his tone. His knuckles whitened on the glass. "I know she did. She resisted and she pretended. She prevaricated and she lied. But she loved me."

"Why resist at all?" I asked. "As you say, you are everything a woman could want in a husband. You are titled and rich and handsome and charming."

"I never claimed to be charming."

"No, that is my personal assessment."

A fingertip reached out to touch my cheek, light as a feather. "Why, Veronica. Perhaps you do care after all."

I turned my head and gave a sharp snap of the teeth. "Careful, your lordship. I am no tame kitten for playing with."

He drew back his hand. "No indeed. You are fully a tigress." He settled into his chair. "She resisted me because she wanted Malcolm."

I nodded thoughtfully and he turned an outraged face to mine. "Are you not going to protest? Will you not demand how any woman could prefer Malcolm Romilly to *me*?"

I shrugged. "But I understand it perfectly. Malcolm is handsome in his own pleasant country squire fashion. There is something quite jolly

olde England and roast beef about him. One could well imagine him in
Tudor velvets or perhaps in plate armor, carrying a lance at the side of
the Conqueror."

"That is the most appalling, sentimental *rubbish—*"

I broke in. "And of course, he has this," I added, sweeping an arm to
indicate the castle. "I am sure your country seat is impressive, but it isn't
a castle, is it? And you only inherited it last year. You didn't even have a
title when Rosamund met you. Besides, I seem to recall that your father
kept you on rather limited purse strings."

"I managed," he said through clenched teeth. He rose and refilled his
glass.

"But your father was not in ill health," I persisted. "He was the head
of the family and there was no indication he would leave you to inherit
for another twenty years. What woman would care to wait for her husband to step into dead man's shoes when she could be mistress of this
castle right at the beginning?"

"You think she wanted him for his castle?" he demanded.

"Oh, not entirely. I meant what I said about his personal attractions.
Granted, he is a bit careworn at present, but I suspect he is capable of
quite pleasurable wooing. And there is something gravely sweet about
him, old-fashioned, as you say. Courtly."

"Courtly!" He fairly spat the word. "You think Rosamund preferred
courtliness?"

I shrugged. "I did not know her. But I can tell you that it is easy to see
why a woman would rather throw her lot in with a pleasant and easy
gentleman of wealth like Malcolm Romilly instead of gambling her happiness on you. It is the difference between walking a paddock with a
pony and galloping barebacked over the Downs in a lightning storm
with a stallion between your thighs."

I darted him a look and he broke into a smile, raising his glass.
"Hoist with my own petard."

"Well, what did you expect?" I asked, smoothing my dressing gown. "Of course you are the obvious choice for any woman of spirit and verve. But Malcolm is safe, and for many women, there is no greater attraction than security."

"How dull you make it sound!" he observed.

"It is not dull to want to know that one will always be fed and clothed and have a roof over one's head. Only someone who has never faced the specter of the workhouse could think security to be dull. Rosamund was forced to earn her way in the world. That means the greatest luxury imaginable to her must have been Malcolm's stability. His predictability would have consoled her, would have made her feel safe as nothing else in the world possibly could."

"You would never do that," he said suddenly. "You would choose the lightning."

I turned to look at the fire. "We are discussing Rosamund," I reminded him. "And she chose Malcolm. I presume you did give her a choice. You offered her marriage?"

"I did," he told me promptly. "Or at least I tried. She wouldn't let me finish. We were sitting on the little shingle beach overlooking the Sisters. Her hair had come loose, masses of dark hair, tossing in the wind. She sat there, plucking the petals off a flower, offering each one up to the breezes. 'He loves me, he loves me not,' she teased me. And that is when I took her hard by the shoulders and told her of course I loved her. By way of response, she broke the flower in half, throwing the pieces of it to the beach. 'Then you're a fool,' she said, with such maddening coolness you would have thought we were strangers. And only the previous night she had been in my bed, clawing at me like a wild thing."

His hand tightened again around the glass and for an instant I thought he meant to throw it. Instead, he put it with great care onto the table at his elbow. "She told me that she intended to marry Malcolm and that was the end of it. Nothing I could say would dissuade her. I am sorry to say I was ungentlemanly enough to threaten to reveal our dalliance. The previous night was not the first time we had been together. Four, five times over that month. It was like a game to her at the beginning. She was reserved and cool, as untouchable as a Renaissance Madonna during the day, when others were around. But when we could steal a few moments alone, she was unleashed, like nothing I had ever known, demanding and violent in her passions."

I said nothing. He went on, talking almost more to the fire than to me. "When I threatened to go to Malcolm with the truth, she laughed. She said it was my word against hers and who would believe a libertine like me? The next morning, they announced their engagement at breakfast. I shall never forget the air of triumph about her as she clung to him. He was so damnably proud of it, making everyone look at the Romilly betrothal ring on her finger. I could not bear the sight of them. I left that same day. I told Malcolm that my father required me to accompany him on a trip to Russia and that I had left it too long. He pleaded with me to stay, to stand up at his wedding as his supporter, but I told him Father insisted, and I went. I never saw her again."

"When did you give her the harpsichord?"

A cruel smile touched his lips. "I found it in London, just before I left for Russia. It had already been decorated with the mythological scenes and I thought it would be a grand joke if I had my own face painted onto the image of Jupiter and the striped roses added to garland Leda's head. It took the artist only a day to make the changes, and I had it sent on to her, a sort of secret engagement present. Only she would know what it was meant to represent. She practiced every day, you know. I loved to think of her playing and looking down at the image of us together in a way that only we would understand."

"And so you went to Russia?"

"I did. My father had been increasingly insistent that I travel with him on an extended tour of Russia, where he was bound by his diplomatic interests. He was noticeably pleased when I finally agreed. I could tell he was delighted because he unbent enough to smile at me. Whilst we were abroad, I consented to another of his schemes. I permitted him to arrange a marriage with the daughter of an English duke who had taken a diplomatic posting at the court of the tsar." He paused, then pushed on, unburdening himself of the last. "I loved Rosamund with every atom of my existence, and still I married another woman, a plain and unlovely woman I loathed and whom I punished with silence and unloving attempts to get an heir until she died from sheer disillusionment. There was not a moment of our marriage that I did not make her feel the weight of my disappointment that she wasn't someone else." He went on, cataloguing his sins for me in a quiet voice limned with self-loathing. "I thought to make a decent husband, at least I meant to try. I went along with Father's arrangements for my marriage. I played the dutiful husband, whatever the cost. I gritted my teeth and made love to my wife. Until the telegram arrived."

"What telegram?"

"The one Rosamund sent on the eve of her wedding to Malcolm," he said. "I didn't receive it, you see, not for a month. My wife and I took a wedding trip." His lips twisted as he said the word "wife." "Her family had a villa on the Black Sea and we went there for some weeks. Our communications with the outside world were spotty. Few letters and no telegrams were forwarded. We collected all of it when we returned to St. Petersburg, a pile of correspondence that had been accumulating for four weeks. Four weeks during which Rosamund believed I received her wire and did not care enough to respond."

"What did the wire say?" I asked gently.

He shrugged. "She had bridal nerves. Thought of calling the whole thing off and coming to me. I had only to say the word and she would be mine. I suppose it finally got to her, the notion of spending the rest of her life with a fellow so profoundly unexciting that his notion of hedonism is to take two baths a week instead of one."

"Would you have responded?" I asked. "Would you have told her to call off her wedding to Malcolm and come to you?"

"I would have torn down the Caucasus with my bare hands to get to her," he said simply.

"Even though she had already broken your heart by refusing you?"

"Nothing would have mattered to me," he insisted. "Only that we were together. But by the time I received it, she had married Malcolm and vanished. I learnt of it from the English newspapers the same time I received the telegram."

"What a cruel irony," I said. "I wonder what became of her?"

"That is the question which torments me. It tortured me then, it tortures me still. The idea that I had been so very close to my dearest wish annihilated me. I am afraid I became rather unhinged. I lashed out, principally at my wife. The night I learnt of Rosamund's disappearance, I made my wife sit up until dawn, pointing out her every shortcoming. I told her about Rosamund, in detail, lurid, disgusting detail. She was a gentle creature and I flayed her with my scorn, choosing each word with care so it would wound the deepest. I never struck her, but by God, I opened her to the bone with every word. I broke something within her that never recovered. She had conceived a child, and heaven only knows what sort of little monster it might have been, gotten in such circumstances. She suffered in childbed, and when they told her she had to rally, to fight for herself, she simply turned her face to the wall. She had no will to live because I took it from her. And all because I could not forgive her for being someone I did not want."

His eyes were veiled with tears, and I slid to the floor in front of him, holding out my arms. He collapsed into them with a suddenness I could not have anticipated. He clung to me as a drowning sailor will grasp a spar, too desperate even for hope. He did not weep, at least he made no sound. But his shoulders heaved once or twice, and when he drew back, I kept my face averted until I was certain he was once more in command of himself.

"So now you know the worst of me," he said in a ragged voice. He cleared his throat hard, smoothing his hair with one elegant hand, trying to regain something of his dignity.

"You must have been in such terrible pain," I told him.

He gaped. "I just told you—"

"I know what you said. And I know from my own observations that you are difficult and capricious and sexually rapacious. But I hope you will credit my experience where men are concerned. You might have been monstrous to your wife, but you are not truly beyond redemption, no matter how diabolical you care to think yourself. You could not be such a blackguard and still regret your treatment of her, Tiberius. You are warm and generous and you are a man of honor, at least by your own lights. You must have suffered acutely at Rosamund's hands to have paid back your pain upon your innocent wife."

He shook his head as if to clear it. "Dear God, no wonder Stoker—" He broke off. "I have never, until this moment, known true loyalty, Veronica." He seized my hand and kissed it. "Whatever you ask of me, from now until I draw my last breath, I am your sworn cavalier."

I retrieved my hand. Tiberius had, as was his custom, taken refuge in gentle mockery, but I knew he was sincere.

"What happened after your wife died?"

He passed a weary hand over his eyes. "We were still in Russia at the time, so I consoled myself with every imaginable sort of Slavic debauchery. I marinated myself in vodka and slept with half the court, including the tsar's brother. A few months of that should have been the end of it."

"But it wasn't," I reminded him.

"No. Rosamund haunted me, I dreamt of her," he said, shutting his eyes. "I used to drink enough to stupefy me into sleep because then I would be certain of seeing her."

"Did Malcolm ever know of your attachment to one another?"

He paused. "I don't know. We had to be very careful because of

Rosamund's reputation. She had a living to get, and the merest hint of a dalliance would have ruined that. Anything short of an engagement would have spelt doom for her prospects of employment."

"But it's possible?"

He shrugged. "Anything is possible. She might have told him. Someone else may have discovered it. She may have been observed in the act of sending that telegram. It is not significant in any case." He spread his hand in a gesture of magnanimity. "You know why I have come, my dear. I am here because Malcolm requires my friendship and support and I mean to give it."

"Liar," I said pleasantly.

His gaze narrowed. "I beg your pardon?"

"Oh, don't come over lofty now, Tiberius. I have no doubt you've been called worse by a much better class of woman. You had an ulterior motive in coming here. You want to know what became of Rosamund and you suspect Malcolm had something to do with her disappearance."

"If I did, I was a fool," he told me in a silken voice. "Perhaps there is nothing to be gained by raking up the past."

I knew that tone. He was playing games as only Tiberius knew how. But I knew a game or two of my own, and I answered him in the same cool voice. "Your ulterior purposes have purposes, my lord. And I mean to find them out."

"Is that a threat, my dear Miss Speedwell?"

"It is a warning," I told him. I rose to take my leave. I opened the door and nearly fell over Stoker, his hand raised as if to knock.

His expression of shock was one I shall remember all of my life, and it was compounded as he studied me from tumbled hair to disarranged robe and bare feet peeping out from my hem. He looked past me to his brother, who lounged lazily in the armchair by the fire, and it was painfully obvious what conclusions he was drawing.

"Stoker—" I began.

He gave me a smile that was icily polite as he held up a hand. "Silence, if you please, Veronica. This is between Tiberius and myself."

He stepped sharply around me, gave me a gentle push onto the stairs, and closed the door behind me. If his preternatural calm had not alarmed me, the sound of the bolt shooting home would have done it.

CHAPTER

12

I dared not knock; such noise might rouse the household. But neither could I retire to my room without knowing precisely what sort of damage the Templeton-Vanes were inflicting upon one another. Stoker had the advantage of inches and weight, but the viscount was older and frequently armed. I wrapped my nightdress about my legs and seated myself on the stone step, awaiting the outcome. I harbored no illusion they were fighting over me. I might have provided the spark, but the tinder was old and dry. This battle had been brewing from the cradle, and—truth be told—I was rather glad they were finally getting on with it.

Few sounds penetrated the stout oak door. I heard breaking glass and a long groan—whose I could not have guessed. This was followed by the sound of splintering wood and an odd gurgling noise, as if someone were being strangled with the belt of his dressing gown, I decided.

At long last, silence reigned, and I rose, shaking out the folds of my nightdress. I knocked softly upon the door, and after an impossibly long time, it was answered. Stoker sat upon the hearth, covered in ashes and broken glass with a small knife stuck into his arm, while Tiberius attempted to staunch the flow of blood from his nose. One of his eyes was swollen nearly shut, and his left arm dangled at his side.

"I believe you have suffered a dislocation," I pointed out helpfully.

"Nothing he hasn't done to me before," Tiberius returned with a lowering glare at his brother.

"I told you I would remedy it," Stoker rasped. He rolled onto all fours and levered himself up after a moment, staggering only a little. Without preamble, he grasped his brother by the neck and waist and slammed his lordship's shoulder into the bedpost, setting the joint neatly back into its socket with a growl from the viscount.

"Now, what about this?" Stoker demanded, gesturing towards the knife still quivering in his arm.

"The merest scratch," the viscount assured him. "That knife is hardly more than a child's toy."

Stoker curled his lip as he tightened his fist, but before he could lay hands on his brother again, I grasped the knife by the handle and jerked it free. Stoker smothered a howl of pain, and I saw Tiberius' eyes light with pleasure.

"Do it again. I like it when he screams."

"Mind your manners or I will use it on both of you," I warned them.

"How you do tempt me," Tiberius murmured.

"Is there no end to your flirtations?" I demanded.

"Where you are concerned, never," he assured me.

I wiped the knife blade clean upon Tiberius' dressing gown. "I am keeping this," I told him as I slipped it into my pocket. "I cannot trust that you won't hit something vital the next time."

"My dear Veronica, if I meant to wound him properly, I would have."

"You did not have to stab him," I pointed out.

"Of course I did," Tiberius returned patiently. "It is a widely known fact that the mentally defective are impervious to all but the sharpest pain."

"Oh, for the love of Christ and all his pretty angels," Stoker began, but I put up a hand.

"Enough! I am glad the two of you have indulged in your little brawl. There is nothing like a healthy bout of coitus or fisticuffs to drain the tension out of a man. But the time to quarrel is finished. We ought to talk about the results of the séance tonight."

Tiberius made a gesture of dismissal. "A bit of mischief, nothing more."

"I am not certain," I replied. "Helen Romilly seems genuinely distressed, as does Mrs. Trengrouse."

"Of course she does," Tiberius shot back. "She is the one responsible for keeping Helen away from the brandy snifter."

"Not very gallant," I reproved. "But you raise an excellent point, Tiberius. Helen seems quite upset for someone who ought to be accustomed to such things. She saw me in my nightdress and nearly levitated with fright."

Tiberius stirred. "Did you make yourself known to her?"

"I suppose I ought to have done so, but I was afraid if I spoke she might shriek down the house or fall into a fit of hysterics. It was all most curious."

Stoker lifted a brow. "How so?"

"Helen does this sort of thing for a living. Madame Helena and all that. She contacts the dead with the same frequency that the average woman might speak with the butcher. And yet the manifestations this evening seemed to distress her."

"Veronica, she does not actually contact the dead," Stoker said flatly. "She is a charlatan."

"Perhaps," I temporized.

"Perhaps nothing," he said. His tone was always dismissive when we discussed anything that could not be explained perfectly by scientific inquiry. "She takes money from grieving and desperate people to make them think she is doing something which is quite plainly impossible. The woman is no better than a common cutpurse, stealing money from the unsuspecting."

"How very uncharitable," Tiberius murmured.

"Charitable! What cause have I to be charitable to a person like that?" Stoker demanded. "She sits in a room and puts on a voice and suddenly everyone behaves as if it were the Second Coming. It's maddening."

"Maddening, but not the point. Helen Romilly was deeply shaken. I think she was as surprised as everyone else at that table at what transpired. She seemed sincerely distressed by the music. In fact, that particular manifestation has left everyone closely connected with Rosamund ill at ease," I said, trailing off suggestively.

Tiberius' grey eyes widened. "Except me, you mean. Are you seriously suggesting that I have anything to do with that childish trick?"

I shrugged. "You have the best motive," I pointed out.

"Motive?" Stoker asked, his expression suddenly bright with curiosity.

I paused and Tiberius took a moment to summon his usual sangfroid. "Very well, Veronica. Tell him. He will enjoy it mightily, I have no doubt. But if you don't mind, I would rather not be witness to my own exposure. It is a conversation best conducted in privacy."

"In other words," Stoker supplied, "'Get out.'"

Tiberius' handsome mouth thinned cruelly. "Precisely. I will lock the door behind you. Or ought I to try holy water? A little friendly exorcism might send you on your way."

I rose and smoothed the skirts of my dressing gown. "Come, Stoker. Tiberius is in a pet, and I cannot blame him. His shoulder must be hurting dreadfully." I turned at the door and blew him a kiss.

He responded with a muttered profanity and I smiled. No matter how much they brawled, the Templeton-Vane boys were the proverbial peas in a pod.

A distinctly unpleasant interlude followed during which I stitched Stoker's wound under his exacting instructions. He gave my handiwork a long, measured look before nodding his grudging approval. "I suppose it will have to do, although it would have been a damned sight neater if I'd been able to wield the needle myself," he grumbled.

I dressed the wound, none too gently, and settled myself into an armchair while he stirred the coals. He was silent a long moment as he watched the flames catch, then turned to me, his smile tinged with mischief. "You realize there is no possible way to explain my presence here should I be discovered," he said, mocking my objection of the previous evening. "Whatever would they think?"

"I am beyond the opinions of provincials," I retorted.

"I thought you liked the Romillys," he replied, taking the second armchair and stretching his feet towards the fire now crackling merrily on the hearth.

"I do rather. But it is difficult to become friendly with people who are cohabiting with a ghost."

He snorted. "Surely you do not believe that nonsense."

"No," I said, drawing out the syllable.

"I swear upon my mother's moldering shroud, if you expect me to believe that there is an actual phantom lurking in the corridors of this castle, I will put you over my shoulder like a sack of wool and carry you away," he warned.

"It isn't that I think Rosamund is present," I protested. "The trick with the music is the product of a nasty imagination—a human one, I have no doubt. But what if there is something beyond that, a presence from beyond prodding the living to do the bidding of the dead?"

His brows knitted together. "A scientist must consider every possible hypothesis," he said seriously. "And after giving that idea very careful consideration, I can tell you that it is the rankest horseshit."

"Language," I murmured.

"Well, honestly, Veronica. You cannot seriously believe that."

"I did not say I believed it," I pointed out coolly. "I merely suggested it is a possibility."

"It bloody well is not."

"If all scientists were as stubborn as you, we would still be expecting ships to sail off the edge of the world and thinking the sun revolved around the earth."

"I am *not* stubborn—"

"Spoken with the obstinacy of a bull," I said sweetly. "It is not your fault that you suffer from a lack of imagination."

"A lack of imagination! To refuse to entertain the possibility of an actual ghost playing harpsichords and blowing out candles!"

"I did not mean those things," I said, striving for patience. "Those were clearly tricks. Drafts can be manufactured with ventilators or candles can be tampered with. As for the music—"

He held up a hand. "It can only have been managed by a human hand. A clockwork mechanism is a damned likelier explanation than a phantom."

I shook my head. "We searched the harpsichord from tip to toe and found nothing to suggest it had been meddled with. I think someone must have played it and fled through the hidden passage," I finished. "Which means it could not have been anyone at the séance."

"Or our miscreant might have left a music box in the passageway and been with us all along," he countered. "Any of the guests or family might have done that."

"Or some supernatural agency—" I began.

He snorted. "I still don't believe it."

"Of course you don't. Neither do I. I simply think we ought to consider every possibility before settling on one. There must be an explanation we have not yet discovered. But we will."

He tipped his head to give me a curious look. "Why?"

"What do you mean, 'why'?"

"Why must we penetrate the mystery here? Why do we care?"

I blinked at him. "Because it *is* a mystery? Have you no proper curiosity? No feeling for the challenge?"

"Veronica, we have upon three occasions involved ourselves in such exploits. We have been almost drowned in the Thames, very nearly immolated, chased through the vilest sewers of London, and—no little thing, I should add—I was shot. Explain to me the allurements of such activities, if you will."

"You were abroad in the night, ready to investigate the music room before I was," I reminded him.

"Only because I knew you were going to do it and I meant to keep you from trouble," he countered smoothly. "I should far rather a calm and quiet life with my specimens and my studies."

"Now, *that* is the veriest horseshit," I returned succinctly.

"Language, Veronica," he said with perfect mimicry. Oh, how I exulted then! To be engaged in an investigation once more, sparring with Stoker, was to be more myself than at any other time. I felt a rise of excitement and a sudden ferocious joy as heated as that of any butterfly hunt. Even taking a Kaiser-i-Hind on the wing had not afforded me as much pleasure as this.

"You thrill to the chase as much as I," I reminded him happily. "You simply like to pretend that such feats of bravado are entirely at my instigation so that you can appear to be the rational and steady one whilst I am given to flights of fancy and ridiculous adventures. And yet, not a single one of those escapades was undertaken without your eager assistance."

"Assistance?" His voice rose incredulously. "I thought I was the hero of our antics."

I tipped my head, studying his tumbled hair and bruised face. "No, I have always thought of you as my Garvin."

"Your Garvin. As in Arcadia Brown's half-witted sidekick," he demanded.

"Garvin is not a half-wit," I reminded him. "He is simply less gifted than his female companion and must defer to her courage. And expertise. And intuition."

He said something far fouler than his brother had uttered and slid lower in his chair. "That's a fine how-do-you-do," he muttered. "Nothing but a bit of muscle."

"Nonsense," I soothed. "You are also quite pleasant to look at. Not now, of course, with your lip stuck out like a sulky mule and that bruise blossoming on your face. But when you make an effort, you are very nearly handsome."

It was the rankest lie. Stoker was not *nearly* handsome; he was utterly delectable, not in spite of his flaws but because of them. The scar and the untrimmed hair and the signs of rough living only made him seem all the more real. Tiberius might have presented the picture of a perfect gentleman, fresh from his tailor's bandbox, but Stoker was everything true and vibrant and alive in the world.

To my astonishment, he did not continue to sulk. He suddenly sat up straight, fixing me with a sharp eye. "What did you mean about Tiberius? How is he connected to all of this? And how did his portrait come to be on the harpsichord? I presume he was in love with Rosamund."

I related to him all that Tiberius had told me of his ill-fated relationship with the lady and his subsequent disastrous marriage. Throughout the recitation, Stoker was silent, studying his feet, his expression inscrutable. When I had finished, he blew out a deep breath.

"That unspeakable bastard," he murmured. "Who knew he could actually make me feel sorry for him. I never knew things were so bad. He was Father's pride and joy, you know. The heir to the kingdom," he said, throwing out his arms expansively. "I was only ever the cuckoo in the nest."

"Your father does not sound the sort of man to accept his wife's indiscretion easily," I mused. "Why did he acknowledge you as his son?"

Stoker gave me a thin smile. "Because he knew it would hurt her more to have me there, every day, under his power and her with no means of protecting me. Under the law, I was his child, and he could beat me or starve me and there wasn't a bloody thing she could do about it. It was a subtle and sophisticated cruelty, like everything he did."

"Did he often beat you?" I asked, careful to avert my gaze. I had learnt some time before that looking upon Stoker's pain was a thing I could not easily bear.

"No," he answered. "That was the subtlety at work. He knew it was far more effective to do it only very occasionally and without provocation. I would never know when it was coming or why. He thought that would keep me in line, and for a while it did. His tortures of Tiberius were of a more mundane variety."

"Such as?"

He shrugged. "Breaking things that Tiberius loved. Giving away his favorite horse. Yanking him from a school in which he thrived to place him in one he detested. He did those things to all of us, really. They were designed to toughen us, to make us Templeton-Vanes," he added with a curl of his lip. "Rupert kept his head down and did as he was told. He never rebelled, never fought back. Merryweather was too young for the worst of Father's games. Besides, the old devil had his hands full with Tiberius and with me."

"You fought back," I guessed.

He grinned. "Every chance I got. And then, when I was twelve, I left altogether. He didn't much mind. He made inquiries and sent detectives and eventually dragged me back home, but the sport had gone out of it when he realized I would just leave again. And Tiberius had developed his own strategies for dealing with him."

"What sort of strategies?"

"Tiberius learnt never to love anything or anyone lest it be used against him. He developed that mask you know so well, that polished veneer of urbanity, so detached and lofty he might as well live on Mount Olympus. He has no use for us lesser mortals. Or at least, he didn't. That is why this Rosamund business is so very disturbing. It makes him human."

"He told me his wife died in childbed. What happened to the infant?"

"Dead too. Almost immediately after birth."

"How tragic!" I exclaimed.

"All the more so because it was a boy," Stoker told me. "Son and heir to the Templeton-Vanes. Lost at birth."

"What does he mean to do without an heir?" I asked. "Will he re-marry, do you think?"

Stoker narrowed his gaze. "Why? Do you mean to keep up this ridiculous charade of a betrothal? If you do, do not have a June wedding, I beg you. Such a cliché."

"Don't be nasty," I ordered. "Very well. I will tell you the simple and rather silly truth behind the charade. Malcolm Romilly is a Catholic and somewhat conservative. Tiberius thought if he presented me as his fiancée, it would make me more respectable than a woman traveling with a man to whom she is not related."

"I knew it," he said with soft triumph.

"You did not. You were clearly annoyed at the notion of my becoming your sister-in-law," I reminded him.

"Memory fails."

I snorted. "I am very fond of Tiberius, I confess. But that will not dissuade me from my determination never to marry. But Tiberius has a title and an entailment. What will become of them?"

He shrugged again. "Rupert is next in the succession, and he, mercifully, has four sons. The line is secure so long as Tiberius doesn't mind it going eventually to our nephew."

"I cannot see him taking another wife," I told him. "He spoke rather bitterly about the state of matrimony, and having his heart broken so badly over Rosamund—"

Stoker's eyes rounded in amazement. "His heart broken? You cannot be serious."

"Of course I am."

"Impossible."

"Why?"

"For Tiberius to have broken his heart, he would have to possess one in the first place. Believe me when I tell you, he does not."

"Feathers," I said succinctly. "You yourself just said that he learnt to guard his feelings. People who are forced to such stratagems often experience far stronger emotions for having to bottle them."

"If you say so," he replied with maddening calm.

"How can you be so immovable? A moment ago you said you felt sorry for him," I reminded him.

"My sympathies are of the fleeting variety. I have remembered too many of his tortures of me during our youth to waste my tears upon his pain."

"You are in a filthy mood, and if you cannot talk sensibly, you ought to go."

He rolled his eyes. "What do you want of me, Veronica? Yes, Tiberius has experienced pain and loss. So have we all."

"His is freshest right now. Being here is dredging all of it up again."

"His own fault," Stoker pointed out calmly. "He needn't have accepted Malcolm's invitation. All he had to do was refuse and spare himself revisiting his greatest tragedy, but instead he comes and sticks pins into the pain. Don't tell me he is deserving of my pity. He has brought this on himself."

I was silent a long moment—too long. Stoker gave me a searching look. "What?"

"He *has* brought this on himself," I agreed. "But why? It makes no sense."

"What are you nattering on about now?"

"Everything you just said. I am agreeing with you. Try not to let the novelty throw you off your stride," I told him. "But you were right. Tiberius is as imperious and controlling a character as I have ever known. He has arranged every facet of his life to his own satisfaction except losing Rosamund. His correspondence with Malcolm has been spotty of late. They were the best of friends for years, certainly, but with Malcolm imposing exile upon himself, they have not met since before Tiberius left for Russia. Yet as soon as Malcolm asked him to come, he agreed. They both claim it is for the sake of rekindling their old companionship, but is that enough to bring Tiberius here knowing that he would encounter memories of Rosamund? Or does he have another purpose in mind?"

Stoker threw up his hands. "Only the lesser devils in hell could answer that, Veronica."

He stayed another hour, alternately ranting against his brother and idly threatening to return to Tiberius' room to finish the thrashing he had begun earlier. It took considerable powers of persuasion to keep him with me until he was calm.

"You will not beat the truth out of him and I am bored with stitching you back together," I said. "Besides, it is rather flattering, considered properly."

"Flattering? How in the name of seven hells did you come to that conclusion?" he demanded.

"Well, Tiberius might have brought a professional detective into the business. He could have engaged a private inquiry agent to do his sleuthing. Instead, he is relying upon us."

"*Without telling us,*" Stoker stormed. "That is the difference between working with us and using us. He has exposed you to danger without the slightest consideration for your safety."

It was telling that Stoker was more concerned about my own safety than his own. I gave him an indulgent smile. "Do not worry about me. I have brought my knives," I told him cheerfully.

"Knives? Plural? I only gave you one, the little fellow to strap to your calf," he said, his expression startled.

"And I wear it," I promised. "But a lady likes to have options." I went to my carpetbag and lifted out the false bottom, revealing a compartment that Daisy the maid had not discovered. I began to extract my weapons, passing them to Stoker as they emerged. "Here is the hatpin I had made—a fine steel stiletto with a very sharp point. I warned you it was sharp," I said, handing Stoker a handkerchief to staunch the bright bead of blood that welled up on his thumb. "Here are the minuten for my cuffs," I added, handing over the packet of headless pins used by lepidopterists to secure specimens to pieces of card. I often threaded them through my cuffs when I desired a little extra protection. I removed a delicate violet silk corset from the compartment, holding it up as Stoker blushed furiously. "This is my favorite, I think. Each stay is actually a slim blade of excellent Italian steel," I told him, demonstrating how quickly I could remove one from the bodice.

"Anything else?" he asked. "A beehive to hide in your bustle? A poison ring full of arsenic to bung into someone's tea?"

I flapped a hand. "Don't be crude. Poison is a distinctly unoriginal method."

He cocked his head curiously. "So how would you go about it if you were to dispatch someone?"

"I have nineteen strategies at present and I am developing a twentieth. Don't worry," I told him cheerfully. "If I ever decide to kill you, I shall make it quick and creative. You will never see it coming."

"That, my dear Veronica, is what I am afraid of."

He paused and with that peculiar telepathy we sometimes shared, I knew what he was going to say next. "I know you do not wish to speak of Madeira," he began in a halting voice, "but I think we must."

"There is nothing to say," I replied.

"I believe there is." He turned to me, his sapphirine eyes bright with emotion. Anger? Challenge? I could not tell. "I was with Lord Rosemorran when the bills arrived, Veronica. A doctor. A wet nurse. A seamstress's charges for the making of clothes for an infant." He paused and the moment stretched between us, a taut silence waiting to be shattered.

"Yes. All of that." I lifted my chin. "You want me to be answerable to you?"

"I should have thought our friendship would demand it," he said simply.

"I am answerable to no one," I replied fiercely.

"And I am no one?" he asked, his voice edged with some dark feeling I had never heard before.

"Of course not." My voice was snappish and I said the words quickly, thrusting them from my lips. "But I can give you no explanation."

"I see," he said, turning once more to the fire.

He said nothing more and I rose, my hands curling into fists. "I know it looks as if I went to Madeira to have a child," I began.

He rose too, more slowly, favoring the arm that had just been bandaged. The bruise blooming on his face was a slow, spreading purple, plummy and deep. He came close to me, pronouncing each word carefully. "I am not the men you have known before," he reminded me.

"It is time we cleared the air," I told him, planting myself firmly in his path. "I have come to a decision. I do not break promises easily, but I owe you that much."

"That Lady Cordelia went to Madeira to have a child out of wedlock?" he hazarded.

"How did you—"

He sighed. "Veronica, give me a little credit. I may be a man, but I am a doctor, after all. I saw the signs. I also know that she would have sworn you to secrecy and you would have felt obliged to keep your promise to her. Therefore, I will ask you nothing about the child or its father. If Lady C. wishes me to know, she will tell me herself."

"Thank you for that," I said simply.

"The only thing I did not understand was why there were doctors' bills with your name on them." He lifted his brows in inquiry.

"A relapse of malaria," I told him. "I went to take care of Lady C. and instead she nursed me." I smiled, thinking of the time Stoker had cared for me during a bout of the fever that lurked in my blood, bursting out at inopportune moments. "I must say, her bedside manner is rather gentler than yours. But I know whose I would rather have." Something in his face eased and I smiled again. "Did you really never believe the worst of me?"

He shrugged. "I knew you would never be so pigheadedly mysterious about your own child. You don't care enough about public opinion to keep such a thing a secret. But you would go to your grave to protect a friend."

I stared at him, a smile breaking over my face. "You really do comprehend me."

"Yes," he agreed. "And you are a bloody sight more challenging than Latin, believe me." He went on. "I also know that if you found yourself unexpectedly with child, you would put aside your obstinacy and come to me for help."

I canted my head as I moved a step closer, just near enough to see the silver-grey lights in the dark blue of his eyes. "What would you have done for me?"

He shrugged and took his own step closer. "Whatever the situation required. I would have traveled with you to the furthest ends of creation. I would have delivered the child. I would have married you and given the damned thing a name if you wanted."

"I will never marry," I reminded him sharply. He was standing scant inches from me now, his mouth temptingly close. I could smell sweetness on his breath—the honey drops he carried in his pocket at all times.

"I know. Neither will I. I have seen too much of that particular institution to last me a lifetime." I was surprised at his statement but not the sentiment behind it. He had suffered at the hands of his wife, this noble and generous soul who deserved nothing but loyalty.

"Then we are agreed," I replied. "We will never marry."

"Never. Although, no marriage does not necessarily rule out certain marital activities," he observed.

"Stoker—" I murmured. His hand moved up, his palm cupping my jaw as his thumb stroked my earlobe. I tipped my head back, arching my throat towards him as I twined my arms about his neck, careful not to disturb his wound. He put his mouth to the pulse in my throat, kissing a trail from my ear to the neck of my nightdress. I slid my hands into his hair, my lips parting as I said his name again on an exhalation of the sharpest, most exquisite anticipation.

His mouth dipped lower still, his teeth grazing lightly over my flesh with only the thin fabric of my nightclothes between us. I tightened my grasp on his hair as I said his name a third time, an incantation of sorts, a prayer, a charm of summoning.

But even as I moaned my encouragement, he pulled back, letting go of me so abruptly that I nearly fell over.

"My dearest Veronica," he said, his eyes widely, innocently blue, "I must offer my most heartfelt apologies for letting myself get carried away. After all, you were the one who said we must keep our friendship foremost. Such demonstrations can only disturb and confuse us," he finished with an air of feigned contrition.

"Revelstoke Templeton-Vane," I said through gritted teeth.

He held up his hands. "No, no, I am most sincerely sorry. Whatever must you think of me?"

"Give me five minutes and I shall tell you," I threatened.

Instead he patted me on the head in an avuncular fashion and I snapped at his hand as I had his brother's.

"Now, now. That's no sort of way to behave to a gentleman who prizes your friendship above all else," he told me serenely. He gave a broad yawn. "I must say, the exertions of the day have left me heartily tired. I think a good night's sleep is in order, don't you? Good night, Veronica."

He left me before I could throw anything more substantial than a baleful look in his direction, but I was quite certain I heard his laughter on the stairs as he went.

CHAPTER

13

After Stoker's departure, I put the interlude to the side. Clearly, he was determined to punish me for pushing him away yet again, this time using my own physical desire for him as the instrument of torture. I thought back to his languid disrobing on the beach, the artful way he had pressed against me in the passageway. He had spent the better part of the day arousing my appetites and yet refused to sate them. I applied a little cold water to my person to cool my heated blood and put all thoughts of Stoker and his enticing presence from my mind. He was not the only one who could play such games, I told myself.

Besides, I reflected, there were more pressing issues at hand. To begin with, I was worried for Tiberius. Our friendship was a new and tenuous thing. We had seldom spoken of truly meaningful matters. As Stoker had noted, Tiberius had cultivated his air of cool detachment as a means of keeping the world at bay, and it had worked. Too well, I thought. It was difficult to penetrate to the heart of the man. Even his openness about his occasional sexual escapades was intended to alarm and alienate rather than create intimacy. He said shocking things in order to be thought outrageous, not to share anything real of himself. If one managed to remove his mask, he would be sure to have another smoothly settled into place before the real man could be glimpsed behind the façade. It was this very elusiveness that made him interesting to me. (Shall I explain the similarities between discovering his lordship's true character and following the mazy, winding path of a butterfly determined to escape capture? They are legion, I can assure you, gentle reader.) This likeness to my favorite pastime and chosen profession was not designed for my benefit, but there were few people of the viscount's acquaintance more qualified to appreciate it, I decided.

And I had seen enough of Tiberius' true character to see in him much of his younger brother—far more than either of them would have liked. Stoker and Tiberius were wounded things, both of them still carrying the barbs and venom of the attacks they had suffered at the hands of others. Stoker was marked in ways he could never escape, both physically and mentally. But for all his wealth and polish, Tiberius was just as damaged. The only difference was that his money had afforded him better camouflage for the carnage.

Listening to him talk about Rosamund, I had been struck by the pain in his voice, all the more apparent for his efforts to conceal it. He had made his voice light, chosen his words carefully, but I had seen the tightness around his mouth, the white lines at his knuckles, the tautness of his hands. And that moment when he realized I saw and understood, when he had thrown himself into my arms and at last faced his pain . . . it was almost beyond bearing. No matter what happened in the castle, no matter what murderous intent played out around us, I would not abandon him. Tiberius had not thought to ask openly for help from a friend because he did not yet realize that he had one in me. But I would show him.

Thus ran my thoughts for the rest of the night. I slipped into a heavy slumber in the smallest hours, waking just as dawn broke. In spite of my night of broken sleep, I bounded out of bed, determined both to enjoy my holiday upon the island and to make headway into unraveling our mystery. Washing swiftly, I dressed in my hunting costume of narrow skirt and jacket over slim trousers and took up my field notebook and pocket glass. I fitted half a dozen minuten to my cuffs and laced up my boots. A quick stop in the kitchens for provisions—a few rolls and an apple for my pockets—and I was off, making my way through the dew-drenched gardens and into the orchards beyond.

In accordance with my expectations, Mertensia was already about, hands filthy, skirts bemired, perspiration pearling her brow. "Good morning," she said shortly, responding to my greeting with a minimum of civility.

She was near the gates of the poison garden and I joined her without waiting for an invitation. "I had not thought to meet anyone so early," I lied. I offered her a roll, which she took, wiping her hands upon her skirts, streaking the fabric liberally with dirt.

"Thank you." She took the roll grudgingly, her hunger winning out over her obvious annoyance with me. "I ought to have brought something with me, but I came out before Cook was awake," she told me, breaking off large pieces of the roll and stuffing them into her mouth.

"You've been out here awhile, then," I remarked.

She chewed and nodded. "A few hours. I wanted to work with my *Cestrums*," she told me. She finished the roll and moved towards the garden.

"Are you going inside? I should very much like to accompany you," I said, moving between her and the gates.

She paused, then pursed her lips. "Very well." She took a pair of gloves from her pocket. "Put these on and you may come with me."

"Don't you need them?" I asked, tugging them into place.

"I know what not to touch," she informed me with a roll of the eyes. "Now, I know you have heard the warnings, but I shall repeat them again. Touch nothing, smell nothing, and for the love of God, eat nothing once inside these gates."

I swore obedience and she led me inside. The very air within the gates seemed different, charged with an almost narcotic heaviness.

"Don't breathe too deeply," she warned. "That's the *Cestrums*."

"*Cestrums* are nightshades, are they not?" I asked as we moved further into the garden. The air was heavy with the warm, vegetal breath of the plants.

She led the way as she lectured. She might have been reluctant to keep company with me, but her obvious love of her plants won out over her irritation. She warmed as she spoke of them, dotingly, as a mother will her children. "Together with others, yes. All of my *Cestrums* are toxic, particularly the one whose perfume you can smell. That is *Cestrum nocturnum*, night-blooming jasmine," she said, stopping short just in front of a massive shrub starred with small white flowers. "I prefer her colloquial name, lady of the night." The shrub, in reality a clump of vines tangled together in impenetrable union, reached upwards, snaking its tendrils in spirals that rose far overhead, tangling with the structure behind. As I peered closer through the pointed glossy green leaves, I saw a woman's face, withered and weathered, the vines wrapped about her throat. I leapt back, causing Mertensia to laugh, a trifle unpleasantly.

"Some of the lads in the village make a living by salvage," she told me. "They take what they can from ships lost along the islands. Pieces like that they bring to me and I buy them for the garden."

Belatedly, I realized the sculpture was a figurehead, all that remained of some poor benighted ship dashed to doom upon the rocks. "How very unique," I said politely.

She pulled a face. "You needn't worry. There are surprises all over the garden, but none quite so startling as that one. I call her Mercy. Sometimes I talk to her whilst I work."

This last was said in a tone of near defiance, as if she were daring me to judge her for her eccentricities. "You are fortunate," I told her.

She blinked. "Fortunate?"

I spread my arms. "To live in such a place. To have full reign here. It is like your own little kingdom and you are the queen."

She gave a sudden laugh, harsh and rusty, like a child's squeeze-box that has not been used in a very long time. "I am not the queen. I am nothing but a pawn, moved by the whims of the king," she added with a glance towards the windows of the castle.

"That would be Malcolm," I ventured.

"Naturally. The garden, like everything else on this island, belongs to him."

She turned and began to tie up a slender green tendril.

"Still, he seems to interfere little with you here," I said, sitting on a modest stone bench. I don't know if it was my tone—casually inviting—or my posture—relaxed and unhurried—that persuaded her I was not to be got rid of easily. She gave a sigh, then picked up her secateurs, clipping sharply as she spoke.

"Malcolm lets me do as I please," she admitted. "For now."

"You expect that to change?"

"It nearly did. But that's in the past." The words were spoken with no real desire to confide in me; that much was obvious. But I suspected it had been a very long time since Mertensia had enjoyed intimate conversation with a woman near her own age. I might have maneuvered her into further confidences, but it occurred to me a direct approach was the most likely to bear fruit.

"Mertensia, you were cordial enough when I first arrived, but now you seem to have taken against me. If I have offered you some offense, I should like to know what so that I may apologize or at the very least stay out of your way. Otherwise, I shall sit here and wait for your apology for being frightfully rude to a guest in your home."

I settled my hands on my lap as she dropped her secateurs. She retrieved them, giving me a baleful look. "I was cordial because I thought I could like you."

"And you have decided otherwise?"

"Obviously," she said, snipping viciously at a bit of the *Cestrum*.

"Now we are making progress," I said.

She was silent a long moment, the only sound the snap of her shears. Suddenly, she turned to me, bursting out with it. "Helen saw you. On the beach yesterday with Stoker."

"Yes, I know. We had a lively discussion of it over tea yesterday."

She gaped. "Aren't you embarrassed? Ashamed? I said *she saw you*."

"Yes, I heard you, my dear. And I have nothing with which to reproach myself. Stoker and I are very good friends."

"I can imagine," she said, her mouth thinning with real bitterness.

"Not that good," I amended. "But we have known one another for some time and we work together."

"You work?" Her eyes were narrow and suspicious.

"Certainly. You didn't imagine I wanted the glasswings for my amusement, did you? I am developing a vivarium in central London to be associated with the museum that Stoker and I are establishing. It will be the work of a decade or more, but we are confident."

There was a reluctant interest in my work, I could see, but she smothered it swiftly as she turned back to her *Cestrum*. "That doesn't account for you seeing him. Like that."

"Naked? My dear Mertensia, how very Puritanical of you. I thought Catholics were supposed to be more broad-minded about such things. There is no shame in the human form, particularly Stoker's. His is especially well sculpted."

Her hand jerked and a lush blossom fell to the grass. "Damn," she muttered. She turned to me again. "I meant because of your engagement to his brother."

"Oh, *that*. Well, I suppose it will do no harm to confess that my betrothal to Tiberius is a fiction. He thought it unseemly for us to travel together otherwise. He said it was because Malcolm was rather conventional about such matters, but I suspect it was more to annoy Stoker than for any other purpose."

"You really aren't engaged to Tiberius?"

"Shall I vow on something? I haven't a Bible at hand, but perhaps my word would do."

"I believe you," she said finally. "And I think I know why Tiberius would have made up such a story. It isn't because of Stoker or religion. It is because of Malcolm. They have always been competitive with one another, ridiculously so. Malcolm's bride disappeared, so Tiberius appears with a beautiful fiancée. It is a way of keeping score," she explained.

"How very childlike men can be," I observed.

"Frequently," she agreed. She put aside her secateurs and rummaged in her pocket, withdrawing a slender dark brown cigarette. She lit it, scraping a lucifer on the stone bench. She drew in a deep breath of sharp smoke and handed the cigarette over to me. I took it, pulling in enough smoke to blow an elegant ring.

"Oh! Will you teach me how to do that?"

"Certainly." I spent the next quarter of an hour explaining the mechanics of the smoke ring and guiding her. Her first few efforts were lopsided, but the last was even prettier than mine.

"You are a natural," I told her. She ground out the cigarette on the sole of her boot.

"I miss this," she said. "It has been a long time since . . ." She trailed off and I knew she was thinking of Rosamund.

"You were school friends with Rosamund, weren't you?" I asked. "It must have been a dreadful shock when she disappeared."

She shook her head. "The shock came earlier." She looked at me, her dark gaze resting a long moment on my face, assessing. In the end, she decided to trust me, at least a little. "I thought we were friends, truly. I was so happy when it was arranged that she should spend the summer with us. I had had so little company here. I loved Malcolm's friends, but to have a companion of my own . . ." She let the rest of the sentence hang unfinished in the air. "But she was different. I saw it as soon as she arrived. There was something hard about her. The posts she had taken were difficult. She was worn and tired and a little more."

"A little more?"

"Angry. Nothing so obvious that you could put your finger on it, but it was there. A sort of edge to her. She was careful never to make any remarks in front of others, only me. But she would sit here on this bench and look around and I knew she was plotting something."

"What sort of something?"

"To marry my brother and make herself queen of the castle," she told me flatly. "I ought to have realized it sooner. We had talked about the castle when I was at school with her. Our dormitories were arranged with the girls two to a bed, and Rosamund was my bedmate. We would lie awake, long after the others had fallen asleep. I was too homesick to go to sleep. So I talked about the castle and she encouraged it. I told her all the legends, the giant, the Three Sisters, the mermaids and Spanish sailors. And I told her about Malcolm, how he was the loveliest brother imaginable. I think I made him out to be a bit of King Arthur and Siegfried and Theseus all in one. I quite adored him," she said with an apologetic little smile. "Younger sisters often do. And I didn't realize what it must have sounded like to a girl with Rosamund's meager prospects. I was lonely for a castle and a wonderful big brother, and all she had was that bare room at school and the extra chores she had to do as a scholarship pupil. I never realized it was cruel."

"You were a child," I reminded her.

"A fanciful one. I spun her stories and she believed them as much as I did. In the end, she helped me run away. She gave me the little bit of pocket money she had and she lied for a whole day, telling the headmistress that I was abed with a stomachache. She got into terrible trouble. She was lucky not to be expelled. Malcolm helped with that," she said with a vague smile. "He was so horrified that I had run away from school and so relieved I had made it home unscathed. Poor darling! He was so terribly young for such responsibility and not very good at being a guardian. Lucian was running mad at his school and there I was, halfway to getting my best friend expelled. He did the only thing he knew how—he threw money at the headmistress until she agreed to keep Rosamund on. Rosamund had only a glimpse of him that day when he went to settle things, but it was enough. She made up her mind then and there to live in our castle one day and to marry the prince who had appeared as if out of nowhere to save her."

"He must have made quite an impression upon her," I said.

"He did indeed. I am not surprised. To someone like Rosamund, who had known only the stings of privation and no real ease in her life, Malcolm must have seemed like a revelation. He was courteous and wealthy. He represented security, and when he stepped in like a figure out of myth to arrange her future at the school, she idolized him just a bit." She broke off with a small smile. "I know it seems ludicrous that Malcolm could form the focus of a young girl's fantasies. To me, he is so very ordinary. But he is not a bad-looking fellow, and Rosamund was so determined to see him as a hero. I think she was quite surprised to finally come to the island and find him a very regular sort of person."

"Was it a long time between your leaving school and her visit here?"

"Oh, years," she told me. "We kept in touch, after a fashion. I am a haphazard correspondent, but Rosamund wrote the first of each month, without fail. When she finished school, she had to take employment. There was never any question but that she would have to support herself. She wrote of her employers, her duties, her circumstances. At first, she was wildly entertaining about it all. She wrote with a sort of archness and made it seem like a lark. But as she changed posts and never quite found a place that suited her, she had to take smaller wages, less congenial employers. The tone of her letters changed. Finally, she decided to go out to India, but she was not due to take up her post for some time. It seemed the perfect opportunity to let her come to the island for a little rest."

"Let her come?" I seized upon the curious phrasing. "Did she invite herself?"

"Very nearly," she told me. "She sent a rather desperate letter, reminding me a little too pointedly about my promise to have her to stay. It rubbed me up the wrong way, but I realized I was being churlish. I *had* promised her, after all. And I decided it might be pleasant to have her. I thought it would be a few months only, a summer of working in the garden and sailing around the island, teaching her our ways and giving her a bit of respite before she had to charge into the fray again. But I saw it almost immediately, the way she looked at Malcolm, at the castle, at everything. There was such naked longing on her face."

"Like a child at a sweetshop window?" I guessed.

"Not quite. This was something altogether darker, more determined. It was as if she meant to have it all or die in the attempt—"

She broke off, covering her mouth with her hand as she realized what she had said.

"Mertensia, what do you think became of her?" I asked gently.

She dropped her hand and rose abruptly from the bench, taking up her secateurs once more. "I don't know. And I wish people would stop trying to find out."

"You don't want to discover what happened that day?"

"No. What purpose can it serve?" she demanded. "If she ran away— and even with the evidence of the bag, it is just possible—it will only make Malcolm miserable. If she died accidentally, it will make him miserable. If someone—"

She turned her attention to her plants, saying nothing more, her mouth set in a stubborn line.

"If someone murdered her," I finished. "We must acknowledge the possibility that this might have happened. And if it did, who stood to benefit from her death?"

She remained silent, refusing to answer. Just then, Stoker strode into the garden.

"Good morning," he said. "I know casual visitors are not meant to be here, but I heard voices."

She turned in obvious pleasure, her mouth going slack when she saw the bruises on his face. "Stoker! What on earth has happened?"

"I was sleepwalking," he told her. "A family affliction. My brother suffers from it as well." The lie was a smooth one but it would never have fooled anyone more worldly than Mertensia Romilly.

"I have arnica in the stillroom. It will help with the bruising," she told him.

"I am very grateful to you," he replied.

She flushed and I rose, knowing a cue to leave when I saw one. "I should be getting on," I murmured.

"A moment, Veronica," she said. Her face was illumined with a sort of vitality that made her almost attractive. "You ought to see the glasswings."

"The glasswings," I repeated dully. My heart began to thud within my chest. "Are they here?"

She nodded, leading us to a nearby bush. "They were feeding earlier upon the lady of the night. The caterpillars eat her leaves and the grown butterflies—what do you call them?"

"Imagoes," I replied. "Or imagines, if you prefer."

"Imagoes, then. They feed upon the blossoms. The flowers are only open at night and they are already beginning to close. But if we are still and quiet, they may return."

The three of us seated ourselves upon the grass, sharing the last bread roll companionably as we waited. The sky grew overcast as the minutes stretched into long passages of time. The small stars of the jasmine blossoms, mistaking it for dusk, began to fold in on themselves like maidens at prayer, closing their petal-hands together and nodding gently upon the vine. Oddly, the scent of them grew stronger as they faded, almost as if, knowing they were about to slumber, they sent out an invitation borne on the wind to come before it was too late. My head grew heavy with the fragrance of the lady of the night as it wrapped its tendrils around me, holding me fast and coaxing me into a state of torpor. I could not have moved even if I wanted to, so somnolent was I. Mertensia seemed similarly affected, her head nodding quietly upon her breast as the last bit of roll slipped from her fingers and onto the grass. A nimble squirrel leapt out to claim it and scurried back again into the shadows. Stoker stretched out upon the grass, his hands laced behind his head as his lids drooped.

My own eyelids were low when I saw the first flutter of movement. It was a suggestion, nothing more. A wisp of something upon the wind, dancing just out of the range of my perception. I snapped my head up, forcing my eyes open wide. And there it was, a glasswing, the size of a man's hand, flapping lazily towards the *Cestrum*, alighting as elegantly as a queen upon the blossom. I could not breathe, could not speak, and even if I had the power, I would not have roused Mertensia or Stoker. For that moment, the glasswing was my own private little miracle.

As I watched, transfixed, another came into the little glade, moving with the same slow majesty. Another came behind, and yet another, until the shrub was full of them, their wings of clear cathedral glass fluttering languidly against the dark green of the vines. Each stood perched upon a single creamy blossom, drinking deeply, the black veins of their wings stark against the white flowers. Almost against my will, I rose and moved towards them, my footsteps noiseless in the damp grass underfoot.

They did not notice, or if they did, they did not care. They continued to drink, sipping nectar like Olympian gods. On impulse, I put out my hand, brushing gently against the vine. It shuddered lightly, upsetting the nearest glasswing. She hovered in the air, just above my fingertips, as if deciding whether to grace me with a gesture. She alighted upon my upraised hand as if bestowing a favor, her wings beating double time in case she had need of a hasty retreat. But after a moment she slowed them, walking forwards on legs as slender as lines of ink upon a page. She crept up my arm, until she reached my shoulder, perching there and spreading her wings to catch the rays of the changeable sun. For a moment, she was gilded by the flame, a perfect living jewel, and the beauty of it was more than I could bear. She would exist for so short a time, but her existence brought something irreplaceable to the world. Perhaps her beauty was all the greater for the fact that it was fleeting.

Without warning, she gave one great flap of those heavy wings and was gone, disappearing over the iron gates upon the salty sea wind. Her friends followed soon after, each taking its leave of the little glade like nuns retreating after vespers. I watched until the last of them had risen over the gates, disappearing from sight.

"Magnificent, aren't they?" I had not heard Mertensia come to stand behind me.

I nodded, careful to keep my back to her until I had composed myself.

"Come back whenever you like," she told me softly. "There is a spare key in the stillroom if you want to let yourself in."

"That is very kind," I replied.

"It isn't kindness to give a thirsty man water," she said. "It is human decency."

I inclined my head towards a still-dozing Stoker. "I am certain he would appreciate a tour of your garden. It is most interesting." She blushed a little—in pleasure, I thought. She was a curious soul, Mertensia, I reflected. I would be sorely disappointed if she turned out to be a murderess.

Stoker roused himself with a start. "My apologies," he said through a tremendous yawn. "I must beg your indulgence for my bad manners."

Mertensia smiled and I saw the smallest shadow of a dimple at the corner of her mouth. "It is no matter. Island air takes most incomers that way." She dipped her head shyly. "By way of a forfeit, you should come to pay morning calls and carry my basket."

Stoker leapt to his feet but before he could respond, I stepped forward. "What a delightful idea! I should love to see more of the island. How clever of you to suggest it, Mertensia."

She darted a glance from me to Stoker and back again. "Of course. Let me go and get what I need. I will be back shortly and we can go." She vanished from the poison garden and Stoker gave me a level look.

"That was cruelly done," he said in a soft voice.

"Cruel! I think it more cruel to encourage her," I replied shortly.

He reared back on his heels. "I am doing no such thing."

I resisted the urge to roll my eyes heavenwards. "Stoker, you are an exceedingly handsome man, unlike anyone she has likely ever met in the whole of her sheltered existence. You share her interests and you are courteous. I am no mathematician, but that particular equation adds up to a naïve young woman being halfway to falling in love with you."

He flushed scarlet to his ears and muttered something inaudible before clearing his throat. "Do you really think so?" he asked, his expression frankly appalled. "I was only attempting to be kind."

"I know you were," I said, a trifle more gently. "I am not certain if you are aware, but you have an *effect* upon women."

"Not all women," he corrected.

I could not rise to the bait, I told myself fiercely. If I were to admit the depth of my feelings for him, I risked the ruination of the dearest thing in the world to me—his friendship. It was a small and pale shadow of what I wanted from him, but it would have to suffice. Having made a point of refusing anything more, I could not now demand it as my due. I had made this particularly cold bed and it was my lot to lie in it. Alone.

Instead I primmed my mouth, taking a schoolmistressy tone. "Mind that you do not attract her more than you can possibly help," I instructed.

He seemed sincerely puzzled by the direction. "How in the name of seven hells do I do that?"

"Let her carry her own basket," I told him impatiently. "And for the love of almighty Jesus, button your shirt!"

His hands went guiltily to his collar, which—never tidy at the best of times—had come undone, baring a long column of beautifully muscled throat. "I had trouble this morning," he confessed. "My arm has stiffened and doesn't want to reach that high."

"Oh, let me," I ordered. I wrenched the collar tight and pinned it with ruthless efficiency. "There, at least you are decent for the company of respectable women," I pronounced.

I made the mistake of glancing up into his face then. A smile played about his lips, and his eyes were bright with amusement. "Veronica," he murmured.

I stepped back so sharply I nearly lost my balance. "She is coming," I told him. "Try to be less adorable."

To his credit, he did try. He could not leave off his gentlemanly instincts long enough to let her carry her own basket, but he worked neatly around this.

"I am afraid the injury in my arm is playing up," he said smoothly, "but Veronica is hale as a horse. She will be only too happy to carry your basket." He thrust the object into my arms and set off with Mertensia, leaving me to come behind, laden like a donkey. The basket clinked ominously and Mertensia looked around in some irritation.

"Mind you are careful with that," she warned. "Some of the bottles contain remedies that are quite out of season."

I pulled a face and set myself to keeping up with them, not an easy task given that Stoker was determined to make quick work of the outing. He was destined to be thwarted by his hostess's strategy of keeping him at her side for the whole of the excursion. Mertensia attempted to dally at every possible landmark, pointing out every shrub and outcropping along the path, to which Stoker made artful replies. Unable to bring himself to be rude to her by means of short responses, he instead took the opportunity to give her lengthy lectures of such catastrophic dullness that only a saint could have possibly endured them with patience. I caught snatches of phrases here and there as I caught them up, bits of impenetrable Latin delivered with the somber air of a Welsh parson.

Mertensia's eyes glazed over as he extolled the virtues of the rock formations beneath our feet. "Really?" I heard her ask. "I had no idea. I am afraid I do not know much at all about rocks," she said somewhat desperately.

"Oh, are you talking of rocks?" I asked, widening my eyes and setting down the basket for a moment. "I do enjoy a good discussion of rocks."

"Pity we've just finished it, then," Stoker told me. He eyed the basket with an unholy sort of enjoyment. "Come on, then, Veronica. Don't dally. Miss Mertensia has calls to pay." He turned and strode off and only the rocks heard the names that I called him as I trotted after.

In spite of the earliness of the hour, the local folk were all up and about their business. We made several stops in the village so that Mertensia could dispense her remedies, tonics, embrocations, and balms of every variety. The local folk were cordial to us and deferential to Mertensia, accepting her instructions and her preparations with equal respect. She was sure of herself, I noted, missing all traces of her customary awkwardness when she inquired about a child's cough or an old woman's rheumatism. In caring for the islanders, she came out of herself, relaxing enough to discuss the various ailments with Stoker in his capacity as a former naval surgeon. He gave a little quiet advice from time to time, to which she listened with interest, and I found myself excluded, taking the role of observer.

When we reached the last of the cottages, Mertensia preceded us inside to make a private examination of an elderly patient whilst Stoker and I waited.

"Do you ever miss it?" I asked.

"Miss what?" He rummaged in his pocket for a paper twist of peppermint humbugs, popping one into his mouth and crunching hard. The fact that his teeth were even and white and uncracked from such abuses was proof that Mother Nature played favorites.

"Practicing medicine. You trained as a surgeon, and I have seen you play the part several times. You are good at it."

He shrugged. "I am good at many things I no longer do."

I thought of the scores of women he had bedded during the period of enthusiastic debauchery that had preceded the self-imposed chastity of his last few years. I gave him a level look and he colored furiously.

"In the name of seven hells, Veronica, I did not mean *that*," he protested. "And no, I do not miss amputating limbs and mopping up after a flogging."

"I thought floggings went out with Napoléon," I said, plucking a humbug from his palm.

"Just because something is forbidden doesn't mean it won't flourish," he told me. He put the paper twist on a stone and brought another sharply down upon it, breaking the last humbug in half. He handed the larger piece over to me.

Just then, a pair emerged from around the corner of the cottage, young Peter from the inn and Daisy the castle maid. Peter was carrying a covered pail and Daisy was hurrying him along.

"Mind you come along smartly, lad. Mrs. Trengrouse will not wait for that," she warned him. She caught sight of us and bobbed a swift curtsy.

"Hello, Daisy. What brings you down to the village?" I asked.

Peter brandished the pail. "Chicken dung, miss."

"I beg your pardon?"

Daisy clucked her tongue at him. "Do not speak to the lady of such things," she scolded. "Now, get on to the castle and take that straight to the laundry or I will make you the worse for it."

He darted a hopeful look at Stoker, who obliged him with the last piece of humbug. He grinned as he put it into his pocket with grubby hands.

"Thank the gentleman!" Daisy told him.

Peter bowed. "Very kind of you, sir."

"You are most welcome, Master Peter," Stoker replied with a courtly inclination of the head.

Peter scampered off and Daisy looked after him with an exasperated expression. "More trouble than a dozen monkeys, he is."

"Dare I ask what Mrs. Trengrouse requires of . . . that?" I asked.

"The chicken leavings? 'Tis for scorch marks, miss. I was put up from laundrymaid to chambermaid but the new lass scorched a sheet when she was ironing and Mrs. Trengrouse was fit to be tied, she was. Now we have to soak it in a mixture of what the chickens give with a bit of vinegar and fuller's earth to make it right again."

Just then Mertensia emerged from the cottage. "Hello, Daisy. Chicken dung, I presume?"

"Yes, miss."

Mertensia turned to us. "Mrs. Polglase's chickens are the most prolific on the island for that sort of thing. Off you go, Daisy. Mrs. Trengrouse will be looking for you."

The maid hurried off and Mertensia turned to us. "Mrs. Polglase the elder is having a difficult morning, but she wanted very much to meet our visitors. Will you oblige her?"

We expressed our willingness to do so and Mertensia guided us into the cottage. It was neat as a new pin, with freshly whitewashed walls and scrubbed stone floors. It was one main room with a sturdy table and chairs and a set of shelves with a loft made up for sleeping. In the back wall, a Dutch door had been cut, giving onto a hen yard, where a raucous clucking could be heard along with a woman's voice as she shushed them patiently. Inside the cottage, a fire of good hardwood was burning in the hearth, and near it a bed had been arranged and fitted with blinding white linens—no doubt the handiwork of Mrs. Polglase's excellent chickens, I surmised. In the bed, a tiny old woman of indeterminate years, anywhere between eighty and a century, peeped out from a pile of shawls and blankets and scarves, her little head topped by a vast cap of the sort worn by French queens and superior parlormaids of the last century.

"Mrs. Polglase, this is Miss Speedwell and Mr. Templeton-Vane," Mertensia shouted.

The old woman smiled vaguely and a plump figure bustled into the cottage through the Dutch door. Mertensia made the introductions again, presenting us to the younger Mrs. Polglase, a woman of perhaps fifty with a broad, comely face and a hearty handshake.

"Welcome you are, and how kind of you to come and visit Mam," she said with a nod towards the withered little woman in the bed.

"I mentioned we had visitors and she insisted," Mertensia told her.

"She does take an interest," Mrs. Polglase said. "Her mind wanders more often than it stays at home, but she always likes to hear of the castle folk." She turned to us. "My mother-in-law used to provide eggs and chicken feathers for the castle from her own flock before she grew too old to manage. Very proud of her roasters, she was."

"The finest chickens in Cornwall, I have," the old woman piped up. She stared at us with a suspicious eye. "Have they come for a chicken?"

"No, Mrs. Polglase," Mertensia told her. "These are our guests at the castle."

The older Mrs. Polglase pushed herself up just a little, peering out from the assorted blankets and shawls. "Be that Miss Rosamund?" she asked, scrutinizing me with rheumy eyes.

Mertensia sucked in her breath, but the younger Mrs. Polglase merely pushed her mother-in-law gently back onto the pillows. "Now, Mam, you know Miss Rosamund is dead. That is Miss Speedwell, a guest at the castle."

The old woman gave a fretful toss of the head. "I want Miss Rosamund. She were reading a book to me and she hadn't finished. 'Twere a very good book too. About elopements and a brothel," she added with a sharp nod.

Her daughter-in-law tucked in her coverlets tightly, immuring the old woman in the bed. "Brothels and elopements! You've no call to hear about such things at your age," she said firmly. "You need a nice dose of your tonic from Miss Mertensia and a good nap."

"I need a man," the old woman said with a long, thoughtful look at Stoker. He stepped sharply behind me.

"Save me," he muttered into my ear.

"Now, Mam, have done," her daughter-in-law told her. She gave Stoker an apologetic glance. "Think nothing of it, sir. She does wander in her wits, although she was a bit of a light-skirt in her day."

"Reading *Clarissa* cannot have helped," Mertensia put in repressively.

The younger Mrs. Polglase laughed. "Bless you, Miss Mertensia. She has had that book for a decade under her pillow. Miss Rosamund used to read the Bible when she first came calling, but Mam told her she would rather hear about Lovelace than Lazarus, and Miss Rosamund saw no harm in it."

"Miss Rosamund came often to call?" I asked.

Mrs. Polglase canted her head, thinking. "At least twice a week, miss, I should think. She took a proper interest in the folk around here. As the future mistress of St. Maddern should," she added stoutly.

Mertensia seemed to have curled within herself during this conversation. She gathered up her things, leaving behind a green glass bottle. "Mind you give her a spoonful of tonic with breakfast this morning, every meal after, and another dose before she sleeps. It will keep her aches at bay. Send to the castle if you need more."

She turned to go, but not before the old woman pushed herself up again. "Where is Miss Rosamund?" she demanded. She looked accusingly to each of us in turn, narrowing her eyes finally at Mertensia. "Did you take her away? Why did you take Miss Rosamund away?"

Her daughter-in-law tightened her mouth and did not look at Mertensia. "Now, Mam, you know that is not true."

"I know that is what folk say," the old woman told her, her expression baleful as she stared at Mertensia. The younger woman shushed her and herded us gently from the cottage. "I am sorry, Miss Mertensia. Her mind," she began.

"It is of no matter, Mrs. Polglase," Mertensia told her woodenly.

She set off for the castle without a backwards glance. Stoker and I followed behind, slowly, each of us lost in thought.

CHAPTER

14

We returned to the castle without speaking of the incident in the cottage. As we reached the last terrace, Mertensia turned to Stoker. "You ought to come to the stillroom. I have arnica for your bruises," she told him tonelessly. He agreed and I left them to it, going to find the household in a state of some excitement outside the breakfast room. Caspian and Helen were standing next to a pile of baggage, arguing strenuously with Mrs. Trengrouse.

"I am very sorry, Mrs. Romilly, but I am afraid there is no accommodation for a trip to the mainland today," the housekeeper was saying as I entered.

I went to stand near Tiberius as Caspian, his face empurpled with rage, remonstrated severely with the housekeeper. "What sort of balderdash is that? No accommodation? What the devil do you mean?"

"I mean, Master Caspian, that the boat used for trips over is at Pencarron and must be sent for."

"Then do it, by God!" he thundered. His mother stood at his elbow, pale and silent as her son carried on. She seemed diminished now and content to let him take the helm. He put a protective arm about her. "My mother's nerves are flayed to shreds. We'll not stay here another night. Send for the boat."

"It cannot be done," Tiberius drawled. His voice was lazy but held unmistakable authority.

"What's that you say?" Caspian demanded. His obstreperousness faltered a little in the face of Tiberius' cool composure, but he held his ground. Mrs. Trengrouse shot Tiberius a grateful look. She had held her own with dignity, but she seemed grateful to have the matter attended to by a figure of authority.

"I am afraid, Caspian, that Mrs. Trengrouse is quite correct. The sea is running far too high after last night's storm. You can signal until your arm falls off, but no one from Pencarron will come."

"Of all the bloody nonsense," began the young man. He broke off at a touch of his mother's hand. "Very well, then. What of one of the local fishermen? They have boats. One of them can take us over."

"Not likely," Tiberius said evenly. "To begin with, their boats stink to high heaven of pilchards and crab. Not something your mother would find comfortable, I'm sure," he added with an inclination of his head towards Helen.

"I don't mind," she said in a faint voice.

Mrs. Trengrouse spoke up. "The local fisherfolk won't go out in these waters, not when the horses are running."

"The horses? What damned horses?" Caspian was fairly shouting now.

Tiberius replied. "It is a colloquial term referring to the white froth on the edge of the waves, like the manes of horses running in the wind. It simply means the sea is too high and the currents too strong. They will not risk a trip to the mainland when their boats could be dashed upon the rocks."

"But I can see it!" Caspian protested. "It is less than an hour's rowing. How dangerous can it be?"

"Between the currents and the hidden rocks? Very," Tiberius told him. "Even men who have sailed these waters their whole lives won't take chances on a day like today. Now, why don't you let Mrs. Trengrouse have the staff take your things back upstairs and come in to breakfast?"

"I don't want bloody breakfast! I want to get off this island," Caspian said, purpling more than ever.

"Oh, dear. It seems we've missed a bit of theatrics," Stoker murmured in my ear as he came to stand next to me, munching happily on a piece of thickly buttered toast. Mertensia came in behind, pushing a lock of hair behind her ear. The marks on Stoker's face were shiny with some sort of ointment and he smelt faintly of herbs and beeswax. He looked with some satisfaction at the brilliant bruise that had blossomed over Tiberius' nose and the slight swelling above the viscount's eye. Tiberius returned the scrutiny, permitting himself a smile at his handiwork.

Mertensia did not miss the exchange. "My God, Tiberius," she blurted out. "What happened to you? Did you sleepwalk also?"

Tiberius put a hand to Stoker's upper arm and gave him an affectionate squeeze right over his stab wound. "I presume Stoker told you that? How informative of him."

Stoker would not oblige him by wincing, but he gave a growl of warning low in his throat.

I hurried to change the subject, bringing Stoker and Mertensia up to the mark. "Helen and Caspian would like to leave but transportation is proving a challenge."

"It is not a challenge," Caspian contradicted. "It is a damned conspiracy to keep us here!"

"Caspian," his mother said, putting a hand to his sleeve again. He shook it off. "I'll not be told what I can and cannot do, Mother," he told her, his features set in a mask of grim resolve. "We will hire a boat from one of those useless yokels and I shall row us over myself."

We argued against the plan for the better part of a quarter of an hour, but Caspian had decided and he would not be dissuaded. I very nearly confessed that I had been the "ghost" Helen had seen, but it seemed obvious it would make little difference. She looked distinctly uneasy and had surrendered her authority, content to let her son take the lead. He blustered and fumed, but beneath it all, I saw the tightness at the corners of his mouth, the unflinching grip his mother kept on the leather traveling box that held a protesting Hecate.

The rest of us gathered on the terrace of the castle, drawn like spectators to a railway crash. Stoker collected another stack of toast, crunching calmly as Caspian and Helen made their way down the line of fishing boats, each time being waved off with a gesture of dismissal. We could just make out the waving of the arms, the offer of a banknote, and the abrupt, scornful refusals. With each disappointment the youth seemed to grow more enraged until finally, a very old man with a very old boat accepted his money and stood back, letting Caspian hand his mother into the tiny craft, pitching bags after her with more anger than care.

"Ah, old Trefusis," Mertensia said, her eyes alight with mirth. "I'm not surprised. He'll do most anything for a coin."

"Including letting two inexperienced people out on such a sea?" I demanded.

She shrugged. "He won't let a puppy like Caspian get the better of him, you may rely upon that. And if the boy gets a soaking it will teach him to respect the sea," she finished. Her mouth was set in a bitter line.

Stoker offered me a piece of toast. "Stuff this into your mouth and behave yourself," he instructed quietly.

I took it as Mertensia pointed. "Do you see that bit of rock? That marks the change from the calm of the harbor here to the open sea between us and the mainland at Pencarron. If the stupid boy cannot manage her there, he'll have no chance. He will turn back, I promise you."

I did not trust her promises, but she seemed unconcerned, as did the Templeton-Vanes. Stoker was silent and watchful, keeping a weather eye upon Caspian and Helen, no doubt assessing whether or not he would have to intervene for their safety. Tiberius was more amused at the folly of setting off in such conditions, occasionally punctuating his sips of coffee with pungent remarks about the boy's intelligence and judgment. Our host was not present, and I turned to Mertensia.

"I am surprised Malcolm is not here putting a stop to this nonsense."

She shrugged again. "No doubt he has some estate business to attend. Watch now, the bloody idiot is trying to manage the oars." We turned as one to face the shore.

For several minutes Caspian struggled to get control of the little boat, first rowing in a circle and then slowly towards the mouth of the harbor, the vessel lurching like a drunken man. It was easy to see the change in the sea as soon as the boat passed from the safety of the snug little bay. Instantly the whitecaps foamed over the edge of the gun-wale, tossing the craft up and down again as a child will toss a toy in the bathtub. Caspian struggled against it, rowing hard as Helen clung to the side of the boat, one hand clamped to her hat. The boat rose and dove, again and again, making no headway towards the mainland as it faced that implacable sea. The water was grey and the cloud had come on thick and low, obscuring the sun and threatening rain.

"That is all the poor devil needs," Stoker muttered as he stuffed the last bit of toast into his mouth.

"Will you go?" I asked.

"If I must, but I hope he has sense enough to see himself back," he replied with maddening calm. It was surprisingly tense, watching the tiny boat strive against the waves.

"He must turn back," I said, more to myself than to anyone else. I felt a sudden thrust of guilt at not revealing my role in Helen's obvious reluctance to stay upon the island, but Tiberius gave me a consoling shake of the head as if intuiting my thoughts and indicating it would have done no good to confess.

"Another wave like that, and they'll both be thrown overboard,"

Stoker said, pointing to the swell gathering strength and speed as it bore down hard upon them. We watched in mounting concern as they braced themselves, clinging together as the wave broke over the boat, soaking them both and filling the vessel with water.

Stoker stripped off his coat—stiffly, thanks to the wound in his arm—but before he could make his way down to the shore, we saw Caspian change tack, making hard for the harbor again, rowing with all of his might. Helen pulled at the oars with him, her hat forgot as they toiled together to bring the boat to safety.

"How reassuring," Tiberius said dryly. "One does like to see filial devotion at work."

"Shut up," Stoker said through clenched teeth as Tiberius studied his cuffs. From behind us I heard a sharp intake of breath.

"I will go and order hot baths," Mrs. Trengrouse said. "They'll be lucky not to catch pneumonia after this. And not one of you with a proper breakfast yet!"

I had not realized she was there, but I nodded. "Is there anything I can do?"

"Bless you, miss, no."

Mrs. Trengrouse hurried off. As the little boat drew near the shore, the fishermen dashed out to help heave her in. Helen was in a state of watery dishevelment and Caspian looked no better, the tails of his coat trailing seawater as he stomped across the shingle. The fishermen took it in hand to help Helen and convey the bags up to the castle while Caspian argued fiercely with old Trefusis, who refused to give back his money. In the end, the boy left it, shaking his fist as he took his leave of the elderly man, following the men who escorted his mother and their possessions to safety.

We moved into the dining room for breakfast, feeling a little deflated now that the drama was ended. We picked at the meal while Mrs. Trengrouse bustled in and out with pots of tea and clutches of freshly boiled eggs. Caspian and Helen were sent upstairs for hot baths and in due course they trailed downstairs again for some refreshment. Helen was holding Hecate close to her chest, murmuring endearments and feeding bits of bacon to the outraged cat.

"She is put out with me," Helen said to no one in particular. "She doesn't like boats."

"I know you've just nearly died at sea, but do you think you might keep that animal away from the table?" Mertensia asked in withering tones.

Caspian, predictably, jumped to his mother's defense. "How dare you—"

His mother spoke up, in a sharper voice than I had yet heard her use with her son. "Caspian, that is quite enough. Leave it. And, no, Mertensia," she finished with a long, level look at her sister-in-law, "I do not think I will keep the animal away from the table. She has been dreadfully upset and needs consoling."

"Oh, very well," Mertensia said with ill grace.

But Caspian was not to be placated. He flung his napery aside and strode from the room. Helen fed another piece of bacon to the cat and said nothing. After that everyone drifted from the table, Tiberius back to his correspondence and Mertensia to her stillroom. Helen said she would rest in her room, trailing away with the cat still clutched to her chest.

"I believe 'resting' is a delicate euphemism for getting blind drunk," Stoker said.

"Don't be horrid. The poor woman has obviously had a fright—for which I am partly responsible," I reminded him.

He pulled a face but followed me out of the dining room. As we passed one half-opened door, we heard the clash of balls and exchanged a quick glance. A peek inside the room revealed that Caspian had taken refuge in the billiards room, idly knocking the balls around with his stick.

"Ah, thank God!" he exclaimed when we entered, his expression still thunderous. "We can get up a game now. It seemed wrong to go in search of partners, but since you've come of your own accord, perhaps you won't think too badly of me for wanting a bit of diversion."

"Certainly not," I said with a smile. I flicked a glance to Stoker, who went wordlessly to the rack and retrieved two sticks. We chalked the ends as Caspian gathered up the balls and arranged them in a triangle.

"Shall I play you first, Miss Speedwell? And then the winner can play Mr. Templeton-Vane? And shall we say a pound a game?" There was something hectic about his mood, and I realized then that gambling must be his consolation as drink was his mother's.

We all agreed to the stakes and Caspian gallantly insisted that I have the first turn. I leveled my stick and sighted the ball down its length, conscious of Caspian across from me, watching narrowly as I bent over the table. With a single sharp motion I levered the stick, scattering the balls and sinking two.

Caspian's mouth gaped and it remained open for the next ten minutes. I cleared the table, dropping the balls neatly into the pockets. When I finished, I put out my hand with another smile. "My winnings, Mr. Romilly?"

He grinned, although the smile did not quite touch his eyes. "My dear Miss Speedwell, you shall have to accept my word as a gentleman that I am good for it. I am afraid I have nothing in my pockets after that villain Trefusis took my last bit of money."

"I will accept information in lieu of a banknote," I told him as Stoker retrieved the balls and set up the table for the next game.

Caspian's dark eyes narrowed. "I always pay debts of honor. Besides, what information could I possibly offer?"

I waited until Stoker had broken and Caspian had lined up his first shot to step into his sight line. "Information about why you and your uncle were quarreling so heatedly," I said just as he moved. His hand jerked and his stick skidded on the green baize, ripping a tiny hole in the cover. He swore under his breath and stepped backwards, ceding his place to Stoker.

"I suppose it would be foolish to pretend it never happened," Caspian said with a rueful smile. A single lock of dark hair fell over his brow, giving him the look of a very young, rather sulky poet.

"Extremely foolish," I assured him.

Stoker broke the balls, dropping one with his first shot. "Laggard," I said. He gave me a wink and moved around the table, taking his time in lining up the next. He was moving at a deliberate pace, giving me the chance to inveigle information from Caspian.

I gave the young man an encouraging look and went to stand near him, so near that I had to tip my head back and look up at him from beneath my lashes. "Now, if you tell me the truth, Caspian, you will not find me unsympathetic."

He smiled again, but it was a sickly attempt. He looked for all the world like a child in trouble who was not certain if a tantrum or sorrowful confession would carry the day. I put a hand to his arm, and to my astonishment, he burst into tears, burying his head on my shoulder so heavily that I nearly staggered under the weight of it. I patted him as I looked to Stoker, who threw up his hands in mystification.

"Caspian," I began, but this only caused him to sob more loudly. He carried on in this fashion for some minutes as I continued to pat his back and make soothing noises in his direction. Stoker went on sinking billiard balls and rolling his eyes at this display of emotion until Caspian stuttered to a stop, winding down like a clockwork toy.

"I do most sincerely apologize, Miss Speedwell," he managed. "I do not know what came over me."

"You are clearly in great distress," I consoled. "Perhaps it would help to unburden yourself."

He nodded, gulping a few times as he scrubbed at his eyes with the heels of his hands. "You are very kind. Yes. I think it might."

He half turned his back on Stoker, who moved steadily through the game, hitting and sinking and retrieving the balls over and over again, as if he feared interrupting the pattern might cause Caspian to recall his presence and stem the flow of his confidences.

The lamplight fell half across Caspian's features, highlighting the noble brow and handsome nose. He looked like a prince from a tragic play, steeling himself to commit some act of self-destruction.

"Do you know anything of my father? You might have heard that he was talented and much loved. The truth is, he was a sad disappointment to his family. But not to us, my mother and me. He was a second son, superfluous in every way. He left St. Maddern's to make his own fortune. He met my mother in London and decided to marry, although he had precious little to offer. You see, my grandfather made it clear that everything would be left to my uncle Malcolm. Nothing of the estate is entailed, but the Romillys have always aped the customs of the great and good. Primogeniture is the habit here, and my father always knew he could not look to the Isle to sustain us."

"He sounds a unique and interesting man," I said softly.

The large brown eyes, soft as a spaniel's, warmed with gratitude. "He was! The Romillys run to melancholia, you know. But not Papa. He was merry as a grig, always ready with a joke or a tease. He used to turn every situation, no matter how desperate, to something of a game. Even the times the creditors came and took our furniture away, he used to make us pretend we were castaways on a desert island and had to build our lives anew in the jungle. It was magical," he said, his voice dreamy.

It sounded frankly dreadful to me. There were few things in life more tiresome than a man who would not shoulder his responsibilities, and whilst I appreciated an optimistic spirit more than most, a man who played at crocodiles and tree houses instead of securing steady employment would have met with a sturdy kicking were I his wife.

I forced myself to smile. "How resourceful," I said.

"He was," Caspian assured me. "And he brought me up always to believe that I must follow my own north star, that I must never surrender to base ambition but listen to the dictates of my heart."

"And what does your heart tell you to do, Caspian?"

"I mean to go on the stage," he said with such gravity that I only smothered a laugh with the greatest of effort. I covered it with a cough, and he put a solicitous hand to my shoulder.

"Are you quite well, Miss Speedwell? Shall I pour you a glass of water?"

"Thank you, no. I was simply overwhelmed by the force of your passion, Caspian. You are clearly well suited to your chosen profession."

He preened but did not remove his hand. "Do you really think so? I feel it, here," he said, thumping his chest hard with his closed fist. "This is the seat of an actor's life, here in his breast," he added, taking my hand and placing it flat upon his waistcoat. I could feel the thump of his heartbeat beneath his clothes, steady and quick.

"I am overcome with emotion sometimes," he added. "My passions run quite near to the surface, you understand. It must be so, if one is to access them and share them with an audience."

"Quite right," I murmured as I discreetly withdrew my hand. Stoker had not made so much as a sound, but I could sense his feelings as clearly as if he had climbed atop the green baize table and shouted them.

Caspian was shaking his head mournfully. "It is difficult to entertain one's dreams without the support of one's family."

"Does your mother not approve?"

A gentle smile touched his lips. "Well, Mama would approve anything I wanted, I believe. But she is nervous of the insecurity of the life of a player. There is so little that may be relied upon from one year to the next. This matters not at all to me," he hastened to assure me, "but Mama wants a guarantee that I will not starve. That is why she insisted we come here," he told me, pitching his voice quite low. "She wanted to secure Uncle Malcolm's interest."

"His interest?"

"In my well-being. As it stands, Uncle Malcolm is a traditionalist, just like my grandfather. Mertensia may be his sister, but I believe he will leave St. Maddern's and all its encumbrances to me as the only male in the direct line. We both, Mama and I, thought it high time that he make a separate allowance to me as his heir beyond what he gives to Mama."

I thought of the raised voices, the passionate plea and the cool dismissal, and of Caspian's certainty he would inherit. "And Malcolm refused?"

Resentment darkened his eyes. "It is not unusual, you know. Most great estates make a formal allowance to the heir to permit him to establish his own household. A few hundred pounds a year would mean so little to Uncle Malcolm, but it would enable me to pursue my career upon the stage without worrying about taking bit parts and small, unworthy roles. Besides that," he added smoothly, "there is the matter of a few insignificant debts of honor to be paid. But Uncle Malcolm wouldn't hear of it. He said that playacting is beneath the dignity of the Romilly name and he would have no part in my making a career on the stage."

I blinked at the breathtaking arrogance of demanding money from a man he hardly knew simply because he *existed*, but Caspian Romilly was hardly to blame. His mother had cosseted and coddled him from birth, indulging his every fancy. Little wonder he had emerged from her tender care as feckless a creature as his father.

"Very natural that you should have resented his refusal," I said.

He brightened. "Thank you! I thought so as well. So unreasonable of him," he added with a petulant twist of his mouth. It was a pity about that mouth. It was an enchanting feature, fashioned for kissing, but his expressions frequently ruined it.

I patted his hand. "Well, I can hardly think that the quarrel would have lasted. Doubtless Malcolm will come to his senses sooner or later. He is much distracted with this Rosamund business at present."

"Yes," he said slowly. "I suppose that is true." He brightened. "I should go and look in on Mama now. Thank you for a most interesting and entertaining hour," he said, bowing neatly before taking his leave.

"God, the young are so exhaustingly buoyant," Stoker said as he emerged from the shadows of the corner where he had discreetly kept himself for the duration of the discussion.

I looked at him curiously. "I presume you heard everything."

"My hearing is acute, you know that." He took his cue and bent to line up the shot. He paused for the space of a heartbeat, then rammed the stick home, sinking the ball with a gentle click. He straightened. "You don't really think the boy capable of murder?"

"He isn't a boy," I reminded him. "He is eighteen, a man under the law. He only seems young because his mother has treated him like a new-lain egg."

"Of course, it is interesting to ponder," Stoker said, stroking the blue-black shadow at his jaw.

"What?"

"Well, if Rosamund was murdered, that young man has a very strong motive."

"What leap of logic has led you into that morass of a conclusion?"

"Simply this: he stands to inherit a significant fortune. You heard him. The Romillys have always held with the old customs. Under the principles of primogeniture, that fellow is next in line. Unless his uncle Malcolm fathers a child."

"Men have killed for less," I agreed grudgingly. "But would he really murder his uncle's bride just to preserve his place in the succession?"

Stoker shrugged. "He might. We do not yet know enough of his character."

"We know some," I replied. "He is passionate, resentful, impulsive—qualities I rather like, if I am honest—and not entirely trustworthy when it comes to money, I suspect."

"I'll grant you the first three, but how can you possibly know the last?"

"Because the little blackguard still owes me a pound."

Without ever quite discussing it, we somehow found ourselves walking down to the village. The atmosphere of the house had become oppressive, and the late-morning weather had taken a turn for the dramatic, the sea winds whipping color into our cheeks and the falling temperature causing us to walk quickly, drawing in great drafts of fresh, brisk air.

"That's better," Stoker said, breathing deeply.

"The air here is different. Do you feel it?" I asked.

He stopped and breathed again, slowly, savoring the salt-tinged scent. "It smells of the sea, like any island. And apples from the orchards. And something else, something cold and mineral, like flinty wine."

I nodded and we set off again. Something tight within my chest eased a little. We had a mystery to solve, and such a quest never failed to bring out the best in us. As the temperature dropped and the seas swelled, my mood rose, as did Stoker's. He began to recite poetry as we walked, lines from Keats:

> *Souls of Poets dead and gone,*
> *What Elysium have ye known,*
> *Happy field or mossy cavern,*
> *Choicer than the Mermaid Tavern?*
> *Have ye tippled drink more fine*
> *Than mine host's Canary wine?*
> *Or are fruits of Paradise*
> *Sweeter than those dainty pies*
> *Of venison? O generous food!*
> *Drest as though bold Robin Hood*

Would, with his maid Marian,
Sup and bowse from horn and can.

"Is there any occasion for which you cannot find a poem from Keats?" I asked as we neared the Mermaid Inn.

"Of course not," he replied happily. "It was one of the greatest discoveries of my life when I learnt that Keats was a man for all seasons and all situations. There is not a person, a feeling, a moment, that Keats did not address."

I stopped to face him. "He has no poem to fit me," I challenged.

He grinned, a devilish expression that nearly robbed me of breath. "Of course he has. *'I met a lady in the meads, Full beautiful—a faery's child, Her hair was long, her foot was light, And her eyes were wild.'*"

"'La Belle Dame sans Merci'?" I demanded. "That is how you see me? A beautiful woman without mercy who kills her lovers?"

He tipped his head with a thoughtful look. "'Tisn't so much that she kills them. I think it's more that she isn't terribly fussed when they die."

"Of all the—" I broke off when I saw the unholy glint in his eye. "You are in an unaccountably buoyant mood."

"I am near the sea," he said simply. I remembered then how many years of his life had been spent aboard ships, first of Her Majesty's Navy, and then of his own expedition as he traveled to Amazonia in search of undiscovered species and perhaps a little glory as well.

I glanced to the sign above the door, the lascivious mermaid with her hands cupping her breasts and beckoning the weary traveler. "I wonder if you ought to go alone," I suggested. "Mother Nance might be susceptible to your masculine charms. You could ask her about Rosamund and perhaps unearth a little local gossip."

He laughed. "For all your knowledge of men, you still haven't discovered that we are by far more prone to gossip, only we call it telling tales. I will put on my manliest demeanor and speak to the fishermen in the taproom. You can convene a coven meeting with the old woman and discover what she knows."

He turned to open the door and I put out my tongue behind his back. He would enjoy a few pints of the delicious and potent local cider and some decidedly manly talk while I was forced to sit by the hearth and engage in ladies' prattle. I longed to be amongst the men, but I understood his point. He was one of them, work roughened and stalwart for all his elegant vowels and good breeding. They would talk to him where they would not to a woman, no matter how engaging she might be.

Mother Nance welcomed me into her parlor with no sign of surprise. "I've just put the cider on to warm. The lads drink it cold, but I think a bit of warmth is just the thing on a day like today. Put a little heat in your bones, it will," she promised. I looked to the hearth, where two copper tankards were standing expectantly.

"You anticipated company?" I asked as I took the seat she indicated.

She slanted me a look that might have been chiding under other circumstances. "I anticipated *your* company, my dear."

I made no reply to that—there seemed no possible reply to make—so I sat in silence until she had warmed the cider. She snapped a cinnamon stick in two, dropping a piece of the bark into each of the tankards, followed by a pair of cloves she cracked upon her teeth. When the cider was sufficiently hot, she poured it carefully over the spices and added a slender thread of dark golden honey.

"From our own St. Maddern's Isle bees," she told me as she handed me one of the tankards.

I took a sip and nearly choked. "This is not cider," I protested as I wheezed.

"Of course it is," she told me, taking a great swallow of the stuff and smacking her lips appreciatively. "With a bit of rum in it."

"How much rum, Mother Nance?"

"No more'n half a teacup in each," she promised.

Half a teacup. At this rate I would be drunk as a lord by the time I finished our little chat. I made a note to myself to drink slowly.

"Did you hear there was a bit of excitement up at the castle?" I ventured. "Some say Rosamund's ghost has appeared, just as you said."

She shook her head, her expression inscrutable. "I did indeed say it."

"You are a canny woman, Mother Nance. What do you think happened to her?"

She shrugged. "Who can say? Perhaps the merfolk have come at last to take one of their own home."

I suppressed a sigh and took another drink. "A faery tale," I told her. "You do not really believe that merfolk came ashore and dragged Malcolm Romilly's bride to her death."

Her look was pitying. "'Twouldn't be death, lovey. Not to go to the merfolk. Going home, more like."

This line of questioning was clearly unproductive, so I tried a different tack. "The whole business has been terribly upsetting for the master of the island. Surely the rest of you would like an answer for his sake."

She said nothing but merely sipped at her cider, and it occurred to me that an unsolved mystery with ghosts and a missing bride and perhaps a few merfolk thrown in for good measure was bound to be good for business. Travelers and curiosity seekers and other ghouls would be lured from miles around.

"I suppose he shall simply have to reconcile himself to being a tragic bridegroom," I said.

"Like your Templeton-Vane," she said, darting me a sly glance over the top of her tankard. I lifted a brow at her and she laughed. "Of course, the question is, which one?" she added.

"They are neither of them mine," I told her.

She peered at me suddenly, her curious gaze searching my face. "I'd not have thought you blind, my dear. But there're none so blind as they that will not see."

I gave her a thin smile. "Perhaps we might get back to the subject of Rosamund," I suggested.

She flapped a hand. "You're a thruster, you are."

"A thruster?"

"Pushing in where there is no place for you and making one," she explained. I opened my mouth to object, but she held up a hand. "I don't say it's a bad thing, so settle your feathers, my dear. You've had to do it, haven't you? All your life. Ever since you were born under a shadow."

"Born under a shadow?"

"'Tis the sight," she explained. "I know when a person has been born in sunlight and when they've been born in shadow. You are a child of the moon, poppet. That darkness never leaves you. It is your constant companion, and it always will be. And you know it, don't you?"

"Mother Nance," I began patiently.

"Ah, you don't want to talk about it, do you, love? Mother Nance understands. 'Tis a hard thing for a child to know she isn't wanted. It gets into her blood and bones until she knows that she must always find her own way, for none will smooth her path. But that sort of thing makes a woman strong, you know. Have you ever broken a bone?" she asked me suddenly.

"Yes," I told her, my mind whipping back to the summer I was eight and I fell from an apple tree. "My arm. When I was a little girl."

She put out her hand and I stretched my arm towards her. She cradled the wrist a moment, closing her eyes. Then her hands, cupping gently, moved up the limb, pausing halfway between wrist and elbow.

"'Twas here," she said, more to herself than to me. "This is where the bone broke and was mended." She patted my arm. "And it is stronger now. Did you know that? When broken places mend, they are stronger than before."

I said nothing, but as she held my arm, I felt a curious warmth beginning to flow from her palms through my sleeve and into my flesh. A witch's blessing, I thought wryly. After a long moment, she smiled and released me.

"Hearts are the same as bones, you know," she said as she picked up her tankard again.

"Are they?"

"Aye. One may be broken into a thousand pieces, but when they are bound together again and a heart is made whole, the love it gives will be all the fiercer."

I thought of Stoker, so desperately in love with his first wife, and the betrayal that had nearly destroyed him.

She narrowed her gaze. "I could give you a charm for that," she said, watching me carefully. "It wouldn't take much, you know. Just a suggestion of a glamour, the merest whisper of a spell . . ."

She let her words trail off suggestively, and for an instant, I was tempted. How easy it would be! To tip a bit of potion into a cup of tea or a glass of whisky . . .

I shook my head, banishing the rum-laced thoughts that were clouding my judgment. "No, thank you, Mother Nance."

Her mouth twisted into an indulgent smile, very like the one she gave her grandson, I thought. To her I was a child, and a stubborn one, refusing the help that she offered.

"Mother Nance, do you know anything about Rosamund Romilly? Anything that might explain her disappearance or what became of her?" I burst out.

She settled back in her chair, her gaze going soft and unfocused. "She does not rest," she told me at last, her voice small and dreamy. "She walks and she grieves. She must be buried properly for her spirit to quieten."

"Do you know where she is?"

She gave a slight, almost imperceptible shake of the head.

I put my tankard aside and prepared to rise.

She glanced at it, the fire in the hearth reflected in the polished copper. "Beware the sister," she said suddenly, clutching my hand, her eyes round, the pupils dilating wide and black.

"Mother Nance?" Her hand was tight upon mine, the bones grinding a little as she grasped it harder.

"Beware the sister," she insisted.

"Mertensia," I murmured.

Just as suddenly as the little fit seemed to come upon her, it eased. She dropped my hand and sat back in her chair, giving her head a shake as if to clear it.

"Don't mind it, child," she said, her voice returning to normal. "The sight takes me that way sometimes, a force passing through me like the wind rushing through the trees. I do not even know what it means, only the words that I must say."

She gave me a crafty look. "Would you like to buy a charm of protection?"

I tamped down a rush of annoyance. No doubt the old woman had playacted in order to sell a trinket.

"Are you certain?" she pressed. "I sold one just this morn to the one who speaks to the dead."

"Helen Romilly?"

She nodded, a smile playing about her lips. "She's a silly woman, thinking she can talk to ghosts. The ghosts choose you," she told me decisively. "Come here at dawn, she did, to buy a charm; she were that affrighted. And now she knows better than to meddle with things she cannot control."

"What sort of charm did you sell her?"

She waved a hand. "A trinket meant to keep the dead at bay." She poured another measure of cider for herself, adding a hefty measure of rum. "Will you not have another?"

"No, thank you. I must be getting back to the castle."

She nodded sagely. "Aye, there are things to be done. Mind you come back if you change your mind about that love charm."

"I do not think I could bring myself to win a man by slipping him a love potion," I told her frankly, smiling to take the sting from the words.

Her expression was sorrowful. "Nay, child. The potion is for you. There is no heart as pitiable as one that cannot love."

CHAPTER

15

I left Mother Nance in a state of considerable irritation. Her vague meanderings had been a pointless waste of time, and her instruction to "beware the sister" was absurd. Judging from the considerable noise of masculine conversation from the rest of the tavern, Stoker had not yet emerged from the taproom, so I made my way back to the castle alone, walking quickly, as the wind had risen, tossing the tops of the trees about with an unearthly sound. I reached the castle just as the rain started, driving and cold.

"Heavens, miss," Mrs. Trengrouse said as I appeared in the main corridor. "You'll catch your death in weather like this!"

I gave her a wan smile. "Fear not, I have the constitution of a donkey, Mrs. Trengrouse. You'll not be landed with an invalid."

She nodded towards the drawing room. "Everyone is gathered for luncheon. I have ordered it laid in the drawing room as the fire draws better there and the weather has turned. There will be hot soup as well. The trays have only just now gone in, so you haven't missed it. I'll send Daisy to help you change."

"No need," I told her with the flap of a hand. "I can manage more quickly on my own."

I hurried to my room and flung off my butterfly-hunting costume, donning instead my day gown—a plain dark blue dress frogged with black silk braid. It was severely cut as a Hussar's coat and offered the advantage of buttoning up the front so I had no need of a maid to help me into it. I changed my boots for thin slippers, and I smoothed my hair as I pulled my door closed behind me.

To my surprise, Stoker was just mounting the stairs, his black hair sleek with mist, his coat spotted with raindrops.

"Did you learn anything of note?" I asked.

He shook his head. "Nothing save that the local cider is very, very potent. Were your inquiries more fruitful?"

I shrugged. "Mother Nance was amusing herself at my expense. But she did mention that Helen Romilly had purchased a charm from her."

His dark brows rose. "Helen is dealing in love potions? I suspect she harbors a tendresse for Tiberius, but she's wasted her coin if she thinks to lure him into matrimony."

"It isn't a love potion. It is a charm of protection. Whatever Helen fears, her feelings are sincere."

We joined the others in the drawing room, where a sort of truce had been established. The casual meal gave a picnic air to the atmosphere with platters of cold meats and tiny casseroles of macaroni cheese jostling fruit compotes and a vast salad of greens from the castle gardens. Mertensia was freshening up the moss of one of her bowls of flowers while Helen presided over the soup tureen standing upon a sideboard and Tiberius stared out at the rising weather. Caspian was sunk low in a chair, sipping his tea and nibbling a leg of cold fowl. It was a peaceful, homely sort of scene, and anyone peering in from the storm-tossed gardens would have thought us the very picture of domestic serenity.

Or so we thought. Helen had just ladled a small bowl of soup for me when Mrs. Trengrouse entered, her eyes round with horror.

Mertensia paused in the action of rearranging the flowers. "Trenny, whatever is the matter? You look as if you had seen a ghost," she said with a smile that did not reach her eyes.

Trenny clutched at Tiberius' sleeve and looked at us in turn, her eyes wild. "It's the master. He's nowhere to be found."

"What do you mean?" Tiberius demanded.

"I mean that Mr. Malcolm has gone missing. God help us, the ghost has taken him!" And with that, she crumpled into a heap on the floor.

A quiet pandemonium erupted and it took several minutes before order was achieved out of the chaos. I moved at once to Mrs. Trengrouse whilst Caspian and Mertensia exchanged sharp words upon the matter of who should take charge.

"I am the man of the house in my uncle's absence," Caspian pronounced loftily.

Mertensia had to be forcibly restrained by Stoker from applying a sound slap to his cheek. I was busy burning a feather under Mrs. Trengrouse's nose to revive her, when, to my astonishment, Tiberius stepped into the breach.

"That will do!" he said, clipping off the words with icy precision. If he had shouted—as Stoker no doubt would have done—the effect would have been arresting enough. But Tiberius' chilly authority was sufficient to stop everyone in their tracks. "There is considerable turmoil at present without the two of you quarreling like children, and if you cannot behave, go to the nursery," he ordered.

Mertensia and Caspian regarded him with mingled resentment and awe, but they lapsed into silence. Stoker dropped Mertensia's arm, and she let it fall to her side, contenting herself with only a sullen look towards her nephew. Helen remained silent, sitting up very straight, Hecate the cat looking on with interest.

Tiberius went on. "Now, Caspian, I suggest you summon Daisy to help Mrs. Trengrouse to her room. Stoker, will she require further medical attention?" Stoker moved to the pale and distressed Mrs. Trengrouse, gently coaxing her to her feet and putting a steadying arm under hers. He gave her a quick, assessing look and shook his head at Tiberius.

"I think she will be right as rain with a strong cup of tea, perhaps with a measure of brandy thrown in, don't you agree, Mrs. Trengrouse?"

The housekeeper spoke, her voice steadier than I would have imagined. "Bless you, sir. Yes. I apologize. I don't know what came over me."

She stepped away from Stoker's arm, brushing out her skirts and squaring her shoulders.

"You're upset, Trenny darling," Mertensia said. She took the housekeeper's hand in her own, patting it awkwardly.

Tiberius turned his penetrating gaze to the housekeeper.

"Mrs. Trengrouse," Tiberius said. "When was the last time your master was seen?"

She paused to think. "Last night. He was restless and could not sleep and I heard him walking the corridors."

"What time was that?"

Her brow furrowed as she worked out the hours. "Midnight, my lord? Half past? I am afraid I was not paying attention."

I held my tongue. I could give Tiberius the time based upon my own sighting of Mrs. Trengrouse during my investigations of the music room, but that conversation was best held in private. "Does he have a valet or other manservant I don't know about?"

"Oh, no, my lord. He is a very self-sufficient gentleman. I attend to his clothing but otherwise he is content to take care of himself."

"And no one noticed he was missing before now?" Tiberius' tone was frankly incredulous.

"He always rises early," Mertensia put in. "He often has trouble sleeping and even after a good night, he does not lie in."

"You don't miss him at breakfast?"

"His habits are not fixed. He will sometimes take a bit of cold meat and walk out early to look in on the crops or the quarry. Other times he will take nothing and break his fast with the tenant farmers. It is not unusual for him to absent himself through the morning, but none of the estate folk has seen him today."

Tiberius looked to Trenny, who nodded in agreement with her young mistress. Tiberius gave her a nod of dismissal and she left, moving more slowly than was her custom.

"I do hope Trenny will be all right," Mertensia lamented. "And where on earth can Malcolm have got to?"

"There, there," Caspian told her in a surprisingly kindly voice. "It's all right. I'm sure Uncle Malcolm is just off in the village having a laugh with the local lads."

Mertensia snorted at the notion of her brother consorting with the local ruffians but seemed to appreciate his effort at civility.

"In the meantime," Tiberius went on as if no one had spoken, "there is no call for alarm. If it is his custom to be out and about the island, then no doubt he has simply lost track of time and will return in due course."

"But Trenny," Helen began in a halting voice. Tiberius gave her a kindly look.

"Mrs. Trengrouse is no doubt upset after all this talk of ghosts and has leapt to a conclusion. The rest of us needn't follow. Still, Stoker and Veronica will have a look around the castle for Malcolm. Caspian, you might send word to the village and farms to see if he has been spotted, while Mertensia can ask the staff. I will be in the library should any of you discover his whereabouts. I am certain this is all a tempest in a teacup and he will turn up in time for his dinner. I have never known Malcolm to willingly miss a meal," he finished.

It was a testimony to his authoritative manner that no one questioned him. The two Romillys merely nodded and took their leave to do his bidding, the luncheon dishes abandoned. I saw Stoker glance longingly at the casseroles of macaroni cheese before turning manfully aside.

"My God, you would have made quite a Caesar," I told Tiberius when the others had gone.

"I believe taking a firm hand is the best strategy in all situations," he told me with a meaningful look. I sighed. The vulnerable, confiding fellow of the previous evening was gone. Tiberius had resumed his mask and his custom of saying outrageous things.

"I saw Mrs. Trengrouse last night," I told him. "In the music room, shortly before I came to your room. If she were the last to see him, it was most likely at that time."

"So quarter to one, then," Tiberius said.

"Something like that. And now he's gone missing."

"I cannot blame him," Stoker put in. "He must be horrified at how his plan has turned out."

"His plan?" I asked.

"Yes, his plan to embarrass his friends and relations with this idiotic farce of a house party."

Tiberius gave him a level look. "Explain."

Stoker folded his arms over the breadth of his chest and lounged against the mantelpiece. He looked relaxed and yet possibly lethal, like a lion at noontime rest. "Malcolm invited the lot of you here to investigate Rosamund's death."

"Disappearance," Tiberius corrected swiftly.

Stoker waved a hand. "Either. Both. In any event, he brought everyone together and arranged for her flowers to be placed on the table. He organized a séance. He wanted you to talk about her, to stir memories of what she was like and how it was when she was alive. *To what purpose?*"

"To investigate her death," I supplied patiently. "He was quite clear upon the point."

He shook his head slowly. "I wonder. Malcolm presented evidence that Rosamund never left the island alive. What if he has other evidence that he did not share—evidence implicating one of his guests?"

Tiberius did not deny it. He flicked an invisible bit of lint from his lapel. "How very interesting," he said blandly. "Do go on."

"Very well. What if Malcolm intended to lure Rosamund's murderer to the island to take his revenge?"

"You have no proof of that," Tiberius pointed out reasonably.

"No, but it is a working hypothesis that fits all of the circumstances."

"I'll grant you he might have been able to arrange the candles guttering out by means of clipped wicks or some such trickery, but what of the music?" Tiberius demanded. "He can't have done that. He was with us."

Stoker explained swiftly about the hidden passageway between the music room and the library. "Anyone might have managed it by means of a hidden music box or a bit of clockwork mechanism we have yet to discover. But having considered it, I don't think Malcolm did," Stoker said slowly. "His expression was too genuinely shocked. I think the music was a warning to him to let well enough alone."

"A warning?" I ventured. I drew in a sharp breath. "From the murderer!"

"Precisely," Stoker said. "Suppose Malcolm believes one of you responsible for his bride's disappearance. He summons you here to get to the bottom of things, makes a few suggestive remarks, plans a few little surprises like the flowers to keep everyone on edge. Now, someone who genuinely loved Rosamund and was innocent would be upset, but only the guilty would take action."

"By turning the tables," I said, picking up the thread of his idea. "Making Malcolm think that her ghost had actually been summoned."

"That is the rankest, most absurd—" Tiberius began. Stoker held up a hand to silence him.

"I am not saying it is logical. But if someone were responsible for Rosamund's death, then coming here, being subjected to Malcolm's little suggestions—that would be enough to prod the guilty party to act. The candles are blown out, Rosamund's music comes down the corridor.

What is Malcolm to think? He will be overcome with grief and bewilderment. He will not be able to continue his little game."

Tiberius looked doubtful. "I could pick a dozen holes in that theory without taxing my imagination."

"Do it. And then come up with a theory of your own. I shall be happy to wait," Stoker told him.

Tiberius' expression was thoughtful. "Even if what you say is true—"

"It is."

"Even *if*," Tiberius continued as if Stoker had not spoken. "There is no proof. And what has become of Malcolm? He would not be so overcome that he would simply abandon his house party."

"Unless," I began. I let the word drop into silence as I gathered my skirts into my hands and bolted from the room. The Templeton-Vanes were hard upon my heels as I made my way down the corridor and up the main staircase. It took only two wrong turnings to find Malcolm's bedchamber.

"Veronica," Stoker remonstrated. "You cannot simply barge into Malcolm's room."

"I can and I will," I told him stoutly. I rapped sharply at the door, but there was no response. I threw open the door. The bed had not been slept in. The coverlet was still drawn neatly back, by the maid the previous night, the curtains still tightly closed. The wardrobe door stood open with a few items in disarray, as if Malcolm had snatched up clothing with no care.

"He left in a hurry," Tiberius said thoughtfully. "He is always tidy as a monk."

"And he never went to bed," Stoker pointed out, nodding to the pristine sheets. "That is suggestive of a disordered mind. Perhaps he did himself a mischief."

Tiberius' voice was sharp. "You think he might have killed himself?"

"It's one of eight possibilities for his absence," I remarked.

Tiberius' eyes fairly popped. *"Eight?"*

I ticked off the prospects as I named them. "I have been thinking out the possibilities with regard to Rosamund's fate, but they will do just as well for Malcolm. He might have killed himself. He might have met with an accident. He may be trapped somewhere and unable to free himself. He might be hiding. He might have suffered a breakdown of sorts. He might have been murdered. He might have keeled over dead of quite natural causes. He might have surprised smugglers or pirates and is being held against his will in a lair—"

Tiberius made a strangled noise and Stoker shook his head. "You've over-egged the pudding with that one."

"I never claimed all the options bore equal likelihood. I merely said they were *possible*. And you must admit, there is a history of piracy in this place."

"Not since the days of Elizabeth and her privateers," Stoker argued.

"Feathers. As long as men sail the seven seas, those bent upon mischief or profit will find it," I countered.

Tiberius held up a hand. "I have never, in all of my life, needed two people to shut their mouths more urgently. The point is that Malcolm has gone missing and we must determine our next step."

"Our next step," I instructed, "is to search the castle from turrets to terraces. Onward!"

They did as I bade them with ill grace. For all their differences, the Templeton-Vane men were of a masterful bent and never liked being told what to do. As for myself, I never permit petty irritations to dissuade me from my purpose. (For most people, a potentially murderous viscount, a missing host, and a vengeful ghost might seem out of the realm of petty irritations. But then, most people have not led my life.)

We divided the task thusly: Stoker took the wardrobe, Tiberius searched the washstand and water closet—a rudimentary affair whose plumbing arrangements do not bear further discussion—whilst I gave the bed a careful going-over. There was no safe in the room, no strong-box for the keeping of anything of a private and valuable nature. I felt my way through the pillows and between and underneath the mattresses, scattering feathers into the air as I searched. I even went so far as to crawl beneath the bed, where I was impressed to find not so much as a mote of dust. Mrs. Trengrouse was as thorough as she was devoted.

"This is ridiculous," Tiberius said, emerging from the tiny water closet with decided distaste. "There isn't a place to hide as much as a pin."

I crept out from under the bed, straightening my skirts and accepting the hand Stoker proffered. He hauled me to my feet and shook his head. "It pains me—you cannot imagine how deeply—to agree with Tiberius. There is nothing to be found here." After a thorough search of the wardrobe, Stoker had stood in the fireplace, running his hands over the stones and sifting through the cold ashes until his face and hands were black as a badger's pelt.

I tipped my head, looking thoughtfully at the wooden paneling on the interior wall of the room. Like the rest of the bedrooms, this one had been built into a tower, with circular stone walls surrounding most of the space. But a partition wall of stout oak had been installed along one side, dividing the bedchamber from the adjoining water closet.

"Tiberius, how large is the water closet?" I inquired.

"Six feet?" he guessed.

"And how long is this wall?" I asked, running my hands over the elaborate linenfold carving. Finding a likely spot, I rapped it with my knuckles. A dull thud echoed back.

"Nine," Stoker supplied, coming immediately to help. Together we rapped our way down the panels, alternating to listen as the other knocked.

"What are you both doing?" Tiberius demanded. "You look like figures in a fun fair."

"The Romillys are an old Catholic family," I replied. "Malcolm said he found the bag in a priest's hole and Mrs. Trengrouse mentioned the castle has several. Many recusant households boasted them. Some were doubt-less holdovers from the days when good Englishmen feared invasion from abroad and wanted a place to hide, but most were purpose-built in order to conceal a priest or Catholic relics during the reign of Elizabeth."

"And they went on being used through the Civil War," Stoker added. "Many is the Royalist who was hid away as the Roundheads searched fruitlessly for those who fought for the Stuarts."

"Thank you for the history lesson," Tiberius said dryly.

We rapped at the panel for several more minutes before the telltale hollow echo repaid our efforts.

"Here!" I cried. Stoker moved to my side, inspecting the seams in the panel.

"It cannot be a large space," he mused. "You couldn't hide much more than a dog in there." He traced the panel with his finger. It could not have exceeded three feet by two. The linenfold was bordered by a pattern of lozenges and roses and I pressed them all in turn.

"There must be a mechanism," I protested. "There is most definitely a space behind this panel. But how to gain access . . ."

I repeated the process, taking my time as I ran careful fingers over each petal and leaf with disappointing results.

"It appears your efforts are in vain," Tiberius said, inspecting his fin-gernails.

"And I was so certain," I muttered. As I had in the music room, I kicked lightly at the baseboard, a thick panel of stout oak almost a foot high. Suddenly, the panel swung out noiselessly.

"Which of us shall go in?" Stoker asked. I did not bother to reply. The entrance was too tiny to admit a man of his inches comfortably. Besides, the discovery was mine. I would have sooner cut off my own arm than let him precede me.

"Excelsior!" I cried, diving into the dark space headfirst. A strong arm about my waist pulled me back. "Unhand me, Stoker," I instructed.

"Not until you promise not to hurl yourself into trouble," he replied. "That panel may have been closed for centuries. Even if it has been opened recently, the air will still be bad. There is no ventilation and no light. Give it a moment to air out and at least take a candle."

I pulled a face at his precautions but he was entirely correct. In my haste to explore, I had failed to make even elementary preparations, and I was chagrined at my own recklessness. "Very well," I said meekly.

The minutes ticked by slowly, but after a quarter of an hour, I took the candle that Stoker had obligingly lit for me and folded myself once more into the tiny space. The air was, as he had predicted, thoroughly foul. It was cold and smelt of old stone and something else I could not place, a dankness, a rankness that offended my nostrils. I clapped a hand over my nose and peered into the shadows. The candle gave enough illumination to reveal that I was crouched in a space even smaller than I had imagined. The opening behind me was the entirety of the panel—three feet high by two feet wide, barely large enough to permit me to enter while bent double. The back wall was another paneled affair, some three feet from the front, giving approximately the dimensions of a very small coffin. I shuddered. I knew that priests had often spent weeks in their sad little hiding places. I could not imagine any man lasting more than a few hours in such confinement without going entirely mad.

As I raised the candle, the shadows in the corner revealed a dark bundle. I retrieved it and stepped backwards out of the filthy little hole.

"That was vile," I said, brushing myself off. It was a futile gesture. The priest's hole had been free of cobwebs. It was only the atmosphere of the place that clung to me like a spider's silk. I blew out the candle and handed it to Tiberius.

He stared at the bundle clutched in my arms. We had none of us examined it properly when Malcolm had presented it—an eventuality I could attribute to my own delicacy in asking for the thing and a decision I regretted—but we had the chance now and we took our time. The fabric was wool, or it had been once. It smelled like something wet that had never properly dried, no doubt the source of the dankness I had detected. I opened it carefully, but the sodden fabric fell to shreds in my hands. Inside the bundle was the traveling bag.

He had been expecting it, but Tiberius still reared back as soon as he saw the case. I traced the initials worked into the wool with a careful fingertip.

"R.I.A.," I said.

Tiberius managed a nod. "Rosamund Isabelle Aylesworth."

I flicked a glance towards Tiberius. "We ought to examine it."

"Do it," he ordered, his mouth grim.

With as much care as if I were mounting Priam's Bird-wing, I opened the bag and extracted the items inside. A toiletry case marked with the same initials, some underclothes, beautifully embroidered, and two dresses. A pair of shoes and a florilegium of Restoration poetry. The things were all damaged, the clothing stained and smelling of damp, the book pulpy, the soles of the shoes coming away from the leather. I peeled back the cover and saw a signature inscribed in a flamboyant hand. *Rosamund Aylesworth.*

Tiberius said nothing and I repacked the bag silently. When I had finished I sat back on my haunches.

"It would appear Malcolm told the truth, at least with regard to the traveling bag," I said gently. "This is indeed proof that Rosamund never left the island on her wedding day."

Without a word, Tiberius strode to the door, closing it quietly behind him. I think I would have preferred if he had slammed it.

CHAPTER

16

Malcolm had still not made an appearance by teatime, and as we gathered about once more in the drawing room, we were a solemn group. Helen made no appearance at all, sending word that she preferred a cup in her room. Mrs. Trengrouse, pale and fretful as a mother hen, had ordered heartier fare than usual, fruitcake and sandwiches thick with roasted beef to stand with the scones and pastries, and she lingered as Tiberius, Stoker, Mertensia, Caspian, and I settled to it. The rest of us seemed to have little appetite, but Stoker helped himself to a liberal assortment of sandwiches, giving a happy sigh as he bit into the first.

"Is there anything else you require, miss?" Mrs. Trengrouse asked Mertensia. Caspian might be the heir presumptive, but her loyalty clearly lay with her master's sister in his absence. Mertensia flicked her eyes to Caspian, but he seemed lost in thought.

"I don't think so, Trenny," Mertensia replied, giving her a little gesture of dismissal. As Mrs. Trengrouse closed the door gently behind her, I turned to Caspian.

"Has there been any word from Malcolm?"

He shook his head. "No, but I am certain he will turn up. The locals said he is forever wandering about the island. It is part of his responsibility as master of St. Maddern's," he said.

"Is it part of his responsibility not to sleep in his own bed?" I asked.

Caspian choked slightly and Tiberius murmured, "My dear Veronica."

But Mertensia stared at me as she stirred sugar into her tea. "How do you know where my brother was last night?"

"Because Tiberius and Stoker and I took the liberty of searching his room. He did not sleep there last night."

Mertensia put her spoon into the saucer, rattling it a little. "This is bad," she said.

Caspian protested. "Don't be silly, Mertensia. The weather was vile last night. What if he went to check on one of the islanders? He might well have stayed through the storm."

"But the rain had stopped by this morning," she pointed out. "He would have returned."

"The storm is rising again," Caspian said with a nod towards the rain-spattered windows. "He might well have decided to remain right where he was, snug and warm."

"Would he not have sent word?" Stoker asked.

Mertensia nodded. "He would. He is terribly responsible in that way. He knows we would have worried. Besides that, someone in the village would have seen him. Unless you never actually asked them, Caspian? How do we know you looked for him at all?"

"Of course I looked!"

Mertensia shrugged. "So you say. But if anyone had a good reason to wish Malcolm ill, it is you."

The four of us turned curious eyes upon him and he looked to each of us in turn, his eyes rolling white. "I—I say, you all don't believe I had anything to do with this nonsense! You can't. I didn't even know Rosamund, not really."

"You stood to lose your inheritance if she produced a Romilly heir,"

Mertensia went on. "That would have been motive enough to do away with her."

"Do away with her?" His eyes turned heavenwards and then he looked to the rest of us in mute appeal.

"The lady has a point," Tiberius said evenly.

"I was still a boy when she disappeared," Caspian protested. "I hadn't even left school yet. Do you really think I would have murdered my uncle's wife just to inherit this cursed pile of stone? And who the devil said anything about murder before Mertensia's imagination went galloping off of its own accord? For all we know, Rosamund left of her own free will and is living in the Argentine right now."

He finished this rejoinder with a magnificent arch of his brow, the sort of gesture that Tiberius had mastered in the cradle. But Caspian did not have quite the nerve to pull it off. His voice had quavered a bit at the end, and the look Stoker gave him was not unkind.

"Steady, lad, no one's accusing you of murder."

"She is," Caspian said with a jerk of the head towards Mertensia.

"Yes, I rather think I am," she replied.

"You damned, beastly—"

"Now who's being insulting?" she asked with a triumphant air.

"You are both being tiresome," Tiberius pronounced. "And, Mertensia, with all due respect, the greater sin lies with you as you are the elder."

"By a considerable amount," Caspian put in.

Her upper lip curled. "Prick my vanity if you like, boy, but it means nothing to me. Our values, my dear Caspian, are nothing alike. I care for the land and the people here, the history, and the life we lead. You will never understand that."

"You'd better hope I do, or when I am master here—"

Mertensia leapt to her feet, pointing an accusing finger. "There it is! An admission of your ambitions."

He jumped up, squaring off to face her over the tea table, nearly up-setting the dish of clotted cream. "I merely said—"

They shouted for a little while, hurling invective at one another over the scones as Tiberius and I watched. Stoker sat, contentedly eating his way through the sandwiches before moving on to a rather appetizing-looking cake decorated with marzipan.

"Should we stop them?" I asked.

He shrugged. "Why bother? This has clearly been brewing for a while. Perhaps it will clear the air."

"It's not helping us to find Malcolm," I pointed out.

"That doesn't seem to be anyone's priority," he observed.

At the mention of Malcolm's name, Mertensia and Caspian fell silent, both of them looking slightly abashed. "Poor Malcolm," Mertensia murmured. "I wonder where he can be?"

Tiberius took the opportunity to seize the reins of conversation. "While we were in his room, we examined the traveling bag. He was quite right about it. It was most definitely Rosamund's and full of what seem to have been her most prized possessions."

Stoker and I had carefully hid the traveling bag back in the priest's hole before restoring the panel. There seemed no reason to take the evidence from its place of concealment as it seemed far safer there than elsewhere.

"Where is it now?" Mertensia demanded.

"There is no call for you to know that at present," Tiberius replied, every inch the lord. "Now, in Malcolm's apparent absence, I shall remind you that I am the highest-ranking man on this island. Furthermore, I am the lord magistrate for my country estate and I am no doubt more familiar with the law and correct procedure than anyone else here, unless you have some constable or judge tucked away you'd like to produce?" He looked from one blank Romilly face to the other. "No? Good. Then let us be clear. I am taking control of this matter. I will authorize an island-wide search for Malcolm Romilly. Not a stone will remain un-turned while we look for him. My brother and Miss Speedwell will assist me, and the pair of you will either help or keep bloody well out of my way, do you understand?"

Caspian merely nodded but Mertensia clenched her fists against her skirts as emotions warred upon her face. Tiberius' tone turned silken. "You must forgive me, but I am afraid I could not hear your replies."

"Yes, my lord," Caspian said swiftly.

Mertensia gave a sharp nod, seemingly against her will. "Yes, my lord." Her voice was harsh and two spots of bright color burned high in her cheeks.

"Excellent. Now that my brother has demolished that entire cake, I suggest we make our preparations and begin the search, as we will get nothing more to eat here."

Under Tiberius' capable direction, the entire island was searched. The fishermen and villagers scoured the buildings and fields, not omit-ting the various nooks and crannies and smugglers' caves that were in-evitable in such a place. Mertensia and Caspian formed an unlikely alliance and made a careful search of the grounds of the castle. Tiberius remained in the library with the understanding that anyone who dis-covered anything of note would report immediately to him, and Stoker and I were left with the task of searching the castle itself.

"It's a ridiculous notion," I muttered after we had climbed our four-teenth staircase and inspected what felt like our twenty-seventh empty bedchamber. "He might be anywhere. Has anyone even counted the boats? He might have sailed to one of the Three Sisters."

"Impossible," Stoker replied as he poked his head into a mercifully empty water closet. "He knows these waters. He would never have at-tempted such a suicidal act."

I stopped what I was doing and leveled my gaze at Stoker.

"Don't," he ordered, intuiting my thoughts. "Do not even suggest it."

"We must consider the possibility," I insisted. "You will admit he has suffered a great deal, and he seems a sensitive sort of man. Who is to say that finding Rosamund's traveling bag was not the final straw? It has clearly preyed upon his mind. Perhaps having that proof that she did not leave of her own accord was too much for him. He might have brooded on it ever since he came upon it until he could stand it no more. Just imagine—he was deeply in love with her, and losing her must have been a heart-wrenching experience. After years of uncertainty, he finally discovers evidence that she did not leave this island, that she must be dead. He invites a dearest select group of guests to help him discover the truth of her disappearance and instead he seems to have raised a ghost. What horror that must have kindled within him! He must have been nearly out of his mind with grief and shock. What more natural thing than that he should decide to join her?"

"You are forgetting two things," Stoker pointed out reasonably. "First, if Rosamund's traveling bag never left the island, neither did she."

"Your point being?"

"That she was clearly murdered," he stated.

"Feathers. She might have met with an accident. She might have died of natural causes. She might have—"

"She might have been swallowed by a whale, but it's not bloody likely," he retorted. "I forgot your tendency towards melodrama."

"My tendency to melodrama! You are the one insisting Rosamund was the victim of a crime worthy of a penny dreadful."

He folded his arms over the breadth of his chest. "Veronica. I realize that your feelings for Tiberius have clouded your judgment, but do try not to be quite so much a woman."

I gaped at him in mute outrage.

He went on in a tone of such maddening calm that I was tempted to bring an andiron down on his head. "You have, upon many and various occasions, persuaded me that a woman might be just as capable of rational thought as a man. I might even be so generous as to point out that you have, once or twice, been possessed of more sangfroid than I myself. But I find you sadly lacking in any matter that touches my brother."

"Of all the cheap and desperate insults, to attack my scientist's brain," I began.

He held up a hand. "If you mean to rage at me, can you do it whilst we search? Otherwise we shall never finish the entirety of the castle."

He left the room and I had no choice but to trot after him, my footsteps clipping sharply on the stone floors. We continued to search in silence for some time, neither of us speaking beyond necessity.

We discovered nothing of note until we came to the last room. I pointed to the little card written in tidy script. *Mrs. Lucian Romilly.* I rapped gently but there was no reply. We slipped into the room, closing the door noiselessly behind us. The bedside table was littered with tins of pastilles, moist handkerchiefs, a tiny crystal goblet suitable for liqueurs, and a little flask of green glass with a chemist's label. Stoker lifted it and gave a tentative sniff.

"Some sort of medicine?" I asked.

"Only to a Scotsman," he said with a snort. "It's rather fine single malt."

I thought of her gin-filled bottle of hair wash and wondered how many other caches of spirits she had brought. Her slippers—ridiculously high-heeled affairs embellished with feathers and a satin ruffle—had been left where she dropped them. Hung by the washstand was her dressing gown, an impractical confection of lilac silk. "Curious," I said, running a finger over the watery silk. "I should not have thought her the silk dressing gown sort."

"What would you have thought her?" Stoker asked as he rummaged slowly through the drawers of a low chest beneath the window.

"Black satin. A sober velvet at a push. But not something as frivolous as pale purple silk."

"She is a fantasist," Stoker said flatly. "She would rather believe in her own imagination than in reality."

"How can you know that?" I demanded.

He held up the book he had unearthed beneath her shirtwaists. "Her taste in private literature. A rather racy French novel with a dashing hero who risks all for his ladylove. He's always selling himself into piracy to rescue her or renouncing holy orders to clasp her to his manly breast."

I narrowed my eyes at him. "How do you know what the book is about?"

"I've read it," he said simply. "I trade books with the parlormaid at Bishop's Folly, and she has a penchant for French romances. You wouldn't like them," he added with a malicious smile.

"And why not?"

"Because they always feature couples who trust one another." Before I could respond, he canted his head, studying the trunk. "What is that doing here?"

"Perhaps it hasn't been carried back to the box room," I offered. "It was doubtless packed when they intended to travel today and meant to be sent on after."

He knelt in front of the trunk and attempted to raise the lid. "It is still locked. Do you see a key?"

We made a hurried search of the expected places, but there was no key to be found. "I suppose she carries it upon her," I told him. "Many women do."

"Then give me a pair of your hairpins," he instructed. I did as he bade, knowing he would make quick work of the lock.

"Mind you don't scratch it," I warned. "We do not want to tip our hand and let her know that her things have been searched."

He gave me a pitying look. "Do give me a little credit, Veronica. I have been lock breaking since before you were born. One of the many advantages of having elder brothers who locked up their pocket money."

"You mean you stole from them?"

"Every chance I got," was the cheerful reply. "There it is," he said with some satisfaction as the catch clicked open. He lifted the lid and together we stared into the trunk.

"What on earth—" I pulled out a piece of material unlike anything I had ever seen before. It seemed fashioned of cobwebs, almost like a sort of cheesecloth but infinitely lighter and more gossamer. Long filaments of silvery threads caught the light as they rose in the air, dancing a little in the draft from the ventilator.

"Ectoplasm," Stoker pronounced.

"I beg your pardon? That is nothing like the outer layer of a cytoplasm," I protested.

"I am not referring to the scientific definition," he corrected. "This is altogether different. I have only seen it once before, when I worked in the traveling show. We had a medium for a few months who would deliver manifestations and one of her little tricks was conjuring this mess."

"Tricks? Then she was not in communication with the spirit world?"

He rolled his eyes heavenwards. "Veronica, there is no such thing as legitimate communication with the spirit world because there is no spirit world. You are a scientist, for God's sake."

"I am scientist enough to believe that there is much we cannot explain and that it is arrogant to presume we know more than we do," I replied. I took the length of material from him, running the exquisite softness through my fingers. It was so light it seemed to weigh less than the air itself, gossamer as a butterfly wing.

He sighed. "Very well. But in this case, the medium was most definitely a fraud. She used butter muslin and a bit of phosphorescent paint, but the effect was similar to this—a cloud of white to emanate from the mouth."

"The mouth?"

He shrugged. "Most mediums swallow and regurgitate the stuff."

Stoker peered into the trunk, pointing to a curious device. "A squeeze-box with straps to carry between the thighs so it will make moaning noises on cue. Candles with wicks that have been tampered with to ensure they will extinguish at a certain time. Everything in here is designed to trick the gullible." His mouth thinned in disgust. "No music box to hoax the sound of the harpsichord, but she has the means of every other effect. Helen Romilly is a rank charlatan," he pronounced.

"I see you have discovered my secret," Helen Romilly said from the doorway. She stood silhouetted against the light from the corridor, cradling her cat against her bosom. Before we could speak, she entered, closing the door.

"I do not blame you for your disapproval," she said in a calm voice. "I can only plead the need to keep myself and my son fed."

"By preying upon the hopes and fears of the grieving?" Stoker demanded.

She canted her head. "I will not justify myself to you. We all live in a man's world, do we not? And you are a man."

"Are you saying that I cannot understand your choices?" he said, dropping the lid of the trunk with a crash.

"No. I am saying that Miss Speedwell will understand them better. Tell me," she said, turning to me, her eyes wide in the lamplight, "was there ever a time when you worried about keeping the wolf from the door? You earn your bread. Was there ever a day when you were down to your last crust?"

"Yes," I told her. Stoker's head snapped up, but I kept my eyes fixed upon Helen Romilly's. She stroked her cat, running one long white hand down the ebony fur over and over again. "More than once, if I am honest."

"Then you know," she said simply. "You know what it means to have to think about what you will and will not do in order to stay alive."

"I, too, have been poor—" Stoker began.

She cut him off with a sharp laugh, causing the cat to stir. "Until you have been forced to contemplate selling your body, you have not been poor. Do not compare your situation to ours," she instructed. She turned those lamplike eyes to me once more. "Imagine how much greater the consequences of that choice when you have not only yourself to think of but your child as well. I have led an exhausting life, Miss Speedwell. It has been my misfortune to love feckless men, first my husband and now my son. And make no mistake, I love them truly. But it is a tiring thing to be the person upon whom all things depend. If a meal was to find its way to the table, I had to provide the coin. The same with the roof over our heads and the shoes upon our feet. I knew what I was doing when I married Lucian. He made no pretense at being a practical man, but I daresay you are woman of the world enough to understand my motivation there," she hazarded with a glance towards Stoker.

"I might understand the attraction but not the compulsion to marry it," I replied.

"Oh, we should have been friends under other circumstances!" she exclaimed.

"Can we not be friends now?" I asked.

"Not so long as you suspect my son of murder," she answered. She gathered Stoker in with a look. "I assure you both that I know his faults better than he does. I was cataloging them in his father's character before he was born. You have never seen two men cut so closely from the same cloth. But their impracticality, their scenes and dramatics, are nothing more substantial than that bit of muslin in your hands. Caspian has made a hobby of throwing tantrums simply because he thinks it makes him interesting. He might have taken up hunting or the glockenspiel, but he does this instead. There is, beneath it all, not a malicious atom in his person."

I would not quarrel with a devoted mother's assessment of her child.

I tried a different tack instead. "Surely Malcolm would have helped if he had known there were difficulties with money," I ventured.

"Malcolm! Bless you, he was unable to help himself. When Rosamund disappeared, he fairly went out of his mind. The letters I sent went unanswered for months. By the time he was able to respond, I had already chosen. I did not wish to sell my body, so I sold my soul."

"That is when you became Madame Helena?" I asked.

"There was an annuity that Lucian had secured for us from the Romilly estate, but he left debts as well, heavy ones. I have struggled to pay them. In the end, I thought it best to bring Caspian here to see his uncle, to remind Malcolm that he had a ready-made heir in his brother's son."

"And perhaps to feel guilty enough about cutting Caspian out via his marriage that he might make him a separate allowance?" I ventured.

She shrugged. "Why not? It was possible. If nothing else, it meant a few months of room and board I did not have to pay. So I wrote and Malcolm invited us for the summer. We stayed through the wedding and when Rosamund disappeared, it was clear there would be no additional money for us. Malcolm asked us to go. In London, it became apparent that we could not continue on as we had been. I considered every possible method by which I might assuage our financial difficulties. In desperation, I went to a medium and attempted to contact Lucian. I'll admit I was influenced by the effects of the last of Lucian's excellent wine cellar. But I had my wits about me. I knew the woman for a fraud within the first two minutes. I was never going to hear from Lucian, but as I left, it occurred to me that I had discovered an answer after all. I was more presentable and better spoken than that charlatan, and I had a better way with people. I needed only a few props and a new persona. Thus, Madame Helena was born," she finished with a flourish.

"Why have you come now?" Stoker asked.

Her smile was mirthless. "Because I may have kept the wolf from the door but I can still hear him howling. With Rosamund gone, Malcolm's only heir is Caspian. He needed reminding of that. If he wanted to invite me here to conjure her spirit, I was too happy to play along."

"You have never actually been witness to a ghost?" I asked.

Her expression shuttered and her hand stilled on the cat. "Only once."

"Rosamund's," Stoker said gently.

"I don't know what happened. I began the séance as I always do, invoking the spirits. And then things began that I cannot explain."

"How did you manage the rapping?" I inquired.

"Simple," Stoker said. "She slipped her hand out of Caspian's and knocked on the underside of the table."

Helen nodded. "Most people are too suspicious to permit such an easy trick, but I knew Malcolm would not think it peculiar if Caspian were seated next to me."

"And the candles? They were fixed to extinguish themselves?" I asked.

"Yes. We have them timed perfectly so that I know just when to ask a question. The sudden guttering of the candle looks like an answer then. It is most effective under the right circumstances."

"You did not trouble to use the ectoplasm," Stoker pointed out. "Or were you saving it for later?"

Her smile was wry. "One of the guiding principles of my success: I do as little as I need to set the scene. Malcolm was only too ready to believe in Rosamund. It required nothing on my part but a little acting and the candles."

"And the music," I reminded her.

Her expression shuttered again. "That was not me."

"Come, now," Stoker began.

Her fingers tightened on the cat's fur, earning her a growl of protest. She opened her hands, crooning an apology to the animal.

"The music was the climax of your performance," I said. "Surely that was arranged."

"It most certainly was not," she snapped. "I have confessed to everything else. If I had managed to arrange that, I would say it."

"Then how was it done?" Stoker demanded.

"How should I know?" she replied in some desperation. "I was as surprised as the rest of you when I heard it."

"But you immediately associated it with Rosamund?" I asked.

"Yes. She was the only musical one in the family apart from Lucian. When he left for school, the music room was shut up and no one played. But Rosamund asked that Malcolm open it up again and he was only too happy to oblige her. She played for hours on end, maddening Baroque stuff. I used to go for walks just to get away from the sound of it," she told us.

"And when you heard the music you believed you had actually conjured her ghost?" Stoker did his best to keep the skepticism from his voice, I think, but I heard it, as did Helen.

"I know you do not believe me," she said, her voice dropping dully. "But how else can you explain it?"

I flicked Stoker a warning glance and spoke before he could reply. "Is that why you bought the charm from Mother Nance?"

She nodded, lifting her wrist to show the length of colored cord knotted there. Dangling from it was a slim silver medallion with a worn inscription of some sort. "It's a coin, salvaged from a Spanish shipwreck on the beach."

"Rather unlucky for the fellow who wore it last," Stoker ventured. "Spanish sailors have never fared well in these waters."

"It is better than nothing," she returned, lifting her chin.

"Why did you try to leave the island today?" I asked.

"Because of her," Helen said. "If she walks, who is to say whom she will visit? What harm she will do? She died in the prime of her life on her wedding day. She must be angry, so terribly angry." Her voice faded to a rough whisper, thick with fear.

Stoker's pity seemed to stir then. He put a consoling hand to her arm. "I am certain you have nothing to be afraid of."

She gave him a grateful look, and I chose then to speak. "I am not so certain," I began slowly.

She blinked, panic returning to her. "What do you mean?"

"If Rosamund is returning, if her spirit is uneasy, it must mean that she has unfinished business. She wants something—revenge? To make us aware of how she died? A proper burial? Or to punish those who did not protect her in life?"

I stepped towards Helen with each question, coming so near that I could see the pupils of her eyes dilate in terror.

"Mertensia," she said, bursting out with the name. "She would want Mertensia. I heard them quarreling the night before the wedding. In the garden. It was terrible! I thought Mertensia would kill her—" She broke off suddenly, two spots of color burning in the dead white of her face.

I stepped back, giving her a consoling smile. "There. I'm certain Stoker is right and you have nothing to be afraid of. All the same," I added, "I would not leave this room after dark if I were you."

CHAPTER
17

"That was a trifle mean," Stoker observed as we made our way from the family wing. "Even for you."

I bristled at his accusing me once more of small-spirited behavior. "I was not *mean*. And if I were, she deserved it. I seem to recall you carping endlessly about her fleecing the grief-stricken."

"Oh, I object to her occupation on principle, but there is something pitiable about her nonetheless."

I quickened my pace. "The sentimentality of the male sex never ceases to astonish me," I muttered.

"What's that?"

"Nothing," I returned. "Except that for a man who has suffered as much as you at the hands of women, I should have thought by now you would be immune to feminine wiles."

"Wiles! If you think that Helen Romilly possesses *one* wile—"

We were still arguing when we reached the stillroom. I had hopes of bearding Mertensia in her den. She was not there, but the pan gently steaming on the hob intimated a return shortly.

We occupied the time investigating our surroundings, and the still-room offered much to see. The room was fitted with shelves from stone floor to beamed ceiling, spanning the length of the walls. Each shelf held an array of glass jars, some clear, some amber, some green, and every jar was filled with something interesting. There were potions and decoctions, creams and salves, elixirs and balms. From the beams hung clusters of drying herbs, and in the corner stood a copper distillation device and next to it a large sink. A worktable had been placed in the center of the room, its surface scrubbed clean, and behind it a bookshelf had been hung and stacked with herbals, physic books, pharmacopeia, and florilegia. Another set of shelves held an assortment of equipment, glass beakers, pans, spoons, measuring devices.

"I'll be damned," Stoker said in a low voice. "This is nothing like my nanny's stillroom."

"I should have thought the Templeton-Vanes grand enough to have a stillroom maid," I remarked as I thumbed my way through the books. I was still annoyed with him but curious in spite of myself.

"We did, but that was Nanny's first post starting in the house and she guarded our stillroom like a dragon. And if she had seen this one, she would have raised holy hell with my father until he had equipped hers better."

"What sort of things did your nanny brew up?"

"Toothache remedies and jams," he said promptly as he studied the shelves of herbal mixtures. "Nothing to touch this. My God, she has a preparation of foxglove here!"

I glanced over to where he stood enraptured with Mertensia's collection. "For treating heart ailments?"

"Or poisoning people," he returned. "Everything on this shelf could kill a man—or woman—in sufficient doses." He began reading off the labels, each penned in Mertensia's tidy hand. "Peppermint syrup for digestion, lettuce juice for headache, fig syrup for constipation. Those are the harmless ones. But this shelf"—he returned to the foxglove preparation on the top shelf—"this lot is altogether different." He paused, moving closer to the bottles as he extracted one. "Mertensia does more than dabble in digestive tisanes," he said as he lifted the bottle to the light.

I plucked a book from the shelf. It was thick and bound in dark green cloth stamped with a golden mermaid. I flipped through the pages, realizing that it was a sort of receipt book, recording her various preparations with notations and scribbling as she perfected each. Within the leaves were loose pieces of paper, laundry lists and notes from Mrs. Trengrouse, doubtless thrust aside to be forgot in the fever to brew a new batch of potions. I skimmed them, stopping when I came to a sheet of cheap paper headed with the name of a barely respectable hotel for ladies in London. There was no salutation and the text picked up in the middle of a paragraph. Clearly the first page had been lost, but I recognized that flamboyant hand immediately.

—why I am so terribly desperate. I cannot describe to you the awfulness of this place. There are beetles in the beds and blackflies in the bath, and oh, Mertensia! How much better I could bear it all if you were here. Remember what jolly times we had at school? A few short months, but the happiest I have ever known because of your friendship. The lumpy porridge and lumpier beds were nothing at all when I could listen to your stories of St. Maddern's! Mermaids and giants and piskies—I remember them all, just as you told me. How I envied you, my dear, having such a place to call your own. I used to think that nothing in the world could possibly be as wonderful as seeing it for myself, if only to know that splendor like that exists somewhere in the world. I should not tell you this, sweet Mertensia, but I am afraid and a little sad to think of what the future holds. I need not imagine; I know it as clearly as if it were a picture someone painted and hung upon the wall. I shall grow old as a governess, each year thinner and sadder as I hurry to do the bidding of others. Never a home of my own, never a husband or children or a single square inch of land that

belongs to me. Nothing of mine except a shelf of books and a handful of handkerchiefs. What a desolate thought! I know I must go to my fate, as Andromeda to the Kraken, ready to be chained upon the rock and wait for my doom. But there is no heroic Perseus to wing to my rescue. I must break my own chains, Mertensia. Will you help me? For the sake of our friendship, I recall to you the promise you made—

The letter stopped there, the following pages not to be found. "This is fascinating," I breathed. I read the letter to Stoker as he poked about the bottles upon the shelf.

"A genteel bit of extortion," he said when I had finished. I thrust the page back into the book and replaced it where I had found it.

"I feel rather sorry for her. She was clearly dreading her next post in India. Her prospects were grim."

"Not as grim as this," he told me as he scrutinized a bottle plucked from the shelf.

"What's that?" I asked.

"Henbane," he told me. "Used to treat rheumatics or breathing troubles, but even a drop too much is fatal. There's any number of deadly things here—jimsonweed, nicotiana, poppy—each with medicinal properties as well as toxic. She has taken great care to mark them as dangerous." He gestured towards the row of bottles. *Beware the sister,* Mother Nance had cautioned. I went to the bottles and inspected them.

On each, Mertensia had listed the ingredients beside a tiny black skull, inked in lines so fine they might have been silken threads laid upon the label. I pursed my lips in a soundless whistle. "So, not just the odd broken bone or spot of indigestion for Mertensia," I murmured. "She has administered life and death to the people of this island."

"Nothing so sinister as that," Mertensia said as she moved into the room on noiseless feet. She was carrying a basket of wood and Stoker hastened to take it from her. "Thank you. Another small log to keep the stove hot, I think," she told him. He did her bidding, stirring up the fire with a poker before placing the wood atop. She wore a pinafore over her clothes, a long affair that reached from shoulders to hem, and her sleeves were rolled back, her hair tucked haphazardly into a snood.

"I made up the foxglove for Mother Nance. Her heart gives her trouble from time to time, and I ensured the preparation was approved by her doctor on the mainland. The others have their uses as well," she told me as she went to pluck a dried assortment of herbs from the bundles tied to the beams overhead. "More arnica, for your bruising," she added with a glance at Stoker. "And for Tiberius'. The pair of you have managed to use up my entire store cupboard of the stuff."

She smiled a little when she said it, but she could not sustain it. "You are worried about Malcolm," Stoker suggested.

"It isn't like him to be so irresponsible," she said, collecting the rest of her ingredients. "Trenny said I should keep busy. No doubt he will turn up by sundown as Tiberius says and have a good laugh at us all for being so worried." Her tone was light but her eyes were shadowed.

"We have searched the castle and found no sign of him," I told her. "But we have uncovered evidence that Helen is a fraud as a medium."

She snorted. "I could have told you that. She spent an entire summer here without even a hint that she might have sensitivities. Then as soon as she left here, she set herself up as Madame Helena. It's a grotesque joke." She broke the dried arnica into smaller bits, dropping them into a shallow stone mortar. She took up a pestle of the same material and began to grind the brittle leaves slowly.

"Helen said she had to provide for herself and for Caspian," I told her.

"She has a small annuity from St. Maddern's that Malcolm arranged after Lucian's death. If she needed more, Helen had only to ask and Malcolm would have given them a home," she retorted. "Lucian's widow and child would never have been turned out in the cold."

"Perhaps," I mused. "But it seems a hard thing to one's pride to have to come cap in hand to one's relations to ask for money. I seem to have overheard Malcolm refusing Caspian a request for a loan only yesterday. The discussion grew quite heated."

Mertensia's hand stilled for a moment, but she went on, doggedly. "I do not know anything about that."

"Then perhaps you would like to tell us about your quarrel with Rosamund the night before she disappeared," I said sweetly.

She dropped the pestle with a loud crack. Stoker stood beside her, his manner gentle. "Mertensia, I am certain it was nothing—" he began.

She shied away from his hand, looking at him with sudden suspicion. "Is that how the two of you play at it? She hurls accusations and you settle the ruffled feathers?"

Stoker did not look at me. "I know it must seem that way—"

"Seem! You are her creature," she spat. "Dancing to her tune, pretending to be kind when all the time you are waiting, like a spider."

"You did not answer the question," I said sharply, calling her attention back to me.

She returned to her work, taking up the pestle with shaking fingers. "Yes, we quarreled. Rosamund decided to show her true colors at last."

"How?"

The fight seemed to have gone out of her. She ground her herbs as she spoke, her eyes never quite meeting mine, her back half-turned to Stoker. "She told me that things would be different after she married Malcolm. She said she had plans—for the village, for the household. I told her I did not mind if she wanted to make changes in the castle. It was her right as mistress. As long as I had my garden, I would be happy."

Her voice faltered and I saw her knuckles whiten as she pressed the leaves to powder. "She wanted your garden, didn't she?"

"All those years of work and she meant to tear it out. She wanted roses and peonies," Mertensia said, fairly spitting the words. "She meant to pull down the whole poison garden, have the entire thing planted with flowers, pretty things, she said, instead of all those nasty poisonous plants she didn't like."

Stoker held himself quite still, but his voice was warm. "That must have felt like a betrayal," he said.

"It was," she admitted. She looked at him then, reluctantly, it seemed. "I thought I was going to have a sister of sorts. I've never had the knack of making friends easily, but Rosamund attached herself to me at school and for the few short months I was there, we were never apart. But the summer she came to stay here was different to what I expected."

"How?" I asked gently.

"Difficult. Tiberius and Malcolm were always making such a fuss of her, dancing and riding and rowing. She monopolized them, but I was not surprised. Tiberius and Malcolm had always had a healthy rivalry. It was just the pair of them showing off. When Tiberius left, everything was quieter. I saw almost nothing of Malcolm, but I still never believed anything would come of it. He is just so proud of the island and she was interested in everything."

She looked down at the dirty green powder in her mortar. "I have ruined this lot," she said in a dull voice. She threw the powder into the fire and began again with a fresh bunch of leaves. "Then they announced their engagement, and for a few weeks Rosamund seemed different, quieter. I would come upon her at odd moments and she was always just sitting, lost in thought. When she was with Malcolm, her spirits were high. There was a recklessness about her, a sort of devil-may-care gleam in her eye that I could not understand. I would have thought she would have been serene. She had everything she ever wanted. But Rosamund was never serene. There was only brooding silence or that hectic gaiety. Nothing in between. No real happiness, no real love for Malcolm. I finally confronted her the night before they were married. That is when she told me that I needn't bother myself about her. She had everything planned."

Mertensia's hands stilled as she spoke, her voice dreamy, her eyes fixed upon a point in the distance. "She talked for hours, it seemed. She told me all that she wanted to do, every way she meant to take charge of things. I never realized, you see, how much she had resented me when we were at school together. I thought we were equals, miserable little girls bound by our unhappiness. But Rosamund saw things differently. There was a watchfulness to her I had never seen, a brittleness. It created a strange atmosphere that summer. The air was heavy, as if waiting for a storm to break. And then I discovered that she had been taking my place."

"In what way?" Stoker asked, his voice low and coaxing.

"It has always been the family's responsibility to take care of the villagers. My mother did it, and before I was old enough, after her death, Trenny used to make the calls. She taught me how to pack the baskets, what to choose to give the most comfort—a broth with wine and egg yolks for a nursing mother, a calf's-foot jelly for a broken leg, just as I did today. There is not a hearthside on this island beside which I have not sat, warming soup and knitting socks. One day I brewed up a bit of cat's-claw tonic for old Mrs. Polglase. She has rheumatism quite badly and cat's-claw is the best remedy. I used to take her a bottle quite regularly, but that summer there was so much to do, I had left it. I felt bad when I realized how long it had been. I took the tonic and went to the Polglase cottage, but when I got there, Rosamund was already there, reading to Mrs. Polglase. She had taken the last bottle of tonic I brewed and brought it with her. They were having a great laugh when I arrived, and it was only the first of many such times. I eventually forbade her from coming into the stillroom to take my remedies, but it did not stop her. She merely smiled like a cat with a cream pot and went about her business. She persuaded Cook to bottle up soup for her and she knitted shawls and carried books with her. People started to talk about how thoughtful she was, how considerate. She even took to arranging flowers in the church, taking my best roses before I had a chance. Everywhere I went, she had got there first. It was as if I were being erased. You saw what it was like with Mrs. Polglase. The villagers *adored* her. I began to see what it would be like for me once she married Malcolm. There would simply be no place for me here."

Stoker's gaze flicked to mine. Mertensia seemed entirely unaware that she had just confessed to a powerful motive for murder. I gave an almost imperceptible nod and he moved forward slightly, careful not to touch her, pitching his voice to a soft, honeyed tone that had always sent shivers down my spine.

"She must have broken your heart," he said. "You could not leave St. Maddern's. You are as much a part of this place as the sea itself."

She gave a slow nod, the pestle slipping once more from her hand. Tears stood in her eyes and she turned, almost against her will, it seemed, burying her face in his shirt. Stoker embraced her, settling those muscled arms firmly about her as one large hand cradled her head. He murmured something soothing, I could not hear what. The words were for her only. She sobbed for a long while; then her shoulders stilled and she relaxed into his grasp.

"I am sorry," she said brokenly, trying to regain her composure.

But Stoker kept one arm securely about her as he retrieved a handkerchief from his pocket, one of his enormous affairs of scarlet linen. She took it with a grateful, watery smile. "I am sorry I was so rude to you," she said. "I do not really believe you are her creature." She did not even look at me as she spoke. Her eyes were fixed adoringly on Stoker.

"I am very much my own man," he assured her.

I tasted sourness and said nothing.

"Did you ever confront her? Tell her how you felt?" Stoker asked.

She nodded. "Precious little good it did. She merely laughed and said I was being ridiculous, and then she made some casual remark about things changing for the better on St. Maddern's. And I went off to have a good cry in the garden. Helen found me there and I told her what had happened. She took me along to Trenny, who gave me warm milk and put me to bed. She said it was all a tempest in a teapot and everything would seem better with a good night's sleep."

"Excellent advice," Stoker told her.

The feeble smile deepened. "I suppose. The wedding was fairly miserable for me, pretending to be happy for them. But then she disappeared and it was so much worse! I thought the most difficult thing would be for Rosamund to live here, but that was nothing compared to the suspicion, the whispers, the newspapers. The not knowing was diabolical."

"It seems to have affected Malcolm quite badly," Stoker offered.

At the mention of her brother, her face shuttered. She pushed gently out of Stoker's embrace and picked up her pestle. "I am certain Veronica has better things to do than listen to me moan about my family," she said with a forced smile.

"Not at all," I replied. "I am persuaded that Malcolm's disappearance is connected to Rosamund's. If we discover the truth about her whereabouts, no doubt we can do the same for him."

"I hope you are right," she said. She said nothing more and that seemed our cue to leave. As we made our way from the stillroom, I saw the corner of the scarlet handkerchief peeping from her pocket. Her finger reached out to stroke it as we closed the door behind us.

"Well, that might have gone better," I said in some irritation.

Stoker shrugged. "We learnt a little of Rosamund's ability to manipulate thanks to that scrap of letter. And we confirmed there was a quarrel. Whether Mertensia is telling the truth about the fact that it ended remains to be seen, but I am inclined to believe her. She is a simple, forthright woman. I think she has no talent for deceit."

"And with only herself and the missing Rosamund to witness it, we shall never know."

His expression was reproving. "Can you find no charity in your heart for her? Mertensia is a sterling character."

I made no reply to this. I started off down the corridor, the tiny heels of my slippers ringing irritably on the stones. Stoker caught up to me, his hands thrust deeply into his pockets. "Where are we going now?"

"To find Mrs. Trengrouse," I told him. "She saw Mertensia after the quarrel with Rosamund. Perhaps she can shed some light on the matter."

"Excellent," he said, patting his flat belly. "I could do with a bite of something."

"If you're hungry, you needn't have come with me," I told him irritably. "Go and stuff yourself like a Michaelmas goose for all I care."

"Because you can do this all on your own," he replied, stopping short in the corridor.

I turned to face him.

"Forgive me. I quite forgot your refusal to accept anyone else's help, your insistence upon never needing anyone, ever, for any purpose. Very well. I have a few things to investigate on my own."

"Such as?" I demanded.

"Do not concern yourself about it," he instructed, the muscle of his jaw tight as he ground the words through clenched teeth. "But I think it is time we held my brother's elegant feet to the fire."

With that, he turned smartly on his heel and left me staring after. "Whatever has got into him?" I muttered.

Just then Daisy turned the corner, her arms full of freshly laundered sheets, smelling—one thanked the Almighty—not at all of chicken manure. "Oh, I beg pardon, miss. Was there something you needed?"

"I was looking for Mrs. Trengrouse," I told her. "I had a question about Miss Rosamund."

"She is about somewhere, no doubt," Daisy assured me. "Probably looking in on the dinner preparations." She paused, giving me a close look. "I hear as you went to the village proper today, miss, besides Polglase cottage. And had your palm read."

"How did you—" I broke off, suddenly seeing the resemblance to the village witch and remembering how she had scolded young Peter with an air of familiarity. "You are related to Mother Nance. Granddaughter?"

"Great-niece," she said with a grin.

"And I suppose that is how she gets her intelligence of everything that happens at the castle? You keep your ear to the ground and feed her information so when the Romilly guests come, she seems omniscient?"

"Aw, 'tis just a bit of fun, miss! She earns a little extra coin and she always sends a few coppers my way for it."

Her look was puckish and I could not hold a grudge against this enterprising pair. "You told her that Mrs. Helen was afraid of ghosts, didn't you? And that's how she knew to offer her a protection charm?"

She grinned. "It weren't no protection charm, miss. Just a bit of old coin Mother Nance has had banging around since God were in leading strings. But Mrs. Helen feels ever so much better for having it, don't she?"

I thought of Helen's desperate clutching of the charm. "I suppose so." I glanced down the corridor, making certain we were alone. "Daisy, did you ever tell Mother Nance anything about Miss Rosamund? Was there anything you observed about the lady that you found curious?"

Her mouth tightened. "I don't like to say, miss. 'Tisn't fit for proper ladies to speak of."

"I am no proper lady," I assured her. "Now, tell me. Your master's life may depend upon it."

Her eyes rounded. "The master? I can't see how that may be, but all right, miss. Yes. I did note something." She glanced down at the pristine sheets in her arms. "I changed her sheets every day, I did. I washed all her linen myself, bath and personal. And in the three months that she were here, she only had her monthlies once."

I blinked. "I beg your pardon?"

"Her monthlies, miss. She bled the first month she came, but never after that."

"Rosamund was going to have a child," I concluded.

"Yes, miss. She were sick a time or two in the morning. Nothing half so bad as I've seen with my sisters," Daisy advised. "But sick nonetheless. I cleaned it all up and she gave me a shilling to keep quiet about it. And quiet I was," she added firmly. "I never told Mother Nance, although she might have made a few shillings herself out of childbirth charms. But it made it all the more tragic when she disappeared, miss. It weren't just her that vanished, it was the master's child," Daisy said, shaking her head sorrowfully.

But I had a different thought entirely.

After my talk with Daisy, I repaired to my room to wash off any dusty traces of the search, extracting cobwebs from my hair and rubbing a smudge from my cheek. Suitably freshened, I found Tiberius in the billiards room with Stoker. They were not playing but sitting, sunk deep in the leather armchairs, smoking and saying nothing.

I went and sat on the hassock at Tiberius' feet, ignoring Stoker entirely. I leant forward, placing my hands in Tiberius'. "Did you know?"

His brows quirked up inquisitively. "Did I know?"

I tightened my grip, my gaze never leaving his. *"Did you know?"*

He did not speak for a long moment, and when he did, he paid me the compliment of the truth. "I did."

"How? Was it in the telegram she sent you before she married him?"

He gave a slow nod. Stoker stirred but did not interrupt.

"By the time I received the telegram, she was already missing and my child with her," Tiberius said. Stoker's eyes were bright with inquiry but I continued to ignore him.

"Tiberius, you have not been forthright with us. Tell us now why you have come here."

His expression hardened. "Malcolm married the woman I loved and for whatever reason, he failed her—failed her so badly that she fled. Or took her own life. Or was murdered. If someone has hounded Malcolm to death for it, then I would like to know who so that I may take them by the hand and convey my thanks."

I had never heard him speak so bitterly, and it was a moment before I could form a reply. "You surprise me, my lord," I said gently. "I hadn't realized you shared Stoker's capacity for rage."

"Share it?" he mocked. "My dear lady, I taught it to him. Now, I should like very much to discover the truth of what has happened to Malcolm."

"And Rosamund," Stoker put in steadily.

The brothers squared off in a posture that was no doubt familiar to them from their boyhood days of brawling. "Yes. I do want to know precisely what happened to her."

"Well, I am glad you are man enough to concede you have an ulterior purpose."

Tiberius' handsome mouth curled. "Brother mine, I thought you learnt long ago—even my ulterior purposes have ulterior purposes."

Stoker returned the smile. "Such as murdering Malcolm Romilly?"

I blinked at him. "Stoker, what on earth—"

"I searched Tiberius' room when you were talking to Daisy. He has a revolver hidden in his bag. He does not habitually travel with one, and a sleepy isle off the coast of Cornwall is not exactly a thiving hive of dangerous criminal activity. Therefore, why would he choose to arm himself this time, I ask myself. Why come here at all and suffer the tortures of Rosamund's disappearance resurrected? Unless he decided to take matters into his own hands."

"Stoker, you cannot—"

"Accuse my own brother of plotting a murder? Of course I can. In fact, I accuse him of carrying it out."

"You bloody fool," Tiberius began with a thin smile.

"Am I?" Stoker crossed his arms over his chest. "I'll stake my life on you being up to your lordly neck in this business and take my chances."

They stood toe-to-toe for a long, breathless minute. There was no sound except the ticking of a particularly ugly mantel clock until at last Tiberius expelled a deep breath and let his shoulders soften. "Very well. I came here to kill Malcolm. Is that enough of a confession for you or shall I write it in my heart's blood?"

Stoker's expression barely shifted but I caught the triumphant flicker in his eyes. I hurried to speak before he goaded his brother to further violence. "Tiberius, perhaps you would care to start at the beginning."

He shrugged. "There is not much to tell. When Rosamund disappeared, no one knew precisely what had happened. Theories abounded, each wilder than the last. It was suggested that she had thrown herself into the sea or that she had gone off in a passing boat. Some said she was murdered, others that she had turned into a dove and flown away on the west wind. That last contribution was from the more superstitious villagers," he added with a cold smile. "No body was ever recovered, no note or witness ever produced to say one way or another what became of her. Malcolm was advised that he could apply to have her pronounced legally dead if she had not been heard from in seven years. For three years, there has been nothing. Then, quite out of the blue, Malcolm wrote me a fortnight ago. He said he had discovered proof that Rosamund did not leave the island of her own free will and he wanted me to come here because he wanted to discover the truth."

"Did he tell you anything more?" I prodded.

"No. Only that he trusted me because I had not been here during her disappearance and because he knew that Rosamund and I were barely acquainted and therefore I could have had no motive for harming her. It was that bland little reassurance that taunted me. I read it over and over again, and it suddenly occurred to me, *What if he had known?* He might have discovered our feelings quite by chance. Rosamund sometimes kept a diary and she was not always careful with it. What if it had come to light and Malcolm learnt of our relationship? Might he have intended to lure me here under false pretenses? Could a maidservant have known? Had Rosamund confided in her schoolmate Mertensia? The more I considered the matter, the more possible loose ends I imagined. And any one of them might have exposed us."

"And so you determined to come and discover the truth for yourself," I added.

"More than that. I always resented the fact that whatever had become of her, he had not been able to prevent it. Had she run away? Then he must have been the source of her unhappiness. In choosing Malcolm for her husband, she must have believed he would bring her comfort and companionship. Somehow he had failed her. And then his letter came, claiming he had proof she had been harmed, and that is when I became angry, blindly, redly angry. All I could think was that he had been able to do the one thing denied me—marry the woman he loved—and he had lost her. He had not kept her safe. He had not protected her. And I wanted justice for Rosamund's sake, visited both upon her murderer and upon the man who had let it happen. So I decided to come here, prepared to deal justice if necessary."

"How did we fit into your plan?" I inquired.

Tiberius smiled. "I have never done murder before. I thought an accomplice might be necessary."

"And you expected we would provide that help? Really, Tiberius. You go too far," I chided.

"Do I? You are not overly concerned with the law, either of you," Tiberius replied as he looked from me to Stoker. "You care for justice, but not for how it is achieved. If I executed a murderer, would you really give evidence against me? Or would you help me hide the body?"

"Why the pretense?" I demanded. "Why not just explain what you were after?"

"It's hardly the sort of thing one asks casually. One simply cannot invite people to engage in a spot of justifiable homicide," he said. "But I thought that if I could bring you here, if you could see it all for yourself, you would both sympathize."

"You did not invite Stoker," I reminded him. "In fact, when he asked to come, you specifically told him he could not."

Tiberius' smile was patient. "My dearest Veronica, have you not yet learnt that the surest way to guarantee that Stoker will do something is to tell him he may not? He was twice as eager to come for being forbidden the invitation."

"Of all the bloody, manipulative—" Stoker began.

Tiberius held up a finger. "Effective. I've known how to maneuver you since our days in the nursery. You have not changed."

"Neither have you," Stoker replied bitterly. "We are brothers, Tiberius. You could have told me the truth."

"As you did when Caroline de Morgan was trying to put a noose about your neck?" Tiberius asked. "You have never once turned to me for help. Why should I return the favor?"

The question sat uneasily between them, the silence heavy with reproach.

"Did you kill Malcolm?" Stoker asked bluntly.

Tiberius canted his head and gave his brother a curious look. "I cannot decide which answer you would like most. To hear that your brother is as capable of intemperate violence as you are? Or to hear that he is better than you after all and can resist the most primal of urges, that of the killer."

"Tibe," Stoker said in a gentle voice, the nickname one I had never heard before. A relic of childhood? I wondered how long it had been since Stoker, since anyone, had called him that, this elegant and fractured man.

Tiberius drew in a deep, shuddering breath and put his shoulders back. "I did not. I came here with the intention of killing him, and I may do it yet. But I have thus far not harmed so much as a hair upon his head. I give you my word—not as Father's son, but as Mother's."

Stoker gave him a long, level look, then nodded. "I believe you. And I will do everything in my power to keep you from making a murderer of yourself."

"You may try to stop me," his lordship said coolly, "but you will not succeed."

"You should give it another thought," I broke in. "Having a murder on one's conscience is no easy thing. I speak from experience."

His lordship's mouth went slack, but before he could ask anything further, I held up a hand. "Now, on to business. We must be logical and scientific in our method. If you did not murder Malcolm, where is he?"

"Do you want my word upon it?" Tiberius thundered. "I had nothing to do with Malcolm Romilly's disappearance. But I swear to you, I vow by all I hold dear in this world and the next, if we find him and it is proven that he had anything to do with Rosamund's death, I will wrench out his still-beating heart with my bare hands."

He was breathing heavily, the only sound in the taut silence of the room. Just then, Mrs. Trengrouse appeared, her expression anxious.

"My lord! There you are. I don't know what to do," she said, coming forwards in haste.

"Here I am. What is it, Mrs. Trengrouse?"

She hesitated. "'Tis probably nothing, my lord, but I found something on the western beach, outside the tunnels," she said. "I don't know what it means, you see, and I am afraid, so very afraid that it means the master is not returning."

Stoker's manner was gentle. "What did you find?"

She shook her head, the threads of silver gleaming in the lamplight.

"I cannot rightly say. 'Tis like nothing I have ever seen before. But I—" Her voice broke on a sob and Stoker patted her shoulder.

"We will come," he assured her.

We followed Mrs. Trengrouse through the house and down to the kitchens. "Where is the staff?" I asked as we made our way through the usually bustling offices.

"'Tis their suppertime," she said. "Cocoa and bread and butter before they finish the dinner preparations." Stoker gave an appreciative sniff of the aroma of cocoa as she led the way to the tunnels, lighting lamps for us and unlocking the gate. She collected a lantern and went first through the narrow passage; I fell into line behind Mrs. Trengrouse, who kept up a continuous patter of talk as we made our way down to the beach, the brothers walking behind.

We emerged onto the beach just as the sun sank behind the Sisters, the dark rose gold of the light turning to silvery grey. A tiny boat had been beached at the edge of the water, and Mrs. Trengrouse led the way to it, hurrying over the shingle. The waves were rising in the evening wind, lacy whitecaps forming at the crest of each breaker.

"Inside the boat," Mrs. Trengrouse said, lifting her lantern high so we could see. "Just there."

The Templeton-Vanes clambered into the little craft, Tiberius more slowly than Stoker. They stood, looking about for a moment before turning to Mrs. Trengrouse in perplexity.

"Now you, Miss Speedwell," she ordered. "Into the boat."

In one hand she still held the lantern aloft, lighting the way. And in the other, she leveled a revolver at my heart.

CHAPTER

18

"Well, this is unexpected," Stoker remarked with a bit of his old hauteur.

"I know," she said, smiling thinly. "If you had expected it, sir, you'd never have come. Now, into the boat, miss. I'll not ask again."

I did as I was bade for the simple reason that I could see no plausible alternative. I was too far away to disarm her, as were the Templeton-Vanes. Stoker put out an arm and braced one booted foot upon the gunwale, hoisting me swiftly to stand in between them.

"What now?" he asked.

"You will row the boat to the First Sister," she said, nodding towards the rock.

"And if we refuse, you shoot us?" he guessed.

"Beginning with Miss Speedwell," she assured him.

"What if we row out a bit and turn back?" Tiberius inquired.

"Then I will shoot her before you reach the beach," she promised. "Your choice is simple, my lord. You and your brother row Miss Speedwell to that rock or risk her life."

Tiberius opened his mouth, but Stoker thrust an oar into his hands. "Shut up and row, Tiberius," he ordered.

"I have a number of questions," I said to Mrs. Trengrouse.

She smiled again, but it was a tremulous, anxious thing. "I imagine you do, but I am no hardened criminal, Miss Speedwell. I am not steeled to enjoy this sort of thing, and the longer you linger upon this beach, the more nervous I become," she said, waving the revolver again.

"For Christ's sake, sit down," Stoker told me, tugging my skirt hard enough that I tumbled to the bottom of the boat. Without preamble he leapt from the boat and gave it a mighty shove, launching it into the water. He gave Mrs. Trengrouse a long, level look, assessing the distance between them, but she merely kept the gun fixed upon me, and he resumed his position in the boat, taking up his oar.

We were perhaps halfway to the island before we dared to speak, keeping our voices low lest they carry across the water to the villainess waiting upon the beach, watching our progress with her lantern lifted high.

"So much for your arsenal of knives," Stoker said. His face was a mask of pain as he rowed. He had removed his coat with difficulty and a bloodstain was blossoming on the white linen of his sleeve.

"I can only presume that your bad temper is the result of the rowing pulling loose your stitches," I told him coldly. "As it happens, I am not wearing my boots or my purple corset, and it seemed a bit excessive to strap a knife to my calf just to sit down to tea. I shall know better next time."

"Next time," he said in a hollow echo.

"Now, let us turn our considerable energy and intellect to the problem at hand. We might row around the island," I suggested. "We will soon be out of distance for a decent shot and we could risk pulling for the other side of the island. We would find help there."

"The current will carry us the wrong way," Stoker said flatly. "And we cannot row against it all the way around the island."

"Then what if we—"

Stoker gave a jerk of his head. "We cannot do anything other than what she has ordered," he said. He looked down between his feet and I realized that the rising sensation of cold I had been feeling was not simply nerves. Seawater was seeping into the boat, filling the tiny hull.

Tiberius swore and began to pull harder at his oar. "She means to drown us."

"No, she means us to comply," I corrected. "If she meant us to drown, she would have made a bigger hole." I inspected the series of small punctures drilled into the hull. Sawdust was floating on the top of the water, and I realized she must have damaged the boat just before coming to find us. A few other granules floated on the surface and I rubbed them between my fingers, dissolving them.

"Sugar," I pronounced. "She must have packed the holes with plugs of sugar to keep the boat afloat long enough to get us away from the beach."

Stoker and Tiberius pulled hard for the little isle, and we reached it just as my skirts were beginning to float. We were wet through to the waist. Tiberius vaulted over the side and onto the slippery rock, putting out his arms to me. I jumped, rocking the boat dangerously as Stoker steadied himself. The water was nearly to the gunwale in the boat, and with a single nimble rush, Stoker leapt to the rock, the quick motion thrusting the boat under the water.

"Well, that lets out any idea of rowing back," Tiberius mused.

I looked around the island. It was a single large rock, mostly flat, rising a little way out of the water. It was covered in seaweed and dreadfully exposed to the rising wind. I shivered in my wet clothes and without a word the three of us huddled together in the center of the rock. We were silent awhile, watching the last of the grey light fade and the stars begin winking to life. Across the narrow channel, the warm golden light of Mrs. Trengrouse's lantern hovered like a firefly in the gathering darkness for a long time before at last it bobbed away.

Stoker turned towards the horizon, where the sea stretched away as to the end of the world. *"'The vast, salt, dread, eternal deep,'"* he pronounced.

"Keats?" I asked.

"Byron, actually."

"While the two of you natter on about poetry, I should like to point out that Mrs. Trengrouse is well and truly gone," Tiberius said. "And we are castaways."

"And me without a flask," Stoker said lightly.

I reached beneath my skirt. "Have mine," I told him, passing over the small flat bottle of aguardiente I always carried upon my person.

"Thank Christ," Stoker said, taking a long pull. He offered it to Tiberius, who refused with a shudder.

"It is not a very good plan, this scheme of Mrs. Trengrouse's," Tiberius said. "She has got us out here, now what? We pass an uncomfortable night and then hail a passing boat. She might have purchased a few hours' peace for herself to finish whatever diabolical machinations she intends, but she cannot hope to escape us."

Stoker gave me a long look in the starlight before looking to the horizon, where the moon, enormous and glimmering white as an agate, was rising, casting its light across the shimmering sea.

"'Tis the full moon," he said slowly. He picked up a piece of seaweed in his hand and held it. "And the kelp is damp."

"What does that signify?" Tiberius demanded. "I vow, when I get my hands on that witch, I will make bloody well certain she goes to Newgate for this. Who does she think she is, forcibly detaining a peer of the realm?"

He went on in that vein for a few minutes, but I picked up a piece of seaweed for myself and looked at Stoker. "Oh," I said quietly. He nodded.

Tiberius paused in the middle of his diatribe. "What?" he said irritably. "It is bad enough that I am marooned out here like bloody Robinson

Crusoe without the pair of you doing that enraging thing where you seem to read one another's minds."

"The tide is rising," I said calmly, marking where the waters had climbed since our arrival.

"So? They do that," Tiberius returned. "Every twelve hours, I am told."

Stoker kept his face towards the horizon, the moonlight illuminating his profile like an emperor incised upon the face of a coin. "It is the full moon," he repeated. "And the kelp is wet."

Tiberius rolled his eyes heavenwards. "Why does he keep bloody saying that? I can see the damned moon and I do not give a queen's quim for wet kelp."

Stoker turned at last, his expression fathomless. "Today is the first full moon after the autumn equinox. The sea will rise, higher than at any other time during the year. And at the last high tide, it rose enough to cover the island completely."

It took a moment for Tiberius to grasp the full implication of what he was saying. Even in the fitful light I could see him pale, his eyes suddenly bleak. "You mean we shall drown here?"

Stoker shrugged. "I see no boats, brother. It is only a matter of time before the sea closes over us."

"But the other Sisters," Tiberius began.

I shook my head. "Too far to swim and pointless. There is no shelter and they are even further out to sea. No trees to provide fuel for a fire and even if there were, I suspect Stoker's matches are worse than useless."

He reached into his pocket for his matchcase and opened it. The handful of lucifers inside floated on a little puddle of seawater. "Pulp," he said succinctly.

"What if we made a great noise and shouted for rescue?" Tiberius asked, somewhat desperately, I thought.

"The wind is blowing the other direction," Stoker told him with greater kindness than I would have expected. "It will carry the sound away from the island."

We were silent, each of us locked in our thoughts. Finally, Tiberius burst out. "I do not accept this," he said, rising to his feet. He stood, magnificent in his rage. "Damn you! This is your fault, you bloody bastard," Tiberius thundered.

Stoker rose to face his brother. "Say it again."

"This is your fault," Tiberius said with brutal clarity.

Stoker's fist connected with his jaw before the last word was finished. I jumped between them. "Is this truly how you mean to spend our last hours?" I challenged. "Brawling like boys? Tiberius, you are unfair. This is no more Stoker's fault than mine."

"It is," he insisted, rubbing at his jaw. "He let her do this. He had a chance to overpower her on the beach."

"I would not risk Veronica's life," Stoker said simply.

"Why? Because you love her?" Tiberius jeered. "Much good your love will do her now, brother. She dies with the rest of us."

"But for now, she lives," Stoker returned. "If I had acted hastily, God knows what that woman might have done."

"You might have bested her," Tiberius said. "Yes, there was risk, but risks must be taken in life, have you never learnt that?"

"I have learnt that better than most," Stoker told him with icy calm. I stared at him in perplexity. I had seen him so often enraged or in a towering temper, but never this cold composure, this complete and utter placidity in the face of certain death.

"And still it profits you nothing," Tiberius returned. "You risk nothing and so you are nothing. You love her," he repeated, jerking his head towards me. "And yet you have never told her, have you? Well, I am glad of it. She deserves better than you, you bloody fool. She deserves a man who would kill for her."

Stoker's smile was slow and terrible. "You think that is love, brother? That I should kill for her?" He shook his head, his eyes locked with mine. "You are the fool, Tiberius, because you still do not understand. I do not love her enough to kill for her." He stepped to the edge of the rock. "I love her enough to die for her."

And without another word, he disappeared over the edge of the rock and into the blackness of the sea.

For a long while I felt nothing at all, only a bone-deep numbness. Eventually I came to feel Tiberius' arm roped about my waist. I pushed at it, none too gently.

"Let me go."

"Only if you promise not to try to jump again," he warned.

"I did not—"

"You did."

After a moment, I gave him a sharp nod and he released me, moving his hand to my shoulder. "There is nothing to do but wait," he told me.

I looked at him then and saw that he was older now. The moon had risen higher, hollowing his cheeks and deepening the shadows around his eyes. Four long scratches scored his face from cheekbone to jaw, the blood crusted.

"Did I?" I gestured towards the scratches.

"Yes. When I would not let you go after him."

I sat down heavily on the rock, thrusting my hands into my pockets in a futile search for warmth. I felt the familiar form of Chester, the tiny velvet mouse. I tried not to think of the fact that this would be our last adventure together. "I suppose I ought to thank you."

"Don't," he ordered, sitting beside me. "I did it as much for myself as you. I could not have two lives on my conscience tonight."

"Then you think—" I did not finish. I could not.

He shrugged. "The sea is rising, the mist is falling, and the water is as cold as a woman's heart."

"He is a good swimmer," I said stubbornly. "I have seen him."

"He is," Tiberius agreed. He did not believe, any more than I did, that Stoker could survive the swim to St. Maddern's, not with the sea rising and a newly stitched wound in his arm hampering his stroke. Tiberius was simply trying to keep me consoled until we should both fall asleep on the rock, bone-chilled and aching with cold, until the sea crept over us and carried us off.

"Well," Tiberius said finally, his eyes bright with unshed tears. "I didn't realize the boy had it in him."

"You ought to have," I told him. "You have known him longer than anyone. You ought to have seen his worth."

"I spent most of my life hating him," he replied. "For no other crime than being Mother's favorite. I knew the boy, but not the man. He is a stranger to me."

"Is he? You are peas in a very particular pod, Tiberius."

He gave a short laugh. "How did you come to that conclusion?"

"You are both sentimentalists."

"I do not have a sentimental bone in my body," he protested.

"Don't you? A hardened cynic would hardly have to hold back his tears at a time like this."

He pressed his fists to his eyes. "How could he? I cannot bear this, Veronica. I thought losing Rosamund, losing our child, was the worst I would suffer. But this . . ."

He dropped his hands and the tears he had shed mingled with the blood on his face. "How will we bear it?"

"We shall not have to," I told him, nodding towards the creeping sea. It had covered the top of the rock, leaving us a small patch upon which to sit. With every minute, the silvery water came closer, whispering.

"It sounds as if it were speaking," I told him. "I wonder if that is how the legends of mermaids and sirens came to be."

He shrugged. "I suppose. I wonder if Rosamund . . . do you think she walked into the sea? Is that how it happened? It would have been a peaceful end, I hope." I thought of the stories Stoker had told me of the sailors he had watched drown and I knew better, but somehow I found it in my heart to lie a little.

"I hope so too," I told him, taking his hand in mine. It was large and warm, as Stoker's were. I noticed again that where Stoker's were calloused and scarred, Tiberius' were smooth-fleshed and delicate, the hands of a gentleman. I would have sold my soul for Stoker's roughened touch at that moment.

"So, Mrs. Trengrouse is our villainess," Tiberius said, tightening his grip on my hand. "Why, do you think?" He did not care, I thought. He merely wanted conversation to turn his thoughts from the encroaching sea. He did not want to face death alone and in silence. So I held his hand and I talked as the water rose over our feet.

"Perhaps she was acting in concert with Malcolm," I suggested. "She has always been devoted to the Romillys. If he did, in fact, learn of Rosamund's child, he would have a motive to kill her. And if he were involved in Rosamund's death, Mrs. Trengrouse might have played the accomplice."

"Then where is the devil?"

I shook my head. "Impossible to say. He might have taken fright that he would be discovered and Mrs. Trengrouse is hiding him somewhere we have not found. He might have killed himself and she is covering for him. He might have fled to the mainland."

We discussed the possibilities, batting around theories and abandoning them as the tide rose. My skirts swirled in the black water, and I got to my feet, pulling Tiberius up beside me. "We will stand, together," I told him.

"It will only take longer," he replied.

"We will stand," I insisted. "We will meet our end head-on."

"Spoken like a true English gentleman," he said with a wry twist of the lips.

"I am no gentleman," I replied. I put my hand back into my pocket to clutch Chester.

He put his arms about me as the water reached our waists. "We cannot stand much longer," he said. "My footing is about to go."

"Mine as well," I said. I glanced out to the western horizon, where the other two Sisters were shapeless shadows in the silver mist. *Beware the sister,* Mother Nance had said. I felt a rush of hysterical laughter fill my throat and swallowed it down hard.

"Climb on my shoulders," he ordered. "You might purchase a few more minutes—" Just then his foot slipped and he righted himself, clutching me as we both realized the futility of his plan.

His expression was agonized. "You would not be here if it were not for me," he began.

"Do not," I told him sternly. "I came of my own volition. I made my own choice, as I have always done. And if I must go, I am glad not to go alone."

The sea swirled hard about our waists, tugging at us. Tiberius straightened his shoulders and lifted his chin. "And if I must go, I am glad to go with you, Veronica. It has been my honor."

A wave crashed into us then, dragging us apart and tearing us from the rock. Tiberius' fingers slipped from mine and I opened my mouth to call to him but seawater filled it. I turned my face up just in time to see the moon, that beautiful pearled moon, drift from a cloud and shed her light like a benediction. And then the sea closed over my head and I saw nothing except the great black emptiness of the deep, the vast, salt, dread, eternal deep.

CHAPTER

19

I woke to a hot stripe of sunlight on my face and a cool compress upon my brow.

"Finally," Mertensia said with obvious relief. "I thought you would never come round. We were afraid you might have hit your head upon one of the rocks, but we could find no injury."

"I drowned," I said, levering myself to a sitting position. The room swam about me, spinning like a child's top. Mertensia pushed me back none too gently.

"You *almost* drowned," she corrected. "You went under twice before they pulled you out."

"They?" I asked, the losses of that terrible night crashing over me with the weight of a mountain.

"The men from the village," she told me. "They took a boat out to bring you and Tiberius back from the rock. Whatever made you decide to venture out there is quite beyond me, but they launched a rescue boat."

"How did they know?" I asked her in confusion.

"Why, Stoker told them," she said evenly.

Blood rushed to my head, pounding in my ears. "Stoker?"

"Yes," she said with a benign slowness, as if she were speaking to a backwards child. "He swam back to St. Maddern's, God only knows how he managed it. He landed on the beach half-dead and then roused the men with the summoning bell. They had a devil of a time putting to sea—it was the highest tide of the year, you know. And they don't like to be out on the sea on such a night. But he swore and bullied and threatened them until they launched."

"He is alive," I said stupidly. I turned my head to see Chester sitting on the bedside table. One ear was a little lower than it had been, set now at a jaunty angle, and his eyes were different. The beads had been black before but now they shone, winking dark blue in the morning sunlight. I turned back to Mertensia.

She rolled her eyes. "Isn't that what I have been saying?"

"And Tiberius?"

"Downstairs, eating his second breakfast since he had no dinner. The pair of you had drifted apart by the time the rescue boat arrived. They were able to recover him more quickly because he was directly in their path. You were carried a little distance away and quite unconscious by the time they pulled you from the sea. Old Trefusis himself administered the necessary remedies and I am told he quite enjoyed it," she added with a sly smile. "And then you vomited up half the sea on him and he was rather less enchanted. But you were still unconscious when they carried you in, and Stoker ordered you put to bed with hot bricks and ladled whisky down your throat until you slept easily. He said rest was the best cure for you."

"What time is it?" I asked, scarcely able to take in everything she had told me.

"Nearly gone noon. And the weather has cleared at last, nothing but glorious sun and clear skies," she said, flinging the curtains back fully. The single patch of golden light burst into an unbearable brightness that illuminated the entire room.

"I have to dress," I told her. She tried to prevent me, but I forced my way past her and she eventually lent a hand, muttering all the while.

"I could make you a restorative," she suggested.

I buttoned my cuffs and tucked Chester into my pocket. "Where is Mrs. Trengrouse?"

She shrugged. "I do not know. First Malcolm and now Trenny. I do not know what strange happenings are at work here, but I hope soon to have an end to them."

"You will," I promised her. I flung open the door and rushed down to the breakfast room, taking the stairs as quickly as I dared.

Tiberius was, as she had told me, sitting in state, helping himself to plates of eggs and kidneys and piles of toast. As soon as I appeared in the doorway, he rose. He came to me, his expression a mixture of relief and something more. "My dear Veronica," he murmured. "You are looking a fair sight better than when last I saw you."

I grinned in spite of myself. He held out his hand, but I pushed past it and went to embrace him. His arms came around me and he murmured into my hair. "We are more than family now, I think."

"More than family," I agreed. "Where is Stoker?"

He resumed his breakfast, taking his seat at the table and buttering a fresh piece of toast. "He took himself off to the village to thank the lads who came out last night."

I plucked the toast from his fingers and headed for the door. "More than family," I reminded him as he protested.

I met Stoker on the path from the castle to the village. I was fairly flying down the hill, my skirts gathered in my hands, when I rounded a bend and there he was, suddenly before me. I strode towards him, not slowing my pace. I came upon him like a cataclysm, taking his face in mine and raining kisses upon him until we were both short of breath as if we had run a footrace.

"Veronica," he said at last, his expression so full of emotion I could not speak for the fullness of it. I put my arms about him and pressed my face to his chest. "Don't. Not yet," I pleaded. "Tell me something mundane."

A low laugh rumbled through his chest and I felt his lips upon my hair. "Very well. I have just been to see the village men. To thank them for their courage and skill last night."

I nodded and he went on, speaking of things that mattered not at all.

"They were reluctant to go, but in the end, they overcame their fears and if it were not for them—" He broke off and his grip upon me tightened so that I knew I would never breathe again.

"Stoker." The word was weighted with everything I meant to say and could not voice. I retrieved Chester from my pocket. I held the little mouse towards him on my palm with a question in my eyes.

"You were clutching him when they hauled you aboard. One of his ears was nearly off and the eyes were gone, but I still know my way around a needle," he said lightly. I thought of the hours he must have spent, sitting at my bedside, putting each stitch into the velvet, slowly and methodically, marking them off like the pearls on a string of prayer beads.

"Stoker," I repeated, turning my face to his, offering, asking, waiting. He ducked his head, suddenly elusive.

I turned his face towards mine, almost able to master my emotion. "You think we will not speak of what you did?" I asked.

"Not now," he said, and there was a harsh note of pleading I had never heard in his voice before. "I cannot bear to remember, much less to speak of it."

"You risked your life to save us," I reminded him. "Do you regret what you said?" I asked.

"No. I regret that you heard it," he countered.

"Did you not mean it?"

He drew in a deep breath and leveled his gaze at me. "Veronica Speedwell, I meant it then and I mean it now and I shall mean it with every breath until my last. I love you."

I opened my mouth, but he laid a finger upon it. "Not now," he repeated. "Not here with my brother at hand and murderers lurking in the hedgerows. We have played a thousand games with one another, but the time for that is past. Whatever we mean to be to one another, we will speak of it when these other distractions are no more. We will speak of it—when we are free to act upon it," he finished, rubbing his thumb across my lower lip.

His eyes promised much and I shivered with anticipation as I nodded slowly.

"You are right, of course. This is hardly the place for that sort of thing. Does this mean you will stop torturing me by displaying yourself in various states of undress?"

"Not a chance." He grinned. I kissed him again. I did not think of Caroline. She was in his past, buried the moment he dove into the sea to save me. She would not haunt us again.

We gathered Caspian and his mother and Mertensia in the drawing room for a council of war. Tiberius explained what Mrs. Trengrouse had done, breaking the news as gently as possible, but Mertensia took it poorly, dissolving into an unaccustomed bout of weeping. Helen, her fears eased, took it upon herself to console her sister-in-law, putting an arm around her shoulders and murmuring soothing platitudes.

Caspian, to my surprise, rose to the occasion. "We ought to search again," he said. "We can press the entire island into service."

"Where do you suggest we look?" I asked Caspian. He shrugged.

"Damn me if I know, if you will pardon my language. We played sardines all over this house, but apart from the priest's holes, there are few proper hiding places and none large enough to hold a man for any length of time."

I jumped to my feet. "Damn us all for blind fools," I muttered, taking to my heels. Tiberius and Stoker were hard behind, following as I made my way to Malcolm's bedchamber.

"We have already looked here," Tiberius reminded me. I ignored him as I searched for the mechanism to expose the priest's hole.

"Here." Stoker reached past me to press the bit of carving. The panel shifted and I squeezed into the hideaway. Stoker pushed in behind me, holding a lamp aloft.

"Look there," I said in triumph. On the dust of the floorboard was the clear imprint of a shoe, small and pointed. "A woman's," I said. "And left since we were here last."

"What made you think of this place?" Stoker demanded.

"That," I said, pointing to the back of the priest's hole. "It is paneled where it ought to be stone. I only remembered it when Caspian mentioned the priest's holes. It struck me as odd at the time, but I was too interested in the traveling bag to explore further."

Stoker felt the panel on the back of the priest's hole, running his hands carefully over the moldings.

Tiberius stuck his head into the stuffy little compartment. "What the devil are you doing? It is obviously empty."

"And it is obviously only an antechamber," Stoker told him. "Sometimes priest's holes were made up of more than one chamber, and we ought to have realized it sooner."

"How can you tell?" Tiberius challenged.

I explained about the paneling as Stoker resumed his explorations. We started at opposite ends of the panel and pressed towards the center without victory, neither of us having discovered the mechanism. I realized there was a commotion behind us and glanced backwards into the bedchamber to see Caspian and Mertensia and Helen gathered, watching anxiously.

I climbed out of the little chamber while Stoker put out his head to address Mertensia and Caspian. "I do not know which of you to ask, but I require permission to break down the wall."

Aunt and nephew exchanged glances and nodded in unison. Before anyone could speak, Stoker returned to the hole and lifted one booted foot, slamming it hard into the panel. It made an ominous creak but did not break. Stoker braced his arms and positioned himself again, kicking the panel until it shattered with a deep moan of protest. He ripped at the broken boards until he made a hole large enough to admit him. I knew, even before I heard the soft intake of breath.

"He is there," I murmured, eager for the others not to overhear just yet. It would be too upsetting for them to discover his corpse in situ.

"He is," Stoker said, putting one leg over the broken panel to reach into the chamber beyond.

"Shall I tell them to leave?" I asked softly.

"No. Tell them to get out of the bloody way," he ordered. "He is still alive. And he is not alone."

I had to take Stoker's word for Malcolm's condition, for when Stoker emerged from the back passage carrying the man, I thought him certainly a corpse. He was bone white and unconscious, his breathing scarcely detectable. Helen burst into loud weeping, but Mertensia had recovered her composure. Stoker deposited Malcolm onto his bed and issued a series of commands with regard to treatments to be applied.

"Do you think him likely to die?" I asked as he assessed his condition.

"Possibly," he said with a grim expression. "I saw neither food nor water in there. He is badly dehydrated and suffering from shock and the temperature. It is cold as the grave in there."

I hardly dared to ask. "Is it Rosamund—" I began.

"No," he said, clipping the word sharply. "Mrs. Trengrouse."

He made another trip into the second priest's hole to retrieve her. She was unconscious and Stoker handed her off with obvious distaste to Caspian. "Take her to her room. She is responsible for the attempted murder

DEANNA RAYBOURN

of myself, Tiberius, and Veronica, as well as your uncle. You will guard her and make certain she does not attempt to leave this house if she wakens," he ordered, looking for all the world as imperious as his brother.

If the boy resented being ordered about by Stoker, he gave no sign of it. He nodded smartly and did as he was told. Mertensia hovered in the doorway.

"Trenny," she said softly. "I can hardly believe it."

"Believe it," Stoker said in a stern voice as he returned to Malcolm's care. "She's damned near killed your brother as well, I would wager."

Mertensia drew in a deep breath. "I will order whatever you need from the stillroom and Daisy will bring it. I will attend to Trenny myself until you can examine her."

Stoker agreed by way of a grunt and Mertensia left. Helen, rising magnificently to the occasion, organized the maids into producing hot bricks and water in record time. A fire was kindled in the hearth, the applewood logs soon crackling and giving off welcome heat. Counterpanes thick with down were heaped atop the unconscious man and tucked tightly about him. Stoker kept a close watch, marking the slow rise in Malcolm's temperature by the return of color to his cheeks. Through it all, Tiberius sat, still as a graven god, on a chair in the corner, saying nothing.

After a few hours, Mertensia returned, looking tired and deeply sad. "She has come to," she told us. "She said very little before she went to sleep again. But she seemed glad to know that my brother has been found before it was too late. How is he?"

"The same," Stoker told her. She went and shuttered away the sun lest the bright light hurt Malcolm's eyes when he woke. She brought a small chair next to his bed and seated herself, watching over him as he slept.

"Is someone with Mrs. Trengrouse?" I asked her.

She nodded. "Helen has offered to sit with her, and Caspian is pacing outside with Malcolm's shooting pieces. You would think she were dangerous as Napoléon," she finished with a ghost of a smile.

"She rather was," I reminded her.

"I cannot think what happened," she said in a halting voice. "Her mind must have turned for her to harm Malcolm. It is impossible. He was her favorite, we all knew. She always loved him best," she added. And I thought then how terrible love can be when it is not properly returned, thwarting and twisting itself into something unrecognizable—and dangerous.

After another hour, Malcolm roused, blinking hard against the light of the single lamp burning on the mantel. In the dimness, he struggled to make out shapes.

"Mertensia?" he called feebly. His sister went to him, putting his hand to her cheek.

"I am here, Malcolm."

"Was it a nightmare, then? Nothing but a dream?"

Mertensia glanced to Stoker, who gave her a sharp shake of the head. She smiled at her brother. "Nothing but a dream," she told him. "Sleep now. You are safe."

But he did not sleep. Instead, tears began to seep from beneath his closed lids.

"Malcolm?" Mertensia called softly.

He turned his head on the pillow, his face averted. "I have done a wretched thing," he told her, his voice a hoarse whisper. "A wretched thing indeed."

She leant near. "I am sure you have not," she told him.

He protested, shaking his head violently. Stoker moved to Mertensia's elbow. "Keep him calm," he instructed.

Mertensia patted her brother's hand. "Whatever you have done, you must have thought it right at the time," she told him.

"I wish absolution," he told her. "I must be absolved."

"Absolution for what?" she asked.

"For murder," he burst out, the tears flowing freely down his cheeks. "For murder."

CHAPTER 20

After his storm of weeping had passed, Malcolm composed himself and began his confession. Not to a priest, for there was none
present on the island, but to those of us who had gathered at his
invitation. His sister sat beside him, holding his hand as if to give him
strength during his ordeal.

"I hardly know where to begin," Malcolm told us.

"Begin with Rosamund's travel bag," I said gently. "That is what
started this whole sorry business, is it not?"

He nodded. "Yes. I haven't been able to settle to anything for so long.
Eventually, I decided upon writing a sort of history of St. Maddern's. I
pored over the old books in the library, deciding what to include. Trenny
was a great help to me as I put together the legends—all those moth-
eaten old stories of mermaids and giants. And then I thought I ought to
include the building of the castle itself. I dug through the archives and
found the plans. There was nothing from the first construction, but
there were extensive renovations done in the reign of Elizabeth."

"The priest's holes," I murmured.

"Exactly. A few were constructed where old private staircases had
been. One or two were dug out of the living rock. I thought it would be

great fun to explore them properly. They hadn't been mapped in years and half of them had been forgot," he went on. "When I opened this one, I discovered a second built behind it, a sort of double blind to trick the priest catchers into believing they had found all there was to see when they discovered the first hole. I pressed on and found the second and that is when I came upon the traveling bag."

Malcolm paused and Mertensia handed him a glass of water, holding his head so that he could drink. When he had finished, he resumed his story. "I realized then that Rosamund had not left the island. You see, I always believed she had got cold feet after the wedding and run away from me. To the man she really loved." He looked steadily at Tiberius.

"You knew."

"No. I only suspected. I always thought it too good to be true when she chose me rather than you," he said simply. "I had seen her looking at you when she thought she was unobserved. Do you remember that summer? How we pushed one another, spurring our horses to impress her? Swimming further, jumping higher? We were ridiculous. And when she said she wanted me, *me*, I was exalted. It was only later that the doubts set in."

"Doubts?" I asked.

"How could she choose me when she might have had him?" he asked.

I said nothing and waited for Tiberius to answer. It was the opportunity he had anticipated through the long, cold nights of the past three years. It was the chance to tell Malcolm the truth, once and for all, to exult in his victory at last.

Tiberius held Malcolm's gaze. "There is no mystery, my friend. She loved you."

It was a lie told for the noblest of reasons, and in that moment of duplicity, I had never counted Tiberius higher in my esteem.

"She did not come to me," Tiberius went on. "My God, man. I would have had the decency to tell you if she had. I would never have let you suffer these years never knowing if she were alive or dead."

"I realize that now," Malcolm said. "I knew that summer I was her second choice. She was luminous when she looked at you," he added with a nod towards Tiberius. "But I understood her. I knew she wanted, above all else, security and contentment. You were exciting but dangerous. You would never have let yourself be ruled by a woman, no matter how much you loved her. Rosamund knew she could have her way with me. I would have done anything for her, and I was content with that," he insisted. "She did love me. We would have made a good life together and I would have cared for her. I knew something had happened to make her decide so suddenly about marrying me, but I did not question my good fortune. Not at first."

He paused and Mertensia, with Stoker's blessing, offered him something else to drink, a sip of hot whisky this time. He swallowed it down and resumed his tale. "As the wedding drew nearer, I saw how changed she was. There was a hectic sort of gaiety to her, a forced happiness, feverish. And when the harpsichord arrived . . ." He paused again. "It did not take a genius to piece together what had happened."

"I ought not to have sent it," Tiberius said. "It was an ungentlemanly thing to give that to another man's bride."

"She loved it," Malcolm said dully. "As she loved you. I thought I could make her forget you. I thought we would have children and be happy together. So I married her. And that day she simply vanished and all I could think was that she had run away to be with you. There was no note and her things were gone. No one could make a case for harm to have come to her, so there was this limbo, this terrible, awful limbo where I had a bride but no wife. There were no boats missing, so how could she have left St. Maddern's? But the island was searched and she was not here either. I even hired a private inquiry agent to follow you when you returned to London," he told Tiberius. "But there was never any proof that you had seen her again, and no matter how hard they searched, there was no trace of her to be found. It was as if she simply vanished." His lips twisted wryly. "We Cornish believe in piskies and faeries and mermaids. I half wondered sometimes if there might have been truth to some of those ludicrous old legends. It did not seem possible that she might have disappeared. But she had. And so I got on with things as best I could. I did everything I was supposed to do as master of the Isle, but it was a half-life at most. I was sleepwalking, you understand. Until I found the bag."

His eyes were bleak as he took another draft of the hot whisky. "When I discovered it, I knew then that I had been a fool. Rosamund might have abandoned me, but she would not have left in her wedding gown without so much as a change of linen. Something had happened to her—some accident or worse."

He lifted his head, looking at each of us in turn. "And I began to wonder who might have wanted to harm her. I lay awake at night and I could imagine a motive for everyone who had ever known her," he went on. "I drove myself halfway to madness and back imagining every possible scenario, every unthinkable crime that might have been done to her. And I realized I had to discover the truth before the not knowing destroyed me. So I invited you all here to help me. I thought that if we were gathered under one roof, here where it all happened, someone might say something or see something. I thought the truth must be here, just out of reach if only we could find it."

"Did you know Helen was a fraud?" I asked. "She does not speak to ghosts."

He made a gesture of dismissal. "I suspected as much, but I wanted to believe in her. I wanted to believe it was possible that Rosamund could communicate, that she could somehow make herself known to us. If there was the slightest chance she could do so, then I meant to take it."

Tiberius sat in his chair with the solemnity of a judge while Mertensia continued to pat her brother's hand.

"I told no one what I meant to do. I knew Caspian and Helen would come because they are Romillys when all is said and done. They would come for the memory of Lucian and perhaps to further Caspian's chances to become my heir," he added with a thin, slightly cynical smile. "And I knew you would come, Tiberius, because you were too bound up in Rosamund's story. When you asked if you could bring your fiancée, I thought perhaps I had been wrong after all about your feelings for Rosamund. I told myself that you were coming solely as a friend to me, and when I saw you, I realized how much the past few years had taken from me. Not just Rosamund, but you and the friendship I had cherished for half my life."

Tiberius' gaze was brighter than usual, and Malcolm cleared his throat roughly. "In any event, I surprised everyone with my announcement about the traveling bag. I suppose it was childish of me, but I was so afraid none of you would come if I told the truth about why I wanted you. And I was so desperate to put an end to all of this. Trenny was most upset. She kept wringing her hands and saying that the dead must be left in peace. 'But, Trenny,' I told her, 'we do not know she *is* dead.' It was only the next day that I remembered something, a thing I ought to have remembered as soon as I found the bag."

"What was that?" I asked.

"Trenny was the one who volunteered to search all the nooks and crannies in the castle when Rosamund disappeared. She is the only one who could have put the bag there," he said simply. "Everyone had a part of the island to search and that was hers."

"There's something else you forgot," Mertensia put in. "Lucian taught her a few songs on the harpsichord. She must be the one who played the ghost during the séance."

Malcolm's pale face whitened further. "My God," he murmured.

"There is a passage behind the paneling of the music room," I told him. "Did you not know of it?"

"It never occurred to me," he said simply. "I don't think anyone has used it since I was a boy. If I thought of it at all, it would have been to assume it was blocked."

I shook my head. "She had only to slip into it as we approached. It would seem as if the room were empty because no one passed us as we came in. If she were quick and quiet, no one would guess a thing."

"And that was what terrified Helen into believing Rosamund was really a ghost," Mertensia finished. "But why? Why go to all that palaver just to upset Helen's séance?"

"To discourage any further investigation into Rosamund's disappearance. Malcolm was willing to give credence to Helen's abilities," I went on. "But Trenny knew how superstitious Helen is. She realized that if she could frighten Helen, then she and Caspian would leave and perhaps the entire investigation would founder. It was a desperate gambit, but she had little time to plan since Malcolm sprang the thing on us all and took her by surprise."

Mertensia's response was bitter. "I should not have thought Trenny would have it in her."

"She would do anything for the family," I said, working it out slowly. "Including protect him from the bride who was not worthy of marrying a Romilly. She murdered Rosamund."

I saw Tiberius' grip tighten on the arms of his chair. Mertensia made a sound of harsh protest, but Malcolm buried his face in his hands.

"I cannot believe it," Mertensia said finally. "And yet . . ."

I turned to Malcolm. "When did you discover that she was the one who had murdered Rosamund?"

His expression was one of perfect wretchedness. "When she locked me in that bloody priest's hole. She came to me with a glass of wine, as she always did when she had a favor to ask. She protested about the séance, about everyone searching and asking questions. She said it was only going to stir everything up again, churning up the misery we had only just begun to put behind us. I told her that I could never get on with my life properly until I knew what had happened to Rosamund, that the uncertainty tortured me. I told her that we had to carry on until I had discovered the truth about Rosamund's murder, that I would not rest until I had unmasked the villain. And I saw it again, that sudden terror flicker over her face. And I knew. I *knew*."

He paused to take another sip of whisky, shuddering hard as it went down. "We were here in this room. I confronted her and she admitted it. She said that Rosamund was pregnant with someone else's child. It was not difficult for me to guess whose," he added with a glance at Tiberius. "She said that she had tried to accept the idea that Rosamund would be the mistress here, that she would have to take orders from my wife. But as she sat in the chapel, listening to us make our vows, she realized she could not. She said that letting Rosamund come into this castle as the lady of the house, bringing her bastard child into the nursery, that it was more than she could bear."

"Trenny's nursery," Mertensia put in. "She came here as a nursery-maid. She would have viewed it as the greatest betrayal."

Malcolm went on. "So she lured her away quietly after the ceremony and killed her. She did not tell me the how or the where. Just the fact of the deed. And that was when I went for her."

"Went for her?" Stoker asked.

"I did not know what I was doing," Malcolm said simply. "But I put out my hands and they were around her throat. She was going to let me do it, that is the most terrible part. It was as if she were content to die at my hands. But then the room began to spin and I realized she had dosed the wine with one of Mertensia's concoctions. I was dizzy and weak and I lost my senses for a while. I came to just as she hauled me into the priest's hole. I tried to rise, but I could not. And I listened as she closed the panel behind her, imprisoning me in my own house."

I tried to imagine the horror of hearing the door to one's own tomb closing. A goose walked over my grave just then and Mertensia shuddered visibly.

"So I was there, in the darkness, knowing at last what had become of Rosamund, and much good it did me. I realized that I was going to disappear just as she had. No one would ever know what had become of me."

"Forgive me," I put in. "But you spoke of murder. Whose murder have you committed?"

He looked at me in surprise. "Did I not say? Trenny's," he said, his mouth trembling as he spoke the words. "To my shock, she came back to bring me food. I had been senseless for a long while, many hours, I think. She dosed the food and drink as well so that I would not be able to shout for help. I was too weak to refuse."

"Which is why you never heard us when we were on the other side of the panel discovering the traveling bag," Tiberius put in. Malcolm gave a sickly smile. The idea that rescue had at one point been so near was too horrible a thought to contemplate.

"Why on earth would she have left the bag there?" Mertensia asked suddenly.

Malcolm shrugged. "Where else? It had been safely hid there for three years before I found it. If she had made an effort to destroy it, she might have been discovered. Far better to put it back where it had been all along." Malcolm took a deep breath, steeling himself it seemed, and went on. "She said she only meant to keep me there until everyone had gone and she had decided what to do with me. She wanted forgiveness, she told me. And she came too close," he said, something feral lighting in his eyes. "I grabbed her by the skirts to drag her close to me and when she fell, I caught her by the throat. We fell together, and in our struggles, the panel closed again, locking us inside together."

I looked to Stoker, who stepped forwards. "Rest your conscience," he said gently. "Mrs. Trengrouse is not dead. She is unconscious and in her room, under guard."

Malcolm gave a start, pushing himself up against his pillows. "What is to be done with her?" he demanded.

Tiberius spoke. "That is for the magistrates in Pencarron to decide. She will be taken there if and when she becomes fit to travel."

"The scandal," Malcolm said, his voice breaking. "It will come upon us anyway. In spite of all we have done to keep it at bay."

Mertensia tried to soothe him, but Malcolm clutched at her, his knuckles white as he gripped her arms.

"It is ironic, is it not?" Malcolm demanded, the gleam in his eyes brightening feverishly. "She thought to murder me and I turned the tables on her. And then we were locked in there, together, for many hours. So many hours," he added, beginning to laugh. "And now they will hang her. They're going to hang her," he repeated, still laughing. His voice rose higher and higher as he was seized by hysteria, and it was a very long time before I forgot the sound of that laughter.

S toker ruthlessly injected Malcolm with a decoction he mixed from Mertensia's supplies. He ordered one of the kitchen maids to sit with her master, and we trooped disconsolately down the stairs to the drawing room. There was so much to say but we took refuge in silence instead. Stoker poured out stiff drinks for everyone, insisting on our taking them as medicinal remedies for the shocks we had all suffered. I went with Mertensia to look in on Mrs. Trengrouse. Daisy scuttled out when we arrived. "She has just come to again," she told us, darting avid looks over her shoulder to the woman in the bed. Huddled there, stripped of her jangling chatelaine and her air of authority, she looked like exactly what she was, an aging woman without hope.

She opened her eyes when we went to the bed. It was a narrow iron affair with a serviceable coverlet of green wool. A rag rug covered only part of the floor and a single small window was the only source of air or light beyond the shaded lamp on the night table. I wondered if it had ever struck the Romillys that this woman—who had given the better part of her life in their service—lived so modestly, so chastely. It was not a comfortable bower, I reflected. It was a nun's cell, ascetic and plain and devoid of vanity or indulgence. And I was suddenly immensely, terribly sad for the woman who had spent her life within its indifferent walls.

Suddenly, Mrs. Trengrouse spoke, her voice broken and soft. "I should like to speak with Miss Speedwell alone, if I might, miss," she said to Mertensia.

Mertensia gave her a long, level look. "Very well. Mind you take your medicine before too long," she said with a nod towards a bottle on the night table.

Mrs. Trengrouse nodded. "I gave my word," she assured her young mistress. With a long backwards glance, Mertensia took her leave and the room fell to silence.

"I saw it in your face," Mrs. Trengrouse told me. "Pity. Don't pity me, miss. I haven't had as bad a life as some."

"But you might have had a life of your own," I protested.

She made a rusty sound that might have been a laugh. "A life of my own! That is an impossible dream for a woman in service. Your life belongs to them. And I never minded, you know. Not once. I came from the cottages over Pencarron way. Eight of us in the house and never enough food. I was skinny as a rake when I came to be a nurserymaid to the Romillys. Mr. Malcolm was still a babe, it were that long ago. I cared for him as if he were my own. And when he was eight, they sent him away to school. So many years passed before he came home proper, and when he came home, he weren't a boy anymore."

Her diction lapsed a little into the more rustic tones of her childhood. "I loved him, loved them all, but Mr. Malcolm was always my favorite. The burden of caring for Mr. Lucian and Miss Mertensia would have taxed another man, but not Mr. Malcolm. He sent them to school because he feared he wouldn't be able to raise them proper, but as soon as Miss Mertensia ran away to come home, he said he would keep her here always, just as she wished, the kindliest brother you ever did see. I worked my fingers clean to the bone for him. Whatever he needed, I did it. I valeted for him. I cooked for him. I cut his hair and shined his boots. Until at last, I was above it all, housekeeper of this castle."

Her eyes shone with pride as they lighted on her chatelaine, lying cold and pointless upon the night table. "The day I pinned that to my skirt was the greatest day of my life," she said. "And I thought we would always be together, the master and I. Miss Mertensia would marry one day, I expected, and leave us. And then it would be just the two of us, Mr. Malcolm and me, like a pair of bachelors, growing old in our comfortable seclusion. Then she came," she said bitterly. "And it all fell to ashes."

"He loved her," I reminded Mrs. Trengrouse.

"Loved!" The word twisted her thin lips to something ugly. "She weren't worthy of it, weren't worthy of *him*."

I stared at her, feeling the most abject pity for any creature I had ever known. Her doglike devotion was appalling; any woman with spirit or strength could only feel revulsion at the notion of offering oneself up like a sacrificial lamb to the slaughter of one's own independent thought and feeling. For decades Mrs. Trengrouse had effaced herself until she was nothing other than an automaton, moving through her master's life with no thought beyond serving him and thereby winning his regard, taking care of a family that was never quite her own.

"You think you would never do this for love," she said suddenly. "You think you are above such abasement. But you cannot know what it means to love someone so much that nothing matters, nothing at all. Not your pride, not your dignity, not yourself. Nothing but your little ones and their happiness. That was me with Mr. Malcolm and Miss Mertensia."

"That is not love," I told her.

"Perhaps," she replied with something of her old authority. "But it was as near as I have ever known. And when I thought it was going to be taken from me when *she* came . . . I could not bear it."

"Rosamund," I said, drawing out the name like an invocation.

"She was so lovely, it was a pleasure to hate her," she told me. "I am responsible for her death and I know I must pay for that. I do not regret it. I will hang happily for what I did to her. They will jeer and taunt and say I am a murderess, but she did her evil first, she did. She was willing to let Mr. Malcolm play father to another man's child, and that was wrong."

"It was," I agreed. "But not so wrong that she should have paid with her life. Nor should she have answered to you for her misdeeds. It was Malcolm Romilly's business."

"And I was his avenger, righting the wrongs that had been done to him."

"Still, it was not your place to make that choice."

"My place?" Her laugh was harsh. "I would have had no place if she had lived. She threatened to turn me out. I went to her the night before she were married. I knew she had quarreled with Miss Mertensia about the garden, playing lady of the manor. I went and asked her to be a little kind. She could afford to be generous, I told her. She had everything, the master, the castle, the name and position. She laughed at me and told me to mind my business, and I saw red then. I told her Miss Mertensia's happiness were my business and always would be and that's when she said it wouldn't be for much longer if I kept my uppity ways. She said I had got above myself and needed to learn my place and behave better. And that's when I lost my temper. I said I knew she was going to have a child and that the church might put it right but that she had no call to speak to me of proper behavior."

"She cannot have liked that," I mused.

"She did not. She turned on me then and said if I didn't keep her secret, she would see me put off the island on the first boat, and that's when I realized it couldn't be Mr. Malcolm's child. Until then, I thought they had just anticipated their vows, you see. Many's the couple that does, especially around here with the priest coming only once a month to see to marryings and buryings. But she would not have turned so white and begun to shake if the child were his. I remembered then that I had caught her once with Lord Templeton-Vane, nothing shocking, mind. But I had come upon them once and she was looking up at him with such an expression on her face as no woman has ever used except to a man she loves. I knew then what she meant to do to Mr. Malcolm. She meant to put a cuckoo in the nest, to give this place to her love child, to disgrace this family," she finished bitterly. "And I knew I had to take care of my little ones once more and put an end to it."

"You played the ghost after the séance, didn't you?"

A tiny smile played about her lips. "Mr. Lucian taught me a little of music when he was a lad, first learning his chords. I knew it wouldn't take much to bring everyone rushing in. I needed only a moment to nip into the passage and through the library. I thought to take Mr. Malcolm by surprise, to make him wonder if her ghost had really been summoned. He might give it all up then, I hoped."

She faltered then, her eyes opaque with fear.

"Did you see her?" I asked.

She shook her head, one single sharp shake. "No, miss. But I know she were there. Later that night, I went into the music room and I felt a presence. I knew she had come."

I might have told her then. It would have been a kindness to tell her the truth, that I had been the presence in the music room. But kindness is not the foremost of my virtues. And so I kept my silence and let her believe that the spirit of Rosamund Romilly had been conjured that night.

I leant forwards, my voice coaxing. "Mrs. Trengrouse, what did you do with Rosamund after she was dead? If you tell us and she is given a proper burial, perhaps his lordship will speak on your behalf," I suggested. I had little confidence that Tiberius would do anything of the sort. In fact, I rather suspected he would cheerfully knot the rope himself if it meant revenging himself on the woman who murdered the love of his life. But that bridge was yet to be crossed.

I gave her an expectant look, but she waved me off. "I am tired now, Miss Speedwell. I am glad the master is safe, and it is time for me to sleep." She nodded towards the bottle Mertensia had left and I poured out a spoonful of the mixture as she directed. I waited until the housekeeper had drifted off before I left, smoothing the coverlet over her in a gesture of charity.

Mertensia was waiting outside the door when I emerged.

"You have dismissed the guard?" I asked, looking to the empty chair where Caspian had sat, shotgun broken awkwardly upon his knee.

"We have no need of that now," she said simply.

I handed over the bottle I had taken from the night table. A tiny skull was etched at the corner of the label. "Nor ever again, I should think."

She gave me a steady look. "Will you tell them?"

I shook my head slowly. "It is not my place."

"I had to," she said fiercely. "You heard what Malcolm said about the scandal. He is nearly unbalanced as it is. I do not know if he will properly recover, but I can promise you that being dragged through the mud of every cheap newspaper in England will destroy him. It was the only way."

I said nothing and she squared her shoulders. "I gave her a choice," she said. "She needn't have taken it if she didn't like. I would not have forced her. But she wanted to atone and this was the only way."

"It is an easier death than she deserves," I pointed out.

"But it will give Malcolm a chance at a better life," she countered, and I could not fault her logic.

I turned to leave her then and she put a hand to my sleeve. "Thank you."

I nodded to the closed door. "Go and sit with her. Even a murderess should not die alone."

. . .

On my way to the drawing room, I stopped at the castle's chapel, a tiny chamber consecrated for prayer from the first days when Romillys had lived upon St. Maddern's. It was ten paces across and a perfect square, with a tiny altar set before a stained glass window depicting the patron saint of the island. I knew he had other names—Madern, Madron—and that he was a hermit devoted to his gifts of healing. I did not believe in religion, old or new, but on the slimmest chance that the old saint watched over his island, I offered up a fervent wish that he would employ his talents for healing once more and visit his kindness upon the Romillys. Heaven knew they were sorely in need of them. It was restful with a single pew cushioned in scarlet velvet and tiles of black and white marble underfoot while the ancient fragrance of incense hung in the stillness of the air. The ceiling was vaulted and laced with carvings of the fruits and fish of the island, a reminder to those who worshiped here that they enjoyed a rare and wonderful abundance. And as I turned to leave, I saw another figure, tucked behind a bit of carving upon the lintel of the door, so discreet that it would have been easy to miss her—a mermaid, the pagan ancestress of the Romillys, remembered here in this most Christian of places. I wondered if she, too, watched over those who lived upon her island, and I hoped so. I bowed my head to her as I left.

CHAPTER

21

I found the others in the drawing room. Stoker had retrieved the tantalus from the dining room and picked the lock, liberally distributing brandy to remedy the day's shocks. I had not paused long in the little chapel, but it was time enough for the end to come to Mrs. Trengrouse. Mertensia joined me as I entered the drawing room, saying little to the others except that Trenny had passed away quietly and suddenly. Stoker gave me an oblique look and I nodded once, careful that only he should see. I knew what silent question he had posed, and I knew, too, that he would interpret my reply correctly. To the others, I did not explain about the little bottle with the skull upon the label or the choice that Mertensia had given Trenny. The old woman had got an easier death than she deserved but it would spare the family much in the way of scandal.

The atmosphere was unhappy and the cause of this was soon apparent.

"What has been decided? What will you do?" I asked Tiberius.

The gathering turned as one to him, watching with avid eyes. His expression was inscrutable. "I hardly know. Malcolm is half out of his senses. Mrs. Trengrouse has been revealed to be a murderess, and Rosamund is still missing. It is the devil's own breakfast. God only knows what the courts will make of it."

"Is it necessary to tell them?" Mertensia ventured hesitantly.

"I beg your pardon?" he asked with perfect hauteur.

"Well," she began in a slow voice. "We do not know precisely what happened to Rosamund, that is true. But Trenny confessed to killing her, so we know more than we did before. Those who loved her can finally mourn her. As far as justice is concerned, her murderess has met with it. It wasn't a rope at Newgate prison, but it is death nonetheless. Trenny has paid for her crimes. Surely we can agree upon that."

She looked about the group, but no one said a word for a long while.

"So what do you propose, Mertensia?" Tiberius asked at length.

"Let it go," she said simply. "Do not speak to the authorities on the mainland."

He gave a humorless laugh. "Do you think you can simply cover this up?"

"We have covered up worse on this island," she retorted. "Romillys have smuggled and pirated in these waters for centuries and the mainlanders know nothing of it."

Caspian came to his aunt's side in support. "At least in this we are on the side of what is right, even you must admit that," he challenged, lifting his chin as he regarded Tiberius.

"I must admit nothing," he countered coldly. "You forget yourself, Caspian. And you forget the most important thing in this business. Rosamund. She was the beginning of it all, and she has no proper burial. I will report this to the authorities," he promised.

Helen came forward, joining her son and her sister-in-law. "I understand that you have suffered," she began gently. "But must we all go on suffering? Think of the scandal it will cause. For you as well as for us. There will be no escaping it."

Tiberius drained off the last of his drink. "I will report Rosamund's murder and I will insist on a search being made for her body. I will take this island apart, stone by stone, until she is found. And if there is nothing left of St. Maddern's Isle or the Romillys or the Atlantic Ocean itself by the time I am finished, I don't bloody well care."

Caspian stepped forwards, standing toe-to-toe with Tiberius, sloshing a bit of brandy out of his glass as he gestured theatrically. "I will not let you harm my family," he said, his voice cracking only a little.

Tiberius slanted him a thin smile. "My dear boy, you cannot possibly stop me."

He set his glass down with great care and stood, shooting his cuffs as he surveyed the aghast faces. "I will be leaving on the morning tide," he said. "Consider this my farewell to you all."

He turned on his heel and left the room, closing the door gently behind him. Helen gave a low sound of protest while Mertensia uttered a swearword she might have learnt from Stoker, so eloquently profane was it. Caspian went to set his glass upon the mantel, but it slipped through his nerveless fingers, dripping amber liquid onto the hearthstones. Past caring, he threw himself into a chair and covered his face with his hands.

"We are ruined," he said.

"You tried," his mother said by way of consolation. "And it was a valiant effort, poppet. I have never been prouder of you. You stood up to a peer of the realm!"

"What difference does it make?" he demanded, dropping his hands. "I say, we are ruined."

I stared at the hearth, watching the brandy puddle on the dark stone, thinking of Mrs. Trengrouse. Stoker came to stand at my side.

"It seems such a short time ago that I stood with Mrs. Trengrouse, sipping brandy and talking about ghosts," I mused.

"Fortune's wheel turns on a—did you say sipping brandy with Mrs. Trengrouse? She was teetotal."

"She liked a little stiffener," I confided.

"But she avoided the island wine," Stoker pointed out. "Even to test the quality of it before she added it to the barrel in the cellar."

I stared at him. "Do not even suggest it," I hissed.

He grabbed my hand, heedless of the stares of the others. I clasped his as we proceeded at a dead run through the kitchens and to the ironwork door giving onto the cellars. He stopped, cursing. "Locked and no doubt Mrs. Trengrouse still has the key."

I fetched two hairpins out of my Psyche knot and handed them over. He fitted them to the lock and with a moment's deft manipulation had the thing opened.

"You are going to teach me how to do that," I warned. He opened the door and I hurtled through, leading the way down the stone stairs to the cellars, Stoker hard upon my heels. We stopped just short of the great barrel, staring at it in mute horror.

"I cannot bear to think of it," I managed at last.

"It is the only place we have not looked," he said simply. "And Mrs. Trengrouse was tasked with searching for Rosamund in all the nooks and crannies of the castle. Including the cellars."

"She could have taken her body out to sea and dumped her," I argued.

"It is too far. She might have been seen," he countered.

I sighed and gestured towards the axe hanging on the wall. "You will need that."

"The notion of being seen did not seem to trouble her when she sent us to our doom," I said as he retrieved the axe.

"It was dark and the mist was rising and it was the day after a heavy storm. There was little danger of her being seen," he pointed out. "Rosamund vanished on a bright summer's day." He took a firm grip upon the axe and paused. "Veronica," he said, and I turned, seeing the expression of anguished reluctance on his face.

"I know." I stepped back and gestured towards the largest of the wine barrels. "Do it."

He hefted the axe and swung it over his head. It took three blows before he shattered the side of the barrel. There was a pause, a breathless moment where nothing happened, and then the wine burst forth, rivers of it as darkly scarlet as old blood, pouring onto the floor. After that came the arm, a slender limb wrapped in bridal satin, stained the color of grapeskins. At the end of the arm was a graceful hand, and on the fourth finger of the hand, a ring—a slim band of gold—shining dully in the shadows.

"My God," Stoker breathed. And I knew that for once it was not a curse. It was a prayer.

We did not tell Tiberius until we had removed her from the cask, laying her out and straightening her wedding gown as the last of the wine dripped from the barrel. I wiped her face and arms with a clean cloth dipped in vinegar and Stoker found a sheet to cover her to the neck. Her hair was sodden with wine and badly stained, but what was left of her expression was calm.

I do not like to think of the next hours. Tiberius was shattered by the sight of her. He retreated to his chamber without a word and it was left to Mertensia to make the necessary arrangements. It was midnight before Caspian and Stoker had finished the digging, but when all was prepared, Mertensia summoned us to the poison garden, giving each of us a taper as we gathered beneath the solemn watch of the figurehead.

"What is this?" Tiberius demanded.

Mertensia stepped forward. "You told Caspian you would not leave us in peace until and unless she was buried. That is what I mean to do."

"Here?" Tiberius looked around. "This is not hallowed ground."

"This is a garden," she told him. "The first place of God's own creation for mankind. It is as hallowed a place as anyone could wish. If you want hymns, we shall sing them. If you want prayers, we shall make them."

Tiberius hesitated. "Malcolm ought to be here."

"Malcolm is not well," she said, new authority steadying her voice as she stood toe-to-toe with him. "I will explain everything when he is capable of comprehending it. For now, he will rest."

Tiberius turned in a slow circle, taking it in. Just behind was the stone wall covered in lady of the night, the scent perfuming the night air. The serene face of the figurehead called Mercy watched over it all with opaque eyes.

"Very well," he said hoarsely. "Do it."

There had been no time for a coffin. Mertensia had unearthed draperies from the attics, heavy golden brocade, and Rosamund had been wrapped carefully in these. With infinite gentleness, Caspian and Stoker moved to place her in the grave. When she had been laid neatly, we each took up a handful of the piled earth and dropped it onto the shimmering cloth, offering a peaceful passing to the young woman who would rest forever in the garden at the edge of the sea.

Finally, it was Tiberius' turn. We stepped backwards to give him a moment of privacy as he slipped to his knees at the edge of the grave. I heard his voice, a low murmur that went on for a long time as he spoke one last time to the love of his life. I heard, too, the dull noise when the soil in his hand dropped to the golden cloth. He rose and took the shovel from Caspian's grasp. Together, he and Stoker finished the long, laborious task of filling in the grave. When they had finished, Stoker put a hand to his brother's shoulder and Tiberius covered it with his own for a brief moment. Then he shrugged it away and went to the *Cestrum*, the lady of the night, cutting a long sprig of it to place upon the mound of earth. It was white and fragrant and looked very much like a bridal bouquet. We stood for a long time in that garden as the moon rose above us, shedding its pearly light, and over it all spread the scent of the starry jasmine blossoms blowing away and over the sea.

. . .

By the next morning, all was decided. When Malcolm had recovered himself enough to travel, Caspian and Helen were taking him on a long tour of Italy. A foreign country with no acquaintance to ask questions was just the thing. They expected to be gone at least a year while Malcolm made peace with all that had happened. In the meantime, Mertensia would act as master of St. Maddern's Isle, and given the decisiveness and authority she had exhibited on that fateful night, I had little doubt the island would be in good hands.

The news of Mrs. Trengrouse's passing was accepted with relief on all sides, although Tiberius looked as if he regretted the fact that her end had been a tranquil one. It took a little gentle debate before Mrs. Trengrouse's fate was decided and, in the end, it was Stoker's suggestion which prevailed. He had discovered in his conversations with the local fishermen that burials at sea were sometimes held surreptitiously for those who had died quietly at home and preferred the consolations of the deep to those of the churchyard. He explained that the current had shifted and that anything put on the outgoing tide would be carried away. And so her body was taken down to the shingle beach on the western edge of the isle. She was laid into a small boat and pushed out to sea as the tide turned, bearing her over the horizon.

"It is better than she deserves," Tiberius said as we watched the tiny craft bob and toss on the waves.

"Perhaps," I said. "But justice has been meted. And the dead can rest at last."

We packed and prepared to leave the castle the following week. We had all been affected by the strange events, and Mertensia and Caspian, for once, had been grateful of company. I spent much time with

Mertensia in the garden, preparing my beautiful glasswing specimens and learning their habits. Stoker and I still had not talked to one another again about the night on the First Sister, the night when so many things had been said that could not be unspoken. But the anticipation of what lay before us simmered within me, and more than once I caught his eyes upon me, warm with intention.

Our last afternoon, I had gone down to the village after luncheon to take my leave of Mother Nance, which entailed many tankards of cider and a few more cryptic remarks. "A long journey you'll be taking," she told me, winking, as she raised her tankard to mine. "Mark me well, m'dear."

I made my way slowly up the path towards the top of St. Maddern's, the last of the summer sunshine warm upon my back as I walked. I passed through the gate leading to the castle grounds just as Stoker appeared.

He stopped when he reached me, his eyes alight.

"Good afternoon," I said formally. We had spent the last week in a froth of anticipation, hardly daring to be in the same room together, so violent were our longings. I had lain awake more than one night, torturing myself with frankly indecent thoughts, and I had noticed Stoker had taken to swimming in the cold Atlantic waters twice a day to dampen his ardor.

A slow smile spread over his face.

I looped my arms about his neck. "I am rather sorry to see the end of our time here," I told him.

"I am not," he said. "I have plans for you in London."

"London," I breathed, closing my eyes.

"London," he repeated. "Where it will be just the two of us. No Tiberius, no Romillys. No murderers, no former wives, no moldering corpses. Just *us.*"

He bent his head to a fervent demonstration of his intentions. Just as he began to make significant progress, a little cough sounded behind us. Stoker's teeth, strong and sharp, nipped once, hard, upon my lobe as he gave a little growl of frustration.

"*What*, Peter?" he demanded of the little boy who stood patiently grinning behind us, waving a piece of paper.

"Telegram for the lady," he pronounced. Stoker fished in his pocket for a coin whilst I skimmed the lines.

"It is from Lady Wellie. The Whitechapel murderer has struck again," I said. "She does not say what she wants with us, only that we must return immediately and that it is a matter of life and death."

I half expected him to protest, but I should have known him better than that. Adventure roared in his blood as it did in mine, and once more we would embark together.

"So, another adventure," he said, a slow smile spreading across his features, illuminating his face like a pagan god. "Shall we begin? Hand in hand?"

"And back to back," I added with a grin. "The better to see our enemies." Back to back was also how butterflies copulated, but I thought it best to save such an observation for a more intimate moment.

"Come on, then," he directed.

I grabbed his hand and raced with him into the westering sun. "Excelsior!"

AUTHOR'S NOTE

The Romilly Glasswing butterfly, *Oleria romillia*, is fictitious, invented for the purposes of this book but based upon a genus of clearwing butterflies first named in 1934. These brush-footed specimens are native to the Americas and, while smaller than the imaginary Romilly Glasswings, are every bit as beautiful.

ACKNOWLEDGMENTS

For the warmest of welcomes and the utmost support, I owe much gratitude to everyone at Penguin/Berkley with special recognition of my superb and gifted editor, Danielle Perez, as well as Craig Burke, Loren Jaggers, Claire Zion, Jeanne-Marie Hudson, Jin Yu, Jessica Mangicaro, Jennifer Snyder, Christine Ball, and Ivan Held. Huge and heartfelt thanks to the art department for their inspired work and to the sales, marketing, editorial, and PR teams who give so much. I will forever be indebted to Ellen Edwards for seeing the potential in Veronica and bringing her home.

For an exquisite copyedit and coldread, my compliments and thanks to Eileen Chetti and Jeff Campbell.

For two decades of advice, friendship, and business expertise, I am immensely grateful to my agent, Pam Hopkins.

Gratitude and much love to the people who have given me so much support and given Veronica a splendid launch: Blake Leyers, Ali Trotta, Joshilyn Jackson, Ariel Lawhon, Delilah Dawson, Rhys Bowen, Alan Bradley, Susan Elia MacNeal, Robin Carr, and Lauren Willig. Many thanks to Benjamin Dreyer, Duchess Goldblatt, and the Blanket Fort for laughter and consolation.

ACKNOWLEDGMENTS

I am so very grateful for the practical diligence of my assistant, Jomie Wilding, and the Writerspace team for all things digital.

A very special nod of thanks to Kim Wright for telling me a chilling story and ending with the words, "I hope you use this in a book someday."

My love and gratitude, as ever, to the most supportive family imaginable.

For everything, for always, my husband.